The scream echoed across the entire campus, long, loud, and terrified. Then it got cut off midcry.

The moon was half full, its light pale and cold. The lightstone lamps added their sunny warmth to the pools of light, but that still didn't illuminate all of the campus paths.

That scream sounded serious and the longer May delayed, the worse it might be for the screamer.

That screamer had been a woman, which made the time even more imperative.

May saw two student helpers, both boys, putting books on shelves.

"Get security."

The boys looked up and one of them clutched books to his chest when he realized who had barked an order at him.

May pivoted and started to head back to the archway when she remembered she had forgotten the most important detail.

She turned around, saw the boys slowly setting down their books, and snapped at them.

"This is *urgent*. Someone could be *dying.*"

THE FEY SERIES
(READING ORDER)

ALSO BY
KRISTINE KATHRYN RUSCH

THE RETRIEVAL ARTIST SERIES

Writing as Kris Nelscott

THE SMOKEY DALTON SERIES

A Dangerous Road

Smoke-Filled Rooms

Thin Walls

Stone Cribs

War at Home

Days of Rage

Street Justice

AND

Protectors

Writing as Kristine Grayson

The Charming Trilogy, Vol. 1

The Charming Trilogy, Vol. 2

The Fates Trilogy

The Daughters of Zeus Trilogy

THE INCIDENT AT SEREBRO ACADEMY

THE THIRD BOOK OF THE QAVNERIAN PROTECTORATE

KRISTINE KATHRYN RUSCH

WMG PUBLISHING

The Incident At Serebro Academy

Copyright © 2024 by Kristine Kathryn Rusch

Published by WMG Publishing

Cover and Layout Copyright © 2024 by WMG Publishing

Cover design by Stephanie Writt | WMG Publishing

Interior design by Stephanie Writt | WMG Publishing

Background Art © cappa | Depositphotos

Figure and Academy Art © Ravven | Depositphotos

Book & Pen Art © Canva

Map Art and Design © Stephanie Writt | WMG Publishing

ISBN-13 (trade paperback): 978-1-56146-158-5

ISBN-13 (hardcover): 978-1-56146-161-5

This one is for the readers, who are going on this amazing journey with me.
Thank you!

THE INCIDENT AT SEREBRO ACADEMY

SEREBRO
MOUNTAIN RANGE

SEREBRO
ACADEMY

TO TRINOVANTE

PART ONE
A DEATH

LINGUISTICS

ARCHEOLOGY

HISTORY

REGENTS
TOWER

OLD
LIBRARY

ADV. STUDENT
WING

MAIN
ENTRANCE

CLOCK
TOWER

MEDICAL
SCIENCES

CHAPTER
ONE

Lumin hated Dorovich. The entire continent felt cursed, even though he had only seen a small portion of it. Or maybe he felt cursed. Nothing he had done since he started on this journey across the Infrin Sea felt right.

He hadn't said that to his troop—he didn't dare discourage them more than they already were—but they could probably tell. He kept changing his mind about the mission, something that had started almost the moment the merchant ship had landed in this horrid place.

Still, he had thought things would improve when he came to Serebro, and it turned out that they had gotten worse.

He had thought the city of Serebro housed Serebro Academy, which was his primary target. Instead, the city and the Academy were separated by the Serebro Mountain

Range. The Academy, or so his Spies had learned, was almost a village in and of itself, and would notice strangers, particularly people who looked like (and who actually were) Fey.

Because of that, he was stuck in this crummy neighborhood on the far side of the city of Serebro, in a dilapidated rowhouse with five apartments side by side.

He had put his troop in the first and third apartments, taking the fourth for himself and using the fifth for meetings. At the very beginning of this project, he had designated the second apartment for magickal items they found across the Qavnerian Protectorate.

He had decided to buy those, so that he could take them back to the Black King's son, Rugar, when the troop returned to Nye. When this was all over.

Technically, they were supposed to be destroying the magick in Dorovich, but that was harder than it sounded. He was vacillating between studying it and destroying what he could find and bringing the rest back.

Although right at the moment, he would love to destroy it all.

Lumin stood near the door to the unused kitchen, staring at the piles of artifacts. They seemed alive to him. Glowing slightly, as if their magick was consolidating.

He no longer liked how the front room in this second apartment felt. He had forbidden the Domestics from coming to this apartment, because he was worried about the effect on their magick.

Eerie, the Enchanter he had brought with him, had no such qualms. She stood over the piles, hands clasped behind her back. She was exceptionally tall, even for a Fey, and so thin that Lumin had privately compared her to a stick.

An old hollow stick, the kind that had fallen off a tree the year before, suffered through the winter, and now would crumble at a single touch.

He had no idea how she remained so calm. He wasn't. This second apartment put him on edge. He didn't even like being inside of it.

When he had first seen it, it looked no different than the other four. It had a square front area, with saggy furniture—here, a couch and three upholstered chairs that had been clawed to pieces by a cat—and a kitchen that had a cast iron stove that he couldn't get near, an icebox, and a long wooden table covered with scars.

This apartment had smelled of cats, that sharp pungent odor of cat urine that never seemed to leave once the cats had decided to leave their mark. The cat stench was why this particular apartment became the designated storage area.

He hadn't wanted the Domestics to use magick here to dispel the stench. He wanted this place as free of Fey magick as possible, so that it wouldn't interact with any magick in the artifacts.

Now, the cat smell had faded back, even though the Domestics hadn't done anything. Now, the dominant odor was mildew and old paper. The Dorovicians had a love of books and papers and maps and so-called knowledge, all stored in writing. They'd even invented some kind of device that printed words on paper, and bound them with yet another machine. He didn't pretend to understand how any of it worked, although one of his Spies had learned enough to attempt an explanation.

All Lumin noted was the fact that these books were somehow part of the culture here, a part he didn't entirely understand.

As if he understood any of it. He had let the Spies explore the culture. They had found this row of apartments. The Spies knew how to pay for things, like rent and artifacts. They knew how to speak the language and interact with the Qavnerians in particular.

The Spies were the ones who first learned that the Academy was not in this city and that it wasn't possible to go to the Academy and blend in.

So he had done what any good Leader would do. He sent a Doppelgänger in to become a member of the Academy staff and send reports back.

Thus far, the reports had been vague and filled with complaint. But that seemed to be the hallmark of this entire troop. Vagueness and complaint.

Rugar hadn't given Lumin the best of the Fey, nor had he given Lumin the worst of the Fey. The members of Lumin's troop—and the other troops that had come to Dorovich—were the Fey who could be spared. That meant they were good enough to travel, but not really good at what they did.

They were either people with problems following orders or with minimal magick or with emotional issues. The three most talented members of Lumin's troop were Lumin (of course), Eerie, and Hardin, the Infantry leader who had no magick at all.

Everyone else had some kind of problem that made them expendable.

Lumin was learning that Perdu, the Doppelgänger he sent to the Academy, was a complainer and not very efficient. If Lumin had known that, he would have sent the other Doppelgänger, Shyly, instead. She at least didn't complain.

She hadn't even complained that she was still stuck in the body of the Nyeian she had taken over almost two years ago. Shyly was just waiting for her turn, which Lumin hoped would come sooner rather than later.

He took a deep breath and then regretted it. He hated the taste of mildew and dust.

He waved a hand at the Dorovician junk littering the front room.

"I think we should destroy them," he said.

"Attempting to destroy magick is always a bad idea," Eerie said, as if she were the one in charge. She probably wanted to be, which wasn't uncommon in the relationship between Visionaries and Enchanters. Even for the great Visionaries, like Rugad, the Black King, working with Enchanters was fraught.

Eerie leaned toward the center pile, which was filled with tapestries depicting unfamiliar events. They smelled of mold, which Lumin had noted whenever someone dropped another tapestry on that pile.

Another pile, about four away, had even more tapestries, but they seemed to have words scrawled along them—and he could swear that those words were in a different position each time he looked at them.

"Destroying magick is our mission," he said for maybe

the millionth time. He and Eerie had been going round and round and round about this very idea ever since they had acquired the first cache of magickal artifacts.

At least, they had been told the artifacts were magick. Eerie wasn't certain that they were all magick, although it was clear to every magickal member of the troop that some of the artifacts had magickal properties.

The magick was strong enough that Lumin made sure most of the artifacts were carried, moved, and stacked by the six Infantry who were part of the troop. Shamra, one of the complainers, had claimed that Lumin had brought Infantry only to do grunt work like this.

Lumin might have agreed early in their mission, but not now. He could feel something building. He wasn't yet sure what it was, but he knew it was important.

He had been on edge for days.

And being on edge was something he paid attention to. He wasn't a great Visionary. His magick rarely was as straightforward as the magick of the greatest Fey. He had to pay attention to things like feelings and intuition because those approximated a stop-in-your-tracks Vision for him.

At times, anyway. And at other times, they were just feelings, the same kinds of emotions that everyone else in this small troop had.

He hated that. He felt Blind more often than not. He'd had Visions, although most of them had been long ago. He liked to tell himself that was because he hadn't been in a position to have good Visions until he came to Dorovich.

But he hadn't had any here, either.

He started to sigh, and caught himself, not wanting Eerie to hear that. Nor did he want to inhale more dust.

Besides, second-guessing himself was one of his problems. Second-guessing and regretting that he was leading a mediocre troop on what might be a suicide mission.

He knew—because Rugar, the Black King's son, had made it clear—that if the members of this troop had been great at what they did, they would still be in Nye, mopping up the details of taming that persnickety little country, or working with the Black King to plan the next campaign.

Instead, they were in Dorovich at Rugar's command. Rugar, who had been trying for years to take more control over the Fey.

Rugar believed that the Fey were losing their identity in Nye. They needed to move on, conquer someplace else, continue their takeover of the entire world.

We're getting complacent, he had said to Lumin the day before Lumin and his troop had left on that hideous merchant ship. *We're warriors. That's why we're hearing so many stories of atrocities throughout the Empire. Foot Soldiers need something to do besides train. We all do.*

Of course, Lumin had nodded in agreement. He often said nothing when talking with Rugar. It was safer that way.

Rugar was the frustrated oldest child of a man who seemed like he would never give up the Black Throne. It didn't help that Rugar's father had the greatest military mind in generations.

That military mind made the Black King move slowly. He had conquered a lot of territory, most recently on Galinas, but then he had stalled in Nye.

With the capture of Nye, the Fey controlled half the world. Rugar wanted to leave a force and bureaucrats in place, to remake Nye, but the Black King had settled in. He said that Nye and the surrounding areas needed to be consolidated fully under Fey control before the Fey even attempted the next part of the plan.

The next part of the plan meant getting to Dorovich. The Fey had tried that once, or so some of the stories went, attempting to use the Place of Power in the Eccrasian Mountains to get there.

It had gone badly. The Fey learned that traveling from the Place of Power in the Eccrasian Mountains—the one that had given them their own magick—through another Place of Power that had slightly different magick was extremely dangerous. That travel not only destroyed some magick, but also destroyed minds. Most of the stories of what had occurred during that trip through the Place of Power were lost, but they were severe enough to dissuade the Fey from ever traveling through the Place of Power again.

Instead, the Black King wanted to travel to Dorovich. His plan involved Leut, the small continent separated from Dorovich by a sliver of the Infrin Sea. To get to it, though, the Fey would have to bring ships. Conquering Leut would be the first time in Fey history that the Fey had to travel across the sea to take over another country.

The Black King said that such campaign would be new to them, and would require a completely different military mindset.

Rugar studied maps, saw a tiny island in the middle of

the Infrin Sea, and suggested that the Black King use that as his base.

The Black King dismissed all of it, which, Lumin believed, set Rugar off. He didn't like being dismissed and he didn't like being considered lesser than his father, even though he was.

So Rugar was hoping to send troops to Dorovich without the approval of his father. Before he sent the troops though, Rugar was scouting the country. He needed to know what they were up against.

Lumin suspected that Rugar would lead a fighting force on his own just to prove that he was right.

Which wasn't really Lumin's business. He hadn't even told his troop about his suspicions.

What the Black Family chose to do was based in their leadership, the leadership that had come to them through their magick and through the Black Throne, which had picked them long ago.

Lumin's job was to examine one section of Dorovich, which included a famed academy, and to figure out what kind of magick—if any—the Dorovicians had. If Lumin found magick, he was to study it, and then destroy it.

The Dorovicians, he had found, used artifacts to contain their magick, although he hadn't been sure—wasn't sure, really—how powerful that magick was. Because the artifacts held magick, Lumin had been acquiring as many as he could.

The artifacts were worrying him. They were also making him anxious.

One of his Domestics, Thread, had noted how on edge he was. He had told her that he might be reacting to magick. But confiding in a Domestic always led to conversations about healing, rather than a simple acknowledgment. She diagnosed a change in diet. He'd been eating too many foods unique to Qavner, which she said might be interfering with his magick.

He really didn't know what else he could eat. The Domestics hadn't set up a garden in any of the properties the troop had stayed in. He tried to eat what they prepared, but when he was exploring on his own, which was more often than not, he ate like a local.

Thread disapproved of that. But she seemed to disapprove of most things. He thought perhaps that was why she was here, rather than working with other Domestics to redesign Nye.

And she seemed to forget important things, such as the fact that he was a minor Visionary. He had had a handful of Visions throughout his life—especially as a child and a young man, back when there had been hope and promise that his Visions might make him a strong leader one day. Mostly, though, he had feelings.

Near Visions was what one of his mentors had called those feelings. Some Visionaries dismissed the feelings as anything Vision-related, but Lumin didn't. Whenever he felt unease like this, something was about to happen.

The difference between the unease and, say, an actual Vision, was that the unease did not allow for any kind of interpretation.

This Near Vision was a bad one. He had been on edge for days, and it had grown worse.

Eerie peered at the artifacts in front of her. She didn't

seem to be on edge at all. In fact, the artifacts didn't even seem to bother her.

He had no idea why.

"Destroying *and reporting* on magick is our mission," Eerie said. She always seemed to feel the need to correct him. "Rugar wants to know what Dorovician magick is made of. I say we experiment with each of these items to find out what it can do."

Lumin's breath caught. Experimenting with unknown magick could have terrible consequences. They didn't have enough personnel to do this.

Besides, all he could think about were the lightstones, the source of artificial light throughout Dorovich. Lightstone lamps were everywhere.

Fortunately, he had been warned to stay away from them. A minor Fey, a Navigator, had told all of the traveling troops picked by Rugar that lightstone lanterns could completely destroy a Fey, should the Fey get too close.

The Navigator seemed to believe that the diffuse light, from a lamp far from a person, wouldn't do any immediate damage.

Who knows what kind of long-term damage it will do to your magick, the Navigator had said. *That's why I avoid those lamps completely. I stay on the ship or go to places that only use oil lamps.*

As if that were possible outside of the apartments. Lightstone was everywhere.

It was another reason that Lumin left the travel throughout Dorovich up to his Spies and Dopplegängers.

Their magick shielded them against some of the effects of regional magick—in ways that he did not understand.

The lightstone was but one trap in this country. There were others, like the iron stove in the kitchen was one of those traps. Iron could harm many Fey magicks, albeit not all of them. But enough that he hated being around it, because it made him queasy.

He wrapped his arms around his torso, the unease growing. It was making him vibrate. Maybe he was too close to that stove.

He stepped deeper into the front room, but that made him even more uncomfortable.

"You disagree with me," Eerie said, looking at his posture.

"I do," he said, "but that's not bothering me. Are you feeling tense?"

She frowned. Enchanters had bits of every kind of Fey magic. She might actually have a bit of Vision. Lumin had never asked because—if he was being honest with himself—he didn't want any kind of competition.

"I'm always tense around you," she said, and she wasn't being accusatory. She was being honest.

"Yeah, I understand." He tried to smile, but it didn't work. He was actually getting jittery, as if his insides were trying to vibrate outside of his body. "But more tense than usual."

She glanced at the magickal items. The books in the center seemed to glow gold.

"Maybe it's the proximity of strange magick," she said, more to herself than to him.

14

He shook his head. "I don't think this feeling is coming from the artifacts."

She turned toward him, a prodigious frown on her face. The one thing he did value about Eerie was that she took him seriously when he talked about Visions and Fey magick.

She tilted her head, as if she was listening to something.

Then she moved closer to the artifacts. He wanted to yell at her, tell her not to, but he didn't. He might actually be interfering with her magick.

She stepped to the side of the book pile, and looked at the leather tubes beyond it. Each tube held a map—sometimes more than one map.

His troop was just beginning to understand the maps of Dorovich. The mapmakers here had actual magick. Some maps were simply representational, but others actually moved and changed.

Lumin and Eerie had been debating what those maps meant, although they couldn't look at them for long. The special maps glowed brightly. They also had more than one dimension. Images floated off the tops of them, particularly when the magickal maps were in proximity to each other.

Over Lumin's objections, Eerie had used her Links to consult with a couple of the Enchanters embedded with the other troops in Dorovich. Those Enchanters were encountering maps too. The group in Trinovante was trying to steal as many as they could. That group seemed to believe the magickal maps weren't several *different* maps, but one large map showing the entire continent.

Eerie disagreed with that assessment. She believed the maps showed where the magick was.

Lumin wasn't sure what to think. He could barely look at the maps. They hurt his eyes—at least the ones in those tubes.

"Lumin," she said, "two of those tubes are glowing."

He peered around her. Light was coming out of the edges of the tube, where the leather top had been tied down.

"What does that mean?" he asked.

"I don't know." She actually sounded nervous. He had never heard Eerie sound nervous before, and they had served together when they were younger. They weren't in battlefield situations, but they had to quell uprisings which, the Black King once said, could be much more dangerous.

A glow was coming off the tapestries as well. Not the ones in the image pile, but the ones in the changing words pile.

Lumin's heart rate increased, and he again thought of what that Navigator had said about the lightstones.

"Let's go outside," he said. "I'm not comfortable in here."

To his surprise, Eerie didn't argue with him. She skirted around him, then headed through the kitchen and out the back door.

He had to hurry to keep up with her. As he stepped through the door, he hoped that the on-edge feeling would decrease. It did not.

Some of that might have been the air. It was filled with yellow fog.

The fog was foul. It smelled of woodsmoke and burned the eyes. The fog hurt going into the lungs.

Eerie didn't seem bothered by it. She was standing in the middle of the horrid fog as if it wasn't even there.

"What we're seeing with those artifacts," she said, "that magick starting up? We have no idea why. You were nervous in there."

"I'm still nervous," he said. "The feeling has not gone away."

It seemed to have gone away for her. Or maybe she hadn't felt it to the extent that he had.

"But," she said, "we don't know if you have that feeling because something is happening that you need to tend to or if it's because that strange magick in the apartment is having an effect on you."

That yellow fog made her look even more like a dark stick. Almost like a hole in the fog. He shuddered. A hole in the fog. That phrase reverberated through his brain.

"We probably shouldn't have put all of those artifacts in the second apartment," he said, more to himself than to her. At least he hadn't let anyone with magick stay in the third apartment with the adjoining wall.

"I think we need the artifacts off the premises entirely," Eerie said. "We might have to separate them by type."

Lumin's unease grew even more at the suggestion.

Some of the artifacts that his troop had acquired seemed innocent enough—spoons and bowls and tiles. They all had images engraved on them, and much of the silverware was made of actual silver.

But some seemed to be alive. He didn't want anyone in his troop to touch them again. Touching them once might have been too much.

"I agree," he said. "But I don't think we should ignore the magick here. I think we need to destroy them."

Eerie's mouth narrowed. She looked terribly impatient. Then her eyes widened, and her hands went to her head.

She fell to her knees, and toppled forward, a cry he'd never heard before slipping through her lips.

"Eerie?" he asked.

She did not respond. He yelled for the Domestics, and hoped they could hear him.

She fell backwards. He reached for her—

And then she disappeared.

THE
TURNOUT

SEREBRO
MOUNTAIN RANGE

CHAPTER
TWO

The yellow fog had become stupidly thick. Lumin couldn't see his hand in front of his face. He tried to touch Eerie, to reassure her, but his hand found cobblestone.

There was no cobblestone here.

The fog parted enough to reveal a man face down on the cobblestone, one hand up, the other holding a satchel of some kind. Faces peered out of the fog at him, reaching for him.

And then, he too disappeared.

At that moment, Lumin realized he was in the middle of a Vision. It felt real, and terrifying, and unsteady.

He squinted at the faces, but they slid into the fog. Although a hole in the fog revealed a kitchen, very similar to the one he had just left.

Then it all closed up, and some Qavnerians were standing around the empty space where the body had been.

Someone said, *My satchel for yours*. The man on the cobblestone wasn't lying down anymore. He was standing, looking confused—or angry—or worried.

Lumin could barely see his face, and didn't understand what, exactly, he was seeing anyway.

Then the Enchanter Hadley stepped out of the fog. She was wearing a hood that covered her head. He identified her by her long thinness, and her somewhat pointed chin.

She said, "Who *are* you? What do you want?"

Lumin tried to say, *I'm Lumin. You know me.*

But his voice didn't work. It felt as if he was trapped by the fog itself.

Another woman was standing beside him, one he had never seen before. She was tiny. She wore a cloak with a hood. As she pulled the hood down, it revealed a shock of white hair—the kind most Fey Shaman had.

She had the upswept eyebrows, the pointed chin, the sharp cheekbones, but her ears were covered, and her skin was light. Her eyes seemed almost colorless. And she was short. Shaman were never short.

She was holding a knife. A Fey blade. He recognized its thinness and its lack of heft. A very faint image was carved into the blade, almost invisible—a heart, pierced by two swords.

"This knife," the woman said—and she had moved. Somehow she was standing near a pool of blood. "This knife wasn't made here."

She sounded surprised. Lumin wasn't. It was a Fey blade. There had to be a sheath nearby. The knife was too sharp to be carried loosely.

The woman brought the knife up—and suddenly, Lumin was in that kitchen he had seen. Atrü was crouching, his long body half folded, his black hair pulled away from his face. He clutched Hadley, who was bleeding profusely. His hands were covered with blood. Someone else stood with him, and there was shouting, but Lumin couldn't understand any of it.

All he knew was that Hadley was dead.

"The magic," the woman said, sounding terrified. She was speaking through the fog, which was somehow behind Lumin. Behind him, and through a door, as if the door were some kind of magical portal. It might have been. "It comes from the Fey."

Her words sent a chill through him. She seemed to be looking right at him. He was no longer in that kitchen. He was on the cobblestone again, and the woman with the shock of white hair said, "The Fey are here, which means—"

We need a circle.

He didn't know what that meant. He just knew that something felt off. Terribly off.

He turned, about to ask the woman what she meant, when another person fell backwards through the portal, a knife—a solid, chunky knife—in their forehead. He thought he recognized them, but he wasn't sure.

He wanted to reach for them, when the world shifted around him.

He was standing in ground fog, outside a fortress. All that remained of a moat had a stone bridge over it, and people scurried along it, carrying books, like Qavnerians did.

Books. They glowed. Faces reflected in the light, but

those faces looked oddly not Fey, although they had Fey features. Only one or two Fey features. The cheekbones, maybe, the slightly pointed ears. The upswept eyebrows, the straight black hair. The height.

But little more than that.

There was light, and bubbles, and a solid map floating across all of it, with a moving image traveling up the center, near a river. He squinted at the map, thought he recognized it—but he wasn't sure he recognized the map itself or the images it depicted.

A woman sprawled on her back in the middle of the road. Her face was obscured, turned to the side. Something that hadn't yet come to pass, maybe? He didn't know. He'd never had such a long Vision.

If, indeed, this was a Vision.

A man Lumin could barely see toed the body, a woman in a long coat by his side. The air smelled of smoke.

"This *is* a Fey," the man said, looking at the woman, who was staring at the body.

Another shift, something almost impossible to see. A woman said with certainty, *They're Fey.*

And all dead. A man answered. The same man who spoke a moment before. The man who toed the dead Fey woman. *I don't understand.*

You should, the woman said. *You used the same weapon.*

Helia's weapon, the man said, breathlessly, as if he had just had a realization.

There were maps inside the fortress. They floated just beyond Lumin's reach. He saw a web of light. Someone reached up and shattered the lightstone lamps on the walls.

There's an Enchanter here, someone said.

One of ours? Lumin asked.

I don't think so....

He opened his eyes. He hadn't realized they'd been closed. There was no fog, no smoke-filled air, no smell of sulfur.

He was lying on his back, arms spread above his head, legs tangled. His entire body ached, but he wasn't sure if that was because of the fall or because of what he had just been through.

Eerie was holding his shoulders, her face gray, eyes sunken. Thread was beside her, digging in her healing bag. Thread's black hair was piled on top of her head, accenting her sharp features. Her shirt was twisted along her torso, her legs folded beneath her as if she had knelt beside him before turning slightly.

There were grass stains on the knees of her pants, confirming his assumption.

The air was clear, although he could still taste the sulfur and the smoke. The sky above him was blue, the sun a pale yellow.

"What happened to the fog?" His voice grated out of him, little more than a croak.

"Fog?" Thread answered him. She was holding some kind of poultice that smelled of lavender and something sharp and medicinal. "What fog?"

"The yellow fog we've been plagued with for the past week," he said. "It was everywhere."

"There's been no fog," Thread said. "It's been sunny."

Lumin blinked. He'd been walking through fog for days.

His eyes ached because of it. His mouth tasted of it. He went to sleep, wishing the fog would recede.

"How long have I been out?" he asked.

"I don't know," Thread said, slipping a hand behind his head, forcing it upwards. The slight movement made him dizzy. She placed the poultice underneath his skull.

The pungent odor grew even stronger.

"I don't exactly either." Eerie removed her hands from his shoulders. He could still feel the pressure of her fingers. She must have been gripping him tightly. "I was out for a little while myself. When I came to, you were down."

He tried to push himself up, but Thread put her palm on his chest. "Stay down and let the poultice work," she said.

"What happened?" he asked Eerie.

Eerie glanced at Thread, as if asking permission.

"We think you had a Vision," Thread said.

A Vision. He felt a shiver run through him. He hadn't had a Vision like that since he was a young man filled with promise. That Vision, decades ago, had been filled with light and some kind of walls and an explosion.

Other Visionaries had spent weeks trying to figure it out. But it had been powerful, shattering, something that made them all think he would be a great leader.

And then he had never had another Vision like it.

Until now...

He felt fuzzy, barely able to concentrate. He looked at Eerie.

Her mouth was downturned, her eyes impossible to read. She hunched, which he had never seen before.

He couldn't tell if she was injured or not. It seemed like she might have been.

"What happened," he said slowly, "to you?"

Eerie took a deep breath, then said, "Hadley's dead."

Hadley. The Enchanter traveling with Atrü. Lumin had seen her, hadn't he?

"How do you know?" Lumin asked.

"She's—I can't—we're Linked, remember?" Eerie said.

He remembered now, and he remembered seeing Hadley just a moment ago.

Hadley, bleeding. In a kitchen that had showed up twice in a few moments. In Atrü's arms. People yelling. Talking, something. He couldn't tell.

There had been a lot of blood.

He shoved his elbows underneath him, and Thread increased the pressure on his chest.

"You need to stay down," she said.

He started to shake his head, but he couldn't without getting dizzy. He didn't care, though. He needed to see what was around him, not this awful cheerful blue sky.

"Let me up." It wasn't a request. He used his most forceful voice.

She pulled her hand away, but moved it so that it was near his back, apparently so that she could catch him if he fell.

The movement made him queasy. He braced himself with one hand. The back of his head ached, which wasn't good. He needed to be able to think clearly.

The best way for a Visionary to figure out what he had seen was compare it with someone else.

"You know she's dead because the Link severed?" he asked.

Eerie glanced at Thread again. They had had some kind of communication about him before he awoke.

That would stop now.

"You're going to talk to me," he said with as much force as he could manage. "You will not hide anything because you think I'm hurt."

Eerie folded a little more, as if she was protecting her heart. He had never really thought of her as someone who had a heart, so that seemed odd to him.

"Our Link," Eerie said, "just cut off, as if she blocked it. I felt terror just before it did. And then it shut off, and then—someone else reached out along that Link, maybe Atrü? Trying to find her. For a moment, I saw him holding her and there was so much blood."

"A Vision?" Lumin asked. He had never heard of an Enchanter having a Vision, but there was a phenomenon called an Open Vision, in which the Vision was so powerful that everyone in proximity to a Visionary saw it.

"No," she said. "It was more like a sending—as if someone had sent a warning."

"Hadley?" he asked, ignoring the headache that had settled in his forehead.

"Maybe," Eerie said. "Part of it, anyway. It was so powerful, it knocked me down, and I couldn't get up until I saw all of it. It was a message."

Lumin's left arm was wobbling. He was having trouble holding himself up, which he found strangely embarrassing.

A Visionary shouldn't have physical problems after a Vision. He should just move forward with the information.

"What was the message?" he asked.

Eerie swallowed. That glance at Thread again. Maybe it wasn't permission. Maybe it was an acknowledgement of fear.

"The message," Eerie said quietly, almost as if she didn't want to repeat it, "was simple. It was: *They know we're here. And they can destroy us.*"

THE
TURNOUT

SEREBRO
MOUNTAIN RANGE

THREE

The words made sense. Lumin's Vision finally locked into place inside his brain. The confusion he'd felt, the headache that had accompanied it, all disappeared as if they had never been.

He took a deep breath of startlingly fresh air. He still smelled faintly of that poultice, lavender and whatever medicine Thread had used on his head. The ground was bumpy beneath him, hard and dry.

He placed his hands behind himself on the scratchy grass, and sat all the way up.

"I don't recommend that," Thread said, but he ignored her. The back of his head still throbbed, but that was because he had clearly hit it when he fell.

Eerie hunched near him. Something in her expression told him she was feeling defeated before they had even started.

He turned so that he wasn't facing Thread so much as he was facing Eerie.

"You had a Sending," he said. "It was a jumble."

And if he was right, he had the same Sending. Then it triggered a real Vision.

Eerie nodded. "I saw Hadley, dead."

"What did you see before that?" he asked.

She frowned.

"Anything?" He didn't want to prompt her. He didn't want to give her images that she could invent.

"A woman," Eerie said slowly. "She didn't quite look Fey, but her white hair made me think of a Shaman. Only she couldn't have been a Shaman. She was holding a knife, and she was preparing to use it."

Lumin resisted the urge to nod. He had seen that too.

"She said something about it not being made 'here,' so I'm guessing Qavner?" Then Eerie blinked in something like surprise and raised her head ever so slightly. "There was yellow fog. Everywhere. Even around the man with the satchels."

"Man with the satchels?" Thread asked.

Lumin lifted a finger at her, silencing her. He was going to ask the questions, not her.

"He was Old Family. A Kirilli." She looked at Lumin.

He knew what she was telling him. The Enchanters had discovered that the Old Families had artifacts that had to be confiscated. Magickal artifacts, like the ones his team had taken and placed in the apartment.

"The Kirilli was dead a moment later. No satchels. But he was on cobblestone." Eerie shook her head slightly. "I didn't recognize where they were. There were big stone buildings, like the ones in Nye. There's nothing like that here, at least that I've seen."

She looked at him for confirmation, which Lumin was not going to give. He had seen much of Serebro, but not all of it. He wasn't sure how he would have missed a section with big buildings and cobblestone, but it was possible.

Maybe that was Trinovante, which was where Atrü's troop had gone.

"There was a lot of blood," Eerie said quietly.

Lumin nodded at that, then caught himself, hoping she would think he was nodding encouragement so that she would continue.

"Then it snapped away, and I was starting to move, when Atrü appeared on the grass. He was kneeling and holding Hadley and someone said she was dead, and there was even more blood." Eerie raised her gaze to Lumin, as if she didn't entirely understand what had happened.

She cleared her throat. Thread was watching her now, with the same concern she had used on Lumin.

"Then he faded," Eerie said. "That's when I saw you, collapsed on the ground and twitching. I called for Thread and came over to you. She got here not long after."

"It looked like you were having a Vision to me," Thread said. "But you've never had one like that before, have you?"

Irritation rose in him, and he felt like a young Visionary again, suddenly unable to See anything.

He wanted to lash out at Thread, but he didn't. He decided not to answer her question. In fact, he didn't want to talk to her at all.

But he had to.

"You Saw nothing, right?" he said to Thread. "No Atrü on the grass? No blood? No yellow fog?"

That last bit he had added for himself.

Thread shook her head. Either she had arrived too late for the Open Vision or she had been too far away when it happened.

Also, Domestic magick was very different from Visionary magick or Enchanter magick. Both Enchanters and Visionaries could manipulate their Links.

Domestics weren't even aware of their Links until the Links either grew too strong to be ignored or were shattered.

Lumin wanted to sit with all of this, but he didn't think there was time.

He wished he had someone to consult with, someone who understood his magick. He supposed he could contact the other Visionaries, but he had a hunch they were all dealing with the strangeness of this moment. He couldn't believe that Hadley had delivered the Sending just to him. Nor could he believe that the Open Vision had come just for him.

He let out a sigh and almost put his hand on the ache at the back of his head, but if he did that, Thread would try to make him lie down again.

If he understood all of this right, he had received a Sending just as Eerie had. Then an Open Vision arrived, and because Eerie was near him, she had seen the Open Vision as well.

But he wasn't sure where the Open Vision had come from. Lumin had been able to see Atrü. If Atrü had sent an

Open Vision of that death, Lumin would have felt like he was holding Hadley and covered in blood, as if he were Atrü. He wouldn't have seen Hadley in Atrü's arms.

There were no other Visionaries in Atrü's troop, though, so the Sending couldn't have come from them.

Maybe the swirl of magick and the shock of the moment had created it all. Or maybe that yellow fog, which had crept into that kitchen just a bit with Hadley's body, had a different kind of magick with it.

Something in that moment had created the Open Vision. And sent it to him, and maybe the other Visionaries.

That Open Vision had trigged his own Vision. Everything after that must have been future Vision, things he would have to separate out. Things he needed to understand.

He wasn't sure he could. He didn't know enough about Dorovich, even now, to know where most of those future images took place. He knew that Atrü and his troop were in Trinovante, so the yellow fog had been there.

But the rest of it? The moat? The fortress? The rather generic-looking path with the dead Fey woman and the smoke? He had no way to identify that.

Nor did he know how to identify the Fey who had fallen backwards through a portal, knife piercing their forehead.

He wasn't sure that was in the future or in the past.

What he did know was this: they were in more danger than he had thought. He had thought they could go about their business on Dorovich, blending in with the rest of the population.

There had been a lot of Fey here for a lot of generations.

The Fey that had gotten trapped after the trip through the Place of Power, and the subsequent defeat, had mingled with the local population. That had been centuries ago.

There were no pure Fey enclaves that he could find, but that hadn't mattered. He had assumed that there was enough diluted Fey blood that Lumin's troop looked somewhat normal.

He had figured he and the others could slip in with the right clothing and the right attitude.

It was clear now, from all he had seen, that he had been wrong.

Which meant he had to find a different way to proceed.

He had to become the strong leader he always wanted to be.

And he needed to use his Vision to do so.

PART TWO
THREE NIGHTS LATER

LINGUISTICS

ARCHEOLOGY

HISTORY

REGENTS
TOWER

OLD
LIBRARY

ADV. STUDENT
WING

MAIN
ENTRANCE

CLOCK
TOWER

MEDICAL
SCIENCES

CHAPTER
FOUR

The scream echoed across the entire campus, long, loud, and terrified. Then it got cut off midcry.

May Croninshield knew better than to run toward the sound—not that she could run anymore anyway. She set her tea mug down on the tree stump beside the paved path and peered across the dry ditch toward the area where she thought the sound had come from.

The moon was half full, its light pale and cold. The lightstone lamps added their sunny warmth to the pools of light, but that still didn't illuminate all of the campus paths.

Croninshield could see the path leading to the small stone footbridge with the lovely arches, the footbridge itself and the several paths veering off of it, some leading to the dormitories, some leading to the newer parts of campus, and one leading to the Regents Tower, which had once been a part of the Old Library compound.

Half a dozen students were in her line of sight, all

coming to or going from the library even though it was well after midnight. She was on her so-called lunch break, which for her consisted of the hot mug of tea she had made for herself, three pastries she had snagged from the communal pile, and, in her one nod at health, a small bowl of nuts that she begrudgingly ate because she had heard they were good for her heart.

She always smiled at herself when she had that thought. *Heard that they were...* May Croninshield, Chief Librarian at the most important school in the Qavnerian Protectorate. A woman who knew how to research. A woman who preferred to run the Old Library overnight, because—on good nights —it gave her time to read and explore ideas to her heart's content.

She knew more about her library than anyone else living, and she had never before heard anyone scream like that within its vicinity.

She gathered her misshapen sweater around her ample belly, tugged on the heavy shirt she wore beneath it all, and pivoted back to the library itself.

She was standing about six feet from one of the half-hidden staff entrances. This one was blocked by ancient overgrown shrubs that had eaten part of the path. She always thought about cutting them back and she had never given that order.

She liked having some entrances to the big compound hard to get to.

The library had a lot of secret nooks and crannies, some of that a function of its days as an actual fortress and some of it due to its age. There were more parts of the library that the administration of Serebro Academy had forgotten about than there were parts the administration actually used.

Although that comparison was not fair, considering the administration rarely came here.

They kept things in what they termed May's "capable hands."

May's capable hands were shaking just a bit. That scream sounded serious and the longer she delayed, the worse it might be for the screamer.

That screamer had been a woman, which made the time even more imperative. Try as the administration might to limit criminal activity on campus, crime still happened— often because of raging youthful hormones, boys who didn't understand their own strength, and girls who hadn't yet learned how to enforce the word *no*.

Croninshield slipped through the door, wishing for the very first time that she had assigned security to this tiny part of the building.

The door led into an arched passageway that opened behind some of the stacks. She had to run through the passageway—or rather, what passed for running by a woman who had long since done any real exercise. Maybe fast walking, maybe a ridiculous jog.

She felt everything jostle as she moved. She arrived at the edge of the stacks, saw two student helpers, both boys, putting books on shelves.

"Get security." She wheezed as she spoke, which was just plain embarrassing. She hadn't run that far.

The boys looked up and one of them clutched books to

his chest when he realized who had attempted to bark an order at him.

"Send them through this corridor and out that door." Croninshield pointed behind herself. "I'll be waiting for them."

Then she pivoted and started to head back to the archway when she remembered she had forgotten the most important detail.

She turned around, saw the boys slowly setting down their books, and snapped at them. "This is *urgent*. Someone could be *dying.*"

The boys looked even more scared and startled. She was beginning to wonder if she was going to have to go after security herself when one of the boys nodded his head almost as if he couldn't control it, and said, "Yes, ma'am. We're right on it, ma'am."

And then he tossed down the remaining book in his hand and ran through the stacks, toward some security, she hoped.

The other boy looked in both directions—at her and then toward his friend—and ran in a completely different direction.

Irritation rose. She might have to do all of this herself.

But it would be better if she went toward the scream than trying to get help of any kind.

She hurried back through the archway. As she did, light-stone lamps turned on, startling her. She hadn't realized it had been dark when she hurried inside.

She half ran to the door, then burst through, breathing so hard that she felt dizzy. Okay, maybe the days of three pastries at lunch were done. Her heart was racing hard enough that she thought maybe it would explode out of her chest.

Ahead of her, on that bridge, some of the students still stood, almost like they had frozen in place.

One student, a boy, moved his head slightly. He was listening. He had been one of the students who had stopped when the scream echoed. Maybe he was still listening for another one.

Croninshield stood upright—she had read somewhere that standing upright made breathing easier—and amazingly, that did the trick. Her breath was a little less ragged, her heart rate just a bit slower.

No security, so she was going to have to see what she could find.

That silence following that scream was somehow much worse than the scream itself.

She pushed out of the brambles onto the path, just as two library security guards jogged toward her.

One of the guards was tall, with blondish-brown hair that accented his black library uniform. She had insisted on security uniforms, not for the sake of guards, but for the students, so that they wouldn't try anything untoward in front of someone that they thought of as a random old person.

The other guard wore a regular security uniform, an odd silver that reflected the available light.

As he stepped farther forward, she understood why he was wearing a different uniform. It was Herbert Jaxon, the head of campus security. She was surprised to see him here.

"May, you all right?" he asked. He was of an age with her, but lean and strong, just like he had been when they were in school together as very small children.

She couldn't break him from using her first name if she tried, which she never had.

"It's not me," she said, waving a hand toward the bridge. "Somewhere over there, a woman screamed. It was a serious scream, Jax. Long, and loud, and terrified. I don't know if there's been something since. That kid on the bridge, he heard it, but he hasn't moved toward it. And I'm thinking there's been nothing. Which is worse somehow."

Jaxon nodded, although she couldn't tell if he agreed with her or not. Then he loped toward the bridge, his companion following.

Jaxon stopped near the kid, talked to him, and the kid pointed toward the small copse of trees that some long-ago chancellor had ordered, thinking there wasn't enough green space on campus. As if kids needed green space.

Croninshield followed the two men because she couldn't stay back, but by the time she reached the footbridge, they were already gone—running toward something in the trees.

The kid was sitting on the footbridge's low stone railing, clutching a book to his chest.

As Croninshield reached him, she realized he was young —maybe eighteen, maybe even seventeen, one of the early admittals. His brown face was dotted with acne, his dark brown eyes worried, his swooping eyebrows meeting in the middle because of a frown so prodigious that it looked like his face might get stuck that way.

He was shaking.

"What happened?" she asked. "Was there another scream?"

He shook his head, still looking at the trees. There were half a dozen of them, some saplings, some full grown. Two lightstone street lamps had been placed a discreet distance from the trees because the campus gardeners believed too much light at night would stunt their growth.

Those lights created more shadows in the center of that grove than Croninshield had ever liked.

The security guards were heading toward it now, and there was movement inside, which made her feel somewhat relieved.

The kid was obviously traumatized. From his position, he could have seen that area clearly.

She was torn between talking to him—taking care of him, really—and following security.

"Did you see anything?" she asked, keeping her tone businesslike. Maybe that would calm the kid.

"I-I-I...don't know." He raised one shaking hand to his face. "It-It-I don't know."

This was beyond her. She became a librarian so her interactions with the students would be prescribed. *That book is on the fifth floor.... You don't belong in this section of the library.... Where's your pass?* Not so that she would have to mollycoddle one of these creatures.

"Okay," she said. "Stay here, and someone will talk to you."

He grabbed her arm, which irritated her. No one— certainly not some young student—grabbed her without permission.

She was about to say so, when he said in a near whisper, "There were two people. And then there wasn't."

She frowned at him. "Did the other one get away? I'll get more security on it."

The kid shook his head. "I don't....I don't...I don't know. I think he might still be there. Or not. It was like...she absorbed him."

Croninshield felt her face flush. This kid was probably as young as he looked and probably too naïve by half. He most likely had never seen humans in sexual congress.

She dislodged his hand, then patted it. "Just stay here until security comes back," she said, and hurried down the other side of the bridge.

The footpath was empty now, as if the scream had scared everyone away. It probably had.

The fact that there weren't more students around simply meant less time had passed than Croninshield thought. The campus was too big, and students too oblivious to change routines just because something awful happened.

And from the kid's description, something awful had happened.

Croninshield made herself walk toward the small grouping of trees. She wouldn't be any good to anyone if she arrived out of breath and sweating.

The tall guard was gesturing. He was easy to see in the half-light that filtered between the trees. Jaxon was barely visible, but the light caught his silver hair. He was shaking his head.

Then he pointed away from Croninshield, toward the Campus Security Building. The tall guard took off at a full run toward that building, which made Croninshield's stomach clench.

The kid *had* seen something, and it required more security rather than less.

Croninshield almost stopped and headed back to the library. The guards had it under control; she didn't need to be there.

But she did need to be there, for herself if not for anyone else.

When she reached one of the many forks in the path, she turned toward the trees. Someone was crying—one of those messy cries that came in huge gulping sobs.

Croninshield was about to turn around—this kind of thing was beyond her—when Jaxon saw her and beckoned her over.

It was her own damn fault. She shouldn't have let her curiosity get her into these kinds of messes.

She finally got close enough to see past those lightstone lamps, into the shadowed darkness of that copse of trees. A girl—a woman?—was on her knees, her entire body convulsing with sobs.

Well, that meant if the kid had seen something sexual, it hadn't been consensual.

Croninshield had had a hunch from the beginning that was the case. She hated that it had been confirmed.

And...the last thing she wanted was to be the person in charge of the injured girl because Croninshield was female.

"I sent for more assistance," Jaxon said as Croninshield got close enough to hear him. "Medical staff, more security. We're too late, though, May. He got away."

The person Croninshield had thought of as a girl had the long limbs of a woman. She was wearing a day dress with ruffles along the bottom. They were ripped, as were the shoulders of the dress, which the woman was barely managing to hold into place.

The woman's face was red, her nose swollen, eyes nearly closed, tears dripping off her chin, but Croninshield still recognized her.

One of the overnight librarians. Louella Vance. She must have been on her way to work...late, as usual. But on her way.

"Lou?" Croninshield asked gently, as she crouched.

Louella didn't even look at her, didn't react to her name at all.

"They're sending someone to help you," Croninshield said, hoping she wouldn't have to gather this blood-covered, damaged woman in her own arms. "They'll be right here."

"She's not saying what happened," Jaxon said. "I don't even know where the assailant went."

Just what we need. A rapist on the loose on campus. Croninshield caught the words before they escaped from her mouth.

All she could do was nod.

"Lou," Croninshield said, keeping her voice as gentle as possible. "Where did your attacker go?"

Louella sniffed loudly, then raised her head and met Croninshield's gaze. To Croninshield's surprise, Louella's eyes seemed cold, almost emotionless.

Croninshield had expected sorrow, fear, maybe even anger. Not that ice-cold stare.

Then Louella blinked and tears formed.

"May," she said, her voice rasping oddly. Then she seemed to catch herself. "Ma'am. I'm sorry, ma'am."

"It's not your fault." Croninshield felt off balance, and she wasn't entirely sure why. She had had no idea Louella Vance thought of her as "May." As far as Croninshield knew, most of the staff didn't even know her first name. "Can you say what happened?"

The first part of Louella's response was mumbled, garbled—almost deliberately so, Croninshield thought, and chastised herself for thinking something so uncharitable.

"...attacked me." Louella's voice was thick with tears, but her eyes still didn't match. There was something chilling about them, almost as if the attack had had no real effect on her, and all of this was for show.

"Where did your attacker go?" Croninshield asked.

Louella waved her hand vaguely toward the darker part of campus. The movement was not precise though, and once again, Croninshield had the sense of deliberation behind the movement.

Then footsteps echoed on the path. Croninshield started, and would have expected Louella to do the same, but she didn't. She just remained, crouched, on the grass.

More security arrived. Six men, all bulky, none of them wearing library security guard uniforms. They were wearing the silver uniforms, which made them look bigger than they were.

Jaxon briefed them and pointed firmly in the direction that Louella had gestured at vaguely. More people were coming up the path. Croninshield recognized two of them as the medical team that was usually working overnight.

She tried not to let herself sigh with relief. She wanted nothing to do with this. Clearly, she wasn't emotionally up for any kind of reassurance, any kind of empathy.

Thinking someone who had just been attacked, who was reeling from the strangeness of what happened to her, looked cold and detached was more of a sign that something was wrong with Croninshield than with Louella.

"I'll find someone to cover for you the next few days." Croninshield stood, slowly, knees cracking, thighs protesting. "Don't worry about anything here."

As if Louella was worried about any of that. She probably wasn't thinking at all.

The medics showed up. One of them was a talented woman Croninshield's age. The woman had surprising gifts. She had ways of making the injured feel safe.

Croninshield nodded at her, then stood, swaying a bit because she got up too fast.

Jaxon put a hand on her arm, steadying her. Croninshield nodded at him, then moved away as quickly as she could.

"I shall leave this to all of you," she said, using her librarian voice, somewhat stentorian, quite precise, and always commanding.

Then she turned, so ready to leave, not willing to let anyone know how much this was upsetting her. One of her own, attacked on the way to work.

And Croninshield had things to take care of as well. She would need someone to cover for Louella, not just for tonight, but maybe permanently. Croninshield had seen cases like this before.

Sometimes the women did not recover.

Croninshield took a few steps forward, walking on the grass since some of the security officers were clogging up the path. None of those men wanted to get near Louella, even though they had to question her, to find out who had attacked her.

Croninshield wanted to shout at all of them, just tell them to do their damn jobs. By milling about, they were letting the attacker get away.

She stepped on something, her foot slipping out from underneath her. She had to grab a nearby branch to keep herself from falling.

She was a little lightheaded from the running and all the drama, but not enough to lose her footing on plain grass.

She looked down, saw a pile of something on the grass, and frowned. Then, off to the side, she saw what she had slipped on. A femur. A long one. Human, because there were no animals here that had long thigh bones like that.

Her breath caught and she toed the femur with her solid black shoe. The bone rolled over slightly. It wasn't white or even yellow. It was covered in liquid...

She let out a tiny involuntary yelp. That was blood. Blood. The entire area was covered in blood, which was soaking into the grass.

A shudder ran through her. She had stepped in it. Stepped, slipped, and nearly fallen.

She started to whirl, to let security know what she had

seen, when something shiny and dark caught her eye. Shiny, dark, and a familiar shape.

A skull.

This time, she whimpered, a sound she wasn't sure she had ever made before.

No one seemed to have heard it, and she wasn't about to scream. But she didn't want to walk through the wet again. She wasn't sure what she would do about her shoes.

Then she shook her head. This, *this* was what she had seen in Louella's eyes. This feeling—this—

Except beneath it all, the disgust, the shaking, the whimpering, Croninshield felt a visceral kind of terror.

Identifying the feeling made her step across the soggy blood-covered ground and step back into that small clearing.

Louella wasn't crying anymore. She was snuffling. The medics were bent over her, trying to help her to her feet. Her dress hung about her like rags and it too was covered in blood.

On the upper part. Handprints on the shoulders. Marks that looked like the kind a child would make with fingerpaints.

There didn't seem to be any blood on Louella's legs or the lower part of her dress.

Croninshield frowned, noting the discrepancy, figuring the medics would solve it. Maybe—well, clearly, Louella hadn't fallen into that soggy patch of blood.

Jaxon was giving orders to the other security guards, gesturing with his hands, trying to get someone else to run in the direction that Louella had pointed out.

Croninshield had to force herself to move her feet, to get

to Jaxon's side. She had never thought of herself as someone who would freeze in terror, but then, this wasn't a direct threat, now was it? It was something awful, the remains of something...

Something that bothered her, on more than one level.

She set that thought aside, the way she had set the thought aside about Louella's legs, the blood, the coldness in Louella's eyes.

Croninshield caught one of Jaxon's arms mid-gesture.

"I have something you need to see right now," she said, and tugged him away from the group.

LINGUISTICS

ARCHEOLOGY

HISTORY

REGENTS

TOWER

OLD

LIBRARY

ADV. STUDENT
WING

MAIN
ENTRANCE

CLOCK
TOWER

MEDICAL

SCIENCES

CHAPTER
FIVE

axon knelt over the pile of bones, swallowing hard to keep his gorge from rising. He was not law enforcement, not really. He was pretend law enforcement, the man who kept his own security guards in line.

In fact, he always had to remind the night crew that they were in charge of keeping order on campus, but they weren't supposed to manhandle the students or threaten them with jail.

If someone did something wrong, they were to take that student (and usually it was a student) into the security office, and keep them there until a pair of constables arrived from Serebro.

The city of Serebro had jurisdiction over the campus for real crimes. The campus security handled the petty stuff, from small thefts to altercations in the quad.

The moment Jaxon had seen Louella Vance, crouching, sobbing, covered in blood, he had known that this would not be something his small security force could solve. He had sent two of his guards out to find the assailant, already knowing it was too late to really do so, and one more to the Academy vehicle lot to commandeer a vehicle to travel to the Serebro West Office of the Constabulary.

The cold night air had smelled faintly of fish and saltwater from the nearby Infrin Sea, but now the air also carried the stench of fresh blood. His stomach kept roiling, and he was afraid he might lose the ham sandwich he had had before coming to work.

This, blood, bones, attacks—this was the reason he had never joined real law enforcement. When he learned he had such a sensitive stomach that he wouldn't be able to handle a dead body.

There was no body here. Just bones. A lot of them, the proper amount, he would guess, for an entire human body.

He swallowed hard again, made himself look at the pooling blood. It was starting to coagulate, but there was still a lot of it. Maybe this was what had gotten all over Louella's clothing.

The girl had been damn reticent about what happened, couldn't even tell him exactly where the attacker had gone or even what he looked like.

There was something off about the entire night, and not just because there had been an attack.

Jaxon stood up, wiped the back of his hand over his nose, hoping the smell of onions—which he could not get off for hours after one of those ham sandwiches, not even with a good scrubbing—might overcome the smell of blood.

The onion smell was faint, though, and made him think of food, which made him feel even queasier.

He looked at May Croninshield, who was hovering, hands threaded together and clasped against her breastbone, a posture he had never seen her hold before, not in all of their decades of casual friendship.

"What do you think it is?" she asked.

"Oh, it's human all right," he said, "but whether or not it came from one of the anatomy labs isn't something we can figure out right now."

His words actually made her shoulders go down, and she released a small breath like she had been holding it.

"Anatomy lab," she said.

"Aye," he said. "What else do you think it could be?"

"I don't know...." Her voice trailed off. But he knew the expression on her face. It was one of those expressions he'd seen her get over the years, the one that didn't entirely believe what she had heard, the one that would send her off to investigate something, just to prove the speaker wrong.

"I'll be handling this," he said. "You don't need to worry about it. I believe you'll be one short at the library tonight...?"

He raised his eyebrows, reminding her that Louella was on her staff, not his.

"Yeah, yeah," May said, that damn expression still on her face. "You're right."

"I already sent someone to Serebro," he said. "They'll figure out the bones, the blood, and what's going on. If I had to guess—"

"Don't guess," May said. "Just find the man who hurt Louella."

May could be so irritating. He had never liked that about her. Her commanding voice, her precision. Not many liked that about her. She'd never married or even, so far as he knew, had a relationship. At least he'd had Elaine to go home to for thirty years.

He still missed her. She would've calmed him after this night. She would have made him feel like he had done everything he could.

Even though he doubted he had.

"You're the one who's guessing now," he said, mostly because May rubbed him the wrong way. "You said 'man,' which means you think you know what's happening here, and we don't, May. We don't. There's things that don't add up...."

He stopped talking, but it was already too late. May's gaze focused on him, all sharp and pointed.

"Like what?" she asked.

He wasn't going to tell her, wasn't going to say that he didn't like the way that Louella's hands were clean—all of her was clean—even though her clothing was covered in blood. It didn't make sense.

He'd never seen anything like it, not in all of his years as security on this campus. He'd helped maybe fifty girls over all the years, and none of them—after some kind of assault —had been cleaned off.

He'd thought it was an assault—at first. And now, the blood pool, the bones, the strange marks on Louella's clothing—he wasn't sure what kind of assault. Maybe she was shoved aside by someone who was doing this, whatever this was.

"I can't tell you, May," he said. "I might be a little off myself tonight."

That might explain, to her at least, why he had turned a faint shade of green, the shade that Elaine had always giggled about. *When you get queasy, you turn colors*, she'd say. *And that way I know just how sick you are.*

Goodness, he missed her, never more than at times like these.

May gestured at the bones. "That's enough to make anyone feel off," she said, without using that commanding voice.

She knew the cause of his stomach upset then. No hiding it from her. And there wouldn't be any comfort there either, because May was the prickliest woman he had ever met.

"Go," he said, with more force than he intended. "I'm taking care of this."

She nodded, and her expression softened. For a moment, he thought she was going to say something kind, but she didn't. Instead, she trudged back to the path, head down in a way he'd never seen before.

This had clearly gotten to her as well.

He wiped his hands on his pants, then glanced at the clearing. Some of his men were canvassing, looking for footprints, even though the ground wasn't wet. They would probably destroy any prints, not that it mattered. This was a campus and students cut across the manicured grounds all the time.

One of his men waited behind the medical staff. Jaxon had asked that guard to keep an eye on Louella, just in case she wanted to say something.

The medical staff was bent over her, doing whatever they did. Jaxon hated watching that, because sometimes the staff did private things on site, making sure the girls were okay, checking their wounds, which, in most cases were both personal and extensive.

He sighed, glanced toward the path that May was trudging down. She was moving slower than she usually did, still hunched, as if something had happened to her.

Then there was that kid on the footbridge, leaning against the railing. May stopped and said something to him. The kid put a hand over his mouth, as if he was shocked or surprised, and then he nodded. He left the bridge and headed toward the dormitories, which had probably been his destination earlier.

The kid had been on the footbridge when he heard the scream, and he had stayed there, watching everything. The kid hadn't seen the assailant, though, which bothered Jaxon.

Another strange thing to monitor, among so many strange things to monitor. Because the kid should have seen the assailant as something more than someone who attacked Louella. The kid should have seen the assailant run off, and the kid hadn't.

It would take hours for the constables to get here. The guards Jaxon had sent to fetch them would request at least two, and Jaxon knew that he'd be lucky to get that many.

A crime like this, on the Academy's campus, was too frequent to bother the Serebro constabulary, who seemed to like focusing on property crimes and the infrequent murders. Jaxon always had the sense that the constables that arrived here would be distracted, in a hurry, and unwilling to listen to someone like him.

If the past was any guide, anyway.

Not that he had much to add. Unless his guards found the assailant, which Jaxon doubted they would. Louella hadn't identified the person by name, which either meant she didn't know who had attacked her or she didn't want to admit that the person who had hurt her was someone she knew.

He'd seen both instances, and a dozen in between.

None of them involved bones, though.

Bones and a pool of blood.

His stomach turned again, and he moved away from all of it.

In a few hours, this would be someone else's problem.

He just had to do his best until the constables arrived.

CHAPTER

SIX

Croninshield sat in the librarian's staff room in the Advanced Student Wing of the first floor, not too far from the corridor that she had so innocently meandered down to eat her lunch only an hour or so earlier.

The staff rooms were usually empty at this time of night, unless someone chose to eat their mid-shift meal somewhere other than the library's so-called cafeteria in the very center of this incredible complex.

Usually Croninshield was proud of this place. Usually, she spent as much time walking through it as she could.

But right now, this particular staff room, tucked behind the stacks only available for Advanced Students to browse, seemed safer than anywhere else in the building.

Not that she expected to be attacked. Oh, no. She wasn't thinking of that at all. No one would go after someone like her unless they thought she had money, and Croninshield never looked like a woman who had money.

She came from one of the oldest families in Qavner and, as the last member of a fairly unpopulated branch, she had more money than she knew what do with. But she had gotten rid of her branch's manse in Trinovante decades ago, bought a small apartment in Serebro for the times when she was forced to vacation away from her beloved library, and spent most of her time in the apartment here on campus that the Academy gave her as part of the job.

Over the years, that apartment had become a haven, filled with books culled from the stacks to make room for new arrivals, and furniture that had seen better days because she didn't let anyone up there to replace it.

Even the furniture in the staff room was better than hers at home, but this stuff wasn't as comfortable. Although, she couldn't really compare, because she was sitting a straight-back chair now, looking at her cold and aging feet, with the yellowing toenails and the peeling skin.

She had never taken care of her feet. Okay, truth be told, she didn't take much care of herself, but she hadn't realized until she sat in a room illuminated by three lightstone lamps how ragged her feet looked.

Her shoes were off to one side, covered in blood. Apparently, she had stepped in that pool after all. None of the blood had seeped into her socks, but she had taken them off to make sure.

She really didn't want to put the socks back on either. Or the shoes. She had brought a bucket of water in from a nearby sink along with some rags, so that she could clean the shoes off, but she didn't want to that either.

Then she would have to acknowledge that blood pool. And the bones. And the lessons she had learned, not just from her great-grandmother, but also from all the books she had read over the course of her life.

Croninshield had grabbed a few of the historical tomes off the shelves as she came back here, leaving bloody footprints in her wake. As she had come to the back, she had stopped at the Librarian's Desk in the Advanced Student Wing, told them that Louella was ill, and had asked them if they could handle the work without her.

Of course they could. The students who spent all night in the library were either writing a thesis or they were regular students facing exams. Regular students went to a different wing of the library, and the thesis writers—well, they were usually in the stacks, near the books on their areas of expertise, so that they didn't have to walk far to find out what kind of research had been done on their particular topic.

There were more students in the Thaumaturgical stacks these days than there used to be, but she wasn't ready to go there. The History students were apparently not on deadline or perhaps they had already gone through the secondary sources stage.

She didn't know. She had stopped answering student requests nearly fifteen years ago, when she was promoted to Chief Librarian and had gotten her pick of shifts. She liked the overnights for their quiet.

Their usual quiet.

Her hands were still shaking, and that annoyed her.

They had to settle down before a janitor arrived. She had ordered one to clean up after her. The bloody footprints in the corridor had become bloody heelprints by the time she reached the Advanced Students Librarian's Desk, and were nearly invisible by the time she reached the staff room, but she could still see them.

The janitor was going to have to scrub the floors very, very well, just to satisfy her. Because she would see that blood for a long, long time.

It bothered her. It was so fresh.

Blood that had been carted to that scene shouldn't have been reddish brown. It should have been coagulating, and it should have been mostly black.

Then there were the bones.

The door to the staff room opened, and the janitor entered, dragging a cart. He wasn't really a janitor, just one of the Library Science students whose family didn't really have the money for him to continue his education past the regular student stage.

Otto Arkes was still skinny, even though he had to be in his mid-twenties now. He had a thin mustache that made him look even younger, because it announced his inability to properly grown facial hair.

He was one of her favorites, considerate and hard-working, and true to form, he had brought her a pair of boots from her office several floors above this.

She wanted to tuck her ugly feet under her legs, but that would require a movement she hadn't executed in decades.

He saw her socks hanging from the edge of the battered

couch and said, "Oh, I'm sorry. If I had known, I would have brought some socks."

"The boots are great, thank you," she said, taking them from him. She was surprised at how relieved she was that she wouldn't have to stick her feet into those soggy shoes.

"I'll clean the shoes so you don't have to," he said.

She shook her head. "Let's just throw them away," she said.

Otto frowned at that. "I'm sure there's someone who would want shoes that nice."

The very idea made her stomach twist. There was something bothering her, something to do with history and very old magic.

She was probably being overly cautious, but she had learned to trust these feelings over the years.

"No," she said. "That blood—I think it might be contaminated. Use gloves when you pick up those shoes."

His dark eyes widened, and he looked alarmed. "Contaminated with what?"

Magic, she wanted to say, but she had no proof.

"I don't know," she said, "but there was a puddle of it, and it looked off. I'd rather waste a pair of shoes than cause someone inadvertent harm."

He was already wearing gloves, which she hadn't realized. Of course he would be. Otto was the kind of young man who was extremely cautious about everything, and followed every rule to the letter.

He set her boots near her quite ugly feet, keeping his gaze on her the entire time, which she appreciated, and then he grabbed the shoes and put them into a garbage container on far side of his cart.

She knew the procedures well enough to know there were at least two containers. One for paper, one for food and combustibles. He had put the shoes with the paper, so that they would not get put into the gardeners' bins.

"You might as well take the socks too," she said, "because I'll never wear them again."

She had already checked the hems of her pants to make sure that no blood had splashed on her clothes. She wasn't sure, though, if she would wear these pants again or not.

The night was proving costly in so many ways.

She slipped her feet into the boots. The leather felt rough against her damaged skin, but at the same time, she was relieved to be wearing something else.

"Thank you for this," she said, as she laced the right boot. She was bent over, so she couldn't see his face, for which she was relieved. She felt very vulnerable right now.

"You're welcome," he said. "I'll take the bucket too, if you're not going to use it."

She had forgotten about it already, now that she no longer had to clean the shoes.

She laced the left boot, and then sat up, feeling a little lightheaded. If the night had taught her nothing else, it had taught her that she needed to take better care of herself.

"I'll come back and mop," he said.

He was a good kid. He knew she still needed a moment alone. Or maybe he was as uncomfortable around her vulnerability as she was having him there.

"Thank you," she said. "I'll let you know when I leave."

He pushed the cart out, then closed the door. He was probably going to deal with the shoes right away.

She waited until she heard the squeak of the wheels fade on the other side of the door, before she turned in the chair and faced the books she had stacked on the tables.

She had one of those memories regarding books. If she had seen something on a particular page in a particular book, she could find that something quickly. That skill had served her well in her training as a librarian, and it had served her well as she assisted students over the years.

It also served her well as she figured out which books would remain in the library forever and which ones she needed to sell or, in one case, destroy.

The top book on the pile was the one she wanted. It was a history of Khēmía, written in ancient Khēmíanì and later translated into Qavnerian. She grabbed some gloves that the librarians always kept on nearby tables and slipped a pair on.

This book was valuable, but too important not to have on the shelves. Its value put it in the Advanced Student stacks. There were two other copies of the book—one in the original Khēmíanì, and another more pristine copy of this version—in the special Vault.

That Vault, in the very central core of this library, where the heart of the old fortress had been, opened to Scholars only with special permission and even then, the Scholars couldn't touch the books.

All they could do was watch as someone else—someone trained like her—paged through the volume and showed them the information they wanted.

This copy was considered damaged. It had some unidentifiable black marks near some of the maps in the center and on the endpapers. Those marks could not be cleaned by standard measures.

Still, she handled this volume with extreme care. She slipped her gloved forefinger between the paintings near the front, the paintings that showed the Fey swarming the regions around the Hidden River. Some of the Fey were drawn clinging to the sides of Mount Vitaki.

In the years since she first saw these tipped-in paintings, she had actually gone to Mount Vitaki at the behest of the Forbidden Valley Antiquities Service to see some books that had surfaced in a dig.

Mount Vitaki was not as thin or as smooth as it appeared in these drawings, and in no way could anyone, not even the magical Fey, wrap their arms and legs around the mount as they climbed it.

So, those illustrations, while beautiful, were not representational. But the history contained in the volume, as far as she knew, was accurate. Or accurate enough to cause the book to be on the destroy list during the worst of the Thaumaturgical Purges.

There were events in this book that could only be understood in the context of existing magic. And those hideous Purges had wiped out most of the references to magic throughout the Protectorate.

Except here, in the Old Library, where books like these had been preserved, often to the cost of librarians' lives.

That was another reason she respected these books so very much. They had been survived all kinds of threats already.

The page she was looking for was not that far into the book. There were two full chapters on the Invasion of the Fey. Most Scholars, Advanced Students, and researchers focused on the fact that no one—to this day—knew how the Fey had entered Khēmía in such large numbers without anyone seeing their arrival.

No one ever discovered ships either. There was speculation that they had flown to Dorovich, but not all of the attacking Fey had the magical gift of flight.

Or so it seemed.

There was much Dorovicians did not know about the Fey.

Years ago, Croninshield had read these chapters with great attention. She hadn't been interested in the how of the Fey arrival. She had been looking for how they had been defeated.

Most of the details on the defeat had been light as well. But as she had read for that, she had seen the passages she was now looking for.

The sections on the destruction of villages and enclaves and compounds throughout Khēmía had included a detail that had bothered her when she first read it, and that detail had stuck in her brain.

Throughout the area, especially after the defeat of the Fey, people kept finding piles of bones, sitting in a pool of blood.

She needed to confirm this, though. She needed to know if her memory was correct.

So she scanned until she found the section she had been looking for. It described the aftermath of the battles, the

injuries to locals, the destruction of buildings, the importance of lightstone and windstone in the Fey's defeat, and
then a listing of the "important" dead—the leaders, their
families, the wealthy, and the magical, all who had died at the
hands of the Fey.

In the first instance, though, the ancient Khēmían had
said,

*OTHER DEAD WERE UNCONFIRMED. But the discovery of
bones in pools of blood, often in doorways to important buildings or in dining halls or in secluded parts of compounds of the
wealthy, suggest that many more people died than anyone
could account for. Speculation from the time was that servants
or soldiers had died in a hideous manner defending ruling
classes.*

*The hideous manner—whatever it was—appears to be
unknown. No one discussed it. Most survivors had no memory
of magic that would leave blood and bone, and little else.*

*Some of the Fey magic was obvious—the flaying of skin,
the use of violent creatures like birds with tiny Fey guiding
them—but this magic was not. And the survivors of these
attacks remained vigilant to their dying days, always worried
that something would attack them, pull the bones from their
skin, cast them aside, and leave a blood pool behind.*

LATER DESCRIPTIONS only mentioned that the blood and
bones were discovered in every single village, town, enclave,
and palace that the Fey had ventured into.

No one had known what caused this phenomenon. The blood-and-bones detail showed up in other histories as well.

She thumbed through those books, searching for something—anything—that might give an insight into what had happened. Some of the books went into more detail. They mentioned skulls near the bone pile, intact pelvic bones, so that the people who found the pile knew that the bones had once belonged to a man or a woman, and, in at least one case, a child.

There were so many people missing after the various battles that no one could correlate the missing with the bone pile. Nor could anyone figure out whether the pile had come into being during a one-on-one fight.

The one thing the historians noted was that the piles had a curious uniformity. A blood pool, the bones of the body in an actual pile, and the skull off to one side.

The historians could never find anyone who had seen the magic that created the bone pile performed. No one knew what exactly occurred.

Not even the handful of people found near a bone pile.

When Croninshield read that, the hair on the back of her head stood on end. She had forgotten this, or maybe she had never read it. The detail was in one of the newer histories, one written by a very cautious and renowned Scholar from the city-state of Razbitay.

This book, too, had been translated. Only this time, it was from Razbitos. The Fey had made it into Razbitay, with dire consequences for both the city and the Fey themselves. Eventually, the force that had entered the city had been destroyed, but with much loss of life.

The historian noted that in Razbitay, five different bone piles had been discovered, two after the battle had ended. In those two cases, men were found near the piles, their clothes covered in blood, but their bodies curiously intact.

Speculation was that those men had somehow killed their Fey attackers and did not remember doing so.

Some theorized that the bone pile belonged not to someone from Razbitay, but to the Fey themselves. When killed in a certain manner, the speculation went, they become blood and bone, and nothing more.

Croninshield let out a breath and set this book aside. She needed to consult with someone who understood real magic, someone who had spent their life studying the Fey attack in the Forbidden Valley.

Maybe Croninshield hadn't overreacted when she didn't want to touch her own shoes again. Maybe she had been right to keep that blood away from skin.

The problem was that she couldn't talk to someone knowledgeable tonight. She would have to stay up past her usual post-dawn bedtime and talk to someone in the Thaumaturgical Department. They had an entire History of Magic degree program that had somehow survived the Purges.

She'd met the Honored Professors who had taught in the program and had assisted some of the Scholars they had sponsored. There were very few Advanced Students in that program, by design, because anything to do with magic was considered dangerous these days.

She moved the books to a table on the far side of the staff

room. That table was designed for work in progress, so none of her colleagues would touch the books.

Then she looked at the couch. Maybe if she took a very short nap, she would better ready to face the morning.

But as she approached the couch, she realized two things: the first was that she wasn't tired at all, and the second was that she was too jangled to sleep even if she was tired.

She might see those bones, that blood, that skull, forever.

She wiped a hand over her eyes.

If only her great-grandmother was still alive. Her great-grandmother had lived through the early Purges and had come up with ways to keep the family secure, despite their history of powerful magic use.

Much of what the Croninshields had known was lost to future generations. Croninshield herself had learned the discipline of tamping any magical tendencies down.

She never used magic for casual things, although sometimes it slipped out. Sometimes she believed that her ability to remember where words were on a page of a book she hadn't read for years was part of her magic.

Often, she speculated that her magic—so strong in her childhood that her parents had sent her to live with her grandmother and great-grandmother to learn control—had found ways to reinvent itself.

Once, she had heard someone—a Scholar now long gone —muse on the fact that the Old Library had a magical soul, which meant that it probably had a magical caretaker.

People had laughed at that, and Croninshield had been careful to be one of the amused.

But the idea had floated around her mind ever since then. She knew things about the library no one else did. She was able to find rooms long sealed and books that had seemingly disappeared. She could make her way across this old fortress with ease, despite her increasing age and mediocre health.

She always felt that she and the library were bound together. Sometimes she was convinced that was ego, but it didn't explain the feeling of welcome she had every time she entered the building. Almost as if the library was happy to see her.

She sank onto the couch, and felt its frame dig into her thighs through the thin cushion.

In many ways—non-magical ways—she *was* the guardian of the library. She looked after it with much more care than her daytime counterparts ever had.

And in that role, she needed to keep an eye on Louella. When Louella came back to work—if Louella came back to work—she might have knowledge she didn't know she had.

She might have encountered a Fey, and lived to tell about it.

Which meant that Louella had magic she didn't know she had or that she had never confessed to.

This attack might have been something bigger than any of them realized.

Only Louella could know that for sure.

LINGUISTICS

ARCHEOLOGY

HISTORY

REGENTS

TOWER

OLD

LIBRARY

ADV. STUDENT
WING

MAIN
ENTRANCE

CLOCK
TOWER

MEDICAL

SCIENCES

CHAPTER
SEVEN

Dawn was peeking pinkly over the tops of the jagged mountains on the other side of the Hidden River. The mountains were barely visible from this copse of trees, more like a grayish barrier on the eastern horizon.

Jaxon almost never noticed those mountains, as far away as they were, except at dawn, and only when he was waiting for a shift to end. He wanted this one to be over.

It felt like a complete failure.

His guards hadn't found Louella's assailant. In fact, no one had seen the assailant after the assailant left this little grouping of trees. Not even that kid that Croninshield had found, and whom one of Jaxon's men had tracked down later, had seen the assailant leave. Louella was quiet about all of it, claiming sullenly that she didn't remember anything.

Jaxon hadn't even tried to question her, leaving it to the medical personnel, and the constables.

The constables. What a waste of air they were.

He had been quietly worried about the constables, even before they arrived. The relationship between the Serebro Constabulary and the Academy had been fraying for some time.

The Constabulary wanted the Academy to hire its own constables, all answerable to the Constabulary in Serebro. The Academy's administration had rightfully rejected that idea, but it had caused problems ever since.

The Academy had no legal system, no way of handling crimes on its own, and Jaxon's security team were simply witnesses and the first on the scene, not investigators. So they needed investigators whenever there was a serious crime.

Sometimes the Constabulary sent good investigators. More often, though, they sent whoever was available.

And on this day, that had been two constables who were young enough to have no experience whatsoever. Both were men, which, in hindsight, was his fault. He should have made certain one of the constables was a woman. Women tended to trust each other more with information in delicate situations like an assault.

Jaxon had prepared everything properly for them. He had stayed on the scene. He'd had one of the guards return to the Campus Security Building and bring back red braided rope—a lot of it—which Jaxon had tied around various tree trunks, preventing students from crossing this way.

He had thought that the constables would do a proper

investigation, figuring out where the blood had come from, what the bones were, and if that skull had been stored somewhere.

But the two constables had ignored those things, and instead had talked alone with Louella.

They had returned to Jaxon, who was still on scene, and they seemed angry.

He thought, perhaps, her inability to remember what had happened had irritated them. But before he could ask, the constable in charge, a thirtyish man named Bertie, said, "Y'know, it's a heck of a trip over those mountains."

He wasn't referring to the mountains that were now pinking with the dawn. Those were closer to Trinovante.

Nor was he referring to the Coastal Mountains, to the south and west, which were also tall and jagged.

He was talking about the Serebro Mountain Range, the lowest of the three. The trip was a little over an hour long in any kind of conveyance, and was easy if you were used to it.

Apparently, Bertie and his companion, who had to be all of twenty-five, were not.

"I am familiar with that road," Jaxon said drily. "I've traveled it often."

"Then maybe you should have considered the distance when sending for us," young Bertie snapped. Apparently no one had taught him to respect his elders either.

"I did," Jaxon said. "I always do. We have a woman who was assaulted—"

"She says." Bertie crossed his twig-like arms. The uniform he wore, gold with red and black piping, was beginning to catch the sunlight through the leaves. "She couldn't identify anyone."

"The attack was seen," Jaxon said, working at remaining calm. He would have been better off having one of the college students investigate this matter than these two.

In fact, Bertie's companion, whose name Bertie had garbled on introduction (deliberately so, Jaxon thought), was currently walking the campus with the only female guard who had been on duty last night.

That alone made Jaxon queasy. She was a pretty thing, and he suspected good old Garbled was more interested in her than in this case.

The only reason Jaxon had let Garbled join her was because Jaxon had trained her himself. She was more than capable of shutting Garbled down if he tried anything untoward.

"Not credibly," Bertie said. "And then there are these bones. I spent a year here—"

"You went to the Academy?" Jaxon asked, then silently cursed himself. He hadn't anticipated how much surprise he had let into his voice.

Bertie straightened, lifting his chin as if that movement alone made him as tall as Jaxon.

"I did," Bertie said. "Why does that surprise you?"

Jaxon hesitated before responding. One year meant that Bertie knew very little about the Serebro Academy. One year also meant that Bertie wasn't Academy material.

Jaxon couldn't think of a diplomatic way to approach any of that, but he had to try.

"I think it was the single year," he said. "Generally, students spend four years here."

"Waste of time, that is," Bertie said. "To be the law, you don't need to study the History of the Qavnerian Protectorate. You need to understand the streets."

His implication was that Jaxon did not, and strictly speaking, if the streets were Serebro, Jaxon did not understand them at all.

But he had talked to enough students, particularly angry ones who had been sent away from the Academy, to hear and understand the defensiveness.

Apparently, Jaxon hadn't hidden his contempt well enough, because young Bertie's lip curled.

"If you understood the streets," Bertie said, "you would understand that this crime was not major enough to warrant using the precious resources of Serebro's Constabulary."

"We have remains," Jaxon said, sweeping his right hand at the bones, which no one had touched so far. "We have blood. An injured woman—"

"Please." Bertie mimicked his tone. If Jaxon hadn't worked with students so long, he would have though Bertie was being serious.

But Bertie was actually making fun of him.

"The girl might be covering up for some tryst," Bertie said. "No one saw the assailant. Now, I'm giving your people the benefit of the doubt here. Because if there was an assailant and you couldn't find him, that doesn't reflect well on you, now does it?"

Jaxon didn't move. He'd been goaded by far smarter young men than this one. What was starting to annoy Jaxon the most was that he was going to have to travel to Serebro himself in the next day or so and lodge a complaint against young Bertie.

Maybe Jaxon could do it by letter. Or maybe, he could get the Chancellor to do it.

After all, Bertie and his attitude were wasting time here.

Jaxon could even use Bertie's vaunted *one year* against him.

The thought made Jaxon calmer as he dealt with this idiot.

"And," Bertie was saying, "we both know that the anatomy labs have skeletons of all kinds. I'm sure someone stole one of those, along with some pig's blood. Or maybe they worked together with the local campus butcher and got the blood and bones there."

Well, Bertie had gotten to know parts of campus that most students never saw. Most of them stayed as far away from the Agriculture Departments as possible.

"The bones are human," Jaxon said, keeping his voice level.

"Well, then, Anatomy it is, then, with a contribution of pig's blood. You still do have campus pranks, right?"

Jaxon didn't answer that. Campus pranks were rampant at certain times of year, usually at the beginning of a term when the youngest students felt the freedom of their first absence from home and as yet had no idea how much work faced them.

"The girl probably interrupted someone laying out a prank," Bertie was saying. Apparently he loved the sound of his own voice. "It was midnight, wasn't it?"

"It was," Jaxon said.

"For students to stumble on bones and blood in the dark, well, that would make a prankster very happy."

Jaxon wondered if this whelp knew that from experience.

"The prankster probably shoved her or something, and got blood on that pretty dress of hers—that would explain the handprints—and she overreacted and screamed, and everything tumbled down from there."

Bertie unfolded his arms, shrugged one shoulder as if none of this concerned him, and then glared at Jaxon.

"You can solve pranks like this on your own, you know," Bertie said. "I wish you had checked with Anatomy before bringing us across that mountain."

The sun had finally crested the mountain peaks. The air wasn't warm, and the light was thin, but it did show the mess that this area had become.

There were footprints everywhere, from a variety of sources, including—most likely—him. The bones were piled but the skull had rolled to one side.

There were divots in the ground near the path, in the area where Louella had been kneeling. The divots probably came from the medics.

"You're here now," Jaxon said, drily. "You can check with Anatomy to see if any bones are missing."

"Oh, we're heading back," Bertie said. "I don't know if you know, but the Office of the Constabulary wants us to keep track of our time on every single call. This one cost much too much time for the seriousness of the occurrence."

"An assault on a woman," Jaxon said, "and a probably grisly murder."

"A prank and a shove," Bertie said.

"What proof do you have of your theory?" Jaxon said, unable to take this whelp anymore.

"What proof do you have?" Bertie asked.

"The woman's word, an eye witness, and a disturbing mess in these trees," Jaxon said.

"See, now," Bertie said in a tone that implied that Jaxon was the stupid one, "if you had street experience, you would know that women lie, particularly over so-called assault, especially if they're out when they shouldn't be at night—"

"She was coming to work," Jaxon said.

That actually stopped Bertie's little rant. "At midnight?"

"We have people on staff all night at various locations," Jaxon said.

"Women too?" Bertie asked.

"Just like your Constabulary," Jaxon said, making a note of young Bertie's attitude. His bosses wouldn't like this, particularly since a good half of the senior officers that Jaxon had dealt with in Serebro were female. "I take it you never went to the library at night in your *one year* here?"

"Well, it doesn't matter," Bertie said, recovering, but not before shooting Jaxon another glare. "If there had been something untoward, like a killing or something, there'd be more than this very organized situation."

"Unless the person died elsewhere," Jaxon said. "But you haven't investigated that, have you? If you had done any work at all, you would have known that the young woman was on her way to work, that she was traumatized by her experience—which liars never are—and that we have a situation here important enough to roust *someone* from Serebro who has *proper* investigative experience."

"Well, you rousted us," Bertie said, with a slight sneer. "And *proper* investigative experience tells me that this was something you shouldn't have bothered us with."

He nodded once, then moved onto the path.

"I will make a note of this time-waster," he said, as he started to head back toward the Campus Security office where he had left his vehicle. "I'm sure your boss would like to hear about it."

Jaxon sighed, just a little. He *was* the boss, and if the whelp had done even a little research, he would have known that. He could also have figured it out from the introduction.

But young Bertie had a chip on his shoulder when it came to the Academy—and, Jaxon would wager, when it came to life. Jaxon would use young Bertie's dislike of the Academy in his report. He'd mention it in the letter in the proper position, so that it would be clear that Bertie had not done his job because he disliked the Academy.

If Jaxon ended up having a meeting on this, he would have more difficulty giving this information without sounding bitter, but he would do it.

Bertie had interfered with this investigation in a way that bothered Jaxon. He wasn't sure what the upshot of that interference would be, but he knew that something had gone sideways.

He just wasn't sure what that something was.

LAW BUILDING

TLER
L

REGENTS
LODGING HOUSE

MEDICAL
SCIENCES

CAMPUS
MEDICAL UNIT

ANATOMY

CHAPTER
EIGHT

S hyly staggered her way out of the double doors in the Medical Practice Wing of the Medical Building. The entire place had smelled of some kind of antiseptic, which had made her nervous. She had no idea what the antiseptic was made of, primarily because Louella Vance had no idea what antiseptic even was.

Shyly hated the first few hours in a new body. It usually took her nearly two days to assimilate her memories and knowledge with the memories and knowledge she stole.

But Shyly had had to act quickly here, and she was paying for it now. She was sorting through Louella's memories as if they were organized. They were not.

Not to mention that Louella had very little experience with the Medical Building. Louella had only been in the Medical Building once to pick up documents and some boxes of ancient items that a professor had donated to the Old Library, but that had been years ago.

It had also been on the other side of the building, which was quite far from here.

The Medical Building wasn't as large as the Old Library —few buildings were—but it was large enough, the size of one city block, the chancellor liked to say.

The building was square and five stories high. It had been partitioned as it was built into classrooms, offices, a place of medical research, a wing dedicated to "old traditions," which, if Shyly had to guess, she would have guessed that the "old traditions" were some kind of magickal healing, and then, of course, the Medical Practice Wing, dedicated to treating all kinds of medical problems that occurred here on campus.

The room she had been in had had lightstone lamps along the ceiling, so she had kept her head down the entire time she was there. It hadn't been hard. Every member of the staff thought she was so traumatized that she could barely talk, and she let them think that.

Lightstone was a particular danger. Doppelgängers were protected against some forms of local magick but not all. Perdu, the other Doppelgänger in this troop, told her that he believed they were safe from diffuse light from lightstone— far away light, like ceiling light—but anything concentrated, like light from a nearby lamp, would be very dangerous.

In fact, he had reported feeling a deep sharp pain in the middle of his forehead when he had looked directly in the light from a lightstone lamp.

Shyly didn't want to test any of that, so she stayed as far from lightstone as she could, except in circumstances like this, where she had very little control.

She had chosen a small grouping of trees to take over Louella because it was shadowed and there hadn't been a lot of lightstone nearby. Just two tall lamps that illuminated the paths, but not the cluster of trees.

She had been fortunate to have that darkness. It had allowed her to complete the takeover before anyone noticed anything was wrong.

That had seemed like days ago, but it had only been hours. The sun was coming up and sunlight was spreading across campus, dousing the lightstone lanterns that were scattered along the paths. Dozens of students, all clutching books and looking quite determined, were heading to the first class of the day. Some of them were arriving at the Medical School, and all of them—if they saw her—gave her a sideways look of surprise.

Shyly knew she was a mess. She wore some kind of loose shift garment over the dress that Louella had been wearing when Shyly attacked her. That dress was ruined, but it was all she had—that, and the unfamiliar undergarments, and the intolerable shoes.

They pinched at the toes, something Louella had thought of all the time but felt was worthwhile considering their stylishness and beauty.

One of the first things Shyly would do when she got to Louella's room in the staff apartments would be to toss those shoes out. Shyly would say that they reminded her of the attack, but in reality, they were just about the most painful things she had ever had on her feet.

She probably should have taken them off in the Medical Wing, for all the protection they gave her feet. The medical staff would have seen that as more traumatized behavior, and pretended at understanding it.

They all believed that Louella had been sexually assaulted, even though there was no evidence of that.

And Shyly was so good at transferring herself into a new body that there was no bruising on Louella's skin either.

The attack had gone quickly.

Shyly had simply stopped Louella on the path and asked for directions. Louella had smiled at her, and then launched into some kind of convoluted explanation.

From Louella's point of view, Shyly had been a foreigner, someone who was either new to the campus or new to Qavner. She had been wearing a Nyeian body from her last transfer, a middle-aged woman whom everyone in Nir, the capitol city of Nye, had thought an expert in the lands across the Infrin Sea.

The woman had presented herself as someone who had been to Dorovich many times, but, Shyly had discovered upon the transfer, she had only gone once, as a child, accompanying her father on a merchant vessel right after her mother had died.

The woman's memories were scant and useless. Shyly had been about to find another host when Lumin had approached her. He wanted her to come to Dorovich with him because he needed Doppelgängers. He claimed she was the best, but they both knew that was wrong.

If she had been the best, she would have properly researched her Nyeian host.

She hadn't even researched Louella. That information had come from Perdu, who was already on campus in the body of a visiting professor. Perdu had taken over the man as he traveled to the Academy, figuring that it would be easy for him to pretend ignorance of everything Serebro and the Qavnerian Protectorate in the guise of someone who hadn't been to either place.

Apparently, that had paid off. And Perdu had sent word that what they needed was someone with a lot of knowledge of the Old Library. He had suggested a librarian.

Shyly had watched the library for two days, and settled on Louella. She seemed to know everyone, and she appeared quite competent.

Shyly figured that was exactly what she needed.

Now she wasn't so sure.

She was standing outside the door of the Medical Practice Unit just for a moment. She had to let Louella's map of the campus fill her head. Shyly's few days on campus had not allowed her to understand everything she was seeing.

It hadn't helped that the place felt both unfamiliar and terrifying. It had the feel of the magickal places that she had encountered throughout L'Nacin, in particular, places that had a long history of magickal contact.

She knew vaguely about Dorovich's difficult relationship with magick. There had to be strong magick here because of the horrid Fey defeat centuries ago. But as she learned more about the Protectorate, she realized that the Dorovicians had let their knowledge of magick recede.

She wasn't sure if that was a benefit or a hindrance. She would figure that out in the next few days...she hoped.

Right now, she had to find her way to Louella's apartment, without encountering too many of Louella's friends.

Shyly hadn't realized how many friends Louella actually had, but it seemed that everyone knew her, from campus security to random students to professors. Perhaps that was because of her job at the library.

Shyly was just beginning to understand that job. The Fey did not keep knowledge in books, although they had encountered a few cultures that did.

The Fey believed in keeping the magick with them, usually as part of them, not imbuing it into objects. The cultures that used objects always seemed to have a difficult relationship with magick, one that made it easy to forget how magick worked.

Even though she was starting to assimilate the memories of this woman, Shyly didn't entirely understand how these people could acknowledge that magick existed, and yet somehow determine that it either wasn't for them or it wasn't something they wanted to use.

It was a dichotomy she would explore later, when her head wasn't aching from the converging memories and the familiar struggle of taking over someone new.

A shiver ran through her, reminding her to get to shelter. The morning air was cold and there were too many curious glances in her direction. At some point, one of those friends of Louella's would want to talk to her or take care of her, and Shyly wasn't ready for that.

She needed to lie low for a day or two so that she could absorb Louella's memories enough to don Louella's personality.

Right now, it was a bit of a mystery—a woman who made friends easily and often, and yet one who preferred time alone with books. That made no sense at all and Shyly wasn't certain how she was going to become that person.

She couldn't even tell at the moment if Louella was someone who dominated a conversation or not.

Perhaps this trauma would provide cover, though. It would make others allow for a slight personality change because of what Louella had been through.

Right now, though, Shyly was just confused. There was little that she had in common with Louella. She had an entire group of memories that didn't appear to be hers, and yet seemed quite alive—things she couldn't have known, such as historical incidents.

Shyly hoped that would all sort itself out, because she couldn't go about being confused about who she had taken over. She had to pass for Louella credibly.

It wasn't as important as it would have been in a battle-field situation with someone who understood Doppel-gängers and Fey tactics, but it was still important.

As was getting past this takeover.

Shyly had chosen to take over a body in a somewhat public place, which meant that the bones of her previous host littered the ground, not to mention all of that blood.

Other cultures knew what that meant, but as far as she could tell, this one didn't. The Dorovicians didn't seem to know much about what happened outside of this continent, and here in Qavner, the Qavnerians didn't seem to care about what was going on in the rest of the Protectorate.

Lumin believed the Fey could use that to their advantage. He planned to let Rugar know when everyone returned —*if* everyone returned.

Shyly shuddered just a little and wrapped the overly large —and overly thin—shift-dress thing around herself. She needed to get to that apartment.

Shyly stumbled forward, wobbling on the painful shoes. More and more people were looking at her.

It seemed that the number of students and professors on the path had grown. She stopped, turned, and looked up at the clock tower, which she hadn't even realized was there a moment ago, and saw that the first classes of the morning started in just a few minutes.

No wonder everyone was hurrying and looking stressed. She would wager that some of the glances she got were because no one wanted to stop and help her, although some would feel obligated to do so if she asked.

She wasn't sure if those assumptions were from Louella, but Shyly had to assume they were. Which meant that the memories were starting to tie to emotions.

This was one of the most dangerous points for a Doppelgänger, and easiest time in which to make a mistake. Right now, separating herself from the host was almost impossible, and yet Shyly felt like herself, with a few new memories crammed in.

She needed to get to that apartment and be alone. And she had to trust Louella's memories to get her there.

Shyly put her head down and walked quickly, not acknowledging anyone. She thought she heard a familiar voice say, "Louella?" but the use of the name meant the voice belonged to a friend of Louella. If Perdu had found Shyly, he would have approached her differently.

Shyly was envious of Perdu. He had corralled the visiting

professor as the professor on the way to the Academy. Somewhere in the mountains, Perdu had taken him over.

Shyly didn't know, and no one had said, whether or not Perdu had taken an extra day or two to assimilate the memories of the new host, but the one thing Shyly did know was that the bones and blood of Perdu's previous host were still hidden in the forests between the Academy and Serebro.

Here, the bones were going to cause a ruckus.

Ruckus. That was a word she had never used before.

A bemusement rose in her. Word choice was only one of dozens of changes ahead. And even those—and her own emotional reaction, like bemusement at the wrong time— would cause others to think she was acting strangely.

She finally reached the staff apartment complex. It had been built a hundred and fifty years ago, which made it "new" in Academy parlance. The area was called a complex because there were at least ten buildings that she could see.

They had clearly been built in segments, some taller and wider than the others, some shorter and narrower. She didn't have to ask which building was hers. Her feet took her directly to it.

The apartment building was medium-sized for this little complex. Two stories, with what looked like two apartments on the first floor and three on the second. All of them had windows which overlooked the other apartment buildings.

Children laughed in the back, and her Louella memories told Shyly that there was a central play area set aside for the little ones. Closer to the edge of campus were two schools for children, both considered practice schools for teachers.

Shyly would avoid the schools. They were dangerous for

her. Children could sometimes see magick much more clearly than adults. On previous missions, she had had very young children wonder aloud if she was two people instead of one.

She didn't dare have that happen here, not when she was working alone with no assistance.

Stone steps led up to the building's main door. The door was wood, with scratches along its face—not from an attack or someone trying to get in, but from use.

In fact, the entire building was both stone and wood, unlike the older parts of campus, which were mostly stone.

She was grateful for the wood. Deep down, she'd been worried about lightstone threading its way through the building.

She had mentioned that concern to Gray, their Spy, and he had laughed. *If the Dorovicians had lightstone threaded through the building, they wouldn't sleep. The lightstone would make the entire interior light as day.*

And windstone? She had asked.

It's too thin and porous for building materials, Gray said. *Not to mention loud. Any time a wind would blow, the windstone would either sing or it would howl.*

She had no idea where he had learned this stuff, but it was his job to do so. And he had had to do it early, before Lumin sent Perdu up that mountain. Sometimes it wasn't safe for Doppelgängers to exist in an area filled with wild magick.

That magick could either reveal the Doppelgänger, or kill them.

Lumin had to assure himself that his Doppelgängers would be safe so that they could be useful.

Eventually, when the memories finished merging, Shyly would know everything that Louella knew. If Louella knew what materials were common in construction, then Shyly would know it too.

Right now, she hesitated before climbing those stairs, uncertain if she needed keys. She had none. Louella hadn't been carrying a purse or a bag or anything that would bring her possessions into the Old Library.

Yet, Shyly knew that the door to Louella's apartment was locked, because she had vivid recent memory of Louella locking the door as she left the night before.

And if she had a memory of locking the door, that meant she had used a key but Shyly had no idea where it was.

The panic she had been barely keeping at bay rose inside of her. She had no idea how she would get inside, what she would say to anyone who tried to help her. She was afraid someone might figure out that she wasn't Louella.

Or they would have, if she lived in a place that had actually studied Fey magick.

Shyly let out a breath, reminding herself to be calm. The Fey had fought one big battle here, and they had lost. No one had studied how they operated. No one perceived them as a threat.

Hardly anyone paid attention to what the Fey were doing all the way across the Infrin Sea.

Louella had met scholars who studied international relations, and they seemed to know how the Fey operated politically, but had no interest in Fey magick at all. The military throughout the Protectorate seemed focused on conquest of non-Protectorate countries and keeping the countries inside the Protectorate in line.

If someone thought she was acting in an uncharacteristic fashion, they would think it was because of the attack, not because they had encountered a Doppelgänger.

Shyly straightened her shoulders and walked up the stairs, still wobbling in the damn shoes. Her ankle twisted, and she nearly fell, catching herself on the corner of the entry.

The exterior door burst open, nearly hitting her. A man (oh, she recognized him but couldn't access his name) scurried past her, sending a "Sorry, Louella," over his shoulder.

She grabbed the door, and let herself inside.

The hallway was narrow, and now that the door was closing behind her, dark. There appeared to be one light-stone lamp affixed to the wall in the center of the hallway, but either the fixture was dirty or the lamp wasn't very powerful.

She didn't look at it, keeping her head down.

The hallway smelled of cooked onions and garlic, a smell that seemed baked in rather than something coming from one of the apartments. Part of her found the smell pungent and eye-watering, and another part of her found it to be so familiar that she barely noticed it.

Which meant that the hallway usually smelled like this.

There was a door to her right, with a number on it. That door was not hers. There were two more doors at the opposite end of the hallway, one on either side. Neither of those were hers either.

To her right, a wide staircase went up three steps to a landing, and then turned to her left. She mounted the stairs. They felt familiar. She knew how to avoid the thin spots in the wood, the places that Louella, at least, had thought just a little dangerous.

Shyly put a hand lightly on the wooden railing before pulling her hand away. The Louella part of her warned of splinters, because, apparently, Louella had gotten some shortly after she moved in here.

But Louella had loved her home. She had waited for it, signing some kind of document that put her on a list for a one-bedroom with indoor plumbing.

That was what Shyly hadn't seen—she hadn't seen a bathroom door or facilities outside. This was an upgrade from some of the places she had encountered with previous hosts, particularly in L'Nacin, where they hated adding private baths into construction.

Shyly felt her shoulders relax just a bit. Once she got inside, she could take her time cleaning up.

Her door was the first one she saw as she reached the top of the stairs. The far corner, with good light and a nice design, or so her Louella memories told her.

Shyly stood on her toes and slid a key off the top of the doorframe, almost without thinking about it.

Then she frowned. That was a stupid way to keep the apartment locked. Maybe Louella had felt very safe here.

Shyly couldn't access any memories of another key.

Which meant that this was one habit that Shyly would change almost instantly. It was almost as dangerous as keeping the door unlocked.

She bent slightly, put the key in the lock, and turned to the left. It felt new and it also felt like she had done this every day for years.

She pushed the door open and slipped inside, relaxing immediately at the scent of lavender that Louella had purchased at the small store inside the Alchemy Department.

Shyly froze at that thought. The *Alchemy* Department. For magick. Which meant there was magick in the lavender, even though Louella had probably not been aware of it.

Shyly actually rummaged through her memory, finding the purchase, and thinking about what she had been told (what Louella had been told).

She had been told—by a student, not a professor—that the lavender was calming, perfect for relaxation after a stressful day.

Calming.

If she could, Shyly would have spoken to the Domestics about that. But she wouldn't be able to see them, maybe for days or weeks. She was on her own.

The lavender scent did feel soothing. She was going to have to trust the memory and hope that the magick inside that one fragrance wouldn't reveal who she was.

She leaned on the door, wondering if she should get rid of whatever caused the scent.

No one trained Doppelgängers for small unknown magicks, especially those of foreign origin. Most of the people Doppelgängers overtook were soldiers or political leaders. Never a librarian in a country that seemed to think magick was something that had to stay hidden.

The apartment was nice—or would have been, if it wasn't so messy. Books covered every surface, except a long couch, positioned a few feet away from one of the windows.

The windows were dramatic, covering both walls, and separated by a reddish brick. The window directly in front of her had a window seat, which had a blue cushion along the bottom, a cushion that was sunken in one spot, and was covered with more books everywhere else.

Shelves were built into the walls where there were no windows, so apparently, it was expected that the resident would fill them. Louella had filled them with books, and nothing else. A kitchen stood off to one side, with full cupboards and a flat area on top of an iron woodstove.

There was no smell of smoke here, though, and the single kitchen counter was covered with books, not cooking equipment. Apparently, Louella did not cook here or even use the stove for heat.

Someone had stacked wood beside it, but the wood actually had a cobweb across one side.

Shyly ran a hand along her face. She was shaking, for reasons she didn't entirely understand. But she had come to trust that. She would have to find whatever caused the lavender scent, and get rid of it very quickly.

First, though, she needed to see what else was here.

She stepped deeper into the apartment, disturbing dust motes on the rugs that led to the back room. Clearly, Louella had not been a cleanly person, which actually made Shyly shudder.

Shyly was a cleanly person. She had to be. She needed to know where everything was for each of her identities. She even had to be tidy within her own mind, setting the old personalities aside so she could focus on the new one.

She pushed open the door off the kitchen, which led into a bedroom. There were more windows here, but they were blocked with a plain covering that had clearly come with the apartment. A bed was in the center of the room. End tables with two lamps stood on either side.

The lamps appeared to be made of lightstone. They looked new, compared to most of the fixtures in this place.

The bed was made, which was a surprise, but one entire side was covered with more books. There were books on the end tables and books on the floor as well, but there were no shelves in here. There was some kind of bureau, with potions on top.

Those would have to go.

Another door opened into the vaunted indoor bath. There was a tub that could barely fit one person (if they had their knees up) and a toilet beside it, as well as a bucket sink that appeared to be the only one in the apartment.

The bath was on the wall between this apartment and the next, so if Shyly splashed around in there or made too much noise, she would wager that the people in the other apartment would be able to hear her.

She would be careful.

She scrounged around for a bag, something that she could use to remove the potions. None of them seemed to be the source of the lavender scent. She would have to go on a hunt for that.

She needed to make this place comfortable for herself before she started her actual mission. Besides, everyone would expect her to take some time for herself after the attack.

She would look through these books, stack them properly, and figure out what they were.

A culture like this one probably hid a lot of secrets in books.

She knew they hid a lot of magickal items in that Old Library. Gray had learned that even before Perdu had chosen his new host.

Apparently, there were magickal items scattered throughout this campus. Some of them would be accessible to Shyly and the secrets of others might be in the various tomes stored in the library's locked rooms.

She would figure out all of that.

But first, she needed to take care of herself.

First, she needed the time to become someone new.

ALCHEMY, SCIENCE & THAUMATURGY

GOVERNMENT

LAW BUILDING

WHISTLER HALL

CHAPTER
NINE

Croninshield stuffed her hands in her misshapen sweater. She walked along one of the paths in the oldest part of campus. Generally, she liked this part of the Academy. It felt like a contained city, and she loved the feeling of history, the fact that she was walking on paths that so many others had trod over hundreds of years.

She still wasn't tired, even though the sun had been up for more than an hour now. The light was diffuse, coming through an accumulation of cirrus clouds, some lodging near the mountains.

It was colder than she expected, and the air had the faint smell of the ocean, meaning the wind was coming off the Infrin Sea. She doubted the sun would rise high enough or be strong enough to defeat that chill.

Or maybe the chill lingered inside of her because of the events of the night.

Her mouth was dry. She was getting to a corner of the

old campus that she hated, and she was slowing down. She needed to go to the Thaumaturgical Department.

She wasn't sure she had ever *needed* to go there before, even though she had gone too many times in the past.

The Thaumaturgical Department had lived forever in the Alchemy, Science, and Thaumaturgy building, the oldest building on campus. The building appeared to be a small stone hut built into the side of a mound that some maps listed as the beginning of the foothills leading into the Coastal Mountains.

The mound wasn't a foothill. It wasn't even really a mound, at least as far as Croninshield could tell. The AST building was as difficult to see as a tall mountaintop.

No matter what the weather, AST was always enshrouded in fog. Some claimed that was because the potions the students were always mixing in the Alchemy Department had created a permanent fog. Others thought it a weather phenomenon created by the confluence of trees, a nearby marsh that no one could enter without getting trapped, and a lake on the building's opposite side, all interacting with the mountains themselves.

Croninshield had no idea what caused it. All she knew was that she tried to avoid the building—and the fog—as much as possible.

Part of the reason she stayed away was because of the magic.

She had been a young student, studying Library Science and practically living in the Old Library, when a chancellor (who ended up not staying very long) decided to close the building, with the idea of eventually tearing it down. He had found a spot for the Thaumaturgy Department in one of the new buildings, which would have given the department less room but more security (in theory), something that the professors in that not-quite-post-Purge era had asked for.

Eventually, the Alchemy Department would move as well, and Science was supposed to get its own building. Thaumaturgy needed to move first.

The area was prepped, the building finished, and professors started moving their belongings...which would mysteriously return to the original offices in AST overnight.

Croninshield had always been a late-night person, and one night, she had seen a trail of books heading across the path, floating over the marsh, and into that fog.

The books were traveling on their own. Others later testified to that, but Croninshield had never told anyone, because of the Purges were still too close. Her family had told her to never ever discuss magic with anyone, and she rarely did, even now, except when there was a library reason to do so.

Or something like today.

Because of that experience, though, and a handful of others that had also unnerved her, going to AST made her very uncomfortable. She was almost more afraid to go into AST than she had been to stand near those bones.

But she wasn't a green student anymore. She was the Chief Librarian, and she knew all of the professors inside that building.

She could easily go in without an appointment. She could stop classes. She could do whatever she needed.

That thought didn't make her feel better. The only good

thing about going to the Thaumaturgical Department more than once was she knew that some of the nerves she felt had nothing to do with her.

The area around this ancient building always made her feel nervous, and the feeling wasn't unique to her. It seemed that a wide variety of people were reluctant to come here. Most professors who were not part of the departments housed in this building insisted on meeting with anyone from those departments in one of the cafeterias or in the library.

One of the reasons that long-ago chancellor wanted to move the departments was because he felt uncomfortable near the building, and thought perhaps it was because the building itself was old and falling apart.

As far as she could tell, AST wasn't falling apart. It seemed to renew itself. No one ever fixed anything around it, but nothing ever broke down there, either.

She swallowed hard and forced herself to continue. She also forced herself to breathe evenly and to attempt to slow down her rapidly rising heartbeat.

Nothing bad had ever happened to her in AST and she had never had a bad encounter with any of the staff who worked there, but that didn't stop the emotions from building.

It didn't help that she had had a difficult night, and she was going to have a difficult conversation.

Although she wasn't certain about that part. It was just that she had never had an easy conversation with anyone inside that building.

She took a sharp right on the path before her, leading to

that illusion of a stone hut surrounded by fog. Four students walked ahead of her, all of them tall and thin, and two of them wearing the golden robes that Alchemy insisted on if the student had a lab day.

They walked single-file, heads bent, as they hurried down the cobblestone path that led to the arched door of the so-called hut. They had the look of students heading to class.

The student at the head of the line, a young man with a shock of black and silver hair, pushed the door open as far as it would go, but didn't hold it for the student behind him. The others trailed in, each touching the door with their fingertips as they went by, holding it open.

Croninshield hurried, so that she wouldn't have to ring for entrance—something else she hated about this place.

For a moment, she thought the door would close before she got there. Instead, it stood open as if someone had blocked it.

The door bothered her as much as the building did. It was made of very old wood, which apparently had come from the Razbitay Mountain Range. There was a lot of reddish brown Razbitay wood in the old buildings on campus, even in her precious library.

She didn't mind the wood. She thought it pretty, especially when it was properly polished—something she made sure of in the library itself.

But this door was more than an entry point. It was covered with art, some kind of cross between a carving and a sculpture.

Parts were recessed. Other parts were either attached or carved outward. And even more parts were etched into the door's face, which was one reason why she didn't want to touch it.

People said the design was beautiful, but she could never accurately see it. She could see the mountains, carved as they appeared around the building, and the hut itself, cut into the wood.

Along the top, however, was an image of the crest that the Academy stopped using during the Purges. The crest showed a crown floating above a heart over the tip of a broadsword.

At least, that was what the crest looked like in illustrations around the Old Library and in stone carvings in some of the other buildings.

This crest seemed to move. Sometimes she saw the sword's tip pointing at the heart. Sometimes she saw the heart wearing the crown. And once, she saw no heart at all.

On this day, she didn't even look at it. She didn't want to know what had changed, if anything.

She had never told anyone what she saw or how it changed. Her great-grandmother had told her once, in a very hushed tone because they had been discussing magic, that sometimes Croninshield would see things no one else could. Her great-grandmother had told her to get used to that.

Croninshield never had gotten used to that, but she rarely experienced it the way she experienced this door. It was almost as if the door were a live thing, trying taunt her in some way.

She slipped through it, half afraid it would try to close on her as she entered.

The interior was dark—or, at least, darker than outside.

She knew from experience that a flight of stairs would take her to the main floor, so she walked toward them, her footsteps echoing on the stone floor.

She reached for the banister, when the lightstone in the steps flared on, nearly blinding her. She blinked hard, unable to stop the thought that this building actively hated her.

The scent of burning sage floated toward her, making her wonder what Alchemy was doing at the moment. The smell made her eyes water.

If she hadn't felt so strongly about what she needed to do, she would have fled the building. Instead, she climbed the stairs, gripping the stone banister tightly, half afraid that the stairs would buck her off and send her tumbling back to the entry.

She turned right when she reached the top and went through a stone arch into a corridor with an arched ceiling. The doors along this corridor belonged to professors. Classrooms in the Thaumaturgy Department were on the top floor of this wing for reasons she didn't understand.

There was also a library filled with tomes about magic, most of them written in languages other than Qavnerian. She had once said that those books needed to be in the Old Library, but the then-head of the Thaumaturgy Department had said something that had chilled her to the bone.

If someone wants to destroy all we know about magic, the worst thing we can do is keep the literature in one place.

He had lived through the worst of the Purges. She had thought at the time that his comment had come from that experience.

Now, though, she wasn't so sure. She wasn't certain

what had changed her mind, but something had in the intervening years. Maybe it was the Regents Library, which was filled with tomes that she hadn't entirely understood and more maps than she wanted to think about.

The Regents had moved it to the Old Library years ago. Now, it was housed in one of the oldest wings of the Old Library. She had supervised the move, and to this day, the Regents Library felt alive whenever she walked into it. Sometimes she saw materials floating in the air, materials that seemed to scurry toward their respective storage places when she entered the room.

She hadn't seen anything like that here, but she felt the same kind of energy, something that seemed both alive and edgy, the way the air felt during a lightning storm.

The door she wanted was at the right on the end of the long corridor. She hoped that Honored Professor Wolfgang Sauer was in this morning. She knew he didn't have class until later in the afternoon, only because his survey course on the History of Magic had come to the Old Library the week before to learn how to properly research a complicated topic. She had scheduled that class, but had one of the day librarians conduct it, because she hadn't wanted to get up in the middle of her night to talk with young students who were only trying to fulfill a requirement.

Sauer's door was made of Razbitay wood planks that ran vertically. There were no carvings and no fancy designs, unlike a couple of the other doors on this floor.

Still, she pulled a sleeve over her fist and knocked hard to overcome the fabric muffling the sound.

"Come!" Sauer's deep bass voice reverberated down the corridor.

She grabbed the handle with her sleeved hand, pressed on the latch, and pushed the door open. A wave of that vibrating energy nearly pushed her back against the door on the other side of the corridor.

The energy felt warm and smelled faintly of gunpowder. The hair on the back of her neck stood on end. She resisted the urge to tamp it down.

The office was long and narrow, filled with bookshelves and two desks. One desk was covered with pens and inkwells, as well as piles of parchment.

Sauer sat behind the other desk, his long white hair curling along the edges. His matching mustache and eyebrows seemed to have lives of their own.

He looked like he had been crammed into the back of the office, but he always looked that way everywhere he went. He was one of the tallest men she had ever met, and he had extremely broad shoulders. He did not hunch, not even when he was sitting his desk chair.

"May!" he boomed. "To what do I owe this pleasure?"

She had forgotten how much he liked her. He had even asked her to dinner a few times. She had gone once, enjoyed it until he said something about being kindred spirits, and then used her late-night work as an excuse to stay away ever since.

She entered the office, which was too warm, and pulled the door closed.

"Did you hear about the attack last night?" she asked.

"Louella," he said, voice still booming. Croninshield

wanted to gesture for quiet, but she didn't feel right doing so in his office. "Poor thing. Is she all right?"

"I don't think so." Croninshield gestured at the only chair that was not covered in books and papers. "Mind if I sit?"

"You can stay all morning if you want," he said, his voice softening. His brown eyes had a bit of tenderness in them. Or perhaps it was sympathy. "This is late in your day, isn't it?"

"I should be asleep by now," Croninshield said. "But I can't shut off my mind."

"After an attack like that," he said, "I completely understand. I heard you saw it?"

"The attack? No," she said. "I heard screams and went for help."

He folded his hands over the calendar that covered the top of his desk. Even his fingers had tufts of white hair on them, and hair peeked out of the sleeves of his shirt.

"Still," he said. "You saw the aftermath."

"I did," Croninshield said, "and that's what I want to discuss with you, in your professional capacity."

He raised his oversized eyebrows. Strands of hair from those almost touched some of the strands from his scalp falling along his forehead.

"My *professional* capacity? This attack?"

She nodded. "When I got back to the library, I did some reading on some of the things I saw. I want to know what you think."

"What did you see?" he asked.

She wasn't going to tell him about Louella's lack of

obvious injuries. Croninshield did not want people to use that information to deny that Louella had experienced something traumatic.

"Bones," Croninshield said. "A skull. And a pool of blood."

She described it in more detail, leaving out the fact that she had tripped on it. She barely wanted to contemplate that part herself.

He listened attentively, especially when she cited the books she had looked at.

She almost asked him, *Am I delusional? Overreacting?* But they both knew she was not the kind of woman who ever overreacted to anything.

He let out a gust of air, leaned back and put his hands behind his head, revealing the beginnings of sweat stains under his arms. Apparently, he wasn't comfortable in this warm office either, but he hadn't done anything about it.

"Bones like that are sometimes caused by Fey, although in what capacity, we've never been able to determine." His brows came together, almost matching his mustache in size. "Some of my students over the years have conjectured that these are attacks of some kind. They cite battlefield reports from L'Nacin and Nye, but those have always sounded histrionic to me."

"How so?" Croninshield asked.

"The L'Nacins in particular claim that the Fey have a magic that allows them to take over someone's body and memories. That magic then creates a bone pile."

Croninshield shuddered, despite herself.

"It is a battlefield strategy, to learn how an enemy plans

an upcoming attack and, perhaps, to use the host body to alter that attack."

Croninshield frowned. "But we're not in a battle."

"Indeed," Sauer said, bringing his arms down. He tugged on one end of his mustache as if the entire thing annoyed him. "But....we do not understand their magic, and we have never made a point of studying it. We prefer to study texts rather than eyewitness accounts, and the Fey have been circumspect about avoiding anything written. They do not keep their histories in books."

"How do they keep their history?" Croninshield asked.

"So far as we can tell—and honestly, I have not studied this since I was an Advanced Student decades ago—they have people in each battlefield campaign who can recite the events of the campaign moment by moment, incident by incident."

Croninshield shook her head just a little. "That sounds tedious."

"Yes," Sauer said. "I have a hunch they then give the highlights to another such person who is the keeper of record. But that is merely a hunch, and useless to us at the moment. Are you correct to think that what you saw is a feature of the proximity of the Fey? Yes. Is it the result of Fey magic? We don't know. If it is, why would they be here? There is no battle. And the local Fey enclaves—which are illegal, by the way, throughout the Protectorate—they would never draw attention to themselves like that."

"Illegal?" Croninshield asked.

"Something rarely enforced now," he said. "After the last battle, when we had defeated them, we allowed some Fey to remain in Dorovich so long as they did not congregate. That rule was on the books of Khēmía as well as in several other countries, and was negotiated for when Khēmía joined the Protectorate."

"Negotiated for by whom?" Croninshield asked.

"The Khēmíans. They see it as some kind of protection." He shook his head, making some more hair tumble onto his forehead. "However, those laws have not been enforced in our corners of the Protectorate for generations."

Our corners of the Protectorate. She had not heard that phrase in decades. It was a polite way of talking about Qavner.

"There are local Fey enclaves?" she asked. "In Serebro, I would presume."

"I don't believe so," he said. "It would be difficult to find pure Fey in Dorovich these days anyway. They've intermarried throughout Dorovich. There was a ban on Fey to Fey relationships for decades after the attacks. That diluted their blood."

She nodded. She remembered that detail from her schooling.

"There were reports of blood and bone for nearly a century after the Fey attacks," he said. "And then those reports faded. I have no idea if people stopped reporting those incidents or if there were no more incidents. I would think, given the ghastly nature of such a discovery, that the number of incidents decreased."

Ghastly was right. She shuddered despite herself, still feeling the slip of the bones beneath her now-discarded shoes.

"I don't believe there was ever such a finding on campus," he said. "Ever, even during the worst of the Fey years."

She let out a breath. "So, could this have been a prank gone awry? One of your students, perhaps, who thought that they would cause an incident at the Academy?"

"And attack a woman on her way to work?" Sauer sounded appalled. "Our students in both Thaumaturgy and Alchemy are highly vetted, not just for innate talent—"

Which she knew was code for magic.

"—but also for strength of personality. They learn difficult things here and in both departments, they learn how to make what the Protectorate in its wisdom has sought to classify as weaponry."

More magic. The Purges had a terrible legacy. It was amazing these departments even survived.

"We cannot allow anyone into our departments who has a tendency to taunt the Academy or try to harm one of our students," he said.

She had heard that, but she hadn't thought how that would play out.

"And the Science Department?" she asked.

His laughter boomed. "Science. May, I would not have taken you for someone easily duped."

Her cheeks flushed. He had just insulted her and she didn't know why.

"We do not teach 'science' here," he said, "not as most understand it anyway. The so-called Science Department does teach a systemic study of the structure and behavior of the so-called natural world. It even teaches rigorous experimentation and testing of various theories."

She sat very stiffly, trying to listen with her mind open.

"But it's just a different form of magic, my girl," he said.

Her flush grew deeper at his tone. She had never thought of it that way. But, then, science as a discipline had never interested her. And she had stayed away from magic for her entire life, except as presented in books.

"The Science Department figures out how to use such things as lightstone to create effective lighting throughout the Protectorate. But as to what lightstone is, at its core? The department has yet to figure that out, despite multiple studies."

Sauer leaned back and folded his hands over his stomach. She hadn't realized until now that his stomach was as flat as a student's. She had always thought of him as a large man, so she had assumed he carried a lot of fat.

He didn't. He was just taller and wider than most.

"We do not invent the power that we use," he said. "We *harness* it. And it has taken generations to get that harnessing right. The windstone vehicles that we all use are a product of the Science Department, in consultation with Thaumaturgy. The Academy owns the so-called technology behind the building of the vehicles."

Then he smiled, but the smile was not warm. It was contemplative.

"That is why," he said, "this Academy has so very much money. We could stop all of the obvious fundraising, stop demanding that the alumni send additional funds, and refuse all the estates that leave us their fortunes, and still keep the Academy functioning at the level it is now."

Now her flush was even deeper. The warmth from it moved to her neck and upper chest. She was the librarian. She was the one who should have the most knowledge of the two of them. She was the one who should be telling him things, not the other way around.

"All right," she said, trying not to sound annoyed. She *was* annoyed, but more at herself than at him. "I will grant you that your students are exceptional. Exceptional does not always mean sensible. I ask again, could this have been a prank?"

He took a deep breath, then sighed.

"To my knowledge," he said, "we don't focus on the bones and blood in any of our classes. We barely discuss the Fey these days. I used to offer a class in the Fey incursion, but no one took it for two years running, so we stopped offering it. There just isn't much interest in the Fey—or in our magical history, for that matter—not anymore anyway."

She sat very still, feeling the flush recede from her skin. His response disturbed her more than she had expected it to.

"So," she said quietly, "what do the blood and bones mean?"

He shook his head slowly, as if he was contemplating all of this as well.

"You said that, according to the L'Nacin, the blood and bones were evidence of a battle tactic." She was the one speaking slowly now, because she was coming up with an idea in real time. "The history of the Protectorate shows us that warfare does not start with soldiers and military might."

Sauer's gaze brightened. His brown eyes focused on her with an intensity she hadn't seen before.

"It starts, sometimes, with small events. Spies figuring out a potential enemy's weaknesses. A frontline guard of some kind, placed into position so that a military operation, when it comes, has soldiers already in place."

Sauer leaned forward just a bit.

"Could that be happening here?" Croninshield asked. "The Fey are, unless I miss my guess, quite the military force in other parts of the world. I do know that they have said, repeatedly, that they wanted to conquer the whole world. Perhaps we're next."

"There's a lot of speculation in your statements," Sauer said. "By 'we,' I assume you mean Dorovich? Or the Protectorate?"

She shrugged one shoulder. She had been thinking aloud. She wasn't sure which she meant.

"If they come by sea, wouldn't they want Leut first?" he asked.

"You taught a class that showed they arrived in Dorovich first, and were defeated," she said.

"And we don't know how, exactly, they got here, although many Khēmíans claimed the Fey force poured out of Mount Vitaki."

She frowned. She hadn't read that.

"It has not been corroborated," he said. "I have no idea how it could be, either."

He tapped one thick finger on the edge of his desk, making a drumming noise that would get on her already frayed nerves if he didn't quit soon.

"The question is," he said, "if they are planning some kind of attack on Dorovich, or even on the Protectorate, why start here, at the Academy?"

Croninshield barked out a laugh. She couldn't suppress it.

"You know the answer to that, if you think on it, Wolfgang," she said. "We are the center for all learning in the Protectorate. Our Board of Regents determines what each school teaches—"

"But it's well established that the Fey do not appreciate education as we do," he said.

She shook her head. "They're not about education, are they? They're about conquest."

He frowned, which made all of the hair on his face point downward.

"We store magical items here, at the Academy," she said. "We put our history in books, so our knowledge is stored in books. We determine which magic is legal and which magic is not. Members of the Old Families meet here on a regular basis to discuss the future of the academic system. If I were going to attack the Protectorate, I would send in my spies to figure out why this place is so important to our culture."

Sauer let out a gusty breath, then popped up from his chair. He pivoted, grabbed a book off the top shelf near him, and thumbed through it.

She let him. He was clearly remembering something.

The book was old. Its pages were illustrated with color, clearly tipped in by hand. She must have been very tired because it seemed like the images floated on top of the book, almost as if they had a life of their own.

The images were mostly color. She couldn't quite make out what they illustrated. She saw bright golds and blues, with red threaded through all of it.

She blinked, but the images didn't recede. It looked to her as if his fingers were in the middle of an image, rather than touching one from above.

She waited for him to finish. He was clearly looking for something, and he did not have her gift for finding details in text quickly.

Finally, he shut the book with a loud and dusty clap. The floating images vanished, for which she was grateful. Her eyes ached after seeing them for just that short period of time.

"Advance teams," he said, as if she already understood him.

"What?" she asked.

"A very, very, very long time ago," he said, "before the Purges, before the Protectorate was a force in Dorovich, the Academy sent some of its Thaumaturgical researchers to study the Fey appearance in Khēmía. Not much came of that, but one scholar asked to travel to L'Nacin to discover what he could about the Fey. He took some students with him, including a member of the Kirilli family who had a great deal of artistic talent."

"Those were his illustrations, huh?" Croninshield asked.

"Hers," Sauer said, as if it weren't important who the illustrator was. But Croninshield thought it important. The Kirillis were one of the Old Families.

"They learned a great deal about Fey tactics and methods," Sauer said, "and one thing that caught their attention were the advance teams."

"Which are what they sound like, I assume," Croninshield said.

"They are exactly what you described a few moments ago," Sauer said. "They were sent to scout new territory, figure out the customs, and discern what the threats were to the Fey, if any."

"Any description of the blood and bones?" she asked.

"Not that I saw just now," he said, "and I scanned the section on advance teams. But that doesn't mean the description isn't in there elsewhere."

Croninshield wanted to get her hands on the book. She wanted to see for herself.

"Is that book in the library?" she asked.

"I doubt it," he said. "There were very few copies made. I paid dearly for that one."

It took all of her effort to keep her librarian self from chastising him. She did what she could to keep her expression impassive, even though she was now appalled at him.

He had a rare book and he just kept it loose and open at the top of a shelf in his very messy office?

Then she realized that she was focusing on the book as the source of her discomfort when, in reality, everything about this day upset her.

"I feel like we should talk to the Administration," she said. "Something is going on that they need to be aware of."

Sauer shook his head ever so slightly. "You can talk with them if you want, but you'll have to leave me out of it."

126

"What?" she asked. "You're the expert on the Fey on campus."

"I also work for the Thaumaturgical Department," he said. "They're constantly looking for reasons to shut us and the Alchemy Department down. Did you know that we actually have a plan to merge with Science if the Administration destroys what we've built here?"

She didn't know that. "Surely they wouldn't. You're one of the oldest departments on campus."

"And we barely survived the Purges. We're still here because other cultures in the Dorovich—outside of the Protectorate—have a much more tolerant attitude toward magic."

She made a small acknowledging sound. "And they want this department here in case we decide to conquer one of those places."

"Conquer is not a word we use with the Protectorate," he said, a half smile making his eyes twinkle. "We say *invite* or *coerce*. But never *conquer*."

"Still," she said. "We should talk to someone. There's bound to be a meeting of the Board of Regents soon."

Sauer shook his head. "I'm not liking what I hear from them. Besides, May, what do we have? Theories and supposition. Nothing more. You can't go to the Administration, and certainly not the Regents, without some kind of evidence."

"The blood and bones aren't enough?" she asked. "Especially when books—"

He put up a hand. "There's too much risk, May. I know you understand that."

The flush returned. The stupid man made her blush like a child, and not because of any attraction. He was, perhaps, the only person on campus who could make her feel as if her education was inadequate.

"I think," he said, perhaps sensing her discomfort, "that you need to keep an eye on Louella."

"I plan to," Croninshield said. "She's been through a lot."

"I mean," he said, "given what little we know about the blood and bones, there's a possibility that—"

"She was overtaken by a Fey?" Croninshield asked, then let out a small bitter laugh. She finally understood what Sauer had been saying about proof. "We don't know that or even if those kinds of magic exist. We have no way to know—"

"Exactly, May." He spoke gently. "We don't know. But if she acts strangely, then we have a theory with a bit of teeth, right? If she doesn't seem like Louella at all, then we have even more to go on."

Croninshield let out a small breath, remembering Louella's eyes after the attack. How cold they had been. How strange she had seemed. How uncomfortable she had made Croninshield, which Croninshield had brushed off as a result of the attack.

Maybe it had been a result of the attack, but not the kind of result she thought of. Maybe not trauma but a different personality entirely.

Croninshield shook her head ever so slightly. She was finally beginning to understand Sauer's objection to going to the Administration, at least at this moment.

She was having trouble believing that Louella's body could be present but the essence of her was not—and Croninshield had seen her after the attack. Croninshield had seen the blood and bones.

Sauer was watching her closely, as if he was trying to figure out what she was thinking.

"Well, then," Croninshield said. "I guess we keep an eye on Louella."

"That'll be you more than me," he said. "I'll watch for Fey."

Croninshield looked at him in surprise. "You expect to see actual Fey?"

"If what we believe is true, yes, I do. We don't look twice at people with Fey facial characteristics, or tall people, or people who have slightly pointed ears. Other cultures, in L'Nacin or in Nye, had always kept a close eye on anyone resembling the Fey." He didn't even seem disturbed by what he was saying.

"You're talking about half the population of Dorovich," Croninshield said. Not to mention the fact that he was tall. Or that the ears beneath her slightly curly hair were more than slightly pointed.

"I suspect actual Fey will look different from mixed Fey," he said.

"You suspect," she repeated with a bit of an edge.

"This is new territory for us, May," he said. "We've never experienced anything like this in our lifetime. So yes, *I suspect*. I can't very well say that I know, because I don't. But I have a hunch. Just like you. We're willing to act on our hunches."

She nodded and hoped, deep down, that their hunches would come to nothing. Because if their hunches were right, the Academy—the Protectorate. Or maybe all of Dorovich —would be in big trouble.

LAW BUILDING

...LER
...L

REGENTS
LODGING HOUSE

MEDICAL
SCIENCES

CAMPUS
MEDICAL UNIT

ANATOMY

The Anatomy Department was housed in a small free-standing building between the Medical Sciences Building and the Agriculture Complex. Anatomy had once been the campus's medical unit, but in those days, when healing was a bit less reliable, that building had become a makeshift morgue.

Students didn't know that the campus morgue was in the basement of the Anatomy building—at least the first-years. Third and fourth year students, particularly those on a medical track, worked in the morgue, doing small tasks. And the Advanced Students with an eye toward a medical career had to spend at least one full year in the morgue, dealing with corpses or, as some professors said, *The results of the medical profession's failures.*

Jaxon had always thought that statement unfair. Sometimes the medical profession could do nothing. Sometimes the failure was in law enforcement to keep peace on campus or in the administration for allowing violent students who had no business being around others onto campus.

It felt odd to him to enter the building from the front doors, rather than the half-hidden side door built into the foundation. This was the first time in maybe years that he had entered without going directly to the morgue.

He went through the metal double doors with a scrum of students beside him, some of them carrying books and looking intent, others laughing about their own reactions to a class that involved the dissection of a frog the day before.

He had taken some of these classes when he still thought he would work with the Constabulary. It was in this building that he learned he had a sensitive stomach. No one had bothered to teach him how to overcome it either.

One professor had even gone so far as to say that he would never be able to find his way out of it.

Jaxon had figured his way out of it. This case was doing it for him. He carried the bones in an oilskin bag that he had to sling over his shoulder. All together, they were heavier than he expected. He'd had to shift the bag from hand to hand on the way over, and he slung it over his shoulder only as he got close to the building.

He tried to move slowly so that the bones wouldn't bang together, but that scrum had shoved the bag against his back.

He had felt the hardness of several bones digging into the sensitive skin under his arm, and his gorge had risen. The last thing the Chief of Security for the entire campus needed to do was vomit on an entire group of students, so he willed himself to toughen up.

As he did so, the queasiness died. That made part of him

angry. If it had always been this easy, he might have had a different career.

Although having a different career might have meant that he would have to work with a twerp like Bertie. Spending half the morning with that idiot had been more than enough.

Inside the building, the stench of lye mixed with the smell of boiling meat. No one cooked here, although often people in the lab boiled skin off bone, so that they could have clean skeletons to rebuild.

The queasiness returned with that thought, or perhaps it was just the smell of the boiling flesh.

This part of the building was humid and a bit too hot as well, and he didn't want to think about the causes of that.

He veered left, through swinging doors, into the reception area for the Anatomy Department.

A girl with long black hair sat in one of the uncomfortable chairs near the reception desk, a book open on her lap. She looked engrossed in her reading, although she did look up as Jaxon entered.

The receptionist, on the other hand, did not look up. She too was young, probably an Advanced Student who needed to work for her tuition. She was separating a pile of papers and clipping them together with some kind of fastener.

He stopped in front of the desk and cleared his throat.

"Security Chief Jaxon for Professor Loughty," he said. "She's expecting me."

He hoped that last was true. He had sent one of his

interns over to inform the Anatomy Department that he needed an hour of Róisin Loughty's time.

The receptionist looked up, one hand holding four papers and the other gripping a clip as if it was going to get away. She had noticeably pale skin and hair that was so light it looked like it was made of sunlight. Her eyebrows were pale, and so were her blue eyes.

Over his years at the Academy, he had only met a few people who looked like her and they had all treated him poorly. He fought back an instant dislike, because he knew she hadn't earned it.

"She is expecting you," the receptionist said, her voice as light as her hair. "She's in the Anatomy Lab."

His right hand gripped the oilskin bag tighter. He had said he had something that needed investigating, but part of him wanted to start this little meeting in Loughty's office, not in the lab.

"Thank you," he said, but the receptionist had already returned to her task. If she was any good at her job, she should have asked him if he knew how to get to the lab.

He was being picky, because he didn't want to be here. He wanted to find fault with everything, from the receptionist to the building to the smell.

Well, the smell was bothering him. The stench of boiling meat was giving him a headache.

The lab was on the first floor, situated above the morgue, although few casual visitors to the Anatomy Building knew that. A single stout door made of iron led into the lab.

The entire wall around the lab had iron threaded through it. That wall had to be rebuilt at least twice that he knew of, once due to fire that had started during a dissection and another that had happened overnight, when something attacked one of the corpses.

Fortunately, the attack had happened before his time. The fires had been inexplicable, although there had been whispers of magic. He had never seen evidence of that, but he didn't know what to look for.

When it came to magic, his training was lacking, because the bulk of it happened after the Purges. What he had learned, he had learned from his predecessor, who had been ancient when Jaxon started, and had given him some lessons on magical threats even though such discussions were supposedly forbidden.

One thing that his predecessor had said was that iron could defeat some magic, so when the Administration had asked Jaxon if he thought security needed to be beefed up here, he had said yes, then he had suggested the iron door and wall.

Right now, the damn thing made his back itch. Or maybe he was just tired. He hated having those bones resting against his skin.

He grabbed the solid iron door knob and yanked the door open. It squealed, which it shouldn't have done, given that it was only ten years old. But, he supposed, the increased humidity from all the bone boiling probably rusted something prematurely.

His stomach turned again.

He needed to stop thinking such things.

The lab was large and bright. Instead of lightstone lamps along the walls, the lab had long tubes of lightstone built into the ceiling, controllable by a switch near the door.

The lightstone could be very bright or soft or completely off, something that he had never experienced with lightstone anywhere else. He had never asked who designed the lights, even though one of his guards had asked, after the fire, if the lights could have caused it.

That guard had known nothing about lightstone, which wasn't even warm to the touch. It never started fires. It was made of stone, which did not burn.

In fact, stone was what had saved the lab during the fire. The lab was almost all stone, except for the bodies in their storage cells, the papers that Loughty and her team made notes on, and the reference books in the far back. The reference books were in a cabinet, though, which had a glass front, also added after that disastrous fire.

To the right, as far from the door as possible, was the massive fireplace. It had interior hooks for hanging pots, which were almost always filled with bone. Three pots boiled at the moment, which explained the stench.

Loughty stood near one of the stone tables. She was a large woman, with muscles in her arms that some of his guards could use. Jaxon had seen her lift bodies of people twice her weight and flop them on a nearby table as if the movement hadn't winded her at all.

She wore one of her thin, dark work coats, over a pair of dark pants. She had a long face with a sharp chin. Her hair, cropped short, peeked out from the tight cap she always wore when she was working. She held a pair of gloves in her right hand.

"I thought you were going to be here sooner." Loughty had a deep voice, with an accent that revealed her family's roots in Feltshyon. "I've been waiting."

He wasn't going to apologize, but he knew he had to respond somehow. He also knew his nerves were frayed from the night and his temper was short.

"It's been a strange several hours," he said.

Her expression, which had seemed tense, softened just a bit. "I understand one of the librarians was attacked."

"Louella Vance, yes," he said.

"Is she all right?" Loughty asked.

He realized he had no direct answer for that. "The medics took her."

"Hmmm." Loughty's response was as noncommittal as his answer had been. "You have something for me, though?"

He set the oilskin bag onto the table with a clatter. He winced. He didn't want to damage the bones.

"These were at the scene," he said. He then explained how they were found and the large pool of blood. "I don't think a person could lose that much blood and live."

Loughty slipped on her gloves and slid the oilskin bag toward herself. "The blood didn't come from the librarian?"

"No," he said, a little surprised that she didn't call Louella by name. But, then, not everyone used the Old Library. Loughty's work was mostly inside this building, not in the libraries themselves.

She had stopped teaching first- and second-year students decades ago, so she didn't have contact that way either.

Loughty opened the bag. "No one else was attacked there?"

"Not that we know," he said. "Róisin, really, there was a lot of blood. It formed a large puddle."

She reached inside the bag, seemingly unperturbed by its contents or his words.

"I'm just getting my facts straight," she said. "I want to make sure I approach this with the correct information."

He usually valued her thoroughness, but the smell of boiling flesh was making him so queasy he wondered if he would ever eat again.

She pulled out the skull, held it in one gloved hand, and frowned at it. Then she wiped some grass and dirt off the left side, grabbed a rag, and made sure her glove was clean.

The skull seemed to bother her.

"This is what you found?" she asked as she set it down.

"Yes." He was trying not to let his irritation into his voice. "One of the idiots from the Serebro Constabulary said he thought maybe this was all a prank, that everything had been stolen from the Anatomy Department or maybe even from the slaughterhouse in the Agriculture Department."

Jaxon had leaned a little too hard on the word *idiot*. He hadn't been planning to discuss the prank theory yet, but he was tired and annoyed and he wanted out of here.

"I had one of my Advanced Students double-check. Every intact skeleton is still in the lab. I suppose you could check with Medical Science, but I doubt this is one of theirs either."

She really didn't seem bothered by his word choice or even by the suggestion of a prank. Loughty wasn't always known for her equanimity, so he was a bit surprised by her reaction.

She pulled the longest bones out of the bag and set them near the skull. She stopped at that moment, grabbed a femur and ran a hand along it.

"This is decidedly odd, Herbert." She pulled the bag toward herself and stuck her face in the opening.

His stomach turned violently and he thought for a moment he would lose everything inside of it, not that he had eaten since midnight.

But he managed to take a few deep breaths.

"What is?" His voice sounded strangled.

"These bones," she said. "They're clean."

"Meaning what?" he asked. He didn't want the young idiot from Serebro to be right. Maybe the bones had been stolen from somewhere else. "They're human, right?"

"Yes," she said, "although..."

She poked a finger on the side of the femur. It seemed softer than it should have, almost like it was made of cloth. Her fingerprint stayed for a moment, and then vanished.

"...they seem malleable. That's odd," she said.

He didn't like the word. "They came from somewhere else? Maybe they're fake?"

"No," she said. "They're not fake. They're bone. But maybe they have a disease that weakened them? I'm not sure. May I study them?"

He didn't want them.

"Just tell me what they are," he said.

She pulled the pelvic bone out of the bag, along with some smaller bones he couldn't identify. She moved the pelvic bone toward herself.

"This belongs to a woman," she said.

He almost asked how she knew, but then decided he didn't want to know. He wanted to leave now that he realized there was no way any of this could be a prank.

"And the skull suggests the same thing. I think after I put the bones together, we'll discover that this is all from the same woman."

"With squishy bones?" he asked, swallowing hard.

"Most likely," she said. "There are some features here I've never seen in person. But there might be something in my reference library."

"Something?" he asked. "Something like what?"

She shook her head. "I don't want to say, because I'm not sure. It's all somewhat strange."

"How did you see the squishiness before you touched them?" he asked, then wished he hadn't. She would probably go into a level of detail that he did not want to hear.

"I didn't." She set the pelvic bone down, then flattened her hands on the table and looked at him. "These bones are clean."

"There's a little dirt," he said, "and some blood—"

"No," she said. "When I boil bones, I sometimes have to scrape—

"Okay," he said, putting up his hands. "There's stuff on them. I get it."

He must have looked green, because she smiled gently at him. "Yes. It takes quite a while for bones to become clean. And then they show the effort of the work. And, unless I add something to the water, the bones are never this white."

He frowned at them. "I don't understand."

"Even if I slice open your arm," she said, "and pull your humerus out—"

Oh, he wished he wasn't having this conversation. He kept his hand up, trying to stop her.

"—it wouldn't look like this. It would carry blood and musculature and—"

"Okay," he said. "I get it. Stuff is attached."

"But nothing is here. I'd like to see your blood pool. I wonder if I would find some material there."

He waved a hand side to side, warding off more information. He didn't want to think about what she meant by *material.*

"I didn't collect anything from there," he said. "Just the bones and the skull. The puddle is marked off, so no one steps in it. It's going to sink into the ground eventually."

"Not to mention a smell and a stain," she said. "And it will be interesting near that path when it rains."

He didn't want to think about any of that. "That's either your problem or the groundskeepers' problem."

"By my problem, you mean that I can do what I need to with the site?" she asked.

He nodded, once. "I just need to solve this. What do we have here? Evidence of a different crime?"

She frowned at him. "Crime is your area."

"But the bones, you said they're new."

"I have no idea how these bones got to that location or why there's a blood puddle," she said. "I don't know if that's evidence of a crime. I can't even see it as a prank, because it would take a great deal of effort to get all the pieces to that location. You carried the bones. That's no small amount of weight. To make a puddle of blood like the one you describe, you'd need two large buckets of fresh blood, and those would weigh almost as much as the bones. This isn't a one-person job. Someone would have noticed."

"Would they, though?" he asked. "After all, people carry a lot of strange things across campus."

She sniffed. "I would think that people would notice."

She moved the bones around, putting them in order— the skull at the top, the bones of the arms along the sides, the leg bones closer to him, the pelvic bone in the middle.

"Also," she said, "where would these materials come from? Your so-called idiot from Serebro was right in that the slaughterhouse would have a lot of blood. But it would be dark and coagulated—"

This conversation was filled with difficult moments. Whenever he got his stomach settled, she'd say something that would twist it again.

"—and if someone wanted some fresh, they'd have to cut a jugular and capture the blood."

Loughty's frown grew deeper and she peered sideways at the body itself.

"Someone would have noticed that," she said, more to herself than to him.

She moved an ulna so that it pushed against the humerus.

"To answer your question," she said, without meeting his gaze, "I think there is a good chance that a crime occurred. Something that caused the blood and bones."

"Not just the attack on Louella, then," he said.

Slowly, Loughty raised her head. "You said she was injured."

"I said the medical staff took her to the Medical Science Building," he said.

Loughty's eyebrows lifted. "I heard she was covered in blood."

"She was," he said.

"Is she the kind of woman who would play a prank?"

The quiet librarian? The one who, years ago, on her first day of work, asked him if she would be safe crossing the campus after dark? The woman who barely said a word to anyone outside of the library? That woman?

"I can't imagine it," Jaxon said, and he couldn't.

"She might have your answers, then," Loughty said.

"She doesn't seem to remember the attack," he said.

"Hmmm." Loughty adjusted the bones again. "Have you ruled out magic?"

Irritation surged through him. "You know I don't understand magic."

They'd had this conversation half a dozen times after the fire. Loughty thought that magic had been the cause. He hadn't been certain. But her insistence had led to the iron all over this department.

"I think you understand it better than you say," she said. "We're seeing some impossible things today."

"We are?" he asked.

"Blood and bone with no obvious source. Bones that are malleable."

"That seems strange," he said, "but not magical. There has to be an explanation."

Loughty nodded. "There always is. But it might not be one you want."

He let out a gusty sigh. He was so tired he could hardly remain upright.

"I don't know what answer I want," he said. "I want to know what happened to her. I want to know if I have some kind of criminal on my campus or an elaborate prankster."

"Or someone with a high command of unfamiliar magic?" she asked.

He couldn't take it anymore. "And what does that matter? There are a lot of people on campus who have magic. I am not Chief of the Purges. I don't police magic. I don't want to."

She reached out, almost as if she was going to put a hand on his arm. Then she stopped and pulled her hand back.

"I'm not saying you should," she said. "I'm just asking if you considered the magic angle?"

"I never do," he said. "You know that."

"Because you're overcompensating," she said quietly.

"What?" he asked.

"Your predecessor saw magic everywhere, and tried to purge it from campus. You want to be as different from him as possible."

Jaxon put a hand on the cool stone, mostly to keep himself upright. That observation was too close to the truth.

"He destroyed a lot of lives," Jaxon said. "He didn't have the right to do that. I'm just trying to keep everyone safe."

Loughty patted his hand. "I know that, Herbert. The campus is a much nicer place than it's been in years."

Even though she was humoring him, he didn't mind. He needed that at the moment.

"Why don't you go home and get some sleep?" she said. "I'm going to take a look at that area where your librarian was attacked and see if I find anything. Come on back here at the start of your day, and I'll tell you what I've found. If anything."

He didn't move. He should move, but he didn't want to stop leaning on the table.

"Please, Herbert. Go home before you fall over. You can't sleep on one of these tables."

The very idea made him shudder, and it gave him enough energy to stand upright. He had to go home. He wasn't any good to anyone when he was this exhausted.

"I'll be back at the end of your day," he said.

She patted his hand again. "Good," she said. "I'll be waiting."

And somehow, in his tired state, he almost heard that as a threat.

LAW BUILDING

LER
L

REGENTS
LODGING HOUSE

MEDICAL
SCIENCES

CAMPUS
MEDICAL UNIT

ANATOMY

CHAPTER
ELEVEN

Honored Professor Róisin Loughty hurried out of the Anatomy building, carrying a small kit filled with several oilskin bags and at least two pairs of gloves. She had forgotten to put on a coat, however, and she needed one. Despite the rising sun, the morning air was cold and damp.

As she left the Anatomy Building, students passed her, heads bowed, books under one arm. Most of the students used their free hand to clutch their coats closed, if they wore one at all. If not, they had the arm wrapped around their torsos.

Clearly, no one expected the chill. Everyone had clearly been happy to see the sun after days of intermittent rain and fog.

Students usually cut across the campus, going near the Old Library and its grounds, but they weren't doing so today.

At first, she thought they had heard about the attack and were avoiding the little cluster of trees for that reason. Then she saw the braided red ropes, preventing anyone from walking through that area.

She never really thought of Security Chief Herbert Jaxon as brilliant, but that move was truly smart. It protected the area and made certain that no one stumbled on something they shouldn't have.

The path leading to those trees was well worn, but empty. It felt odd to be out here without the chatter of conversation or the occasional late student running past and trying not to bang into anyone. Strangely, too, at least from her perspective, no one even gave her a sideways glance as she headed toward those trees.

Her heart was pounding and it wasn't from the exertion. She didn't like what Jaxon had told her. The attack was horrible, even without the blood and bones. Loughty knew that the campus wasn't always safe; she attended the security meetings unlike many of her colleagues, and she knew because of those that such attacks weren't as rare as everyone wanted to believe.

But this one had the added blood, bones, and skull dimension. Even if those bones meant nothing, even if they were a prank (and she couldn't imagine how they would be), the attack was bad enough.

This was the center of campus. Even though the attack had happened in the middle of the night, someone had still thought they were be safe enough in this little dark and enclosed group of trees to harm a woman who was just passing through.

Loughty reached the rope that cut across the path. The rope was hip-high for her, which meant it was stomach-high for most. She couldn't step over it either. She was going to have to go under.

She grabbed the scratchy thick braid and lifted it, twisting her torso so that nothing along her back caught on the rope. She hadn't moved like that in years. She was in good condition for most things, but apparently bending and twisting at the same time was something that her body no longer liked doing.

She stepped into the group of trees and noted the ground, turned up with dozens of footprints. There was a bit of torn fabric near the path.

Loughty didn't pick up the fabric, but she looked in the opposite direction from the fabric. The grass was dark. It took a moment to make sense of what she saw.

The blood pool.

She let out a small breath. She was upwind from it, so she couldn't smell it, but she would wager that students heading toward the library could. The blood pool had been there since midnight, so it would have started stinking once the sun came up.

It was also turning black. It almost looked like a tiny version one of those natural tar pits she had encountered on her medical internships in Pahrucii. There was so much blood that it hadn't all sunken into the ground yet, causing it to give the optical illusion of rising out of the ground instead.

She shuddered. That blood pool was larger than she had expected from Jaxon's description.

Loughty had expected to arrive and find the blood crusted along the grass, which it wasn't doing yet.

There were fewer footprints over here. Just three different kinds of shoes, so far as she could tell. One set had stepped into the pool—those had to belong to May Cronin-shield. The others were probably Jaxon's. Loughty could see where the bones had been. The grass was still depressed near them.

She crouched and looked at all of it. She wasn't exactly certain what she was looking for. She had read about these blood and bone piles as a student. They had been a curious feature of the northern cultures in Dorovich for several generations, and anatomists had tried to figure out what caused them.

A few had noted the squishy bones, but hadn't said much more. She would have described the bones she encountered as spongy, not squishy, but they were still disturbing.

There were several theories about the blood and bone piles, and she didn't want to contemplate any of them until she looked at the entire area. She set her kit on the path itself, near all the footprints and the depressions and scuff marks, figuring that particular area had already been examined enough. She wouldn't find anything else there that someone else hadn't touched.

Then she walked around the perimeter of the blood pool, careful not to get too close to it or to step on the depressed grass where the bones and skull had been. There were some small shrubs nearby, most of them barely reaching ankle height. Those shrubs surrounded two different tree trunks, almost like a decoration to hide the plainness.

She walked slowly toward the shrubs, careful where she put her feet. She saw some threads still clinging to blades of grass.

Whatever happened to that librarian happened here, not where all the footprints and scuffed dirt was.

Loughty moved closer to the shrubs. Something brownish poked out of some of the leaves. The slight breeze tickled her hair, bringing with it the sour smell of the blood pool. Not quite rotted yet, but on its way.

This area was going to smell terrible in a day or so.

She couldn't quite see what was poking out of that shrub. Whatever it was seemed entangled in branches and budding leaves, almost at the ground level. She had to get lower to see whatever it was.

It was brownish, with hair on parts that were visible. It was folded and shoved into the branches, pushed down as far as it could go, almost hastily.

The part on top—that was skin—but she didn't know what it covered.

She went back to her kit, took out one of the bags, and slipped on a pair of gloves. Then she got the tongs that were an essential part of the kit no matter where she went.

She walked in her own footsteps as she returned to that shrub, then crouched. Delicately, she used the tongs to grab the edge of the skin, afraid that it would rip.

But it didn't. She knew how to handle loose skin, and that's what was on top.

She pulled, and the skin stretched. She saw hair and

nipples and beauty marks on one side. On the other, parts of blood vessels, still weaving in and out of the musculature, which wasn't all there either.

She carefully placed her free hand underneath the skin, bracing it, the way she would a fragile old dress that she was taking out of a trunk. The skin continued upwards— dimples, what looked like a belly button and pubic hair, and depressions that might have been knees.

This part of the skin was loose and still moist, although the top part had started to flake.

She carefully transferred it into the oilskin bag.

She didn't find anything that seemed to have come from a face, though—no lips or ears or scalp hair.

Once she got the entire skin thing into the bag, she looked for more. She was acutely aware of what was missing. Organs, like the heart and kidneys. The intestines, which she should have been able to smell when she came over here. And all the parts of the face.

She wasn't shaking. She wasn't even surprised on some level. She had come here hoping to find nothing except a puddle of blood, perhaps placed here by someone who wanted to upset the campus for some reason.

Instead, she found an old mystery, one that had never— to her knowledge—been found in Qavner before.

Blood, bones, a skull, and skin.

The history of medicine and magic had flagged these combinations before.

Medicine couldn't figure out what had happened. No one ever found the intact bodies.

But those who combined their medical histories with

their magical knowledge theorized that the blood, bone piles, and flesh were not abandoned randomly. They had been left as spell builders for someone who practiced magic.

Some magic, particularly the magic practiced in the north, used just a bit of blood to augment powers that already existed. Sometimes spells worked better with a drop of the caster's blood.

Magical theoreticians figured that the Fey used blood and bone to create their very powerful spells.

There was no direct evidence of any of this, but alchemists experimented later with more blood spells and found an enhancement fifty percent of the time.

In fact, the alchemists found that some people's blood worked to enhance a spell every time.

Khēmíans in particular believed that these piles were designed to empower the Fey left behind after the invasion, almost as a way to either keep them mostly invisible or to make sure they had weapons should Dorovicians decide to slaughter the Fey they had originally let stay on the continent.

There was no evidence for any of it.

Just an acknowledgement that these piles hadn't existed before the Fey had come to Dorovich, and the piles slowly disappeared as the Fey generation that had attacked the continent died off.

Disappeared until now.

Loughty slipped the skin in the bag and sealed it. Then she took the bag back to her kit. From the kit, she removed one of several glass vials and pulled out the glass stopper, setting it upside down on the dirt path.

She walked over to the blood pool and dipped the vial into it. The blood was still viscous enough for her to fill the vial.

She set the vial on the path next to its stopper, removed her gloves (turning them inside out as she did so), and set them on the grass. Then, using the very tips of her right thumb and forefinger, she removed a cloth from her kit, and wiped off the vial.

She set the cloth next to her gloves, and took another oilskin bag out of the kit. She grabbed the bag from the outside, using it like a glove to pick up the gloves and the cloth, then shook them free. They went deep into the bag.

She sealed it, and grabbed one more bag. She balanced it on her thighs as she stoppered the vial. Then she carefully placed the vial inside the bag, closed it, and rolled it up tight.

Loughty doubted she would be the one to do more than a cursory examination of the blood. She would confirm that it was human, but she doubted she would find out much more. And she wasn't even certain she would discover that. She would look for similarities from it and any blood she might find in the remains of those blood vessels.

Then she would hand it over to the Alchemy Department. Eventually, she would have to relinquish the bones too —or at least some of them. She would make sure she had an intact skeleton first. Then she would lay out the skin over the skeleton and see if they matched—or matched as well as they could.

She stood, and closed her kit. She walked around the periphery of the little grove of trees, keeping watch for any of the missing body parts or even another skeleton, blood pool, or skull.

Her walk was slow and careful. She stopped often to inspect something, which usually turned out to be a berry or old decaying tree bark. Twice, she found more fabric, which told her that the librarian's outfit—whatever it had been— must have been badly torn.

Finally, Loughty stopped near her kit. She hadn't found anything else.

What she had found had been more than enough.

The Fey connection bothered her. She wasn't sure how to proceed with that. Her work usually didn't involve historical issues, unlike the work of many here at the Academy.

Her work usually only involved the past few years, not something that had occurred centuries ago.

But she had a lot of basic magic knowledge. She needed it for her work with the Chief Coroner in the morgue. Not all deaths in the area were from natural causes. Sometimes magic was involved.

It was usually what the coroner called "rogue magic" or out-of-control magic, but it did exist, and she knew most of the local tricks.

This trick—if that was the word she wanted to use—was not local. Even the occurrences of it that she was aware of had happened outside of Qavner. The Protectorate hadn't even existed when the last blood-bone combination was found—at least, that was what she remembered.

She'd have to research that.

But first, she would have to talk with Jaxon. He would

want to know how to proceed, and she wasn't sure what to tell him.

Should they discuss this with the Administration? If so, what would be the point? Or should Jaxon and his guards simply be on alert for someone who might be pure Fey—or someone who used Fey magic?

Loughty didn't know, and she was glad she wasn't the one who had to decide. It was probably cowardly of her not to offer him some advice, but she had no real advice to give.

It felt alarmist to go to the Administration, at least at this point. There hadn't even been Fey sightings on campus.

Not pure Fey, anyway.

She wasn't even sure if there were pure Fey on Dorovich at all anymore.

Maybe the impulse of the Serebro Constable had been correct: maybe what they were all looking at here was a prank.

Then Loughty shook her head.

Whatever this was, it was no prank. The spongey bone had led her toward that conclusion, but the skin, as perfectly intact as one sloughed off a reptile, was not something the average prankster would know about.

Only a handful of books discussed the skin issues, and most of those were ancient magical-medical history tomes. She wasn't even sure the Thaumaturgical Department had any of that information.

She would talk to Jaxon, show him what she had, and then provide him with the relevant citations.

Everyone else could take it from there.

She stood, her back cracking just a little. No one seemed

interested in her. The students had disappeared from the paths, meaning that the second class of the morning was underway. A lone professor stood on the stone bridge near the library, a sweater tied over his shoulders.

When he saw her, he nodded, then continued over the bridge toward the Government building. He was too far away to get a glimpse of his face, but she knew she had seen him around before.

She half-expected others to be watching, but it seemed that the events of the night had scared everyone away from the site rather than sending here as onlookers. Even that professor had seemed a bit embarrassed by his interest.

She gathered her belongings, gave the area under the trees one last look, and then shook her head. She had no real magic, no sense of anything other than what she could see and feel.

But even with that, this area made her slightly uncomfortable, as if the night's events had left the reverberation of violence among the trees.

Or maybe she was reading into that as well, because she knew that something awful had happened here.

Something awful and inexplicable.

She would see what she could do about the inexplicable part when she returned to her lab.

Because she certainly couldn't change anything else.

LINGUISTICS

ARCHEOLOGY

HISTORY

REGENTS
TOWER

OLD
LIBRARY

ADV. STUDENT
WING

MAIN
ENTRANCE

CLOCK
TOWER

MEDICAL
SCIENCES

CHAPTER
TWELVE

That woman was thorough. She actually seemed to know what she was looking for.

Perdu leaned against the footbridge's railing, the riverstone cutting into his back, watching a woman he didn't know search the copse of trees. He wore the heavy wool suit coat that Elmuccio Bascherini seemed to prefer. Bascherini's entire wardrobe seemed to consist of woolen clothing, even though he had come from a temperate area.

Perdu's search of the man's memories told him that Bascherini had been terrified of spending an entire year in the Qavnerian climate. Even though Bascherini had been honored by his appointment as a visiting professor in the newly formed Dorovician Studies Department, he had been afraid of almost everything else, from the weather to the cuisine to his own potential loneliness, since Qavnerian was his third language, and one he did not think he spoke nearly well enough to teach in it.

If Perdu had had it to do all over again, he would have chosen a different host. He had thought he was so smart, taking over a visiting professor. Instead, it put him at a disadvantage. He understood a lot about Bascherini's home state of Razbitay, a tiny city-state that bordered several countries to the north, but he hadn't learned that much about Qavner, except what Bascherini had been afraid of.

The only benefit that Perdu had found was that people here expected him to be ignorant of almost everything. He could ask stupid or obvious questions, and no one would blink an eye.

But he didn't know things that other people here would have known, such as who that woman was.

She looked somewhat official. She wore pants, some kind of cap over her head, and she had carried a large kit into the copse, deliberately stepping underneath the braided rope that surrounded the area.

She was one of the tallest Qavnerians he had ever seen, which he took to mean that she had Fey blood. He still wasn't sure if that assumption was a good one. This woman was a bit too broad in the shoulders to be fully Fey.

The Fey never really became muscular. They relied on magick too much for that.

But she didn't seem to have an obvious magick, not that he expected her to use it out in the open on a Qavnerian campus.

Then she had gone directly to a single spot, one he hadn't had a chance to investigate yet.

Perdu let out a small sigh. He had a class to teach in less than an hour, and he didn't have time to wait. He wished he had gone to breakfast earlier, because the gossip he had heard there had brought him here.

The faculty dining room had been abuzz with the news of an attack. He had carefully taken his usual breakfast of hot mixed grain cereal, a spicy orange tea that seemed to be unique to the area, and some delicious fresh red berries with a dollop of cream, moving slowly so he could eavesdrop.

A librarian, everyone noted, attacked on her way to her job at midnight. Her injuries were not obvious, but she was covered in blood. The rumors were that she had been sexually assaulted, but had somehow injured her rapist. Other rumors said that she was hurt so badly that she couldn't talk.

No one knew exactly what had happened.

He had shoveled his food into his mouth, and left quickly. He needed to check the scene of the crime. He knew that Shyly was coming to campus, but he hadn't known when.

He had recommended that she take over one of the librarians, because they seemed to know everything.

The timing was right; the descriptions were right.

And Shyly would have had no way to reach him before she made the change.

The other detail that caught him was that the attack happened at midnight. He had told her, the last time he had seen her, that she needed to find one of the librarians who worked at night. There were fewer people on campus after eleven p.m., and she could make the transition without a lot of prying eyes.

The rumors made it sound as if Shyly had just finished

the transition when someone summoned security. Shyly wouldn't have had time to clean up everything.

He knew he would have to do it for her.

He had made it all the way to this bridge when that woman showed up. She searched everything and then she picked something up using tongs.

That something, from this distance, looked like a thin cloak or piece of clothing. She stretched it over one arm the way that one did with a long dress or a blanket, and he knew.

He knew.

Shyly hadn't had time to clean up any of the remains of her former body. Security had probably found her when she was still disoriented and trying to figure out who she was.

That worked on a limited basis—attack victims often seemed traumatized. But it wouldn't help with the other details.

And he was eight or more hours late. Someone had noticed how strange it all was.

Students passed him on their way to class. A few looked at him sideways. He'd been on campus long enough to know that people didn't generally lounge on the footbridges.

But this one gave him a good view of the goings-on in that little copse of trees.

The woman folded the skin and put it into a bag that she had pulled from her kit. He didn't see her pick up bones or the skull. There wouldn't be much else there except a pool of blood, which he wouldn't have been able to clean up no matter what.

The internal organs were fuel for the transition, so those

wouldn't be nearby, although sometimes an errant eyeball would escape as the skin sloughed off.

He hoped the woman wouldn't find anything like that.

He had no idea what she would make of any of it. He had gotten to know enough about the Protectorate to realize that it did not consider the Fey a threat. A few people on campus specialized in foreign relations, and felt that Fey-dominated territories needed to be watched and monitored.

But no one had done that. No one here really under-stood Fey magick. And ever since the Purges, the Qavnerians had decided to let a lot of their own magick slide.

He hoped that no one would realize how useful body parts were in certain types of magick.

"Professor Bascherini?"

A dark-haired woman stood in front of him. She was tiny with avid green eyes. He recognized her from his upcoming class. She always sat in the front row, and always asked too many questions.

"Yes, Ysabel?" He tried hard not to let irritation in his voice. A lot depended on his ability to blend in, to make everyone believe he was harmless.

"I have a question about the upcoming exam...?"

Of course she did.

"Can we talk about it on the way to class?" she asked.

He resisted the urge to look at the copse of trees, to see where that woman was in her investigation. He wouldn't be able to go there for hours now, because he had duties in his position as visiting professor.

Not that it mattered. Clearly the woman was collecting

what she found. He wasn't sure how he was going to figure out who she was, or even if he needed to.

Because he could do nothing with those items. And if he was lucky, the ignorance of the Qavnerians would prevent them from understanding what they had found.

"I am certain we could talk on the way to class," he said, deliberately mangling his response in the way that Bascherini would have. "Let us go."

Ysabel waited for him. The moment he pushed himself off the bridge railing, she started into her worthless question, speaking breathlessly, as if the most important thing on campus on this day was her study plan for an upcoming exam.

He tried to pay attention as they walked toward the classroom. He shot only a sideways glance at the copse of trees as they passed.

The woman was still gathering things. She held a glass vial in one hand.

He wasn't panicked. Not really. But he was going to have to figure out which librarian was attacked, and who Shyly was now. He would need to talk with her, stress the fact that the Qavnerians knew something was off about that incident.

He wasn't sure when they could do about it, but he didn't want them to be on alert about any incidents on campus.

He certainly didn't want them uttering the word *Fey*. Not with Lumin itching to retrieve artifacts from the Academy.

Perdu wasn't sure how long he could hold Lumin off.

He would have to talk with Gray about that, when Gray showed up for their weekly meeting.

Perdu wasn't sure if he should tell Lumin to act quickly or to be even more patient.

He supposed he had a few days to figure that all out.

PART THREE
FOUR DAYS LATER

REGENTS
TOWER

ADV. STUDENT
WING

M
ENT

CLOCK
TOWER

CHAPTER
THIRTEEN

Ludmilla Odenkirk sat nervously in large meeting room at the top of Regents Tower. The room was round, and clearly ancient. It was in the main tower part of the building. A larger rectangular section had been built around the tower, long after the tower itself was built.

This room smelled of mildew and damp. The windows were made of some kind of bubbled glass. Through them, she could see the Infrin Sea, gray and stormy, threatening like it always did.

She had hated being close to the sea when she went to school at Serebro Academy, and she hated it now. The sea was the source of mist and storms and a plethora of smells, from dead fish on some heavily misty days to salt and sea foam when the wind glanced off the water's surface.

The windows up here weren't meant to open, so they were coated in white salt around the edges. Someone had to climb down from the top of the building just to clean everything, which happened only a few times per year.

The cleaning was supposed to happen before a meeting of the Board of Regents, but this wasn't a normal board meeting. This was an emergency board meeting, called two days ago.

This was her first emergency board meeting, and only her second meeting overall. Her first board meeting had not gone well. She had been nervous and grieving for her father. She had sat quietly through most of it, unable to figure out what, exactly, was going on.

She hoped this second meeting would go better, but it wasn't starting that way. She was the first to arrive, which made her feel foolish and too eager. But the summons had said *emergency* and it had told her to get here as quickly as possible.

She had done that. Quicker, even, than she had expected. Maybe she lived closer than the others. She would have thought they would all have arrived ahead of here, and none of them had.

At least someone had stoked the fireplace in the boardroom. Someone had put out paper and pens, as well as cups for tea and plates for snacks, none of which had been served yet.

The majordomo of the Regents Tower, Reginald Mumsbury, had shown her into the boardroom with a sniff and a smirk, clearly finding some amusement in her early arrival.

Or maybe he had been smirking at her clothing. Not that he had the right to smirk about that. He wasn't dressed that dissimilarly. He wore pants and a long waistcoat, made of some kind of dark wool material.

She wore pants gathered at the ankle and tucked into the sensible pair of boots that had served her well when she had been a student here. Her coat, given to her by her mother as a going-away present more than a decade ago, actually repelled the rain. Ludmilla had drip-dried off on the several flight of stairs up to the top of the tower. She had carried the coat over her arm as she met Reginald at the top of the stairs.

He had taken the coat from her and put it in a closet in the entry. Then he had smirked again.

Maybe he thought her warm cable-knit fisherman's sweater wasn't respectable either. But she had learned in her years at the Academy, to dress for the possibility of soaking rain, which had been prudent on this day. The soaking rain started the moment the carriage she had hired had dropped her off as close to the Tower as she could get.

She had thought she was going to be late. She had traveled by rail from Trinovante, expecting the train to arrive late like it always did. For the first time, maybe in its entire history, the train had arrived in the city of Serebro early, and she'd managed to hire a carriage to take her over the mountains to the Academy with no fuss at all.

She had noticed, though, that any time she mentioned that she was a regent, she got much better treatment than she had ever gotten in her life. When she had gone into Serebro as a student, the entire town had done its best to ignore her, even though she had been one of the best students in her class.

Students had no place in Serebro, but Regents...apparently Regents were quite important.

At least she had her father's apartment in Serebro to return to at night. The notice of the emergency meeting of the Board included a room number at the lodging house that the Academy provided for the Regents during any board meeting.

If the meeting ran late, she would stay in the lodging house. Otherwise, she would make the trip over the mountains and stay in a place that was familiar.

She hadn't known about the lodging house at the time of her first meeting. No one had bothered to tell her. No one had bothered to tell her a lot of things about being a regent.

At that first meeting two months before, the other regents had done little more than nod a greeting at her, which she had done her best to return. That first meeting would have been difficult and scary even if she hadn't been mourning her father.

Add in the grief, and much of what she experienced had coalesced into flashes, rather than a clear memory of what had really happened. She hadn't been treated in a welcoming manner or even with any kind of respect, which had surprised her, considering how recent her father's death had been.

She had inherited everything from her father—the apartment in Serebro, the country house between Serebro and Trinovante, the family manse in Trinovante, and of course, this seat on the Board. Her father seemed to believe the seat on the Board was the most important thing he was leaving her.

He had given her a lot of instructions about it, in the days before his sudden death.

All that had done was make her nervous about everything.

It didn't help that she was the youngest person on the Board by about five years. When she had been a student, she had always thought of the Regents as elderly. They weren't, not really. Most of them were adults in their prime.

But they all had lifetime appointments, and some of them, like her father, stayed throughout that lifetime.

She threaded her hands together and resisted the urge to get up and pace. The room wasn't quite cold, but it wasn't warm either. She had taken a seat as far from the fire as she could, thinking—hoping—that she wasn't taking someone else's seat.

Her first meeting had been so traumatic that she hadn't been able to map where people sat. All she remembered was that she had had to move twice. She hoped she had the same seat she had ended up with at that meeting, but she didn't know.

She took a deep breath, and hoped someone else would get here soon, or she would start doodling in the notebook she had brought, which would probably be considered unprofessional behavior.

Not even her father had told her how to behave at a board meeting. He also hadn't told her who most of the other Regents were. There had been introductions at that first meeting, but the names had blurred. In the interim, she had made a point of learning the names of her colleagues, but she couldn't learn a lot about them.

That information had proven difficult to find.

Right now, though, everything was difficult. She tried to review the names on the way here, but she was having trouble. Learning twenty-one names shouldn't have been beyond her, particularly when her father used to complain about several of them, but she had been so panicked that everything had gone out of her head.

Part of her panic was the tower itself.

The Regents Tower was one of the the oldest buildings on the Serebro Academy campus. The ten-story-high Tower was in the center of the Old Campus. She had seen it every day when she had been a student, and she had felt the way she was supposed to feel about it—that the Regents were above her, much more important than her, and that everything they did was both important and archaic.

The rumors about the Tower didn't help, nor did the layout. Every single path wended its way around the Tower which, some students claimed, had once had a moat.

Research had long ago proven them wrong. But their sense of the Tower was correct: it had been part of a large fortress, built here at the edge of the Infrin Sea. The fortress had been the original site of the Academy and had had four towers, done in what was now known as Blue Island style—quite plain and yet elegant, balancing the entire fortress as if the towers weighed the edges down in the gale force winds that sometimes hit this part of Qavner.

The fortress itself had been torn down centuries ago, but its outline remained, because the library was also housed one of the fortress's towers, just not as tall as the Regents Tower. The rest of the fortress had been disassembled to make way for individual buildings, some of which served as dormitories for the students and some for actual classrooms. Few of those buildings stood anymore either.

The Architecture Department loved to experiment with new building styles, until the History Department finally stepped in and claimed that the Academy should actually preserve its architectural history as well as its academic one.

Her father had reinforced that decision years ago. He had been proud of that. The Academy had tried, all over again, to destroy their architectural history, and he had led the fight to stop it—which was how Ludmilla knew about it.

She knew about a lot of the fights because of her father. He was supposed to keep matters confidential, and he probably had, within his friends network and his work itself, but he had always told her about the work of the Regents, probably as he groomed her to take his place.

He never told her mother, though, or her siblings, which irritated all of them. They had wanted to be part of his life as well, but that had proven difficult. He had his work, the estate, and his position with the Regents. He had sometimes spoken to her mother, but mostly he had spoken to Ludmilla from the time she turned ten.

He had talked to her like she was an adult, even when she hadn't been, which, she had to admit, had been a blessing. It had enabled her to do better in the Academy than almost all of her peers. She knew how to listen, and she knew how to understand adults imparting information.

The massive oak door opened with a pop. The wood had swelled long ago in the damp, but no one wanted to replace it. Reginald leaned in, holding the door, his amused gaze on Ludmilla.

"You have company," he said in his deep voice, as if he was warning her to behave—not that she hadn't been.

"Cole Mahan," Reginald said formally.

Ludmilla nodded, and stood, because she couldn't remember what the protocol was. Apparently, it wasn't standing, because Reginald's egg-shaped eyes twinkled, and a smile touched the edges of his thin lips. His bald pate shone in the artificial lighting as he bowed, moving out of the room backwards, as a young man walked in.

Mahan had brown hair that needed a trim, broad shoulders, and an athletic grace. He looked like a man who was used to being outside doing things rather than inside studying—at least until she had seen his blue eyes and realized that Mahan tried to mask a massive intelligence behind an insouciant attitude.

She remembered Mahan now. He had been the youngest regent until she came on board. He was five years older than she was, also there because his father had died unexpectedly.

Mahan smiled at her as he deliberately pushed the door closed.

"Reginald is an ass," Mahan said. "He's harassing you now like he used to harass me. Just remember he's the *staff.*"

She didn't believe in treating the staff any differently than anyone else, but she didn't say so, because it would sound pompous. She had worked her whole life to avoid sounding pompous.

"He doesn't seem to recall it," she said.

"Oh, he knows," Mahan said. "That's why he bullies people."

Then Mahan walked to her side. He was taller than she was, which surprised her. He hadn't looked very tall when he had arrived.

He bowed, just a little.

"We were never properly introduced," he said. "I'm Cole."

She was pleased that he had noticed. No one had introduced themselves to her at the previous meeting. She had been introduced to everyone rather quickly—*This is Ludmilla Odenkirk. She's taking her father's seat*—and that had been that. The meeting had then gotten underway.

"I'm Ludmilla," she said, probably unnecessarily, since she, after all, had been the one introduced two months ago. "Do you know what this meeting is about?"

"No," Cole said. "The messenger didn't bother to enlighten me. And then I had to figure out how to get here and if I wanted to stay at the lodge."

None of the members of the Board of Regents lived on campus, as was once required. Only ten of the twenty-two Regents lived in the nearby village of Serebro. The remaining Regents lived in Trinovante and had to travel to the Academy whenever a Board of Regents meeting was scheduled.

Emergency meetings were particularly problematical. Contacting the Regents meant one day's worth of travel minimum just for the summons, and then the Regents had to travel to Serebro.

Apparently, Ludmilla hadn't been the only one who had struggled with transportation.

"Of course," Cole said, "I'm not privy to a lot of the stuff the old bastards know. They don't respect the newcomers or the younger Regents."

Ludmilla had noticed that, but she had thought it had just been about her. She had become used to being ignored, even as a student. She wasn't sure why that was. Maybe she had forgettable face.

She didn't think it was forgettable. Whenever she looked in a mirror, she saw her father's face underneath her long black hair. Her eyes were black as well, unlike her father's, which had been a sky blue. But the rest of her face —the narrow chin, the high cheekbones, the slightly upturned eyebrows—those had come directly from her father.

People used to laugh when they saw her, and say, *Well, Franklin, no denying whose child she is.*

He had always laughed uncomfortably, an acknowledgement, perhaps, that all of his other children looked more like his wife than like him. Or maybe the commentators knew something about Ludmilla's mother that Ludmilla suspected, but didn't know for certain.

Or maybe it was just a comment.

Ludmilla grabbed the high back of her chair, the wooden edges cutting into her palms.

"Do they ever do an initiation or anything?" She felt stupid asking, but she also felt like she had no choice. Even though her father had continually talked to her about being a regent, she felt out of her depth.

Cole's eyebrows went up and he smiled, almost involuntarily, it seemed.

"An initiation?" he asked. "You mean like some ceremony or ritual?"

Her cheeks warmed. She hadn't realized what that sounded like. It sounded like one of those secret societies that had been banned during the Purges.

"Not like that, no," she said. "Just, you know, when new students come to the Academy, they go through a few days of getting to know the place, being told the rules. Something like that."

Cole's smile faded just a bit. He nodded, then let out a small laugh.

"I wish I had thought to ask that," he said. "I've been muddling through since I got here. Which is, I guess, the answer to your question. No. They don't initiate anyone. You show up and you get to work."

"But what is the work, exactly?" she asked. "I know we run higher education in the Protectorate, but it seemed like my father was doing a lot more."

Cole frowned. He moved closer to her as if he was going to answer her in a whisper. He pulled back the chair next to hers—and then the door opened.

Reginald leaned in. Again.

"Mavis Packingham," he said in an even more theatrical tone than he had used before.

He hadn't announced anyone at that first meeting that Ludmilla had gone to, but then, she had arrived late, because she hadn't had directions to the meeting room.

Ludmilla stiffened, waiting to see which Regent Mavis

Packingham was. She was, to Ludmilla's surprise, the solid middle-aged woman whose curly hair had been purplish black the last time, but which was now a lavender white.

She wore a matching white and lavender sweater, a dark purple skirt, and gray suede boots that somehow seemed to survive the mists and the damp. She carried a matching gray suede cap under one arm, and a gray suede bag draped over the other.

"Ah," she said with a smile, dumping her bag in front of a chair near the head of the table. "The children. Welcome to you both."

Cole's return smile was tight. Ludmilla felt her breath catch in her throat. The condescension in Packingham's tone was thick.

"And to you," Cole said, heroically matching her tone.

Packingham didn't seem to notice.

"Do you know why we were called to this meeting?" Ludmilla asked.

Packingham gave her a withering look. "You don't?"

Cole laughed. "In other words, she has no idea."

Packingham started to answer when the door opened again. This time Reginald did not lean in. Instead he held the door with one long arm as two men entered.

One was elderly. His wisps of white hair barely covered his thin pate. His eyes were a watery green, his skin a mottled brown. He was Eustace Wallingford, and he had been a sometimes friend of her father's.

They had been on the outs when her father died, so Ludmilla hadn't seen Eustace in a few years. He looked older and frailer than she remembered.

But she didn't recognize the man holding Eustace's arm. That man was long and thin, so thin, in fact, that he seemed almost skeletal. His long nose hooked, his chin bent slightly upward, and his mouth was a thin line.

His hair was a yellowish-white that curled upward like his chin, and his skin was an unnatural whitish yellow, almost the color of parchment.

When his dark eyes rested on Ludmilla, she shivered.

She remembered him now. He had watched her through that first meeting as if he had been waiting for her to make some kind of fatal mistake.

"Eustace Wallingford and Horace Rogov," Reginald said, and eased out the door almost before both men were completely inside.

Eustace shuffled forward, and said querulously, "I need to sit close to the fire."

Rogov didn't respond. He just led Eustace to the chair closest to the fire. As he sat down, Eustace noticed Ludmilla.

"You should sit, girl," he said. "Standing through the meetings is damned uncomfortable."

"Not everyone is here yet, Eustace," Rogov said quietly.

"Oh," Eustace said as if he hadn't noticed. "Well, we don't stand."

Then he peered even closer at Ludmilla. "You're Franklin's girl."

"Yes," she said, suddenly uncomfortable. Eustace had been a regular at her childhood home. He used to give her candies and books. He would wink at her during dinner if her father was being too full of himself.

She had always thought that Eustace had liked and

valued her. The fact that he didn't recognize her on a deep level bothered her.

Had she changed that much?

"Sadly," Eustace said, "you have the look of your father."

Her cheeks warmed even more, and she looked down.

"For the sake of all that's decent, Eustace," Packingham said, "shut your mouth."

"Leave him be," Rogov said. "He's had four incidents just in the past month. He's lucky to be walking."

Incidents? Ludmilla looked at Cole, who shook his head slightly.

"We don't need him for a quorum," Packingham said.

"I'm not dead yet," Eustace sounded even more querulous than before.

"But you're not completely here, either, are you?" Packingham asked. "Why don't you let your nephew take over?"

"Nephew?" Eustace asked.

"Eustace's lawyers are keeping his nephew away from the estate," Rogov said. "The boy is under the mistaken impression that Eustace is leaving him everything."

Packingham made a dismissive noise. "This is how we're in this mess," she said.

Ludmilla looked at Cole again, hoping for more clarification, but he was frowning.

Then the door opened again, and once again, Reginald held back.

"Yana Hoodwinkle, Pasha Volkovich, Devin Chaban, and Wilma Blankenship," Reginald said, pressing himself against the door, as four people entered more or less single file.

He was about to close the door when he stopped and added, "Sorcé N'lman."

Ludmilla barely looked at the four who had come in earlier, because Sorcé N'lman caught her eye. She remembered him from the last meeting, long black hair pulled away from his face, sunken cheeks, and haunted eyes.

Something about him made her leery—or maybe even frightened. She had the feeling the last time, and it had gotten worse this time, even though he didn't look at her.

He didn't look at anyone. He tugged his gray sweater over matching gray trousers, shifted a black satchel from one hand to the other, and headed to the foot of the table. He greeted no one, and no one greeted him, even though there were low murmurs as the other four took their seats.

Ludmilla realized she had been staring at him. She made herself look away, made herself focus on the four.

None of them were as old as Eustace or her father had been in his last few meetings, but none of them were young either. Or even middle-aged.

Yana Hoodwinkle, who had come in first, had a cap of gray curls that encircled her head and lively gray eyes. She seemed almost cheerful as she nodded at Ludmilla and then sat down across from her.

Pasha Volkovich had long white-blond hair that looked like silk. He had pulled it back, like N'lman had done with his hair, but strands escaped, curling around Volkovich's square face. His skin was leathery, as if he had spent too much time in the sun. His eyes were recessed in his face, lost in wrinkles that seemed like smile lines, although Ludmilla couldn't be certain.

He said something to Wilma Blankenship, who laughed. Her laugh sounded like chimes on a breeze. She was slight and delicate, almost child-sized, but her green eyes held a lot of intelligence and not too much warmth.

Only Devin Chaban looked friendly, and that was because he made a point of smiling at everyone as he sat down. He was square—square of face, square of jaw, square of shoulders, square of body—and it looked deliberate, as if he had exercised that squareness into being. Even his eyes seemed somewhat square, which was a bit unnerving.

It took work to smile back at him.

"Two more and we'll have a quorum," he said as he sat down next to Eustace and patted Eustace's crabbed hand.

"Do you think that we're going to need a quorum?" Packingham asked. "The messenger told me that no one dared miss this meeting."

"Maybe that's because you've missed three of our last five meetings, dear," Yana said, with fake warmth.

"No one else was told this?" Packingham asked.

Ludmilla wasn't told anything, just the time and date that she had to be there.

"We have an important vote," Chaban said. "And a lot of discussion to prepare for it. I want to start as soon as possible."

"We all do," Rogov said, "but if the vote is important, we need the entire Board here."

The friendliness in Chaban's face faded. "You know that Kirilli is dead."

"Yes," Rogov said.

"Of course," Packingham said.

"Tragedy," Yana said.

"Is it?" Wilma asked.

Cole and Pasha nodded.

"Who?" Eustace asked loudly, and Ludmilla wanted to thank him. She wasn't sure who Kirilli was either.

"Augustus Kirilli," Packingham said with stunning viciousness. "You've known him most of your life."

"I don't recall," Eustace said. "Is he important?"

Chaban sighed. "Kirilli had no heirs. We're going to have to figure out how to handle his seat."

"Kirilli has a number of children," Packingham said. "He always told us that he was leaving his seat to his eldest daughter, the unfortunate Augusta."

"Why is she unfortunate?" Cole asked.

"The name bred the girl," Packingham said. "She is solid and stolid and extremely uninteresting."

"If he had children," Ludmilla said quietly, cautiously, "why doesn't he have heirs?"

"Oh," Chaban waved a hand. "He has heirs for his *fortune*. But his daughter has been very clear that she will not become a regent."

"Then the other children should have a stab at it," Sorcé N'lman said, his voice so deep that it actually rumbled the table.

"They have." Chaban sounded annoyed. "They've never been interested. Don't you pay attention?"

"I do," N'lman said, and tilted his head slightly. The movement made his sunken cheeks look even more shadowed. "Many of us complain about our children. All of them come forward when the time is right."

"Not all of us are murdered," Chaban said.

The entire room grew quiet. Ludmilla had trouble finding her breath. Murdered? Augustus Kirilli had been murdered? And that was why they were having this meeting?

Why hadn't anyone told her? Shouldn't someone have mentioned it before everyone traveled?

"Was he murdered for being a regent?" Her voice betrayed her lack of breath.

"He was stabbed for some papers he had," Chaban said, and peered at N'lman, "which makes Sorcé's choice of words about the children very unfortunate."

Ludmilla frowned. What had N'lman said? That the children should have a *stab* at the seat? She did everything she could not to look at him.

Chaban was right; the choice of words was both unusual and unfortunate, especially if N'lman knew how Kirilli had died.

"You're certain the children can't be talked into the seat?" Packingham asked.

Chaban's cheeks flushed. "I wouldn't have called the meeting otherwise. We are going to need to figure out how to fill his seat."

"If it should be filled at all," Volkovich said.

Everyone looked at him and he shrugged, a tiny half-smile on his face.

"The number of Regents is not set in stone," he said.

"Another unfortunate turn of phrase," Packingham muttered.

Ludmilla did not understand that at all.

"If we have that much to decide," Rogov said tightly, "then we need the full Board."

Ah, yes. That was what had started this entire discussion.

"You should have let us all know before we traveled," Packingham said.

"I'm not in charge of the messages," Chaban said. "I leave that to Reginald. Although he did tell me that Josiah Hopkins the Third did not answer his summons. Which is typical of the younger generation. Which means we won't have a full Board.

"The Third?" Volkovich asked. "What happened to his father?"

"He passed a week or two ago," Chaban said. "The son's not taking it well."

"Murdered, like Kirilli?" Packingham asked.

Chaban shook his head. "I don't think so. Some members are getting older. We shouldn't be shocked by this."

Ludmilla glanced at Cole. He was frowning. He seemed like he was about to say something when the door opened again.

This time, Reginald stepped inside.

"Fedor Garvyn and Paulina Elin," he said, sweeping a hand forward as if he were introducing royalty.

They arrived arm in arm, the illusion of royalty broken by their travel-wrinkled coats, and the raindrops dotting their brown hair. Garvyn dropped Elin's arm as they got inside. They split up and walked to opposite sides of the table, pulling off their coats at the same time and hanging them on the back of their chairs.

"Has Devin tried to start the meeting yet?" Garvyn asked. His deep voice did not match his thin frame. He looked at the entire room, one by one, as if demanding that they each answer him.

He had a small goatee and a long mustache that went down its sides, hiding the corners of his mouth, and giving him the look of a perpetually disappointed man.

Or maybe he *was* perpetually disappointed. Elin had the same expression without the goatee or mustache. Her mouth was downturned, her eyes downturned as well.

Her gaze fell momentarily on Ludmilla, before moving to the others.

"I did not try to start the meeting," Chaban said.

"Oh, so we are late." Elin smiled—sort of—at Garvyn. "He's defensive."

"I am not," Chaban said.

"We're not going to fight," Packingham said. "It's because of the fighting that I don't want to be here."

Her comment stopped the conversation cold. Everyone looked down, as if none of them were responsible for the fighting.

Ludmilla wasn't even sure what the fighting referred to. She felt so out of her depth that she wondered what her father had been thinking, insisting that she take this seat.

She had had no idea she could turn it down. She wondered if she could do so this afternoon.

"We have a quorum now," Chaban said after a moment of silence.

Packingham rolled her eyes. "Oh, for—"

The door opened, interrupting her. Reginald stepped inside again.

"Evander Popov, Jules Dh'stan, Xavier, and Baxter Ivonovich," he said, as each person passed him.

Ludmilla looked at the only person who used a single name. Xavier appeared to be as old as her father, but unlike her father before he died, Xavier's back was straight and his eyes clear.

His skin was the darkest in the room. He wore a robe instead of a suit, but he carried a conventional satchel which he set on the ground beside Eustace.

As Xavier pulled the chair back, he gave Eustace a warm smile, then extended his hand. "Good to see you, my friend."

Eustace took the hand with a great deal of confusion, clearly uncertain whether or not to pretend he recognized Xavier.

Xavier saved Eustace the trouble by saying "Xavier," and patted his hand.

Eustace nodded with even more confusion, and pulled his hand away as quickly as possible.

The others took seats around the table, clearly trying to avoid watching the drama with Eustace.

Was everyone going to pretend he was fine? Because he wasn't. But Ludmilla didn't feel as if she could mention that. She tried to disappear in her chair and let the meeting go on around her.

"Three more need to be here," Packingham said pointedly.

"I say we start without them," Rogov said with a sideways look at Eustace. "Not all of us can spend the day at this."

"We'll need to," Chaban said. "What we have to discuss is not a one-vote-and-done matter."

Packingham sighed loudly, and flounced back in her chair.

"I can't guarantee how long Eustace will be able stay," Rogov said.

Ludmilla wasn't sure what the point was of having him stay in the first place.

Chaban waved a hand. "We have enough without the both of you, if you'd like to go."

His words seemed particularly brutal. Even Eustace picked up on it, although all he did was look at Chaban and frown.

"Just get the meeting underway," Packingham said.

Chaban looked at her, clearly assessing whether or not to take her advice.

Elin leaned back in her chair. "If this is about Kirilli," she said, "then we need details."

"We have enough details," Chaban said.

"*I* don't," Packingham said.

"Do they know who did it?" Garvyn asked.

"No," Chaban said. "The murderer is at large. Augustus was killed on a public street, in the late afternoon. It was very odd."

"Why was he killed?" Evander Popova asked. He was heavyset, the folds of his face hiding his eyes, at least from the angle where Ludmilla sat. He seemed old, but he couldn't have been—not given the smoothness of his pale skin and the thickness of his reddish hair.

"I don't know," Chaban said. "I know only that nothing was taken from him. His office believes that the murder had something do with a case he was working on."

"Case?" Packingham asked. "He was a lawyer?"

"Forensic accountant, at least at the end," Jules Dh'stan said. He was a small man, who hunched over his end of the table as if the surface had to hold him up.

"Lawyer before that?" Packingham asked.

"I don't think so," Dh'stan said. "It wasn't really relevant."

"I always thought he was a lawyer," Packingham said.

Cole sighed audibly beside Ludmilla. She had forgotten he was there. She glanced at him. He looked annoyed.

"Maybe," he said pointedly, "we should give each other our biographies so that we never have conversations like this one. We can start with what all of us do for a living."

"Assuming we do anything at all," Packingham said.

Ludmilla shot her a sideways glance, then quickly looked away. Ludmilla was beginning to loathe Packingham. Ludmilla just wanted the meeting to go forward without Packingham injecting her vicious comments every few minutes.

Cole's eyes narrowed as he looked at her. "It would be good to know if someone *didn't* work, as well as if they did."

"When I ascended to the Board," Packingham said, "no one was allowed to work."

"Lying is not going to help us," Chaban said to her.

"I'm not lying," she said.

"I've always worked," Eustace said quietly.

Everyone looked at him, as if they were surprised he could inject a rational comment into the conversation.

"Yes, you have," Rogov said, almost as if he were talking to a three-year-old who had just fed himself. "And so have I. Mavis has a selective memory about many things."

"It was an unwritten rule," Chaban said.

"It was recommended that no one *had to* work," Hoodwinkle said. "That way, they could come to these greatly amusing emergency board meetings."

The door opened yet again, and as it did, Ludmilla realized she hadn't seen it close the last time.

Reginald stood to one side and said, "Sonia Petroscu," as if he didn't even want to speak the name.

A small woman with dramatic black-and-white hair swept into the room. She wore a cape that matched her hair, as did her pants. One leg was black and the other white. Her boots were black and white, and seemed to be made of some kind of leather.

She made it past the door, which Reginald hurriedly pulled closed.

"It took forever to get here," she said. "It was raining, and I had little warning. Was that by design, Devin?"

"Emergency means emergency," Chaban said.

She whipped off her cape and tossed it over an empty chair. Then she took another chair as far from Chaban as she could get.

"Then we'd better get to it, shouldn't we?" she asked, and sat down.

Ludmilla didn't remember her from the first meeting, but then much of that meeting was a blur.

"As I was saying," Chaban said, "Kirilli was murdered. He—"

"Oh, my," said a male voice from the door. A heavyset man wearing a yellowish-gold suit and too many rings put a hand to his mouth. "You're saying that Augustus is dead?"

"He is, Dao," Chaban said. "Are you going to join us?"

The man nodded his head, loosening black curls that fell around his florid face. "I hadn't realized."

Reginald came to the door. "I asked you to wait," he hissed at the man standing there.

"And I told you I was late, and I didn't care about your stupid announcements." The man glared at Reginald. "For those of you who don't know, I'm Dao Kwin. I've been a member of this Board since infancy, it seems like."

"Longer," Packingham muttered.

"And if you don't know who I am," Kwin said, "well, then you're either Eustace or the lovely young lady sitting next to Mahan."

Warmth again flooded Ludmilla's cheeks. She hadn't expected to blush this much. She was glad her skin tone hid most of it, but she was sure the others saw the slight change in color. Of maybe just her discomfort.

"I'm Ludmilla Odenkirk," she said quietly.

"Ah, Franklin's daughter, that's right." Kwin let his hand fall away from his face. He gave Ludmilla a quick smile that didn't meet his eyes at all. "You were here last time."

"Yes," she said.

"Because your father passed too," Kwin said.

"He did." Her voice trembled on the last word. She still had trouble talking about her father.

"Was he murdered as well?" Kwin asked.

"Dao!" Rogov and Chaban spoke in unison, sounding shocked.

"No," Ludmilla said, ignoring them. "He'd been ill for some time."

"Good." Kwin made his way to the only seat at the table that wasn't covered with a satchel or a coat or a cape. "I don't mean that it's good he was ill, I mean it was good he wasn't murdered too."

"No one thinks the murder has anything to do with us," Chaban said.

"Even better." Kwin pulled his chair back. The legs squealed against the floor. "We don't want people killing off Regents for their own agenda, now do we?"

Ludmilla stiffened. Was *that* a possibility? The others looked down, as if they didn't even want to think about it. She glanced around, saw Chaban staring at Kwin as if Kwin had said something he shouldn't have.

"Please," Dh'stan said quietly. "You're scaring the new member."

"She should be scared," Packingham said. "We haven't lost this many Regents in such a short period of time before."

"Three in one year?" Chaban asked. "That's not true—"

"Four," Packingham said. "In five years."

"We're all getting older," Rogov said, with a sideways glance at Eustace. "I'm sure the generation before us felt the same way."

"Yes, but this time there's a problem," Packingham said. "This time, most of us do not have heirs."

Ludmilla frowned. "How can that be? I know that—"

Cole put a hand on her arm, stopping her. But she didn't want to be stopped. She knew that Eustace had five children, and she remembered playing with other children of the Regents when she was a child. There was even an area in the tower that children could play or study while their parents were on the Academy's campus.

"'How can that be?'" Packingham asked, quoting Ludmilla while deliberately mocking her. "It's a simple problem, one you apparently don't have. How many children do you have?"

"Mavis, please," Chaban said, waving his hands in exasperation. "She just ascended to the Board."

Ascended. What an odd word.

"I don't have any children. Yet," Ludmilla said. "I'm not even twenty-five."

And unmarried. She was unmarried. But even if she remained unmarried, she had a lot of family. She would see to it that the seat on the Board, which meant so much to her father, would go to an Odenkirk.

At least, she would do so now that she knew she needed to designate an heir quickly.

"Most of our children," Chaban said, looking around the room, "have made it clear that they do not want to be Regents. My sons don't. I know Eustace's children have declined an offer to be on the Board."

"They were offered?" Eustace sounded surprised. "I'm not dead yet. Am I?"

He posed that question to Rogov, who patted his hand absently.

"You're not dead, Eustace," Rogov said. "I'd tell you if you were."

That answer was rude and impossible, but Eustace seemed to accept it as logical. Ludmilla felt a chill run down her back.

What had she gotten into?

"And that's why we're here," Chaban said. "Because Kirilli died without anyone to take his place. His children do not want the posting. I've contacted them to make certain."

His lips pursed and he shook his head slightly, as if the memory bothered him.

"Out with it," Packingham said.

Chaban shook his head. "They were dealing with the unexpected death. That's all."

It clearly wasn't all, but no one else pushed.

"I suppose he made no contingency plans either," Hood-winkle said.

"Most of us haven't," Xavier muttered.

"Yes, that's true," Chaban said, "and that's one of the reasons we're having this meeting. It—"

"Munira Zubiri," Reginald said loudly, startling everyone in the room. Over half of them jumped.

Ludmilla hadn't heard the door open, which meant that either Reginald had been deliberately quiet or he hadn't closed the door entirely the last time.

A woman with straight black hair stood near Reginald. She wore a long blue dress with fringe on the sleeves, along the waist, and along the hemline, with matching blue shoes peeking out from underneath. Her hands were folded behind her back. Her eyes were as dark as her hair and filled with a terrifying intelligence.

Ludmilla couldn't tell how old she was.

"I seem to be late," Zubiri said in a low, smooth voice. "I thought we had an hour leeway for emergency meetings."

"We do," Rogov said, "but most of us don't take it."

"None of us want to be here," Packingham said, "and yet we are."

"So the rules be damned, eh?" Zubiri said. She waved a hand at Reginald. Bells tinkled at the movement. They were attached to the bottom of her sleeves.

"You may go now," she said imperiously. "And this time, close the door properly."

Ludmilla started. No wonder she hadn't heard the door close. It hadn't.

Zubiri waited as Reginald slunk out and pulled the door soundly closed behind him.

"He needs to be replaced," she said. "Whenever I arrive he's reading minutes or listening in."

"He does keep the histories," Chaban said.

"Because you're too lazy to do so." She walked to the chair with Petrescu's shawl on it. With two fingers, Zubiri picked up the shawl, walked it to Petrescu, and dropped it on her.

Then Zubiri walked back to that chair, brushed it off, and sat down.

"I assume we're discussing Kirilli," she said. "And since we are notoriously uncompassionate, I suppose we're just discussing the issue of heirs?"

"What kind of compassion do you want?" Packingham said.

Zubiri leaned forward and placed her arms on the table. The bells clanged against the wooden surface.

"He did just die, rather horribly," she said. "And most of us have known him for decades. Maybe a moment of mourning would be in order? A few kind words?"

Her gaze passed over Ludmilla as if Ludmilla had no importance at all.

Maybe in this instance, she didn't.

The others were looking down, or staring at the fire, or glaring at Zubiri.

"You'll note," she said, "that I did not give any of you the benefit of the doubt. I knew you wouldn't have honored him."

"We're not here for that." Chaban sounded more angry that defensive.

"Oh, yes," Zubiri said. "We're here to discuss the problem of no heirs. Again."

"How did you know he had no heirs?" Hoodwinkle asked.

"I don't," Zubiri said. "But I assume that Devin wouldn't have called an emergency meeting if Kirilli had heirs. After all, that's what he did when Samantha died."

"That was ten years ago," Chaban said.

"Yes, and we ended up graced with Xavier," Zubiri said. Ludmilla couldn't tell if the sentence was a dig or not. Was Zubiri upset about Xavier?

"I didn't realize I was a problem," Xavier said. "And it's

not that I wasn't an heir, exactly. I am Samantha's second cousin, twice removed."

"The only one who wanted the job," Zubiri said, her gaze touching both Ludmilla and Cole. "The rest of the family thought it was stupid."

"The rest of the family had other concerns," Xavier said. "The Thaumaturgical Purges were difficult on us."

The room became quiet for a moment. Ludmilla stiffened. The Thaumaturgical Purges were something people mentioned as code, but she never knew what they went through as individuals. Most people did not discuss that at all.

"A motion came up then, and I am going to revive it now," Zubiri said. "I move that we disband the Board of Regents."

"Munira," Chaban said chidingly. "We can't do that."

"Traditional shouldn't always win, Devin," Zubiri said. "I made a motion. Is there a second?"

No one spoke for a long moment. Then Eustace said, "Second," in a quavering voice.

"Eustace," Rogov said.

"What?" Eustace asked. "Did I do something wrong? She needed a second."

"He doesn't know what he's doing," Rogov said quietly.

"That hasn't stopped us from using him before," Packingham muttered.

"All right." Chaban snarled the words. "We have a motion on the table. Discussion?"

"We can't disband," Garvyn said. "Who would run the academies?"

"Maybe they could run themselves," Zubiri said.

"It would cause a major upheaval," Popova said.

"Which might not be bad," Zubiri said.

"This is not a serious motion," Petrscu snapped. "This is a waste of our time. She does that deliberately whenever she has the chance."

Zubiri smiled at her. The smile was not kind.

"I move to table this discussion for a later meeting," Cole said.

The entire group looked at him in surprise.

"We need to discuss it, with facts and figures," he said. "The Regents are a relic of an earlier time. It would be good to assess whether or not we're still useful. But not today. This is an emergency meeting. We need to deal with the emergency."

"Young man," Zubiri said. "The existence of the Board in these troubled times *is* an emergency."

"I second the motion to table," Petrescu said, speaking over Zubiri. "Quick, Devin. Call the question."

"Show of hands," Chaban said. "Let's table this discussion to a later meeting."

Hands went up, Ludmilla's included. Only Zubiri and Eustace did not raise their hands. Eustace looked at Rogov in confusion.

"What are we voting on?" Eustace asked.

"Something you agree with," Rogov said, grabbing Eustace's hand and raising it.

"You can't count that as a vote," Zubiri said to Chaban.

"I'm not," he said. "It's an abstention. But it doesn't matter. You still lose."

"I don't think having a discussion is a loss," she said, and then she smiled. "In fact, I think we've just moved my agenda forward, for the very first time in decades."

She bowed her head slightly. The movement chilled Ludmilla and she wasn't sure why. There was so much going on here—so many interrelationships, so much history, that she felt unsettled and slightly terrified.

"Thank you, young Mahan," Zubiri said.

Cole's mouth formed a thin line. He looked angry. Was this because he felt used? Or because he didn't want attention placed on himself? Or something else entirely?

"Let's move on," he said to Chaban.

"Indeed," Zubiri said. "Let's move on. Are you all ready to destroy the Regents from the inside? Because Devin is."

Ludmilla frowned. She truly did not understand what was at stake here.

She finally stood up for herself.

"We need a break here," she said ,and everyone looked at her like she was Eustace suddenly having a moment of clarity. "*I* need a break."

"You can't call a break, dear," Hoodwinkle said.

"That's the one thing I do know," Ludmilla said. "You all were very clear on this point in my very first meeting. We all have the power to call a break. I'm calling one."

"She's right," Chaban said. "Fifteen minutes."

He stood and walked out of the room. The others sat still, as if they hadn't expected this at all.

Ludmilla grabbed Cole's arm. "You're coming with me," she said.

He let out a small snort. "You're quite demanding."

She was, in her normal life. Not here though. She hadn't been demanding here. Not until now.

She had just realized how very dysfunctional this organization was. She had thought, based on what her father used to say, that this organization was not only one of the best in the entire world, it was also one of the most important.

She was no longer sure whether or not he was right. But Ludmilla did know one thing: if he was right, then this chaotic and difficult meeting was going to decide something critical.

And she needed to understand what that something critical was before the voting got underway.

REGENTS

TOWER

ADV. STUDENT
WING

M
ENTI

CLOCK
TOWER

CHAPTER
FOURTEEN

Cole Mahan had deeply underestimated Ludmilla Odenkirk. He hadn't expected her to call a break, and he certainly hadn't expected her to order him around. The woman he had seen her first meeting two months ago seemed meek to the point of nearly disappearing.

He had actually forgotten all about her until he arrived at the emergency meeting to find her sitting alone, nervously twisting her fingers together.

But she had watched the entire meeting so far, and had seemed deeply interested in what was going on. The contentiousness seemed to bother her. She had actively flinched once, but that hadn't stopped her from asking for a break the moment Zubiri started discussing shuttering the Board of Regents again.

Then Ludmilla had grabbed Cole by the arm and

demanded that he talk to her. He was so intrigued, he had said yes.

And, truth be told, he didn't mind talking with her. The others treated him like he wasn't important, which had bothered him.

He hadn't stood up for himself the way that Ludmilla Odenkirk had. When she hadn't understood something or when it had all gotten too fraught, she had asked for time to regroup.

He had never thought of that.

He followed her out of the main hall. Chaban had already left, but none of the others had. Cole couldn't hear anyone talking behind him either, so they remained, apparently feeling stunned that Ludmilla had taken control.

Cole allowed himself a small smile. Having her on the Board might make these meetings interesting after all.

The two of them entered the antechamber. There, Reginald sat like a disappointed slug in his small desk near one of the fogged windows.

The antechamber was chilly, the fireplace empty. Reginald was ostentatiously pouting, the kind of person who wanted others to notice his suffering.

Cole loathed people like that. He hadn't much liked Reginald, and the feeling had grown stronger over the past year or so.

Ludmilla stopped, looking at Reginald with dismay. She clearly did not want to have the conversation here. And she was right not to.

The antechamber was a natural listening chamber. With the door to the main meeting room slightly open, Reginald, or anyone else who wanted to, could hear every word spoken in the room.

"This way," Cole said, and led Ludmilla into the hallway to a flight of stairs. The stairs were not the ones that everyone had to climb to reach the meeting hall.

He had found these stairs much later, when he truly needed to escape the others but had no idea where to go.

The stairs were narrow and old. They led to a little-used room at the top of the tower. Cole had since learned that there were several such rooms at the very top of this place, some blocked off and others impossible to open without the right key.

This one didn't need a key. The door's latch had been broken long ago, and no one had fixed it.

Once, Cole had even asked Reginald why no one had repaired the door, and Reginald's answer had been simple: *No one knows who is responsible for this building's upkeep.*

It had sounded like Reginald expected Cole to research that little bit of information, but Cole didn't see that as his job either. If anything, it was Chaban's job as Chairman of the Board.

But Cole hadn't spoken to Chaban about it. Such a conversation risked losing Cole's refuge.

The stairs twisted their way up, growing more and more narrow as they reached the top. There were two landings, and on each, other staircases branched away.

"What is this place?" Ludmilla asked, sounding nervous.

"Private," he said, leading them up the last part of the staircase.

Her breath caught, as if she didn't like the idea of someone she barely knew looking for privacy.

He didn't blame her. She was a woman alone in a strange new place. If he tried something, no one would believe her—at least no one among the Regents.

Or maybe she hadn't been thinking of her personal safety in that way. Maybe she had been thinking about Augustus Kirilli's murder. She had probably met him only once, but that might have been enough to bother her.

It certainly bothered Cole. That and the fact that yet again, the heirs had refused to sit on the Board.

It didn't seem right. Chaban hadn't even sent Cole a message after the death of his father. No one had informed Cole about the next board meeting. He'd found it listed on his father's daily diary and had come on his own, startling Chaban.

That look of shock had bothered Cole then, and it bothered him now. He found himself ruminating on it more as time went on.

The air was dank on this upper level and smelled of mildew and old wet wood. The stone walls had ancient water stains layered one on top of the other. The most recent was white, but beneath, the others were varying shades of orange and black.

He was careful not to touch any of it, and he hoped Ludmilla was smart enough not to either.

The last part of the staircase was dark. Lightstones had illuminated the landings and the lower parts of the stairwell, but this part was so old that it only had holders for torches. No one had replaced them with lightstones at all.

But he had come here so many times that he knew how many steps there were before he reached the door. He bent his arms, and pushed the door open with his elbows, always careful not to touch the continually soggy wood with his fingers.

Light flooded the stairwell, revealing a startled Ludmilla. She had her arms wrapped around her torso, a clear sign that this entire thing had made her deeply uncomfortable.

This upper room held one round table and a handful of broken chairs. The layers of dust had receded a bit since Cole had started using the room, but each time he came here, he saw no other footprints beside his own.

There were windows on three sides, curved with the tower itself. Once he had looked up from the ground and realized that the windows on that upper level had been added later and were so out of place they looked like wooden teeth.

The windows leaked, and were part of the cause of the water coursing down the stone in the stairwells. He wasn't sure what created the other part.

"My," Ludmilla said. "Are you sure it's safe up here?"

"Safe from the others," he said. "You wanted privacy. Here it is."

She nodded, clearly not sure what she wanted anymore. She gingerly picked her way inside, a sour expression on her long thin face.

In this light, he realized she was older than he initially thought. He hadn't really given her a good look in the previous meeting, and as this one started, he had dismissed her as young and naïve.

She was younger than he was, but she wasn't young. And the naïveté might have simply been about the Board of Regents and some kind of innate shyness.

She walked over to the windows, which were streaked with rain, and kept her arms wrapped around her torso.

Then she turned toward him.

"I'm confused," she said. "Everyone is at each other's throats—"

"That's normal," he said.

"It wasn't at the last meeting," she said.

He barely remembered the previous meeting. But it had been unusually amiable.

"That was the anomaly," he said.

She sighed. "How does anything get done?"

"With a lot of backbiting," he said. "But we do achieve things."

She nodded, glancing at the windows again. "Everyone seems on edge. Is it because of the murder?"

So it had been the murder that bothered her. Maybe it should have bothered him as well. The fact of it bothered him, but the loss of Kirilli really didn't.

Cole had worked very hard not to get close to any of them, particularly if they were people like his father. His father had not been a kind man. If someone had murdered him, Cole wouldn't have been surprised.

Perhaps Cole had been more surprised that his father had died in his bed, alone and ill, without family beside him, because he had sent everyone away.

"No," Cole said. "People aren't on edge because of the murder."

He didn't want to tell her, at this junction anyway, that most likely, no one cared about the murder.

"People are on edge," he said, "because Devin Chaban wants to change the way things are done."

Ludmilla frowned, which made her look even older. "Why would he do that?"

"He's been complaining that the heirs don't want the seats," Cole said. "I didn't want the seat either, but I hadn't realized there was a choice."

"Me, either," Ludmilla said. "My father said that it was the right of the Odenkirks to sit on the Board."

The phrasing caught Cole, because his father had said the same thing about the Mahans.

"Can't we just reduce the number of seats?" Ludmilla asked. "If someone doesn't want one, can't we just close down the seat?"

Cole felt a little uneasy. He had never thought to ask any of these questions. He had the sense that this woman was both smarter than he was and a lot more clear-sighted.

She certainly was a great deal more blunt.

"I don't know if we can close down a seat," he said.

Her lips thinned. She was disgusted at him and not trying to hide it. "So what do you know?"

The sharpness of her words actually stung.

"I know that the old-timers think this is a bad change," Cole said. "They are worried about the future of the Board."

Ludmilla shrugged. "Isn't it a relic? Shouldn't the academies run themselves, just like Munira Zubiri suggested?"

Cole let out a small laugh. He couldn't help himself.

Munira Zubiri always tried to shut down the Board in one way or another.

But when he'd first become a member, she had tried to take Chaban's role as chair. Cole always thought that Zubiri's continually attempts at shutting down the Board had more to do with her failed political ambitions than any belief that the Board should be done away with.

He pressed his lips together. Apparently, he had just decided that he wouldn't badmouth the others to Ludmilla —at least not at this point.

Cole also realized that not badmouthing the others might be more difficult than he had thought.

"Well?" Ludmilla asked. "Are you going to answer me or are you going to just stand there with that sour expression on your face?"

He raised his eyebrows in surprise. He hadn't realized that he was making a sour expression, but it didn't surprise him. He was deeply uncomfortable whenever he came to a board meeting, more uncomfortable than he realized.

"When she first made that suggestion a few years ago," he said, "I thought it sounded reasonable. You do too, from the sound of your questions."

"I don't know enough to know what's going on," Ludmilla said, her eyes narrowing. That look made her already narrow face seem even thinner. "I am just trying to figure out what's really going on here."

"That's an entirely different question," Cole said. He didn't want to get into any of that. "Let's just talk about the purpose of the Board instead."

She nodded, rather condescendingly, if someone could be condescending without saying anything.

He was beginning to like her, and that worried him. So he decided to ignore the feeling.

"The problem is financing," he said. "Serebro Academy more than earns its keep. It has professors in all disciplines who make money on their discoveries and ideas, and even on speaking engagements. That money goes into the Academy's coffers, and is used to augment their salaries and their departments, which is why some departments are more influential than others."

Ludmilla nodded once. He couldn't tell if she knew that or if she just wanted him to move on.

"There are other, small academies," Cole said, not sure if she knew this information. "They're not as self-sufficient. Some of them have been around longer than Serebro. Many of them lost a lot of professors and students during the Purges. Those academies are only just beginning to recover."

"And we get them money," Ludmilla said.

"We also approve their faculty," Cole said.

"That's a change since the Purges?" she asked.

"No," he said. "We've always done that, but it was *pro forma* before the Purges. Now we analyze before a new hire or before someone's contract is renewed. It gives the academies cover. It also ensures that nothing like the Purges will happen again."

Ludmilla's frown grew deeper. "My father was involved in that, wasn't he?"

"That change?" Cole said. "I believe both of our fathers were."

She turned away from him, facing the windows again. The rain was coming down harder. From his position at the door, Cole couldn't see if the rain was dotting the windows or the bubbles in the glass made it look that way.

"It's fascinating to me," Ludmilla said, "that the Board suddenly has a lot more power and now no one wants to sit on it."

"More power?" Cole hadn't thought of it that way.

She inclined her head sideways but didn't turn around. It dawned on him that she could see his reflection in the glass, because the exterior was so gray and stormy.

"We're in charge of the entire education of the Protectorate, right?" she said. "And if we pick who teaches and how doesn't, we have even more control over what is acceptable knowledge and what isn't."

Cole hadn't thought of it that way. He wasn't sure he'd ever heard the phrase *acceptable knowledge* before.

"You make this sound like a conspiracy," he said.

"Isn't it?" she asked.

He took a small involuntary step backwards. He hadn't thought of it that way, and it didn't feel right. Or maybe he didn't want it to feel right.

"I think that the Board has always been in charge of what everyone in Qavner learns. That it has spread to the Protectorate isn't a conspiracy," he said. "And just because a few people no longer inherited their seats, doesn't mean it's a conspiracy either. Do you want the power of your *acceptable knowledge* to rest in the hands of a few families?"

She shrugged, still not turning around. "That's how it's always been done."

"That doesn't mean it's right, though," he said.

"I suppose." She didn't sound convinced. She moved away from the window and started back across the floor. "We need to return."

It was almost as if she had shut down. He had a lot more to tell her, but she didn't seem interested. That bothered him somehow, almost as if he had said something wrong.

He wanted to continue, but he didn't. She had asked for this meeting, and she was ending it.

Besides, they had probably been here too long anyway. He swept his hand toward the door, like Reginald often did, and waited for her to pass through.

She did, wrapping her arms around her torso again, clearly as unwilling to touch the walls as he was.

He left the room almost reluctantly, and pulled the door closed behind him. It banged but didn't latch.

The stairwell was darker than it had been before. Ludmilla had gone much farther ahead of him. He could no longer see her.

She seemed calmer as she walked down the stairs. Maybe he had answered the questions she thought she had.

She might have been calmer, but he wasn't. He was no longer calm at all.

He had no idea if she was seeing things more clearly than he was or if she was making something up from whole cloth. Her suggestions seemed plausible though, and that disturbed him.

Her word *conspiracy* disturbed him more. But not in the way that she had used it.

Control of knowledge meant that everyone worked off

the same set of facts. That was what he would have told anyone who asked.

But what if those facts were wrong? Or incomplete? Or tailored to some agenda that he couldn't see?

What was he supposed to do about that?

He hurried down the last bit of stairs, happy to see the lightstones. They were already illuminated because Ludmilla had passed them.

He had thought of his presence on the Board as a silly assignment, something he had to do for his family legacy.

She had shattered the assumption of silliness. It worried him now. What was the family legacy? What was he protecting?

What were the Regents protecting?

He had no idea. In the past, he wouldn't have cared. But she had challenged him and made him worry about things he had never thought about.

His position on the Board of Regents worked better if he didn't care. But he wasn't sure he could go back to that.

He wasn't sure at all.

REGENTS
TOWER

ADV. STUDENT
WING

CLOCK
TOWER

CHAPTER
FIFTEEN

Ludmilla's skin crawled as she walked into the meeting room. Those stairs that Cole had taken her up, that room where they had talked, left her feeling like she had been coated in spiderwebs, dirt, and mold. The dank smell, which had been everywhere, lined her nostrils and made her want to sneeze.

The meeting hadn't resumed yet, which surprised her just a bit. Chaban had said fifteen minutes and it had been longer than that. But Chaban wasn't even at the head of the table. He was near one of the sideboards, talking with a woman that Ludmilla hadn't seen before.

The woman wore a white apron tied around long skirts, her brown hair pulled up on the top of her head. She was wide, but she looked strong, with big beefy arms that didn't seem to have an ounce of fat on them.

They kept moving as she talked with Chaban. Behind them, on the sideboard, were a variety of meats and cheeses and various sliced breads, as well as cut vegetables and several different kinds of cookies.

None of that food had been there earlier. Ludmilla hadn't realized just how hungry she was. She wondered what the protocol was for getting something to eat. She almost asked, but changed her mind. She had called enough attention to herself.

Someone had placed mugs on the meeting table in front of everyone's place. The mugs were made of ceramic and were engraved with last names. Ludmilla's was gray with black lettering, and the word *Odenkirk*, in Gothic script, went halfway around the mug's widest point.

She picked it up and hefted it. It was as heavy as a vase. Her father had used this. She knew it as clearly as if his fingers had made grooves in the ceramic.

Her hands cradled the empty mug. She missed him. She wanted to talk to him. She wanted to ask him all the questions she should have asked him before. He had tried to tell her, reminding her that she would sit in his seat for years after he died, and she needed to understand things.

Sorry, Papa, she thought, squeezing the mug. *I did need to know, and I didn't listen to you.*

She watched the others mill around, talking. Most of them had inherited their seats, maybe all of them. But the inheritance was getting shaky.

Her eye rested on Xavier, who was standing beside the fire. She had instinctively liked him. He had been kind to Eustace, who clearly should no longer be on the board, but no one seemed to know how to get rid of him.

Kindness seemed rare in this group, and she was well

aware that Xavier's kindness was the only reason she had to like him. She knew very little else about him, except that he was a previous board member's second cousin, the only family member who wanted the job.

And he was not young, which meant that his tenure on the Board would not last as long as hers, provided they both lived as long as people normally did.

His robe was interesting as well. It looked like it was one uniform color—a silvery gray—until she studied it. Then she realized it was decorated with marks that looked like pieces of a language she should have been familiar with.

A language that maybe she *was* familiar with. She had seen those marks before, on something of her father's. It had been on—

"It looks like everyone has returned," Chaban said. "Let's be seated."

Ludmilla felt a thread of irritation. That realization she had been on the verge of remembering had vanished, almost as if Chaban had planned to interrupt her thoughts.

Chaban had left the sideboard. He was standing near his chair, his square hands on its back. His oddly square eyes rested on her, and when he saw her looking at him, he gave her a tiny half smile.

Had he known that she was trying to figure something out? Had he realized he had broken her concentration?

Then she made herself take a deep breath. Of course he hadn't known. It had been a coincidence. And he was probably watching her because she looked ridiculous, standing in front of her chair, cradling the mug.

"I take it there's tea?" she asked, lifting the mug ever so slightly.

"And snacks, since it seems like we'll be here a while," Chaban said. "You are free to get whatever you want throughout the meeting, but the meeting is starting."

Even though half of the regents were now standing in front of the food table, holding tiny plates as they filled them to overflowing.

"We really should break for meals," Zubiri said, following Ludmilla's gaze.

Ludmilla jumped. She hadn't realized that Zubiri was standing so close. It was amazing that she could move so silently, when she had tiny bells attached to her sleeves.

"Feel a little out of your depth?" Zubiri asked.

She was shorter than Ludmilla had thought, coming up to Ludmilla's shoulder. But Zubiri felt like a looming presence anyway, and her dark eyes, lined by thick black lashes, seemed avid.

She wanted Ludmilla to admit that she was uncomfortable. Ludmilla wasn't going to give her the satisfaction.

"A new situation is always a little difficult," she said.

"I'm starting the meeting," Chaban said, louder than he had before. He slapped the palm of his hand on the tabletop, twice, the sound filling the large room.

The Regents in front of the food table turned to see what he was doing. The woman he had been talking with a moment before stuck her hands in her pockets and tilted her head, as if she was amused.

Reginald stood near the back, pouring tea as people held out their mugs.

"We don't dare start until those who do not belong here leave," Zubiri said, pointedly.

"Do we have to leave?" Eustace asked Rogov.

"We belong here," Rogov said curtly. He wasn't watching Eustace, whose plate was so covered in food that bits of cheese were falling off the side.

Rogov's gaze met Ludmilla's, then moved away from her to Zubiri. Because Zubiri stood so close, the others seemed to think that she and Zubiri were plotting something.

Had Zubiri wanted it that way? Was she trying hard to compromise Ludmilla somehow?

Ludmilla shook herself a little. This group was making her paranoid. There was an undercurrent of fear in the room, which she should have asked Cole about.

He was at the food table, carefully placing rolled-up cuts of meat on his plate next to some slices of white bread.

Ludmilla had better get food now, or she would not eat. She separated herself from Zubiri and walked to the table. She let Reginald pour her some tea, then set the mug down for a moment so she could get something to eat.

"We're starting," Chaban said pointedly.

Ludmilla ignored him. She grabbed a plate, put a slice of heavy dark bread on it, then used one of the forks to stab some rolled-up, thinly sliced ham. She set that on the side, along with some cheddar cheese. She topped off the plate with some dark red local berries that had half a dozen different names.

Cole hadn't moved away from the table. He nodded at her plate. "Good idea. Who knows how long we'll be here."

She smiled thinly at him, not wanting to engage.

Chaban slapped the table again, making her jump. "I'm going to start anyway."

"Oh, for goodness sake, Devin," Zubiri said as she walked to her place. Now the bells on her sleeves were tinkling. "We can hear you even as we're stuffing our faces."

Was that for Ludmilla too? She didn't want to know. She studied the food for a moment, then took one of the tiny pastries, before grabbing her mug and heading back to her chair.

Cole followed, one hand near the left side of his plate so nothing fell off.

Ludmilla set the mug down, then the plate. She met Chaban's gaze, then ostentatiously sat on her chair and folded her hands in front of her.

Zubiri let out a small laugh. "My, my, my," she said. "The new girl is ready."

Ludmilla bit back a retort. She wasn't sure what she was going to say, which was probably the point. Zubiri seemed to be one of those people who poked until she got a reaction, so Ludmilla was going to ignore her, and not react to anything she said.

Xavier turned away from the fire, his robe shimmering in its light. The letters seemed clearly, like letters—

On her father's map. That was where she had seen the letters before. There had been lettering just like that on one of her father's maps. The map that didn't look like the others.

Her father had a lot of maps. He had never let her touch

them, even though, as a child, she wanted to. They had been so beautiful—hand drawn and colorful.

All except one. That map had seemed utilitarian—and it did look like it had been used, a lot. It had been folded dozens of times, and ripped in a few places, and there had been stains on it that she had asked about the first time she had seen it.

I'll tell you what those are some day, sweetheart, her father had said, making a promise he had never kept.

But had he tried to keep it? Had she walked away from it later?

She had forgotten about all of it until now.

"What I would like to do," Chaban said loudly, apparently trying to start the meeting, "is discuss the matter of—"

"Reginald," Cole said loudly. "It's time for you to leave."

Cole was standing beside Reginald. Cole no longer held his plate. It was on the tea table. Cole had his hand out for the teapot.

"I'll just finish this," Reginald said, holding the pot.

"You will leave," Cole said. "In fact, you'll escort Mrs. Halmann back to the kitchens, giving her our thanks, of course, for this incredible spread of food."

Reginald's expression darkened, his face suffusing with blood. He looked at Chaban, as if expecting Chaban to defend him, but Chaban kept his head immobile, his gaze on the table before him.

Cole had surprised Ludmilla. She hadn't thought he would be willing to take on the Regents again. He had done so by tabling Zubiri's proposal, and now he was standing up to Reginald.

Cole's gaze met hers, his face impassive, but his eyes alive with...merriment? He was enjoying this? That seemed almost odd.

But she felt a little giddy too, as if the two of them were somehow changing the meeting just by their presence.

Maybe they were.

Reginald handed the teapot to Cole with such force that some tea sloshed out the spout. Cole took it, seemingly unconcerned that some of the tea had splashed on him as well.

"I'll mop that up," Reginald said.

"Later," Cole said in a tone so filled with sarcasm that it was hard to miss his point. He was forcing Reginald to admit—without words—that he was eavesdropping on the Regents.

Cole turned toward the woman in the apron.

"Thank you, Mrs. Halmann. We will not leave a mess for you, I promise."

She chuckled. "The mess would not be for me, Mr. Mahan. 'Tis others who must clean up the kitchens. I'm in charge of creating the messes."

"Well," Cole said with amusement, "we shall let you get back to that."

His tone was amused, but his eyes were not. They had turned dark and almost angry.

Ludmilla felt a jolt of energy, as if Cole had suddenly become someone else, someone with power that he was just beginning to reveal.

Chaban watched as well, seemingly startled. Reginald

looked around the room, as if he were searching for someone to support him.

No one spoke up. All conversation had died out. Everyone, it seemed, was watching this interaction.

"Well, then," Reginald said, "I've never seen Regents clean up after themselves, but I'm ready to be surprised."

Ludmilla's eyebrows went up. No one in the staff at her family's household would dared have talked to the family that way.

Reginald walked over to Mrs. Halmann, and gave her an insincere smile. "You don't need an escort, do you, dear?"

Her chin jutted out. Ludmilla couldn't decide if Mrs. Halmann looked angry or panicked. Or maybe both.

"If she doesn't," Cole said, "then you're excused."

Reginald flushed again. His eyes narrowed.

Ludmilla had the sense that Cole had just made an enemy.

"In fact," Cole said, "we won't need you to be on call. We'll break for dinner—"

"You don't know that, Mahan," Chaban said.

"Oh, stop being pissy because you've lost control of the meeting," Packingham said. She looked exasperated. And exhausted.

"We will be breaking for dinner," Cole said. "We can use you after that to clean up, since apparently we're so bad at it."

Reginald's jaw set. "I see, sir. Where would you like me to go?"

Cole waved a hand. "I don't care where you go, as long as you're nowhere near this meeting. I'm tired of having you overhear everything we say. I have no idea who you're working for—"

"I'm working for the Regents, sir," Reginald said in a very prim tone.

The fury in Cole's eyes grew worse. "I don't believe you. But that's for another day. Right now, though, I'm putting an end to your nosiness. You will leave and do whatever you do when you're not up here. You can return after the dinner hour."

Reginald sputtered, as if he couldn't find the words. Chaban's face was flushed as well. His hands, palms still on the tabletop, started to clench.

"You are dismissed," Cole said coldly. "You as well, Mrs. Halmann."

"Ah, thank ye, lad," she said, and scurried toward the door.

Reginald still hadn't moved.

Cole walked over to him, moving very slowly. Cole wasn't as tall as Reginald, but Cole was stockier. He had more muscle. And his deliberate movements made him seem much more threatening.

"Would you like me to remove you myself?" Cole asked softly, but with a lot of force.

Reginald glanced at Chaban, as if expecting help from that quarter. Only Chaban had his back to Reginald.

Chaban seemed to be unwilling to watch any of this. None of the others spoke either.

Ludmilla's heart was pounding. She hadn't expected Cole to be so menacing. And she had ordered him about earlier, as if he had worked for her.

Reginald's gaze met hers. She quickly looked away. She wasn't going to give that man any encouragement at all.

"All right then," Cole said, and reached for Reginald. Reginald ducked and scampered sideways.

Ludmilla was a bit surprised at how quickly he could move.

"I do the best I can here," Reginald said.

"It's a damn shame there's no room for improvement, then," Cole said.

Reginald looked at a few of the others. Many of them were looking at their hands or the fire or anything except the confrontation going on near the food.

"I do the best I can," Reginald said again, louder.

Cole took another step toward him and grabbed his arm. "We've established that. You're working at the top of your abilities. Too bad, really, that the best of your abilities is so very poor. Now, let's go."

Reginald shook Cole off. Then Reginald stalked away from the food table, angrily adjusting his sleeves. As he passed Chaban, Reginald glared at him, as if it were Chaban's fault all of this happened.

Chaban didn't meet his gaze either.

"And pull the door closed behind you," Cole said. He hadn't moved from his spot near the table.

Reginald's lower lip curled, but he didn't say anything. As he walked past the door, he grabbed the knob and yanked the door behind him. It closed with a loud bang.

Eustace jumped. Rogov put a hand on Eustace's arm, maybe to calm him. Maybe to calm himself.

Ludmilla's heart was still pounding hard.

Cole sat down beside her, then smiled at her. None of the anger remained in his eyes.

"There," he said, just loud enough for everyone to hear. "That's taken care of."

"It is not," Chaban said. "I'm in charge of this—"

"Oh, stuff it, Devin," Sonia Petruscu said. "You run the meetings because the rest of us don't want to."

"I'm beginning to think being passive is not a solution," Kwin said as he made his way to his chair. "Doing everything by default is leading to chaos."

"If you think that Cole's little outburst there is chaos, then you haven't been on the Board long enough," Rogov said.

"I'm not fond of chaos," Eustace said, voice quavering.

No one answered him.

"I don't think we should manhandle the staff," Wilma Blankenship said. Her voice was as tiny as she was. She sounded almost timid.

"Even if they're selling the Board's secrets?" Cole asked.

Someone gasped. Ludmilla frowned at him. How did he know that? Did he know it? Or was he just acting on a grudge against Reginald?

"Do we have secrets?" Eustace said. "Why wasn't I told—"

"Shut him up, will you?" Sorcé N'lman said to Rogov, in a tone so menacing that Rogov cringed.

Ludmilla sank back in her chair. As she did, she realized she was doing exactly what she had done in the first meeting: she was trying to disappear.

She couldn't disappear. Her father had chosen her to sit

on this Board, not any other family member. He had thought the Board was important.

If she didn't participate, she was letting him down. Violating his memory. Not acting in the best interests of the family.

As if she even knew what that was.

CHAPTER
SIXTEEN

Half of the board was looking at their food. Several members stared at Chaban, as if they expected him to do something, maybe reprimand N'lman for the tone he had taken with Rogov.

N'lman saw Ludmilla looking at him, and tilted his head in acknowledgement, his thin mouth in a fake smile. His sunken eyes seemed to glitter with menace.

She had to concentrate to keep herself from shivering.

Cole seemed oblivious to the undercurrents. Or maybe he thought they were unimportant. He shoved his plate to the side and leaned forward.

"We have important things to discuss," he said.

The attention moved from N'lman and Rogov back to Cole. Ludmilla wanted to move away from him so that no one would think she had any part of his outburst.

But she made herself sit still. She wasn't going to be intimidated by this group, no matter how many times she'd been encouraged to respect her elders—and to respect the Regents.

She wasn't sure if she could respect any of them after the displays so far today, and there was still a lot of meeting left.

"Devin here," Cole was saying, his tone sharp, "believes that we have a problem with inheritance, and he would like to propose a solution. Am I right, Devin?"

Chaban's square face settled into squat disgust. His right hand had formed a fist as he looked at Cole.

"You are not in charge of this meeting," Chaban snapped.

"Then take charge," Paulina Elin said. She crossed her arms over her chest, straining the shoulders of her brown blouse. "This back and forth is driving me crazy."

A few of the Regents nodded in agreement. Ludmilla didn't allow herself to agree with anyone, even though the back and forth was driving her crazy as well.

"I'm still trying to understand Kirilli's death." Yana Hoodwinkle spoke loudly, as if she believed that her words might drive the meeting forward. She turned toward Chaban. "You said it was for some *papers*?"

Her gray curls tumbled around her face, making it hard for Ludmilla to see her expression.

"I only know what I was told." Chaban answered her, but continued to glare at Cole.

"Oh, for goodness' sake," Zubiri snapped. "Let's cut through the nonsense, shall we? Devin wants us to take a vote on changing how Regents receive their seats. He wants the position to be elected—"

"I do not," Chaban said.

"—or appointed, or some such ridiculousness, rather than passed down through families." She glared at him. "Right, Devin?"

"It's not that simple," he said.

"It is *precisely* that simple," she said. "We have the power to change this, and Devin would like us to do so."

"Why?" Xavier asked, adjusting his robe. Now it looked almost gray, the symbols fading.

"Yes, Devin," Elin asked. "Why?"

Chaban's mouth tightened. His cheeks had a slight dot of color, and his gaze darted from person to person. He looked like nothing more than someone who had just gotten caught doing something wrong.

"Lately," he said, his voice a bit thinner than it had been, "there has been a dearth of heirs—"

"Oh, spare us," Elin said. "We know what's going on. And there isn't really a dearth of heirs."

She waved a hand at Ludmilla, and maybe that movement included Cole as well.

"I mean," Elin said, "we just got a new one. And we only have your word that the Kirillis don't want their seat. I recall Augustus telling me about his daughter—"

"The unfortunately named Augusta." Packingham pushed a strand of her lavender-white hair out of her face.

Elin half laughed in acknowledgement. "Yes, the unfortunately named Augusta. August-*us*—" and she placed the emphasis on the different suffix "—seemed to see that girl as an extension of himself. He wouldn't have allowed her to give up her seat on the Board."

"Yet she's not here," Chaban said tightly. "She was invited."

"Her father was just *murdered*," Baxter Ivonovich said. At least, Ludmilla thought the slight man with puppy-dog eyes was Ivonovich. He had arrived with Rogov and Eustace, and she hadn't really paid a lot of attention to introductions.

"So?" Packingham said. "The rest of us showed up when summoned, no matter who died."

"I think it was a rather hideous death," Ivonovich said.

"You know something about it?" Blankenship asked.

"I know that it was causing some unease in Trinovante," Ivonovich said, "Particularly since there had been break-ins in some of the estates belonging to the Old Families."

"Recent break-ins?" Blankenship's tiny voice sounded even smaller, as if she was afraid someone would attack them all in the meeting.

"We are getting off track," N'lman said. "I for one would like to get to the point of this meeting before I die of old age."

His snarling voice cut through all of the discussion and made some of the Regents lean back. Ludmilla's heart started to pound hard, but she kept herself still.

One of the few people who didn't seem cowed by N'lman was Zubiri. She glanced at Chaban, who wasn't saying anything, then shrugged one shoulder, pretending at a nonchalance she clearly didn't feel.

"I figured some of this out a long time ago," Zubiri said, "but none of you listen to me. You think I only have one issue, and maybe you can make that argument. But my one issue made me do some research."

Heads turned toward her, and even N'lman seemed interested.

Ludmilla picked up her tea mug, needing its warmth against her fingers. She was feeling chilled, not just by the room and the rain, but by the viciousness in this place.

"Devin," Zubiri said with a sarcastic look in his direction, "doesn't want to disband, because the Regents have more power than almost everyone else in the entire Protectorate. We control the academies, which is where our politicians get trained, where our constabulary receives its training, where our children get theirs."

Ludmilla's grip tightened on the mug. She had touched on that argument with Cole, upstairs.

As if he was having the same thought, he glanced at her, then frowned, like a man whose entire vision of the world was changing.

"We control most everything in the Protectorate," Zubiri said, "from which research gets done to which schools get funding. Devin and his pals would like to control that, wouldn't you, Devin?"

He slid his hands off the table, and let them fall into his lap. "I think you're overestimating some things and underestimating others."

"I'm beginning to think she isn't," Cole said. With one finger, he lightly tapped Ludmilla on the arm in some kind of acknowledgement.

Her own cheeks heated, not because of his touch, but because he was clearly crediting her with that same idea. Only she hadn't spoken to Zubiri or anyone else.

Had they come to this on their own, then?

"If you think we have so much power," Chaban said to Zubiri, "why do you want to disband the Board?"

"Stop!" Eustace stood up. His voice wasn't shaking anymore. His body didn't look frail either.

Rogov reached for him, but Eustace shook him away.

"We are a hereditary body for a reason," Eustace said. "It is in the bylaws. It is part of what we are. That we don't— that our heirs aren't—that nothing..."

And suddenly he collapsed forward. Rogov stood just in time to catch him and ease him back into the chair.

"That we don't what?" Xavier asked gently.

Eustace raised his head. His eyes were wet. He waved a hand. "...the powers..." he managed.

"Powers?" Ludmilla asked, before she could stop herself.

"He's a delusional old man," Chaban snapped.

"And you are a rude one," Dh'stan said.

Eustace bowed his head again, his hands clasped, but still shaking.

"What powers?" Ludmilla asked.

"You're too young to remember the Purges," Pasha Volkovich said quietly. He was sitting close to N'lman, and side by side like that, they looked like complete opposites. Volkovich's hair seemed even whiter, and the wrinkles in his sunbaked skin deeper. "We do not talk about powers anymore."

Ludmilla almost said, *I remember the Purges*, but Volkovich was right; she didn't remember the Purges the way an adult did. She had been very young, and quite protected.

"Are you saying our heritage gives us power?" Cole asked.

"Being on the Board is a form of power," Chaban said quickly.

But no one looked at him, no one spoke to him.

"If you look at the history of this body," Zubiri said, "and apparently, I'm the only one who has—"

"You are not," Rogov said tightly. "Once upon a time, we all had to be versed in the history."

"—or maybe I'm the only one who remembers," she said.

Several others shook their heads.

"But there is language that mentions a power tied to the bloodline. I certainly don't know if that's connected to the Purges. I also don't know if that's hyperbolic." Zubiri rubbed her right hand on her left arm, as if it ached. "What I do know is this: each family was given items to store, away from the academies, away from this room, away from people like that horrid Reginald—who should be fired, by the way. Cole is right."

"I decide who gets fired," Chaban said.

"Actually, the Academy hired him," Dh'stan said. "Which means the Academy has the power to fire him."

"I will speak to them," Cole said. "We need him gone."

Ludmilla nodded. She agreed. Reginald needed to be fired. But his status was a distraction—at least at the moment. This conversation about items bothered her.

"Items." Xavier shook his head. "I was not given any items."

"They were confiscated when it was believed that no one would take Samantha's place," Chaban said. "I'm sorry. I should have returned them to you."

Someone gasped. Not loudly but enough to express the shock of everyone in the room, including Ludmilla. Her eyes narrowed as she studied Chaban. His square face had grown darker. She couldn't tell if he was flushed with anger or embarrassment.

If she had to guess from his tone, it was both. Not that she knew how to read him, not yet, anyway. All she knew was that she hadn't liked him from the first, but she hadn't thought him venal.

The room had grown very quiet, and everyone—all of them—were staring at Chaban as if he had lost his mind.

Ludmilla could hear her father's voice in her head.

There are things I must show you, Ludmilla, he had said. *Things you need to understand. Things we protect—*

"Are you all right?" Cole asked her quietly.

No one else was looking at her. They were studying Chaban as if they were seeing him for the first time.

She wasn't about to confess anything to Cole, so she just nodded.

"How many other things have you confiscated over the years?" Zubiri asked Chaban.

"I think *confiscated* is a harsh term," he said.

"It's your term, you idiot," she snapped. "You used it just a moment ago."

"Only because Samantha's family was going to destroy the items. The Purges have scared everyone," Chaban said.

"Is that true?" Cole asked Xavier.

Xavier shrugged. "This is the first I've heard of any of it. And I had no idea that Samantha had items that made the family nervous. If that's true, no one told me."

"You haven't answered my question," Zubiri said to Chaban. "Have you *confiscated* items from other families?"

"When the families don't want to serve on the Board," Chaban said, "we need to recover our property."

Rogov tilted his head backwards, but not before Ludmilla saw him mouth a curse.

She frowned. Her father hadn't told her that he had important items relating to the Regents, items that did not belong to him.

He would have told her that much, as he was trying to cram information into her unwilling mind. She knew her father. He would have told her.

Wouldn't he?

Eustace raised his head. It was shaking, like the rest of him, but his eyes were still clear.

"You took things from my family then, didn't you?" he asked Chaban in a very calm, very adult voice. "That's why I couldn't find the maps."

Chaban leaned back, as if he was stunned that Eustace had challenged him. Chaban didn't respond, but Cole blurted, "Maps?"

Ludmilla put a hand on his arm. She'd been around people like Eustace before. Their moments of clarity did not last long.

Eustace leaned toward Chaban, and pointed a bony finger at him.

"You took things that belonged to *me!*" Eustace said, spittle flying. "You stole from *me!*"

Chaban glanced at the others, but no one rose to defend him. Half the room was startled that Eustace had spoken with clarity; they were watching him. But everyone else was monitoring Chaban.

"Actually," Chaban said, his voice that kind of calm that some people got when they were humoring a child. "No, I didn't steal. I made sure everything was safe."

"You took my possessions!" Eustace kept wagging his finger at Chaban. "Those maps had been in my family for generations."

"For safekeeping," Chaban said. "You were to protect them."

"No!" Eustace said. "They were for the Wallingford seat in the Regents. That's how the Regents work. We have pieces. We put them together to be a whole. You, of all people, should understand that."

Ludmilla still had her hand on Cole's arm. He was watching, his mouth open slightly. He didn't seem able to believe...something. Was it Eustace's clarity? Or his words?

She hadn't understood most of this, so far, although she was beginning to realize she had nothing to fear from these people as the youngest Regent.

She had other reasons to worry about them, reasons she wished she could discuss with her father.

"Your family does not want the 'Wallingford seat' as you call it," Chaban said. "Your family cannot hold those items."

"That's not how it works!" Eustace yelled. *"I am in charge*

of the seat. I determine who inherits it. I determine who gets the items that go with the seat."

"Eustace," Rogov said quietly. "You need to calm down."

"Are you calm?" Eustace asked him. "Because I am not calm. None of you should be calm. This man, pretending to *lead* us, is stealing from us."

Ludmilla's heart was pounding. She couldn't tell if Eustace's words were upsetting her, if his eerie clarity was making her nervous, or if Chaban's increasing discomfort—which she (and everyone else) could see from the way he squirmed—bothered her the most.

"Who else have you *confiscated* items from?" Zubiri asked.

"Stole," Eustace said, his voice starting to quaver. "You stole."

Chaban's left hand formed a fist, which he held rigidly in place on the tabletop.

"I did not steal from anyone," he said in that same tone he had used before. "You are mostly not yourself, Eustace, so I will forgive your accusations—"

"Forgive me?" Eustace shouted. *"Forgive* me? You are planning something nefarious, Devin."

Rogov reached for Eustace's arm, trying to settle him down, perhaps, or make him sit down. Eustace shook him off and almost fell backwards.

Eustace grabbed the edge of the table. Rogov put a hand behind Eustace to keep him upright, and Xavier caught his other arm.

"Sit down, Eustace," Chaban said. "You're embarrassing yourself."

"No, he is not," Cole said. "Even if you—we—have the rights to the materials, and I don't think we do have the rights to the materials of others, he is very much alive, and working on this Board. You did not have the right to take those items. And since you did not have the right, that means you stole them."

"You make it sound criminal," Chaban said. "It is not. It is—"

"It is criminal," Evander Popova said with great authority. His voice boomed, but not like N'lman's had. "By any definition, it's criminal. You forget, Devin. Many of us here are lawyers."

Heads nodded. Ludmilla tried to figure out who was nodding because they agreed and who was nodding because they, too, were lawyers.

She couldn't.

Chaban opened his mouth, then closed it again, as if he thought better of what he was going to say.

"I want it back," Eustace said. "Whatever you took. I want it back."

Chaban glared at him. "You'll have to ask your grandson. He gave it all to me."

"And you have it now, Devin." Popova put his thick arms on the top of the table, hands folded. He had become someone other than a person in a meeting. Ludmilla could now envision him in a court, speaking with authority. "You will return everything to him, or we see you up on charges."

"I think we need to do that anyway," Dao Kwin said. His

yellowish-gold suit caught the firelight, making the angry expression on his heavyset features look like someone had turned on a light inside of him.

"That would mean revealing Regent business," Fedor Garvyn said. He hadn't spoken at all since they returned to the room.

"No, it wouldn't." Ludmilla finally spoke up. She wasn't a lawyer, and she didn't work for the constabulary, but she did know how the world worked—at least this world. "Mr. Wallingford owns certain items. His grandson took those items, and gave them to Mr. Chaban at Mr. Chaban's request. Mr. Wallingford has now learned of this betrayal and he wants his items back. If Mr. Chaban does not return them, Mr. Wallingford—or the rest of us—can call in the local constabulary."

Heads turned toward her, as if everyone had forgotten she was there.

"Well done," Cole said under his breath. She ignored him. She wasn't sure if he was being patronizing or not.

Besides, Eustace seemed to see her for the first time.

"You're Odenkirk's daughter, Ludmilla," Eustace said. "All grown up. I'm sorry I didn't realize you were here."

Ludmilla smiled, relieved on a deeper level than she wanted to admit that he had recognized her at all. "That's all right, Mr. Wa—"

"Eustace," he said. "You called me Eustace since you were a little girl."

Now he was the man she remembered. Kind and warm and so smart. Her heart twisted.

"Thank you," she said, amazed that her own voice didn't

waiver. Maybe she hadn't lost that little bit of her childhood after all.

Chaban was glaring at her. "You don't have to call in the constabulary."

Strangely, Eustace's comments gave her a strength she hadn't realized she was missing.

She smiled sweetly—and coldly—at Chaban.

"Oh, but we do need to call the constabulary," she said. "I'm curious about what you've confiscated. You're taking items from a living man with no qualms at all. There's been talk of other estates here, but more than that, you claim that heirs to people already in this room do not want to sit on this Board. How do you know that? Have you talked to them? Have you asked for their items as well?"

Chaban's other hand formed a fist. He looked directly at Packingham. His cheeks had grown dark, and the flush had worked its way into his neck.

"She is a new member," he said to Packingham, as if they were alone. "She does not have the right to speak to me like that."

"My goodness, you're upset." Packingham used the same tone that Chaban had used with Eustace. "In my experience, it's only the guilty who question the source, and not the content, of her comments."

"I am not guilty of anything!" Chaban said.

"Then give us a list of the people you've talked with," Volkovich said. He tugged on his white hair, as if the entire conversation was making him nervous.

"And the things they let you confiscate," Zubiri said.

Chaban sputtered, then looked around, clearly searching for allies. No one stepped up.

Cole leaned back in his chair, as if he had relaxed for the first time. "Those lists are important," he said, "but they're not the most important thing."

"They are," Packingham snapped. "You don't understand this because you're new to the Board."

Cole raised his eyebrows. "I've been here for five years," he said laconically.

Ludmilla wanted to say, *I'm the one who is new. Maybe you've forgotten.* Her antipathy toward Packingham surprised her. Maybe Ludmilla's impulse to bicker came because the entire Board seemed invested in bickering.

"The most important thing," Cole said as if he hadn't been interrupted, "is what Devin planned to do with all those items."

Chaban opened his mouth as if he meant to defend himself. Then he closed it, and bit his lower lip.

Cole tapped a finger against the side of his still full plate. His gaze turned toward Eustace.

"There's a reason that the items were to be kept separately," Cole said calmly, "away from the other regents, away from the academies, away from everyone, isn't there, Eustace?"

"Um...what?" Eustace was still standing, but his eyes had fogged. He glanced at Rogov. "Are we leaving?"

"No," Rogov said. "Sit down, Eustace."

Eustace sat heavily, then gripped the edge of the table.

"Why is everyone staring, Horace?" he asked. "Did I do something wrong?"

"No." Cole continued to use that calm voice. "You did something right. You showed a lot of courage, Mr. Wallingford."

"I did?" Eustace asked Horace. "Then why don't I remember it? Am I losing time again, Horace?"

"You're doing just fine, Eustace," Horace said.

"I don't feel fine," Eustace said. "My throat aches. Did I yell out?"

"You put Devin Chaban in his place," Zubiri said.

"Who?" Eustace asked.

Chaban made a sputtering sound. Then he waved a hand. "You all believe the ravings of a madman."

Ludmilla felt her heart sink.

"He's not mad," she said. "He's not well, but he's not mad."

She knew that a lot of people didn't understand what Eustace was going through. She'd seen it with her maternal grandmother, and it had started with her mother, as well, but her mother died before things got worse.

"And you are some kind of expert?" Chaban said, voice dripping with sarcasm.

"Sadly, yes. I've seen this before. Just because Mr. Wallingford—Eustace—" Ludmilla paused over the name, glad to be able to use it, even if Eustace was looking at her in confusion again. "—just because he gets confused, doesn't mean he's wrong. He had a moment of clarity, and it focused on you, Mr. Chaban. Then you confirmed everything that he said."

"Lies," Chaban said.

"Oh, I don't think so." Zubiri said, her voice vicious. "You're afraid of something, aren't you, Devin?"

Chaban's eyes narrowed, but he didn't answer her.

She put her long bony fingers on the edge of the table, and moved as if she planned to stand up, but wasn't quite ready to.

"We need to take some action," she said.

"And what would that be, Munira?" Hoodwinkle asked. All evidence of the cheerful woman who had arrived earlier had vanished. She now looked formidable. "You want to fire him too?"

Zubiri glared at her, but didn't respond. Instead, she stood and looked directly at Chaban.

"We need to see what you've taken," she said. "And then you need to step down as chair of this board. Then you will step down out of your seat entirely."

Chaban laughed. "Do you hear yourselves? You complain that we're not treating the heirs right, and then you tell me to give up a hereditary seat."

Zubiri walked around the table, slowly.

"You have siblings," she said. "I would hope they're a lot more honest than you are."

Ludmilla folded her hands together. She had started something—or rather, Eustace had. Now, she watched as the others turned on Chaban.

She was a bit surprised that it had taken so little for them to do so.

"Where are the items?" Volkovich asked.

"Somewhere safe," Chaban said. Zubiri's comment about having him step down seemed to have the opposite effect from the one she intended. It seemed to give him strength.

Cole sighed beside Ludmilla. "That's enough," he said. "This is going nowhere. I'm going to send for the local constabulary."

"Who will you send? Reginald? Because you told him to go home." Chaban's eyes had narrowed. "You people think you have something on me—"

"No, Devin," Elin said quietly. "We know we do. You're up to something. Why don't you just tell us what that is?"

"Ludmilla has a theory," Cole said. He turned toward her. "You want to tell them or should I?"

Her cheeks heated. She wasn't even certain what he was referring to, not with the stolen items. This was so much more than just a switch in power. Something else was going on here.

"Let's get the items first," she said. "And then worry about the reasons for this strange turn of events."

Kwin frowned at her. Cole leaned back, as if he hadn't expected that. Xavier shook his head slightly.

There was a moment of silence, as if no one quite knew how to proceed.

Then Xavier said quietly, "If the items that we had stored were supposed to remain separate, then we cannot see them together."

"Is that the case?" Cole asked the group. "Are we not supposed to see them together? Or was there an admonition against them being stored together?"

Ludmilla was trying to pay attention and review every

conversation she had had with her father about being a Regent. She couldn't come up with anything.

"Eustace, do you know any details about the items?" Xavier asked him quietly, clearly trying not to upset him further.

"What items?" Eustace asked.

"Your maps. Were you supposed to keep them away from other maps?"

"They've gone missing," Eustace said, his voice breaking.

"I know," Xavier said gently. "We will find them."

Ludmilla was amazed that the patience he was showing. Maybe he had had the same kind of experience she had.

"But," Xavier said. "I need to know something. Can they be around the other maps?"

Eustace sat up just a little taller. His eyes were still troubled, but he seemed to access something, a bit of strength, maybe, or a memory.

"My father said that was a superstition," Eustace said. "But he called everything my grandfather was involved in a superstition."

Then Eustace looked sad. The entire Board was watching him, waiting for his next sentence, even Chaban.

"Then, my father would say that my grandfather should have died in the Purges."

Ludmilla flinched. That was an incredibly mean thing to say to a child. But it was beginning to sound like Eustace's father was mean.

"He died before then, didn't he?" Xavier said.

"I miss him." A tear ran down Eustace's face. "I lost his maps. What'll I tell him? I lost his maps."

Chaban pushed back from the table, his chair squeaking loudly on the floor. "This needs to end. He's spouting a confusing bunch of garbage, and you all are believing him. He's brainless."

"But not brainless enough to be kept out of the meetings," Zubiri said.

Chaban glared at her. "You—"

"So," Cole said loudly, talking over everyone. "The maps can't be in the same place. Does anyone else know about this?"

The room grew quiet. Chaban opened his hands and spread them slightly, as if to say, *Well, then, that's that.*

"We have bylaws somewhere," Volkovich said.

"For all we know, Devin destroyed them," Zubiri said.

"Now, you're all making things up," Chaban said.

"Are we?" Cole's question was sharp. "Tell me, Devin, did you store all the items you confiscated together in one place?"

Chaban clamped his mouth closed, but his flush grew darker. He was answering the question without saying a word.

"It's a superstition," he snapped. "Eustace said so."

Eustice raised his head, his face wet with tears. He didn't seem to recognize anyone. Ludmilla wanted to go over to him, put a hand on his back, calm him, but she didn't move. She knew that any approach right now might scare him.

"So now we listen to Eustace, do we?" Zubiri said. "What is it, Devin? Is he trustworthy or not?"

"Are they talking about the maps?" Eustace whispered to Rogov.

Rogov nodded, but didn't look at Eustace.

"Did he take my maps?" Eustace asked Rogov, who bowed his head. "Is that why I'm so upset? He took my maps? I didn't lose them?"

No one answered him. His words hung in the room. His confusion was upsetting all of them.

Except Ludmilla. She'd wandered through thickets like this before. She knew how to follow the threads.

She leaned forward.

"You didn't lose the maps, Eustace," she said quietly. Quiet was always good with this kind of confusion. He might not recognize her on the surface, but he recognized her deep down.

"Oh, good," Eustace said. "My dad will thrash me if I lose the maps."

She closed her eyes for a moment. Each sentence confirmed the vile nature of Eustace's father. That was part of what they were fighting here. When Eustace slipped into his old memories, he became terrified of a man long dead.

She opened her eyes and gave Eustace a gentle smile. Right now, he was lost in his childhood. She had to bring him forward, but to do that, she couldn't challenge where he was. She had to work with him.

"We all have maps, Eustace," she said in that same voice. Everyone was watching her. No one was watching him. He was clearly making them uncomfortable. "Why can't they be in the same room?"

"Secrets," he whispered.

"Yes," she said. "The maps are secret."

"No!" he shouted like a child would. He was a child. A

giant, confused, wrinkled, sad child. "The maps have secrets."

A chill ran down her spine.

"This needs to end," Chaban said. "He's not well. He shouldn't be—"

"Shut up, Devin," Packingham said. "I want to hear this."

They all did, Ludmilla included. She hoped she could get Eustace to continue talking.

Ludmilla hadn't broken eye contact with Eustace. She willed him to be clear, even though she knew that wouldn't work.

She also knew if she lost the eye contact with him, she would lose the moment, maybe entirely.

"Help me understand, Eustace," she said. "The maps have secrets that you can see when they're together?"

He bit his lower lip, as if he wasn't supposed to say anything. But he nodded the whole time.

"Do you know what kind of secrets?" she asked.

He nodded again, as he wrapped his arms toward his torso. He seemed to be shrinking in front of her eyes, like someone who didn't want to be seen or talked with or even heard.

"Can you tell me?" she asked.

"My father won't like it," Eustace said in a very little boy voice.

"Oh, for goodness' sake," Chaban said, and Eustace jumped.

"See?" he whispered at Ludmilla.

They maintained eye contact, even though she wanted to look at Chaban.

"I do see," she said. "I won't let him hurt you, Eustace."

"I would not hurt him," Chaban growled. "You're hurting him. He's ill."

"If you don't shut up," Zubiri said, "I will shut you up myself."

From the corner of her eye, Ludmilla could see Chaban look at everyone again, as if he were asking for help. No one else seemed to move.

She forced herself to continue to concentrate on Eustace.

"What kind of secrets are in the maps?" she asked.

"Not in all of them," he whispered.

"There aren't secrets in all of them?" she asked.

"Some are pretty," he said.

She smiled. She had a sense that she and Eustace were enacting an old memory of his. Child-Eustace might have found the maps, and thought them pretty. He had probably been punished for handling them, which was why he was so worried about it now.

She almost said, *I'd like to see them,* but stopped herself. That might make Eustace lose focus again.

"The secrets aren't in the pretty ones, then?" she asked.

Eustace shot a worried glance at Chaban, then looked at Ludmilla again.

She held her breath, hoping Eustace hadn't lost his train of thought.

He leaned even closer to her.

"The secrets are in the ripped ones," he said.

"He's making all of this up," Chaban said.

Zubiri sped up her slow walk toward him. Eustace cringed.

Ludmilla did not break her gaze with Eustace, but said through her teeth, "Stop moving."

"I'm not," Eustace wailed.

She couldn't say that she meant the others, because then he would look around and actually see them, maybe even remember that they were here. He seemed to have forgotten them or stopped noticing them or however all of this worked.

Zubiri stopped walking. At least she understood.

Ludmilla said quietly, "Someone ripped the maps?"

Eustace nodded.

"Why?" she asked.

He leaned even closer, his chin just inches from the table. There was a wildness in his eyes, a childish wildness, of a kind she'd seen in her little brothers when they were young.

"Secret," he whispered.

She almost patronized him, almost said, *Yes, Eustace, you've said that.* She needed every bit of her concentration to prevent herself from making a mistake, to make sure that she didn't shatter the illusion.

"The reason they ripped the maps is secret?" she asked.

Eustace smiled, a wide-open, almost happy smile. The kind a little boy got when he knew something an adult didn't.

"The maps *are* the secret," he said. "One big map, my daddy says."

Chaban moaned and tilted his head back. He started to

speak, but Zubiri raised a finger at him, effectively shushing him.

Ludmilla's heart was pounding. If this was true, then the map was important enough to be separated into pieces, too important to be destroyed.

"Have you seen the map?" she asked.

"I put our parts together," Eustace said. "It glows."

Her heart sank. Was he making this up, like Chaban said? She didn't know how to react to that.

"Ask him if the image undulates," Cole whispered.

She almost glanced at him in surprise. What Eustace said had discouraged her, but brought up something for Cole.

Eustace, in this state, probably wouldn't know the word *undulate*. She had to think for a moment to come up with another word.

"Does it ripple?" she asked.

"You saw it too!" Eustace leaned back and clapped his hands together. "It's not pretty."

"No," she said, not sure what she was encouraging. "It's surprising."

He nodded. "Do you have a ripped map?"

"I might." She didn't know. Maybe that was what her father had been trying to tell her. "I'd have to check."

"If we can find my maps, we can put yours and mine together." He looked happy for the first time since she'd seen him.

"We can," she said, feeling a little lightheaded. So that was what Chaban was doing. He was assembling forbidden maps into one big secret map. That undulated.

The word disturbed her.

259

"Do you know what the map is of, Eustace?" she asked.

"Water," he said. "And red sunshine."

"All right." Garvyn spoke up. "It's clear he's making this up."

He was sitting close enough to Eustace to catch Eustace's attention. Eustace frowned at him.

Ludmilla made a small gesture with her right hand, hoping Eustace wouldn't see it, trying to keep Garvyn quiet.

She needed to get Eustace's attention again, before she lost him.

"He's not making anything up," Cole said with the kind of confidence a person had when they had seen the exact same thing. "He's—"

Ludmilla turned toward him, since Eustace had already broken eye contact, and mouthed, *Be quiet.*

Cole nodded, head down, subdued. That surprised her.

She turned back to Eustace, but it was too late. He was shaking, hunched in on himself, more like a broken man than a child sharing a secret.

"Eustace," she said gently.

He shook his head.

"Eustace, can we talk about the maps?" she asked.

"I lost them," he whispered, and at the end of the whisper, a sob. "I lost them."

"He can't keep doing this," Rogov said to her. "He's already stretched. I've seen him like this before. Keep pushing and you'll damage him worse."

She let out a small sigh. She knew that too, deep down inside. She'd seen it before.

"Someone, get him something to drink and something to eat," she said.

"That'll shut him up and make him stop lying," Chaban said.

His viciousness made Ludmilla's skin crawl.

Eustace folded into a small ball. If he hadn't been done before, he was done now. He clearly saw Chaban as some version of his father, and Eustace's father scared him.

"I've got it." Wilma Blankenship stood, barely reaching above the table, she was so slight. "I'm going to get you something to eat, Eustace."

He didn't seem to hear her. He was shivering.

"Something warm will help," Rogov said. "Tea, maybe."

Blankenship nodded. She grabbed an extra mug and poured tea, then brought it to Rogov, who offered it to Eustace.

Eustace shook his head.

Rogov set the tea down.

"He's crazy," Chaban said. "You can't listen to him. He's—"

"He's scaring you to death," Packingham said. "I saw the colors float on my mother's maps when I was a girl. Nothing Eustace said is far-fetched. Not a damn thing, and you know it, Devin."

"He's accused me of stealing," Chaban said.

"Actually, I accused you," Cole said. "I think you are running some kind of scam here. I'm not sure why, but I'm pretty sure we'll figure it out."

"Not with Eustace's help," Rogov said. "You can't push him anymore."

Rogov then glared at Ludmilla, as if Eustace's reaction had been her fault.

"I agree," she said quietly. "We need to take care of him now. I know some healers who can—"

"We're not going to talk about that right now," Zubiri said. "We'll take care of that problem later. Right now, we have Devin to deal with."

Then she smiled, only it wasn't really a smile. It was baring her teeth at him. Ludmilla wouldn't have been surprised if Zubiri had growled.

"You're going to tell us everything you know, Devin," Zubiri said, "and I'm going to make sure you do it."

REGENTS

TOWER

ADV. STUDENT
WING

M
ENTR

CLOCK
TOWER

CHAPTER
SEVENTEEN

Zubiri strode past the fireplace and all the food. She didn't look at any of the other Regents gathered around the table. Instead, she stopped next to Chaban and put her hand on his shoulder, digging her fingers into his skin so deeply that he winced. He put a hand over hers, clearly trying to stop her.

"Don't move," she said.

Ludmilla stared in shock. She hadn't expected violence. Her father had never mentioned violence, not once.

And then a niggling memory hit her: The Purges. What had it been like here during the Purges?

Ludmilla glanced at the others. They seemed to be watching with some kind of fascination. Wilma Blankenship seemed to be the only one unaffected. She brought a plate filled with meats, cheeses, and bread to Rogov.

Quietly, she said to Rogov, "Give Eustace some food. It might help."

He thanked her, and rubbed a hand on Eustace's back. Eustace only wrapped himself up tighter.

Zubiri raised her chin ever so slightly, apparently daring the Board to take her on. She was gripping Chaban's shoulder so tightly that her fingers had turned a weird reddish-white from the strain. Chaban was trying to twist away from her, but Zubiri wouldn't let him.

Her gaze stopped on Cole.

"*We're* going to take care of this," she said to him. "No constabulary. No outsiders. Us."

Cole glanced at her hand as if it made him nervous. Then he half-shook his head. "We'll see."

"I don't even know what that means," Zubiri said.

Neither did Ludmilla. This entire meeting had started poorly and now it had devolved into something else.

"It means," Cole said, "we're going to find out what's going on. If we need law enforcement, we'll get law enforcement."

"We don't use law enforcement," N'lman said.

"Maybe that needs to change," Cole said, as Packingham made a snorting sound.

"You *are* new," she said, reviving the fight from fifteen minutes earlier. "*We* are the ones who control law enforcement."

"Only by choosing what they study," Xavier said calmly. "Cole has a point. I'm willing to take this only so far."

"We need those items," Zubiri said, "and no one outside this room needs to know about that."

"Have you forgotten that the homes of the Old Families

were broken into?" Ivonovich said, his voice trembling. "What if someone was looking for the items we have?"

"Maybe that's why they murdered Augustus," Elin said.

"We're speculating," said Sonia Petroscu. Her skin had paled, making her black and white hair appear even more stark. "We can't do that right now. We need truth."

"We do need truth." Zubiri twisted her fingers into Chaban's shoulder. He yelped. "We're going to take you to those things you stole."

Ludmilla let out a small breath. She could see the pain on Chaban's face. She wanted to stop this, but she also... didn't. Chaban had been awful to Eustace. Chaban was arrogant and difficult. Maybe if the violence didn't go beyond the pressure in the shoulder, it was all right.

Ludmilla wasn't even sure she liked herself for thinking that.

"I didn't do anything," Chaban said. "I had a right—"

"You have no right," Zubiri snapped. "You stole from the families of board members. We need those items."

"You're believing a sick old man," Chaban said.

"And I suspect I'm not the only one," Zubiri said.

Chaban waved his free hand at Ludmilla. "She made him say all of that. She asked him leading questions."

Ludmilla sucked in air. The man was unbelievable. And to think she had been feeling some empathy for him a moment before.

She had to force herself not to respond. He was deliberately trying to bait her, to make her seem crazy.

"Nice try, Devin," Cole said, "but we all listened Ludmilla's conversation with Eustace. And we all saw how nervous it made you. There's something going on here. We just need to know what."

A chair slid back. Dh'stan stood. He had been sitting on the window-side of the table. The gray light made him seem smaller, even more hunched. Or maybe that was his reaction to Zubiri's actions.

Dh'stan surveyed the room and said, "This discussion doesn't need the full Board. You get those materials. Then we will meet again in the morning, to discuss whatever you found, and then we'll determine if it matters."

"Who put you in charge?" Packingham asked just as Zubiri spoke at the same time.

"It matters," Zubiri said. Then she spoke louder, probably to prevent Packingham from fighting with Dh'stan. "Those materials matter."

"We aren't even sure what they are. Let's have facts before we—" Dh'stan waved a hand at Zubiri and Chaban. "—become something we don't want to be."

"And what's that?" Zubiri asked.

Dh'stan frowned. He glanced at a few of the others. Ludmilla couldn't tell if he chose them because he was standing near them or because they agreed with him, and maybe asked him to speak for him.

Dh'stan moved his hands outward, as if he was trying to placate Zubiri.

"Devin might be right," Dh'stan said. "We might have just listened to the ravings of a lunatic."

"Lunatic?" Rogov said, sounding offended. "He's a sick man, but he's not crazy."

"He sounded crazy," Dh'stan said.

"I've seen the same thing on the maps," Cole said.

"You are not a credible witness," N'lman said. "You and that woman had a conversation before we returned—"

That woman? How did Ludmilla suddenly become that woman?

"Yes," Cole said. "I had a conversation with her in which I told her that the infighting didn't matter. We seemed to get things done despite the infighting."

Cole almost sounded defensive.

Dh'stan snorted dismissively, as if he didn't really agree with the idea.

"We'll see if it's possible to get things done," Dh'stan said. "I feel like we've wasted a good day. We're starting fresh tomorrow, once we've all calmed down."

He pointedly directed that last bit at Zubiri. She made a face at him, almost like a child would.

Chaban put his hand over hers again, and she bucked it off without lifting her fingers from his shoulder. His face had become mottled. A bead of sweat ran down the left side of his face.

"And who is running the meeting?" Popova asked. "It can't be Devin, since he's under a cloud of suspicion."

"I will," Packingham said. "I'm senior, and everyone knows that Devin and I don't get along."

"That's the criteria for leadership now?" Chaban asked, then winced as Zubiri's hand tightened on his shoulder.

"If that's the case, then most of us are qualified," Xavier said.

"Here's what we're going to do," Packingham said.

"Munira, Cole, Pasha, and Dao will go with Devin to get the confiscated items."

"I don't think that's a good idea," Chaban said.

Ludmilla wasn't sure it was a good idea either, not with the pain that Zubiri was inflicting on Chaban. She almost seemed to be enjoying it.

Ludmilla had no idea about the others. She trusted Cole, somewhat, anyway. She really didn't know the others. She did remember that Pasha Volkovich had arrived at the same time as Chaban, but she had no idea if that meant anything.

"You don't get a vote," Packingham was saying to Chaban. "I picked people who have been on the Board long enough to be reliable, but not long enough to be worried about their heirs. They will remove the items and bring them here tomorrow. We will reassemble first thing, and figure out what to do next."

"I'd like to go too," Ludmilla said.

"My dear girl," Packingham said, "you have done enough for one day."

Ludmilla started to disagree, but Cole put his hand on hers this time, and shook his head slightly.

"I'm going," he said very quietly. "It'll be all right."

She had no idea if any of this would be all right. She didn't like that Cole seemed to think he could handle something for her. He didn't know her at all.

But she hadn't been here long, and she knew nothing about the workings of the board. She also didn't like the denial that was going on among some board members, like Dh'stan.

She believed Eustace. She figured everyone else would as

well. Couldn't they see the problems he had brought up? Not just the potential theft, but the possible magic in some of the items that the Regents were supposed to guard. Guard against what, she had wanted to ask Eustace.

It was too late now, at least today. His arms were wrapped around himself, his head bowed, and he was rocking. She wouldn't have been surprised if he was crying too, given how young that voice of fear had been when he worried aloud about his father.

Families often made things difficult. That the Regents were tied in with family made this Board more querulous than she had expected.

Cole stood up and walked toward Chaban. Cole pointedly looked at Zubiri's fingers, as if telling her to back off. She shook her head ever so slightly.

Cole leaned on the edge of the long table, his back to the Board as he faced Chaban.

"Where are the items?" Cole asked Chaban.

Chaban tried to sit up, but Zubiri held him in place.

"You think I'm stupid enough to keep them in Serebro?" he asked.

Yes, Ludmilla wanted to say.

"Why is it so hard for you to answer a simple question?" Zubiri asked Chaban.

"Probably because your fingers are making holes in my shoulder," he snapped.

"Where are the items?" She sounded tired.

"What if I tell you they're in Trinovante?" Chaban asked.

"I would think you were lying, given how much you hate Trinovante," Zubiri said.

"You will not play us," Packingham said. "You will take our representatives to those items, and you will give them to us."

"Or what, Mavis? You'll what?"

Ludmilla couldn't believe how defiant the man was, considering how angry most of the Board was.

"We'll have you arrested," Popova said. He seemed calm, even as his voice boomed. When he mentioned *arrest*, it sounded like a real threat.

"An arrest won't stick," Chaban said.

"It will if we have the Protectorate do it," Popova said.

"The Protectorate only steps in on Protectorate issues," Chaban said.

"The theft of historical items for the promulgation of magic is a Protectorate issue," Popova said.

Someone sucked in air loudly again. Rogov looked shocked. Cole let out a small laugh. Ludmilla felt a shiver run down her spine.

The Purges were called Purges for a reason. Not that long ago, people were put to death for stealing historical items for the promulgation of magic.

"You wouldn't do that," Chaban said, his voice shaking. Clearly, he believed that Popova would make good on his threat. "You'd lose the items."

"We don't have them now," Packingham said, taking control of this.

"And, if you're charged and convicted," Popova said, "then those items will be returned to their rightful owners."

"Which could take years," Chaban said.

"Years don't matter to us," Packingham said. "We don't intend to do anything with the items except give them to their rightful owners."

"Which is the Board," Chaban said.

"No," Packingham said. "The families."

"Someone should check the bylaws," Xavier said quietly.

"Oh," Petrescu said, "I'm sure someone will."

She said it with such confidence that it was clear she would be that someone.

"I'll help you," Ludmilla said.

"I'm not doing it tonight," Petrescu said, dismissing her with that simple sentence.

A few of the others stood, gathering coats and peering at the window. Rain still pelted it. The storms lately had been fierce, and for no apparent reason.

"Tell me one thing in front of the entire board," Cole said to Chaban. "What were you planning to do with the items you confiscated?"

Everyone stopped moving. The handful who had grabbed their coats folded them over their arms. The board members looking out the window stopped and turned.

The question caught them all.

Chaban noticed. He looked from one person to another. "I was just going to keep the items safe."

"I mean," Cole said, "what were you going to do with the items if the heirs didn't want them? If you somehow brought in new members, would those members get the items?"

Chaban took a deep breath, like people sometimes did when they were feeling trapped.

"I hadn't thought that far ahead," he said.

It was such an obvious lie that Zubiri let go of him and flailed her free hand in disgust. A few others shook their heads.

Packingham stood. Her jaw was set in a hard line.

"We have not been paying enough attention to this Board and to our duties." She clearly wasn't talking just to Chaban. She was talking to everyone. "We thought of this as something we did every now and then—"

"Speak for yourself, Mavis," Rogov said.

"Well, the bulk of us felt that way, anyway," she said. "We let a lot slip through our fingers. Most of us didn't want extra duties. That changes today."

Ludmilla glanced around the room. Half of the room nodded. Others kept their heads down. But she couldn't tell if they refused to nod because of Chaban or because they still didn't want extra work.

"We will be here early tomorrow," Packingham said. "Be ready to work."

"I'm not sure we can all be here," Rogov said with a nod of the head toward Eustace.

Eustace looked even smaller than he had before.

"Feed him well, and let him get some rest," Ludmilla said to Rogov. "He might surprise you."

"He always surprises me," Rogov muttered. Then he met her gaze and nodded. He seemed to appreciate the understanding.

"What are we going to do about Reginald?" Elin asked.

"We'll deal with him in the morning," Popova said. Clearly he wanted to deal with one problem at a time.

Cole sighed audibly, but didn't say anything. Ludmilla didn't either. Now that the meeting was breaking up, she wanted out of this room. She needed some quiet to think about everything she had learned today—and everything that she hadn't learned.

She had expected this to be similar to the first meeting, which, come to think of it, had been nothing like what she had initially expected.

All those years, imagining how the meetings worked. For some reason (maybe because it was held at Serebro Academy), she had thought this would be like school. She was the newest member, so she would be treated as a beginner.

Instead, she had taken the reins of part of this meeting. But the rest of it...she felt unsettled and vaguely frightened.

The implied violence, and the mention of the Purges, left her distinctly uncomfortable. And Eustace, he broke her heart.

Rogov was packing Eustace up now, trying to get him to move. Eustace kept rocking.

Ludmilla would have gone to help, but she wasn't that familiar to him. That would upset him even more.

The group that Packingham had assigned to deal with Chaban was gathering near him. Dao Kwin stood as far from Zubiri as he could. Pasha Volkovich walked toward them slowly, not making eye contact with anyone on the Board as he did so.

He seemed determined, but about what Ludmilla wasn't certain.

Suddenly, she didn't envy them. She didn't envy any of them.

For the first time since her father died, the future seemed very uncertain. Maybe more uncertain than before, because something was happening—not just to the Board and to academies, but to Qavner Province itself.

And if the Purges came back, well, then, the fear that still underlined every thought, every movement that most educated people had, would become something on the surface, something real and tangible, and maybe even dangerous.

She pushed away from the table and stood, only to find Xavier watching her. Away from the firelight, his robe looked black.

"Would you like to get some dinner, Miss Odenkirk?" he asked. "There is much to discuss."

If he had approached her at her first meeting and asked her to dinner, she would have gone happily. But now, she didn't trust any of her colleagues on the Board. She had no idea what he wanted, and no idea why he would want to talk with her—even though he had been nice to Eustace.

She smiled at Xavier, a smile she really didn't feel, and said, "I appreciate the offer, but not right now."

She didn't have an excuse to offer him, and she wasn't sure she wanted to spare his feelings.

She wasn't sure she wanted to spare any of their feelings, which was unusual for her. Most of the time she was unfailingly polite—until she wasn't. Until she needed to speak her mind.

But to speak her mind, she needed to know her mind,

and right now, information swirled in her head. She had no idea who to believe or what to believe or what, still, was going on.

She knew how she would handle this. The only thing that would calm her was answers.

No one here seemed willing to give her any, so she needed to find them on her own.

She wouldn't be going back to her apartment in Serebro. She would need to figure out her room at the lodgings. Then she'd get dinner, and see what she could discover on her own, before the meeting started in the morning.

With that in mind, she grabbed her own coat from the closet, and left without looking back.

REGENTS
TOWER

ADV. STUDENT
WING

M
ENTR

CLOCK
TOWER

CHAPTER
EIGHTEEN

The meeting room became progressively more and more quiet. The lightstones around the wall had grown brighter as twilight fell outside of the building. The fire was dying out, because Cole had forced Reginald to leave. Reginald normally kept track of everything like that.

Cole looked at the food spread, and wondered, with Reginald gone, whether or not someone would clean it up. Cole supposed it would be his responsibility to make sure someone did.

He hovered near the edge of the table, watching the last of the Regents leave the meeting room. Pasha Volkovich stood near his chair as well, watching Chaban as if Chaban was some kind of bug.

Volkovich's white-blond hair caught what remained of the firelight, making the strands of his hair around his face point at all the lines like little blond arrows. His mouth was thin, his small eyes even narrower than usual.

Cole couldn't tell if Volkovich was angry at being chosen to deal with Chaban or ready to do so.

Munira Zubiri was ready to take on Chaban. Clearly ready, given how she had already hurt him. Cole worried that he might have to hold her back, to keep her from hurting Chaban worse.

She had let go of Chaban's shoulder briefly, but, as the other Regents left, she had grabbed him again, right in the same spot, making him flinch, but keeping him in the chair.

Chaban was watching everyone leave as well, the dismay on his face getting worse as each regent went out the door. Chaban clearly didn't expect to be in this situation, although, to be honest, Cole wasn't sure what this situation was.

He wasn't sure if the four that Packingham had chosen could even complete their assignment by the morning meeting. Chaban had been reticent about the location of the items he had taken and if what he had said was true, then they weren't even in Serebro. They might be a long distance from here, which meant that Cole and the others would be in for a long night.

The only one who seemed truly unconcerned was Dao Kwin. As the others left, he had wandered over to the food. He stood over the table, a plate in his beringed hand. He was contemplating what was left, clearly stocking up before the group did what they had to do.

His yellow-gold suit had become wrinkled during the afternoon meeting—the fabric not up to any kind of prolonged sitting—and his curly black hair looked more unruly than ever.

Horace Rogov and Eustace Wallingford were the last regents to leave. It had taken Rogov awhile to bundle up Wallingford. The man seemed to have only a few moments of clarity, and Cole didn't want to trust them. Because that meant something awful had been going on here, right under their noses, and he hadn't noticed at all.

Rogov propelled Wallingford out of the door, one hand on Wallingford's back in case the man toppled over, which he looked in danger of doing. Rogov grabbed the door knob with his other hand, but paused before he pulled it closed.

He looked directly at Chaban.

"If you do not cooperate," Rogov said, his voice steady, his eyes cold, "I shall tell the remaining Purge Arbitrators that you have stolen magical items for personal use. Do you understand?"

Chaban's skin turned a surprising shade of pale. He clearly understood.

Cole did too. Even now, years after the worst of the Purges, possession of more than twenty magical items without some kind of legal dispensation was a crime whose most severe punishment was death.

"You wouldn't," Chaban said.

"Why not?" Rogov asked. "For all I know, it's true."

"I have no idea how to use magical items," Chaban said.

"Then what are you stealing them for?" Rogov asked.

"Are you coming?" Wallingford asked querulously from outside the door.

"One minute, Eustace," Rogov said, without breaking

eye contact from Chaban. "Devin, who are you stealing them for?"

"I'm not stealing," he whispered.

"Eustace would beg to differ," Rogov said.

"I would what?" Wallingford asked.

Cole watched them. There was more going on here than met the eye.

"You will cooperate," Rogov said. "If not, I will follow through. You're a weaselly, self-important little asshole, and it would give me great pleasure to see you brought to your knees."

"I can do that," Zubiri said with a feral smile.

Rogov gave her a patronizing glare, but didn't respond. "Do you understand me, Devin?"

"Y-yes," Chaban whispered. "I understand."

"Good," Rogov said. Then he stepped through the door, and pulled it closed behind him, the click echoing in the large and nearly empty room.

Cole let out a small sigh. He wasn't going to say anything, not yet. He wanted to see how all of this played out.

Kwin topped his plate with a slice of brown bread, which balanced precariously on top of three different kinds of cheeses and a few slices of apple.

He turned around, his free hand cupping the food pile, and raised his eyebrows.

"Well," he said. "That settles that, then. Devin, tell us where we're going, and we'll have done with this."

Chaban bowed his head, but not before Cole saw Chaban's jaw working off some kind of tension.

"I can't," he whispered.

"What?" Zubiri squeezed Chaban's shoulder so hard that Chaban yelped. "They couldn't hear you."

Cole had had enough. "We can hear just fine."

He strode over to Chaban, put a hand on top of Zubiri's, and slowly removed her fingers from Chaban's shoulder. Her fingers were bony. They felt like claws.

As they released, Cole noted that her nails were long and curved downward. Small specks of blood stained Chaban's shirt.

Cole looked in her dark eyes. She half-smiled at him, then shrugged one shoulder, as if to say *What's a woman to do?*

Cole crouched in front of Chaban and put one finger under Chaban's chin. His skin was hot and surprisingly soft. "What do you mean, you can't tell us where the items are?"

"Can't or won't?" Volkovich asked.

"Can't." Chaban's skin was blotchy, his eyelashes spiked and stuck together. That meant he'd teared up when Zubiri had dug her fingers into his shoulder.

"And why not?" Kwin wandered over. He set his plate on the nearest table as if he didn't care about the food at all.

"I don't have them anymore." Chaban closed his eyes. Tears slid between the lashes, but didn't fall. His chin was trembling.

Cole extended his own fingers, and grabbed Chaban's jaw tightly.

"Look at me," Cole said through his teeth. He shook Chaban's head slightly. "Open your eyes and look at me now."

Chaban opened his eyes. They were swimming in water. He looked like a helpless child who had been caught doing something so awful that he was afraid of getting beaten.

That was probably a healthy fear.

"Why don't you have them?" Cole asked.

"You don't understand." Chaban's words were a bit mushy. He didn't have quite enough mobility in his jaw to enunciate clearly.

"Yes, you're right," Cole said. "I don't. You're supposed to take us to the items. And now, you lie and say that you no longer have them? I have no idea why you would lie right now."

"I'm not lying." Chaban tried to twist his head, but Cole held him too tightly. The cords in Chaban's neck showed with his effort to pull away. "I don't have them."

"Who did you give them to?" Kwin asked.

"I didn't give them to anyone," Chaban said miserably.

"Then why don't you have them?" Zubiri snapped.

"Because he sold them," Cole said, his gaze still on Chaban.

Chaban winced and started to close his eyes, but Cole shook Chaban's head again.

"Am I right, Devin?" Cole asked. "You sold them, didn't you?"

Chaban tried to nod, but Cole held him too tightly. So Chaban whispered, "Yes."

"'Yes?'" Zubiri reached for Chaban, but Cole batted her hands away. "You *sold* items entrusted to all of us?"

"Yes," Chaban said, choking on the "s." "I'm so sorry."

"Sorry doesn't mean anything," Kwin said. "We're all entrusted with these items. They're *sacred*."

Cole hadn't heard that they were sacred, but he did know that they were important. And now, Chaban had sold them?

"How many of the items have you sold?" he asked.

"All of them," Chaban said, either misunderstanding the question or pretending to.

"That is not what I'm asking," Cole said, and heard barely controlled rage in his voice. He hadn't realized until now how very angry he was. "How many items have you sold? One, ten, one hundred?"

"One hundred and thirty five," Chaban said, his voice trembling.

Zubiri cursed and turned her back on them, walking to the fireplace. Kwin's eyebrows went up even higher. Volkovich just stared at the scene, his expression flat, his eyes flatter.

"Maps and everything?" Kwin asked.

"Maps and everything," Chaban said. "I'm so sorry."

"No, you're not," Cole said. "Stop lying or I'll break your jaw."

"Break his jaw and he can't talk," Zubiri said from beside the fireplace. "Shatter his kneecap. He'll be in extreme pain and he'll never walk again."

Chaban shook his head enough that Cole could feel the movement.

"A fireplace poker should do the trick," Volkovich said. "There are two in this room."

"No," Chaban said. "I *am* sorry."

"You're not sorry," Cole said. "You're only sorry that you got caught."

Chaban had the good sense not to deny that.

"Why would you sell our heritage?" Volkovich asked as he pulled one of the pokers from the rack holding all of the metal fireplace equipment.

"I needed the money," Chaban said.

"That's probably obvious," Zubiri said to Volkovich. "And most likely irrelevant."

"Nothing is irrelevant." Cole's knees had started to ache, but he couldn't tell if that was because he usually didn't crouch this long or because the ache had started when Zubiri talked about shattering Chaban's kneecap.

"Why did you need the money?" Volkovich asked.

"Can you let go of my jaw?" Chaban asked Cole. "I can hardly talk."

Cole released Chaban's jaw, and pushed him back at the same time. Zubiri came over toward him, swinging a different fireplace poker from the one that Volkovich held.

"Don't hurt me!" Chaban said, raising his hands.

"Hurt you?" she said. "I've half a mind to kill you."

"That's murder," Chaban said. "It's against the law."

"Not when you kill someone who is misusing magic," Zubiri said. "We just found out you're doing that. We have every right to kill you."

Cole stood. His legs wobbled. Not sympathy, then. He was not as young as he used to be, although he was probably the youngest person in the room.

Zubiri was wrong about killing Chaban. It would be murder, even if it were later discovered that Chaban had violated all those laws that had been passed during the Purges.

Most likely, though, none of the authorities would care. The Purges left everyone terrified of people who misused magic. If this group banded together, and said they were acting in self-defense, who would contradict them? Who would care?

"You were going to explain the money," Volkovich said coldly.

Chaban was the only one sitting. He looked from person to person, but clearly didn't see anyone who would side with him.

Bruises were forming on the side of his face from Cole's fingers.

Chaban licked his lips nervously. "I—um—the family—um—*my* family—we ran out of money a few years ago. The properties are entailed. I can't touch them. Really, no one can. We're barred from selling them."

"So you sold artifacts," Kwin said.

Chaban didn't answer him, not directly. Chaban didn't even look at him. Instead, Chaban was looking at Cole, striving for sympathy.

Cole had no idea why Chaban thought he would be the one to dole out sympathy, but there it was, in Chaban's eyes. Pleading.

"First we let the staff go, on all of the houses." Then Chaban cringed, as if he expected someone to hit him. "Except the gardeners. We didn't want the gardens to go."

"Because then someone would know you were having financial difficulties," Zubiri said with a sneer.

"Yes," Chaban said. "That was five years ago. Then we sold the contents of all of the houses except two, the one in Serebro and the one in Trinovante."

"Where the family is living," Kwin said flatly.

"Appearance at all cost," Zubiri said, looking at Volkovich.

"Sounds like it," Volkovich said, raising the poker and putting the flat of it in his other hand.

Chaban's lower lip trembled. "We shut off most of the rooms."

As if that mattered. Zubiri rolled her eyes. Volkovich lifted the poker slightly and slammed it against his palm.

Cole didn't move, though.

"We're living very close to the vest," Chaban said.

"Not close enough," Kwin said.

"You still haven't told us who has the artifacts," Cole said, determined to keep the focus.

"I don't know, exactly," Chaban said.

Cole's heart sank. He waited, hoping Chaban was lying again.

"You don't know?" Zubiri asked, her entire body alive with tension. "How can you not know?"

Chaban turned toward her so fast that he unbalanced in the chair. It started to topple, but he caught it by moving one foot. He managed to do all of that while cringing.

"We were having sales. Not here. Not in Qavner either. Farther out. In the Hinterlands."

The Hinterlands. The countries that got absorbed into the Qavnerian Protectorate, either through decree or some small battle that they lost before it even started.

"Appearances," Volkovich said to Zubiri.

"We're suffering from an excess of stupidity here," Zubiri said.

"They know what some of those artifacts are, in the *Hinterlands*," Kwin said, emphasizing the last word with sarcasm so deep that his contempt was palpable.

"You paid to have items taken and sold in the Hinterlands?" Cole asked. This family really didn't know how to handle money.

"We hired someone who took the costs out of the profits," Chaban said.

Zubiri rolled her eyes again. Cole didn't feel the need to show his contempt. No wonder the Chaban family had no money. They had no idea how to make it or make it work for them or how to properly pay someone for a service.

"Did they give you an accounting?" Volkovich asked.

"What do you think?" Zubiri said. "He's so stu—"

"Stop," Cole said. "Pasha's question is a good one."

Although he probably asked it for the wrong reasons.

Cole leaned toward Chaban.

"Well?" Cole said. "Did they give you an accounting?"

"Of what?" Chaban asked.

"Oh, for—." Zubiri started, and then stopped herself. "I'm not explaining to this idiot what an accounting is."

"I know what an accounting is," Chaban asked. "Why would someone we hired to handle a problem give us an accounting? We didn't need one. We wanted the items off our hands."

Cole closed his eyes for one brief moment, finally understanding Zubiri's inability to stop rolling hers. He took a deep breath and then opened them.

"A list, perhaps, of who bought which item," Cole said, working very hard to keep the judgement out of his tone. "Do you at least have that?"

"Why would I want that?" Chaban said. "We were done with those items."

"In case, you idiot," Zubiri said, "you—oh, I don't know —sold something you actually wanted to keep."

Chaban pressed his lips against each other, hard, as if he was trying not to say something.

"I told you," he said after a moment. "We wanted to keep it all. But we couldn't afford it."

"And now we know why," Kwin said, reaching for his plate. He somehow managed to pick it up without knocking anything off.

"What's that supposed to mean?" Chaban asked.

"It means," Cole said, before anyone else could speak, "that we have no way of knowing whether you are lying or not when you say you disposed of the items."

"You people are something," Chaban said. "You demand that I tell you what we did with the items, and then you criticize how we did it. I wouldn't lie about this. Do you know how shameful it is to lose everything?"

"Except two houses and a bunch of servants," Volkovich said under his breath.

"And I do have a list of where everything was sold," Chaban said, "as well as how much money we made doing so."

"Before the costs were expensed out?" Zubiri asked, probably because she couldn't help herself.

Cole had almost asked the same question himself.

"They just gave us the one lump figure with the money itself," Chaban said, apparently still not understanding what the problem was. "But everything was tagged to its location."

"Meaning what?" Kwin asked, as he daintily picked the slice of bread off the top of his food.

"We sold the contents of different houses in different regions," Chaban said. "That way, we weren't flooding the market. That's what the selling agents said we should do."

These selling agents were sounding shadier and shadier with each passing sentence.

"All right," Kwin said, after he'd finished chewing. He set a half-eaten piece of bread back on top of the cheese. "Let's assume that's true."

He gave a slight nod to Cole, as if acknowledging Cole's comment about lack of proof.

Kwin had set his plate down again, and walked to the chair where Chaban was sitting. Chaban was bouncing his right foot nervously.

"That still doesn't solve the problem of the items you stole," Kwan said.

"I told you," Chaban said, his voice breathless with obvious panic. "I don't know who got those. And I didn't steal them."

"You're playing games," Zubiri said. "I detest it when people play games."

She took a step toward Chaban, who cringed. She smiled

at him. The smile was so cold that Cole felt the chill all the way across the room.

Kwin put up a pudgy hand, keeping her back.

"The problem," Kwin said to Chaban, "is that you said everything is tied to the location, the house, where the item was. Only, the items you stole did not have a tie to a particular house. In fact, they belonged to someone else. What did you do with them?"

Chaban lowered his head. "We sold them."

"You said that," Zubiri snapped.

"Where did you sell them?" Kwin asked. "Separated into different piles from different houses?"

Chaban was shaking his head even before Kwin finished asking the question.

"We sold them as a unit," Chaban said. "As one thing."

"Where?" Zubiri asked with so much menace that Cole almost cringed.

"In Irbanklu," he said quietly.

Volkovich cursed and whirled away from the conversation, his hair floating around him in the breeze that he had created.

Kwin grabbed his plate again, and Cole had the odd sensation that Kwin was going to shove the entire plate in Chaban's face, not to get him to talk more, but to do some damage.

Instead, Kwin stared at the food as if he'd never seen it before.

Zubiri was shaking her head, slowly, as if she couldn't believe what she had heard.

And neither could Cole. Because everyone knew that

magical items had no place in Irbanklu. Most of the people who died in the Purges had family ties to the Forbidden Valley, or they'd been participants in the Forbidden Valley explorations, or worse, they'd actually worked for the Forbidden Valley Antiques Service.

"You're really stupid, you know that?" Zubiri snapped.

"If I didn't know it before, I certainly know it now," Chaban said with a bit of his old feistiness. "Since you keep calling me that."

"Selling magical items to the magical is a mistake," Volkovich said, his back turned. His voice actually trembled.

"No one knows if the items are magical," Chaban said, but he didn't look at the group as he said it. He knew, just like they knew. He had clearly believed he wouldn't be caught.

"Did you sell everything?" Cole asked.

Chaban looked at him as if he hadn't understood the question. "I just answered that," Chaban said. "The homes, the—"

Cole took a step forward, which stopped Chaban from talking. Zubiri was walking toward Chaban at the same time.

Chaban put a hand to his chin, then looked nervously at Zubiri.

"No," he said hastily. "No, I didn't sell everything. There, anyway."

"What does that mean?" Volkovich's voice was low, as if he was afraid of the answer.

"The maps," Chaban said. "I sold them here."

"Here," Cole repeated, trying to figure out if Chaban meant Qavner or Serebro. "At the Academy?"

"Oh, no," Chaban said. "Then they would have reported to you."

"And that's a bad thing," Kwin said, picking up the bread and then setting it down. "Of course that's a bad thing."

He shook his head.

"Please tell me you didn't sell the maps together," Volkovich said.

Chaban looked down. The hair was thin at the top of his head. He was balding. Usually when Cole saw something like that, he thought it sad, because the person was getting older.

Now, he wanted to rip out Chaban's remaining hair.

Cole clenched his fists, then released them slowly. He couldn't remember the last time he had been this angry.

"How many maps were there?" Cole asked.

"I told you," Chaban started as he raised his head.

He stopped talking when he saw Cole's face. Chaban waved a hand in a gesture that could have been seen as sign of surrender.

"A dozen," Chaban said. "There were a dozen."

"So many..." Volkovich murmured.

"Yes, there were a lot," Chaban said defensively, "but some families had more than one."

And then his face colored, as he realized what he had done. He had confessed to the thefts, in a completely different way.

"Tell me you didn't sell them to the same person," Zubiri said.

Chaban looked between her and Cole. "Well, I—I—I—"

"Be honest for once in your life," Zubiri said.

"There's two kinds of honest here," he said.

"Isn't there always?" Kwin asked with a shake of the head. He clearly didn't believe any of this. "What are they?"

"There was a group of people," Chaban said. "I have no idea if they were splitting up the maps. They came together."

"Came where?" Cole asked.

"Our home just outside of Serebro," Chaban said. "They came together."

"So you were just about to lie and saw that you didn't sell them to the same person," Zubiri said.

"It's not a lie." Chaban's voice rose.

"Might as well be," she said.

Chaban turned the chair slightly so that he couldn't see Zubiri or Kwin. Chaban was looking directly at Cole now.

"They paid really well," Chaban said, as if he thought Cole would understand.

"Somehow, that doesn't make things better." Volkovich muttered. He hadn't turned away from the fire. His posture hadn't shifted.

And somehow, that made Cole even more nervous than Zubiri's volatility and Kwin's sarcasm.

"That money will now go to the families," Zubiri said.

Chaban didn't answer her. He didn't even acknowledge her. He stared at Cole.

"I...um..." Chaban waved a hand again. "I...um..."

Volkovich turned ever so slightly. Kwin froze. Zubiri tilted her head. Cole hoped none of them would say anything, but he suspected that Chaban was about to confess something important.

"They paid really well," he repeated.

Zubiri opened her mouth, probably to let Chaban know he had already said that. Cole raised his hand ever so slightly, stopping her.

"So I asked them..." Chaban closed his eyes, then he opened them quickly as if he had forgotten that he had been assaulted not long ago. He swallowed so hard that Cole heard it.

"I asked them," Chaban repeated, then he shook his head. "I told them that I might be able to get more, and I asked them how I could contact them if I had anything."

Zubiri's eyes narrowed. Cole raised his hand a little higher, so that she wouldn't speak.

"I know it's wrong," Chaban said. "I'm sorry. We're just out of money."

"Did you contact them?" Kwin asked, and Cole mentally thanked him for asking a sane question, not attacking Chaban and stopping this part of the confession.

"No," Chaban said. "Not yet. I've been holding it, and I didn't have everything. I was working on getting the Kirilli maps."

"You were working on the Kirilli maps?" Volkovich whirled, his eyes wild. "You *killed* Augustus?"

"No, no, no, no!" Chaban scooted his chair back as he looked at Cole and then at Zubiri. "Really, no. I didn't. I didn't expect him to die. I didn't know anything about that."

"You knew someone was going to attack him?" Cole asked, voice low.

"No." Chaban said. "I hadn't talked to him. I was thinking, maybe, someone else would leave soon when I asked them to give me their address. But this week, this week *only*, I was working on the Kirilli maps. This week *only*."

Volkovich watched him, eyes flashing. Volkovich seemed larger than he had before.

This was right on the verge of getting completely out of hand.

"When did you last see the group?" Cole asked.

Chaban looked at everyone, quickly, as if he was assessing them, maybe trying to figure out how much danger he was really in. He understood it at the last minute, because he cringed even more.

"A month, maybe," he said. "The money—it's starting to run out, so that's why I was going for the Kirilli maps."

"Didn't I tell you to stop lying?" Zubiri snapped.

"All right," Chaban said. "All right. I heard that Augustus died, and I was thinking that's my opportunity. That's *another* opportunity, don't you understand? My family is in trouble here."

"They're not the only ones," Kwin said.

Chaban understood that. He put his hands up near his face, clearly terrified.

"When did you start working on the Kirilli maps?" Cole asked. He was feeling lightheaded. He hadn't known Kirilli well, but they had been colleagues. Cole didn't want to believe that the Board had something to do with Kirilli's death, but he could no longer rule it out.

"After I heard about his death," Chaban said. "I *swear*."

"Why should we trust you?" Zubiri said, her voice low and menacing.

"Because he was fine the last time we saw him. I didn't try to get anything from someone who is fine." Chaban said that as if it were logical, as if everyone understood it. As if they wouldn't blame him for stealing from people who weren't "fine."

"So you have deduced that Eustace isn't fine," Kwin said. For the first time, he didn't sound calm. He sounded furious.

"Well, he's not," Chaban said. "And his family doesn't want—"

"Stop," Cole said. "Stop justifying. How are we to know that you're not lying about Augustus Kirilli?"

Chaban swallowed. "You could ask his daughter. I sent a messenger."

The poorly named Augusta, as Packingham would say. Cole had to shake that thought out of his head.

"And she didn't respond, so you thought she wasn't interested in the seat," Kwin said.

"I gave her a deadline!" Chaban said.

"A deadline?" Now, Volkovich turned. His eyes glowed, as if they had absorbed the light from the dying fire. "You gave a woman whose father had just died a deadline to respond to you so that you could steal her seat on the Board and her maps."

"I..." Chaban shook his head. "You make that sound bad."

"It *is* bad," Kwin said.

"Is that what you did?" Cole asked.

"Yes, and I haven't heard, so I thought after the emergency meeting, once we've chosen Kirilli's replacement, I'd

298

go to the daughter and get the maps. She clearly doesn't value them."

Cole let out a breath and turned away. It was all he could do to keep from slamming his fist onto the table.

"You can't know that." Kwin said what Cole was thinking. "You really can't know that."

"Look." Chaban sounded panicked. "I can take you to the group who bought the other maps from me. And I can give you what I have as bills of sale."

"We're going to have to search his houses," Volkovich said to Zubiri as if Chaban hadn't spoken at all.

Zubiri nodded.

"The bills of sale should be enough!" Chaban said, again looking at Cole.

"They don't trust you," Cole said. "And neither do I."

"We're going to have to find out where those maps went," Volkovich said. He wasn't looking at Chaban either.

"Let's hope this group broke them up and sold them separately," Kwin said.

But his voice belied his words. He knew the maps had been sold as a unit. Cole had had no idea until that afternoon that the maps worked together, and he wasn't exactly sure where they pointed to.

But they pointed to something; maps always did.

"If the maps were broken up and sold, that group is probably not going to tell us," Volkovich said to Kwin.

"We can bring in the constabulary," Kwin said.

Volkovich shook his head. "This is not something we want known. We need to bring Xavier with us."

"Why?" Cole asked. "We were given this task. It's—"

Volkovich raised his hand and Cole stopped. There was too much that he didn't know, things that the others clearly did know.

Volkovich turned, somewhat ceremoniously, toward Chaban. Chaban bit his lower lip, which still trembled, despite the pressure he put on it.

"Describe them," Volkovich said to Chaban, "these people you sold our heritage to. Describe them."

Chaban took a shaky breath. "They were hard to see."

Zubiri tilted her head back. "Oh, for—"

"Shut up, Munira," Volkovich said in the same tone he was using with Chaban. "Why were they hard to see?"

Chaban shrugged one shoulder. "It was a dim night. Twilight came early, and the lightstones outside the house didn't work really well."

Kwin let out an audible breath. Cole didn't look at him, but kept his gaze on Chaban, who was now focused on Volkovich.

"Tell me what you did see," Volkovich said.

Zubiri stomped toward the fire. No one looked at her.

"There were maybe four of them...?" Chaban said. "I don't know. More could have been waiting at the road. I really couldn't see."

"Convenient," Zubiri murmured just as Volkovich said, "I understand."

Cole didn't, but he also noted that Volkovich was unsurprised by Chaban's admission.

"What else?" Volkovich asked.

"They were tall, all of them," Chaban said. "And thin. And they had an accent."

Kwin set his plate down and folded his hands, a frown line forming between his eyes.

"What kind of accent?" Volkovich asked.

"I'd never heard it before," Chaban said, "and I've traveled the Protectorate."

"Did they all have the same accent?" Volkovich asked.

"Only one spoke," Chaban said.

"Male? Female?" Volkovich asked.

"Male," Chaban said. "I think. It was really hard to see them."

"Yet you gave them our maps," Kwin said, even as Volkovich tried to silence him.

Cole hadn't moved.

"I didn't give them anything!" Chaban said, as if that was worse than selling the maps. "I didn't! They paid me."

"The single person, maybe male, he paid you," Volkovich said.

"Yes, yes, all right," Chaban said. "He paid me."

"Were the others bodyguards?" Volkovich asked.

"I don't know," Chaban said.

"Did you take them inside?" Volkovich asked.

"No." Chaban sounded surprised. "I'm not entirely stupid."

He shot a glance at Zubiri, but she had her back to him. Cole had a hunch she would have disagreed with the self-assessment anyway.

"What happened, then?" Volkovich asked.

"They handed me money—"

"Money? Or something else?" Volkovich asked.

Chaban's eyes narrowed, as if he had been caught at

something. "Jewels. Some gold. A few trinkets that I gave back to them because they weren't worth anything."

"According to you," Kwin said quietly.

"I *know*," Chaban said.

"Like you know how to sell things," Kwin said.

Cole didn't want them sidetracked, but it was Volkovich who remained focused.

"They gave you money," Volkovich said, "and you gave them the maps."

"Yes," Chaban said, sounding relieved to be understood.

"How? In a packet? A satchel?"

"Packet," Chaban said.

"Did they examine the maps?" Volkovich asked.

"The one who paid me, he gave them to the person behind him who looked but didn't take anything out of the packet. Then he nodded or she nodded—or that person nodded—or whatever, and then they all left."

"No more words were spoken?" Volkovich asked.

"They didn't say thank you if that's what you mean," Chaban said.

"Then how do you know you can contact them again?" Volkovich asked.

Cole had the same question.

Chaban swallowed yet again. Then chewed on his lip for a moment, and finally sighed heavily. "When he gave me the money, he said that it might be an overpayment, and if I came into anything else I should contact them, like I did before."

"You contacted them?" Cole asked, unable to hold back.

"The broker who was handling everything, he said he

knew them, and offered to contact them, but I told him to worry about the other things. I'll be honest. I didn't want to pay the commission."

Of course he didn't. Cole resisted the urge to roll his eyes. Chaban was sadly, disgustingly, predictable.

Chaban took a deep breath. "I looked at the information on his desk, and then I sent one of my men—"

"The ones you later fired?" Volkovich asked.

"I didn't fire anyone," Chaban said. "I let them go."

"That's a yes," Zubiri said to the fireplace.

As if the rest of them couldn't figure that out.

"The person you sent," Volkovich said, "did he continue to work for you after that?"

Chaban blinked as if he hadn't understood the question. Maybe he hadn't.

Cole found himself holding his breath.

"I—I—" Chaban said. "I don't know. I wasn't keeping track."

Volkovich shook his head ever so slightly, as if he couldn't believe what he heard.

"You sent someone with a message for that group, and then you didn't notice if that person returned?" Zubiri asked, looking over her shoulder. Her face was flushed from the fire's heat or maybe from her own reaction.

"The group, they came right away after that." Chaban's gaze danced nervously at Zubiri's face, and then flicked away.

Zubiri squinched her eyes. Her rage was palpable. "You fired someone after he did this thing for you? And you didn't even notice if he was still *alive* after talking to those people?"

Chaban inhaled sharply. He clearly hadn't thought of that.

Cole didn't want to explore that part of Chaban's character at all. So Cole spoke quickly.

"You still have the address, right?" Cole asked.

"I do," Chaban said. "I can take you there."

Zubiri turned all the way around, back to the fire. Kwin set his plate down again. Cole shifted. He was ready to go.

But Volkovich wasn't. He hadn't moved, and he remained intently focused on Chaban.

"One last question." Volkovich's tone was almost ominous. His voice wobbled as if he too was repressing fury.

Chaban glanced at the others, saw their collective mood, and looked at Volkovich as if he was Chaban's savior.

Volkovich leaned in. *"Did* they overpay you?"

"No," Chaban said quickly. "Of course not. We're almost out of money."

Zubiri groaned and looked away. Kwin bowed his head. Cole almost swore out loud.

Volkovich let out a small bitter laugh, as if he couldn't believe Chaban had just said that.

"One doesn't necessarily follow the other," Volkovich said.

"What?" Chaban said.

"They're the ones who decide if they overpaid you, not you," Zubiri snapped.

Chaban bit his lower lip. "I would have asked for more money."

"I'm sure you would have," Zubiri said, "if you had the maps."

"Did you tell them about the maps?" Volkovich asked.

Chaban shook his head. "Not Kirilli's maps, no. I haven't seen those people since they came to my house."

"'Not Kirilli's maps,'" Cole repeated. "So, what maps *did* you tell them about?"

Chaban's eyes widened, then he closed them, as if he couldn't believe he had blurted something he wanted to keep secret.

"Devin," Zubiri said, her voice low and menacing.

Chaban opened his eyes. His mouth was in a grim line.

"I told them we all had maps, every one of us. The Regents, and that there were some in the archives at the Academy, and I might've mentioned Kyra Row, but I think I said, Kyra Row Kirilli."

Kwin put a hand on his forehead. "Of course you did."

Cole frowned all of them. Every schoolchild had heard of Kyra Row. She had discovered a large cache of artifacts in the Forbidden Valley and had brought them back to Serebro Academy. Some accounts claimed she brought the items to Serebro Academy to keep from being fired. Others claimed she brought them because she didn't know what to do with them.

The details didn't really matter. The artifacts were beautiful. They had started the Forbidden Valley artifact craze that sent hundreds of people into the Valley to find more. The craze went beyond that, influencing fashion and home décor and so much more....

Until it became clear that the artifacts had some other purpose. Some accounts blame artifacts for the Thaumaturgical Purges. Other histories pointed to the tragedies behind

Row's discoveries. The first one, of some kind of cave, had led to the death of another scholar.

"You called her Kira Row Kirilli," Volkovich said in a flat voice.

"That's how my family knew her," Chaban said. "She used her married name with personal friends."

Kyra Row *Kirilli*. Cole had forgotten she had been married to a Kirilli. The man who had taken credit for many of her discoveries after her death. Some said he actually looted a lot of historical sites in the Forbidden Valley, sites that angered the locals there, and finally forced him to remain forever in Trinovante.

"A month ago," Kwin muttered. "You did this a month ago."

He shook his head, then looked directly at Volkovich, then Zubiri, and finally at Cole. Kwin's gaze seemed both powerful and sad.

"He told them a month ago," Kwin said, "mentioned Regents, and then mentioned Kirilli by name."

"*I did not!*" Chaban started to stand, but Volkovich raised one finger at him, and Chaban remained seated. "I didn't tell them about Augustus."

"You're so naïve," Cole said.

"Let's not get ahead of ourselves," Volkovich said. "For all we know, these people are nothing more than curiosity seekers. They buy collectibles, and bought some maps from Devin."

But it was clear from his dry flat tone that Volkovich didn't believe this any more than the rest of the group did.

"We'll visit them first," Volkovich said.

306

"And if they're killers?" Kwin asked.

"That's why we're bringing Xavier," Volkovich said.

"They didn't look like killers," Chaban offered.

No one acknowledged him.

"What do we do with him while we go to that address?" Zubiri asked.

"I think we divide this group in two," Volkovich said. "Some of us go to that address and the rest go to Chaban's house here in Serebro and look at his records."

"I want to go to the address," Cole said.

"So do I," Zubiri said.

"We can't all go," Volkovich said, "and I need to go."

"Why is that?" Zubiri asked, her chin out as if she expected to defy him.

"Because I have a working theory as to who these people are, and if I'm right, we're in trouble," Volkovich said.

"Aren't you going to enlighten us?" Cole asked.

Volkovich gave him a pitying glance. "If you haven't figured it out by now, you won't understand what I'm telling you. We'll deal with the details later."

"After we go with Xavier," Cole said.

Volkovich smiled, but the smile was cold. "After we go with Xavier," he said. "And not before."

PART FOUR
SEREBRO

THE
TURNOUT

SEREBRO
MOUNTAIN RANGE

CHAPTER
NINETEEN

The night had turned cold by the time Volkovich, Cole, and Xavier reached Serebro. The trip over the mountain road between Serebro Academy and the city itself had been difficult. The rain had been heavy, which meant that Cole had to put up the roof on the windstone vehicle to protect them all from getting wet.

Adding the roof also limited the visibility. The vehicle was so old that it was called a conveyance. The roof had been added later, and didn't fit that well. It leaked. Cole couldn't move away from the droplets. They felt like ice.

The conveyance was built like a horse-drawn cart, only instead of the open front with a bench and a harness and reins, the cart had dials and tubes and windstone innards. Cole had never driven anything like it before.

It had some quirks he didn't like. He had to turn on the lightstone headlamps with a turn of a dial. He had to switch gears manually, something he hadn't done in years, and he had to do it all on a dark mountain road in the pouring rain.

The rain stopped just before they drove over the foothills into the city. Large puddles, some the size of small lakes, covered many of the streets and had turned the dirt roads into mush. But that didn't make the driving any better. If anything, it made Cole more cautious.

He finally pulled the conveyance to the side of the road, despite the protests of his two passengers, and put the roof away. It was soggy. Just touching it made his hands feel like ice.

Volkovich had commandeered an automated conveyance from the Academy, although he did not know how to drive it. Cole did, and as the three of them carefully made their way through the darkened streets, he was beginning to think the only reason he had been allowed to come along was because he knew how to drive something powered by windstone.

Volkovich added to that supposition by casually telling Xavier that he didn't want horses anywhere near the address that Chaban had given them. Xavier had agreed. They either had to take a windstone vehicle or walk from the train station.

To get to the address, they would have had to walk three miles or more. They hadn't wanted to do that, and, given the kind of mission they were on, they couldn't hire a ride once they arrived in the city.

So they had had no choice. They needed the automated vehicle, and they needed Cole.

When both men spoke, which was not often during the

difficult drive, they seemed to use a kind of code, something that suggested a long close relationship. It hadn't been in evidence in the meeting, and maybe Cole was reading it wrong, but he had a feeling the two men knew what they were going to find, and they didn't seem willing to share that with him.

He didn't have much of a chance to ask, either, because driving took all of his concentration. The storm in the mountains had felt overpowering, and once he reached the city, dodging the puddles and avoiding the muddy roads was just as difficult.

It got worse as he drove closer to the address. He had heard that this part of the city was sketchy, and it certainly seemed that way. There were no lightstone street lamps, and half the buildings seemed to be in some form of disrepair—not that he could see them too clearly in the uneven darkness.

Every fifth building or so had an outdoor lamp, usually a torch encased in glass. The light flickered with the flame, illuminating an unpainted door beneath.

The flickering light was, in some ways, worse than the even light of a lightstone. The flickering created moving shadows that seemed to belong to people instead of buildings.

He squinted as he drove. He also went very slowly because he'd had to brake more than once, thinking he was about to run over a person when what he saw was just a moving shadow.

"The building should be one block away, on the left," Volkovich said. His voice, coming out of the darkness, startled Cole, and made him realize just how quiet the neighborhood was.

They were passing building after building, but the streets were empty and the windows dark. The only sound was the crunch of the conveyance's wheels on the gravel road.

"Water ahead," Xavier said.

He had said the same thing a good block away from water several times now. Cole had been unable to see the water, sometimes until they were right on top of it, but Xavier seemed to know it was coming.

He probably knew how to look for it, or, at least, that was what Cole told himself. Because other explanations— along with that color-shifting robe—made him nervous.

They didn't have any weapons. Cole had asked Volkovich if they needed any and Volkovich had given him that cold smile.

If I'm right, he had said, *the kind of weapons you and I can use would be useless.*

Cole was aware that Volkovich had been talking about only the two of them. What little Cole knew about Volkovich included the fact that Volkovich picked his words with precision. He had left out Xavier on purpose.

The conveyance bumped along. The road had gotten more and more uneven the farther they went. When they reached the corner, Cole turned left.

If anything, this street was darker than any of the other streets. He could barely make out the road ahead of him, and the buildings looked like outlines against the darkness.

"Slow down." Xavier sounded irritated.

314

If Cole went much slower, the conveyance would stop. But he didn't say that. He slowed down as much as he dared —and just in time.

The conveyance's wheels hit water so hard that the splash got his legs wet.

He turned slightly to make sure the other two were all right. Volkovich leaned slightly to the left, as if he could peer ahead. Xavier had pulled his robe up to his thighs and tucked it in around the seat. It looked gray in the darkness. He clutched his satchel to his chest. Clearly he did not want the satchel to get wet.

"Watch where you're going," Xavier snapped.

Cole wanted to snap back, *You're not the one driving*, but he didn't. People who didn't travel in windstone vehicles much did not understand that they had an ability to stay on the road even if the driver wasn't paying a lot of attention to his driving.

But Cole turned around anyway. The water poured over the wheels, but mostly remained trapped in the undercarriage. The bottom part of this conveyance was sealed, which was something that Cole had looked for.

Windstone worked just fine when it was wet, but the vents had a tendency to clog when the bottom of a vehicle left the windstone tubes open. The tubes in this vehicle were mounted high on the carriage and had a bit of a protective shell built in.

He would have told the others, if they had asked, that he wasn't worried about the vents clogging, but he would have been lying. They needed to get out of this water as soon as they could.

"There it is," Xavier said. "Stop now."

"I'm not stopping in this water," Cole said.

"That's what they want," he said. "Stop now."

"What?" Cole asked.

"Just trust him," Volkovich said. "This is why we brought him along."

For the very first time, Cole regretted not asking Volkovich why he had wanted Xavier along. Cole should have gotten the details. But he hadn't. Now he felt like a little kid in the face of adults who were talking about something that was over his head.

Still, Cole followed instructions and stopped the conveyance. Water sloshed around them and some seeped onto the floorboards. Cole's shoes were soaked. His trousers clung to his legs, sending a chill through him.

"Shut the conveyance off," Volkovich said.

The conveyance didn't really turn off and on. It could be started, but it wasn't like the lightstone lamps that needed some kind of device to activate them. Windstone needed wind. When the conveyances were not moving, there was no wind. The starter was one of the devices that Cole did not understand, but what he knew about them was that they differed from vehicle type to vehicle type, and yet they all had the same function: they propelled the windstone vehicle forward until the windstone caught.

To stop the vehicle, all he had to do was close the vents.

Which he did.

The conveyance rocked. The sloshing continued, and it was the only sound in the neighborhood.

Until the conveyance groaned. Then a pale silver light illuminated the area around the conveyance.

Cole turned, startled.

Xavier was standing on the seat, or so it seemed. His robe glowed ever so slightly. The light seemed to be coming from it.

"What is that?" Cole asked, not quite wanting to use the word *magic*, but afraid that was what he was seeing.

"Go to the door," Xavier said. He was still clutching the satchel.

"I can't see a door," Cole said. "I can't even see a building."

"You will be able to when you get there," Xavier said. His voice sounded just a little echoey, which was unnerving.

Cole looked at Volkovich, who was still seated. Xavier seemed to float behind him.

"What is this?" Cole asked him.

"The time for discussion was earlier," Volkovich said. "Just do as he asks."

"If something happens to me," Cole said, "you won't be able to get back to the Academy."

"We will be fine," Volkovich said. Not *you* will be fine. *We* will be fine.

Cole felt a surge of irritation, which he suspected was covering a vast amount of fear. He levered himself out of the bench at the front of the conveyance, and braced himself. He was about to land in waist-deep water.

He swung himself forward like he always did when getting out of a vehicle like this and prayed that there was nothing under the water, like a berm or a hole that would catch and twist his legs.

Then he vaulted toward the darkness.

He expected to splash in the deep water. Instead, his shoes landed in muck, but the area around him was dry. There was no deep lake of rainwater. The muck was the only evidence it had been there.

A shiver that had nothing to do with the ice-cold air ran down his spine.

"The water's gone," he said as if it was Xavier's fault there had been water at all.

"Go to the door," Xavier repeated in that slightly echoey tone. "And knock."

Knock. What did Xavier think Cole would do when he got to a door, kick it open?

Then Cole took a deep breath of the frozen air and felt it chill his body all the way down his rib cage. He was angry. He was terrified. And apparently, he was the one they were going to sacrifice should something go awry.

If someone had asked him earlier what could go awry, he would have said nothing—except maybe that they wouldn't get the maps back.

But now, he had a feeling that he didn't understand anything, and that simple fact might just cost him his life.

He wished he had some sort of weapon now.

He had a hunch he was going to need it.

THE
TURNOUT

SEREBRO
MOUNTAIN RANGE

CHAPTER
TWENTY

The carriage stopped at the top of the mountain and rocked just a little. Lumin hated this type of conveyance, but he had never let his people ride in windstone vehicles. None of his Spies had discovered how those vehicles worked, which led Lumin to believe they were powered by magick, even though the Qavnerians seemed to believe the vehicles were some kind of scientifically designed technology.

The night was cold and damp. The rain had left a humid residue that made the air actually feel wet. Lumin wasn't sure if that residue was caused by his own Weather Sprites, who had augmented the rain all week, or if that residue was a normal part of this part of Qavner.

The clouds had been full, coming off the Infrin Sea, but that had only helped make the rain even stronger. They were planning ground fog for the upcoming attack, and had been overjoyed that their work on the rain hadn't taken as much of their energy as planned.

The carriage behind Lumin's eased to a stop as well. There was a little turnout here. Veil, the Spy who had spent the most time at Serebro Academy, had recommended this stop, and Lumin had agreed on its necessity when Veil explained what would happen here.

The turnout overlooked the entire valley below, the one where centuries ago, the Qavnerians had built their first, and most important, academy.

Lumin could feel the history of this place, and he hadn't even gotten out of the carriage yet.

The carriage ride was not something he wanted to repeat, but he hadn't wanted his Enchanter to use a portal. Too many of his troop would have to go through it. Portals worked for limited distances, but became ineffective or just plain dangerous at long distances.

There was enough danger in this particular mission; the last thing he wanted was to increase that danger.

Still, the carriages were problem enough, right from the beginning. The driver of his carriage, a man named Albert, had squinted at the entire troop with great suspicion.

What're you lot headin' to the Academy fer at this time'a night? he'd asked when he had showed up and parked the carriage in front of the new rental home. The rental wasn't that impressive, and Lumin thought that perhaps Albert felt that it showed that Lumin and his troop couldn't pay for the carriage.

So he had Calla, one of the Domestics, hand Albert payment for the entire trip. Calla, in addition to her

Domestic and Healing skills, had just a tiny bit of Charm, enough that she could make someone like recalcitrant carriage driver change his mind and think it was his idea.

Albert had stared at the coins as if there was something wrong with them. Then he had peered at her. For a moment, Lumin had thought Albert wasn't going to succumb to the Charm, which meant he had a bit of magick of his own.

But he pocketed the coins before his partners with the other carriage had even arrived, and then shrugged one shoulder.

Guess it'd be none of my business ta know what yer doin. I'll get ya there, but then I'm headin straight back here. 'Tis late, and I will have work in the morning.

Charm. It was such a useful magick. Apparently, after Calla touched him, Albert no longer thought of the carriage ride over the Serebro Mountains work, at least for this particular trip.

But Lumin had Calla sit on one side of Albert, just in case. Veil should have sat there, because he was the one who had found the man, but Calla turned out to be much more useful.

The carriages were the largest available. They were pulled by a team of four horses, because, Veil had been told, the carriages usually brought people planning to stay at the Academy for months, and those people had massive trunks of luggage.

Albert had thought it odd that this group had very little luggage. Veil had told them that the group would only be at the Academy for a few days, and didn't need much.

Veil had anticipated a problem like this, though. Very

few people traveled in groups to Serebro Academy, and certainly did not do so without luggage. So Veil had sent the third spy in the troop, Stante, to buy a large trunk like the ones students usually used. The troop had filled it with weapons that the six Infantry thought might be helpful.

Lumin also had them bring a few clothing items, and he had packed them in a valise that the troop had used before. He figured it couldn't hurt for his Spies to make their way around campus dressed as much like students as possible.

He already had one Spy there. Gray would meet them later in the evening and tell them what he had learned.

Lumin got out of his carriage, happy to be standing outside, despite the dampness. The air was so wet that very small drops of water formed on his skin. He had experienced this before in actual fog, but he hadn't experienced it on a night with wind and clouds scuttling across the moon.

The turnout was wide enough for both carriages and their horses. The horses smelled, and one had already taken a dump. They seemed restless, maybe because they knew about their fate.

Lumin hated horses, and hated traveling this way, but had seen no other real choice. Still, being downwind from the horses throughout the entire ride over the mountain pass had been unpleasant, to say the least.

He had kept the carriage windows closed, which made the interior a bit close. There had been five troop members inside of a carriage built comfortably for four.

In addition to Calla outside, two Infantry stood in the back, their feet on a running board and their hands gripping the luggage rack on top. Apparently, the carriages had initially been designed for guards to ride on the back, so the extra weight didn't seem to make much of a difference to the way the carriage rode, although, Lumin figured, the lack of heavy luggage probably helped.

The horses had still struggled to get the carriage up a few of the steeper inclines. Albert had warned Lumin that the curvy downhill road to the Academy would be even harder on the horses, and had hinted that maybe some of the stronger and larger members of the troop could walk that downhill stretch.

It was, apparently, only a few miles long.

Lumin looked down at that stretch now, and saw that there were fewer trees than he expected. The entire ride to this point had been along a narrow road paved with some kind of stone, carved through what looked like a forest.

Some of the trees had towered over them, and others had branches so long they had brushed the side of the carriage. After a few moments like that, Lumin wondered if his people on the back of both carriages were getting scratched up.

He had to believe they had been smart enough to move away from the branches as they slapped against the carriage sides.

The road ahead curved and then disappeared into the darkness. That was the other issue: this passage had been very dark, something Albert and Darby, the other carriage driver, had fretted about.

Because Lumin had been very adamant about one thing. He wanted carriages without lightstone lanterns attached to the sides and front.

Ye want old carriages, then? I canna guarantee their condition, Albert had said. *We dinna maintain 'em the way we do the new ones.*

One of our people will inspect them, Lumin had said in that single conversation he'd had with Albert before embarking on this journey.

And one of Lumin's people had. Thread had looked at the carriages, using tiny bits of Domestic magick to fix any cracks and to shore up the undercarriages to make sure the vehicles themselves were strong enough to handle the weight and the journey.

I hadna traveled in such dark in years, Albert had said when Lumin repeated, yet again, that he did not want lightstone anywhere near them.

Then use other kinds of lanterns, Lumin had said. *My people do not like lightstone.*

Yer people, Albert had repeated. *Yer people ain't from around here, now are they?*

Lumin could have answered that with some kind of self-serving lie, but he saw no reason to do so. Strangers who weren't "from here" came to the Academy all the time.

He hadn't been certain of that at first, thinking most of the students came from Serebro and Trinovante. Gray had disabused him of that notion. And then Lumin had learned that Perdu had had a choice of three different visiting professors as hosts. Perdu had chosen one, although only the Spies knew now who Perdu was. One of the few problems with Doppelgängers outside of war. It wasn't always clear who they had overtaken because communication could sometimes be difficult.

None of us are from around here, Lumin had said to Albert. *We're visiting from up north and we've been invited to see the Academy.*

Albert had looked as if he hadn't believed any of that, leading Lumin to think that maybe he wasn't as good a liar as he had thought.

Not that it mattered. Some of Albert's skepticism could be bought off with even more coin.

On this night, Albert had brought two oil lamps, but hadn't lit them.

For emergencies, he had said. He had packed them in some kind of box and kept them beneath his seat, worried that they'd overturn. The last thing he wanted, he said, was to ride in a carriage covered with liquid that could burn if touched by the smallest spark.

Lumin empathized with that. He didn't want to travel in any conveyance like that either. Riding on a hard wooden seat, squeezed between two overly large Infantry, had been bad enough. The three of them would sway as a unit every single time the carriage hit some kind of dip in the road— and there had been too many of those for comfort.

Lumin walked to the edge of the turnout. They were still pretty high in the air. The buildings below seemed small and almost insignificant.

He was not looking forward to that walk into the valley.

The valley spread before him, filled with flickering lights. It took a moment for his eyes to adjust. He had seen versions of this image before, in some of the tapestries that the group had purchased, as well as some paintings in buildings around Serebro.

The layout was familiar from the non-magickal maps he had studied before bringing the troop here. The Academy and its various outbuildings and support buildings filled the valley. He knew there was housing here for professors and staff, as well as gardens and shops that catered directly to them.

Most of the shops were on the west side of the valley, in the foothills of the coastal mountain range. The apartments and professorial homes were on the east, often with a view of the Tamsi, which was the name the Hidden River had in this part of Qavner.

His eye went to the Old Campus, which Veil had said housed the most artifacts. From up here, Lumin could see the outlines of the fortress that had been built in the valley long before anyone had thought of placing a school here.

In its day, the fortress must have been huge. He counted at least seven ancient stone towers, four that formed a large square. Veil said inside that square was the Old Library, which had nooks and crannies and storage areas.

There was another section of the fortress, even though it no longer looked like it ever been directly attached to the main part. A tall tower rose in the night sky. The tallest tower, according to Veil, was the Regents Tower, which was used only by the Board of Regents, whom some said were the most powerful people in the Protectorate.

Lumin didn't see that. It made no sense to him. The two Regents he had met (one accidentally) had seemed like scared, greedy politicians, more concerned with their own livelihood than anything to do with these schools or with the Protectorate itself.

But Lumin did not understand this culture. It wasn't his job to understand it in depth, anyway. His job was to figure out how it used magick, what kinds of magick could harm the Fey, and how to neutralize it.

Sometimes he believed that part of his job would be easy; the Qavnerians had neutralized a lot of the magick on this continent all by themselves.

But the more he was learning about these artifacts, the more he worried. They seemed to be everywhere, left behind by people who had known how they worked or inherited by people who didn't.

Some of the magick was inexplicable to him, like windstone, lightstone, and ironwood. But he had been around long enough and had traveled enough through the Fey Empire to know that magick came in many forms, some of them specific to the culture itself.

From above, the campus looked small, the buildings tight together. Veil had said otherwise. He had said there were trees everywhere, and wide paths that led to every building.

The thing that had bothered her the most, she said, were the students. They seemed to study at all hours. Many campus buildings, including the Old Library, never closed. Someone was in them at all times.

That was why Lumin had sent Shyly with a specific order: to become a librarian and figure out how to get them inside that building. There were magick books in there as well as histories that he wanted, so that he could give Rugar the fullest report possible.

The one building that Lumin couldn't see clearly, and

wasn't sure how to approach, was the building that specialized in what Qavnerians called Thaumaturgy and Alchemy. They mingled it with Science, which made sense, since much of their so-called technology seemed to have a magickal component.

It required special permission to go into that building. Perdu did not have it, and Veil had been unable to acquire it. What he had learned, though, had calmed Lumin somewhat.

He had learned that the Academy no longer gave full-throated support to the Thaumaturgy and Alchemy Departments, had even tried to shut them down at one point. Most of the artifacts in those departments, she had been told, had been moved to the Old Library or destroyed.

He had been unable to verify that information, which was why Shyly was so important. She would give what she had discovered to Gray, who would then lead them to the artifacts, if, indeed, they still existed.

Lumin bounced on the balls of his feet just once, before he realized that his troop would see that as nerves.

Most of them had climbed out of the carriages or off the back. Someone had pulled down the trunk, which was probably a mistake. Albert was watching them all from beside his horses, feeding them whatever it was that horses ate, and trying to calm them.

There was tension up here, and it wasn't just from Lumin.

Eerie approached him, recognizable even in the darkness because of her height and extreme thinness. She looked more at home here among the trees, as if she had been bred for the country rather than any city.

The light from the valley below gave her face a grayish-silver pallor. Her eyes looked bigger than usual, and her mouth was a thin line.

"Something's wrong," she said when she reached him.

He hoped no one else had heard. Everyone else was still near the carriages. He had planned to call them all over, so that they could see what was below, but he had been too lost in his own thoughts.

"Keep your voice down," he said as quietly as he could.

Her eyes narrowed. She stopped beside him and looked into the valley.

"We're not used to this place," he said. "So thinking something's wrong—"

"Back in Serebro," she said. "Something is happening."

He frowned at her. He hadn't even thought of the city. It meant little. They had moved to a new rental because no one wanted to live so close to those artifacts. The artifacts remained at the apartments, and were spilling over into the first and third apartments.

They had acquired a lot of Dorovician magick and it was starting to impinge on all of them. They were having dreams that didn't feel like their own. They were nervous when they shouldn't have been. And then the Domestics claimed their magick had become weaker.

That was when Lumin decided they'd keep the apartments, but they would move to the other side of Serebro, to be as far from the Dorovician magic as they could be.

Eerie had set up protections near the apartments, wards mostly, that would enable her to see or know if someone approached. The Weather Sprites had added their own spells, making it difficult to travel down the nearby roads, mostly by giving them the illusion of flooding—which, they claimed, was easy to do as long as they were increasing the rain in the entire area.

"What do you mean, something is happening?" Lumin asked.

Eerie wrapped her arms around herself as if she was cold. "Someone is neutralizing our wards."

"What?" he asked.

She had spoken softly, so he wasn't sure he had heard her correctly.

"Someone knows how to see through what we've done," she said. "And stop the wards from working."

He didn't ask how she knew this. One of the reasons behind any kind of ward was so that the creator would know if someone had been harmed by it or had breached it.

"Qavnerians don't have that kind of magick, do they?" he asked.

She let out an exasperated sigh. "That is what we assumed when we came here. But the death of Hadley should have taught us that these people are not what we expected."

Lumin shifted from foot to foot. He didn't like to think about the terror he had felt during that series of Visions, particularly the one where Atrü was holding the dying Hadley in his arms. It had been a warning, then, as well as informational.

Lumin did not like that.

"Do you think it's the same people in Serebro?" he

asked. "Have they found us? Has someone told them about us?"

She shrugged, still staring at that valley. "I don't know."

If so, it added to the urgency. He would need to gather what information he could, and then they would have to leave. He would have to figure out how to get his entire troop back to Nye.

He rubbed his hands together. They were getting cold.

He wasn't going to be able to bring back everything from this place. He needed to make some decisions going in, and figure out exactly what to do with the Dorovician magick he was finding.

He had hoped to keep from making that decision now. But this might be the only chance he would get to visit this campus—at least without anyone knowing he was here.

He needed to gather information and he needed to see what the Dorovicians could do.

That might be too much for a single night, a single visit.

But he would do his best.

THE
TURNOUT

SEREBRO
MOUNTAIN RANGE

CHAPTER

TWENTY-ONE

The street was still eerily quiet. Cole couldn't even hear Volkovich or Xavier moving in the conveyance. That vehicle had moaned a lot during the drive here. It should have been making some slight sounds as the two of them moved inside of it.

Cole cast about the edge of the road, looking for the outline of a building, but seeing nothing but darkness.

"I don't see a building," he said, feeling nervous, "and I don't see a door."

"You're facing in the right direction." This time Volkovich answered him. "Just walk. You'll see the building shortly."

Just walk. *You walk*, Cole wanted to say, but he didn't. Somehow he had gotten himself into this thing, and he was going to finish it. Besides, he needed to move or his legs would begin trembling from the chill. He already felt colder than he had since the previous winter.

335

He tried to walk forward, but the muck held his shoes tightly. He had to physically grab himself under the thigh and pick up his right foot with the added leverage of his hands, something he hadn't done since he was a child playing alongside muddy riverbanks.

The foot came free with a sucking sound. He nearly left the shoe behind. He leaned onto the foot, and expected a similar problem with his other foot, but it came out of the muck easily.

The muck wasn't as deep here. After he had taken three steps, there was no muck at all, just a path so hard that it felt like rain hadn't fallen for weeks.

He looked down. He was walking on dirt. There wasn't any greenery around the path he was on. Nor was the path made of stone. Just a flat brown area that had been used as the way to a door, apparently.

The fact that he could see it finally registered. It was lighter here than it had been on the street.

He turned around and saw the glow from Xavier's robe, but little else. The conveyance was as lost to the darkness as the buildings around here were.

Then he turned back. A row of buildings seemed to have appeared out of nowhere, although it was evident from their slightly dilapidated condition that they had been here for years.

Something about the street accentuated the darkness. Now that he was no longer on the street, he could see.

His stomach clenched. He turned again, half afraid he would find himself alone here. But Xavier's robe was a pale beacon against the dark.

Cole shuddered. He didn't like any of this. His father's voice rose in his mind.

If you ever experienced real magic, you'd understand some of the fear behind the Purges.

Cole had argued with him: of course Cole had seen magic. Hadn't everyone? Small things, like making a coin disappear or watching a robe change color.

But there was nothing small here. The air itself felt pregnant with power. And he was walking into it alone.

He almost called out to Volkovich and Xavier, but he didn't. Not because he was afraid of what they would think of him, but because he wasn't sure what he would do if they didn't answer.

He faced the building again. One of the doors in the row had an oil lantern over the door, but it was halfway down the block. Not at all the place that Xavier had indicated.

If the door a few steps in front of Cole was the address he'd been looking for, then there had never been a lantern above it. The door was badly built, too small for its frame. It was almost as if someone had substituted a different door for the original.

There were no stairs, but someone had built a small wooden porch in front of the building. As he got closer, he realized that each doorway was blocked off by two small walls, one on each side of the entry, making the porch mostly impossible to use.

The two doors on either side of the small door had plants growing in that tiny entry space, but this door had nothing. Not even some kind of mat for wiping off dirty feet.

And, he realized, the wood was not wet. Nothing here was wet.

He resisted the urge to look up. He made himself focus on the door.

He realized he was breathing shallowly, because he was so very terrified of what he would find here.

His feet made no sound on the wood, though, and that was because of the mud on his shoes. He had never thought of that mud as protective, but apparently it had that blessed side effect.

He stopped in front of the door and listened.

The building itself seemed silent. He could hear his own breathing, ragged and somewhat shaky, but nothing else. His heart was pounding in his chest.

He hadn't been this unnerved in years—maybe ever.

He balled his right hand into a fist and raised it, slowly, to the cockeyed door. The wood was thin and weather-beaten. It looked like he would get a sliver just from touching it.

"Hello?" he said as loudly as he could. "Anyone home?"

His voice echoed down the entire neighborhood, and then faded into the unnatural quiet. He exhaled, his breath visible in the chill. It had gotten noticeably colder—and the air felt alive than it had a few moments earlier.

That door looked like it was underwater. It wavered, as if someone had disturbed the water image.

He glanced over his shoulder, but didn't see the conveyance. Even the light from Xavier's strange robe seemed to have vanished.

Cole winced. He didn't want to do this, but he had to

know if someone was inside and watching him. He rapped the knuckles of his right forefingers on the wood.

It was soft and mushy and sure enough, he barely avoided getting a sliver.

"Hello?" he called again. "Anyone there?"

The wood vibrated beneath his feet. The building looked like it expanded, and a fetid smell—almost like swamp gas—enveloped him. The smell turned his already sensitive stomach.

He couldn't go inside if he wanted to—which he most decidedly did not.

He turned, wiping his knuckles on his pants, wishing he hadn't touched anything when something sucked the air out of his lungs, making his chest feel like it was collapsing in on itself.

He couldn't gasp. His throat was tight, his chest ached, and his eyes watered.

He scurried away from that building, even though it hurt to move. He thought he was going to pass out from lack of air, but he managed to stagger forward.

He only managed a few steps when something whomped behind him. The sound was visceral, knocking him off his feet. He landed on the dirt, which was cold but not wet. The impact would have knocked the breath out of him if there had been any breath to knock.

The entire sky filled with silver light, and suddenly the air came back. He took a grateful gasping breath. His chest still hurt, and his eyes watered, and he felt like he would never be able to breathe properly again.

But that horrid smell was gone.

His ears rang from the whomping sound, and, he realized his entire body ached from the fall. He wanted to push himself up, but he wasn't able to.

Nothing worked. And the air had gotten warm, stuffy, almost hot. The silver light was blinding him. Now he couldn't see the building or the street because there was too much light, not too little.

He was able to take another breath, and then another, and after the third, his chest stopped feeling like something had slammed into it. He was lightheaded, and his eyes ached from the bright light, but he felt noticeably better.

He pushed himself into a sitting position, then looked for the conveyance. But he couldn't see anything through that light.

He reached a shaky hand out and shoved his right finger into the brightest part of the light. It vanished with an audible *pop*, leaving him unable to see anything except squiggly lines across his eyes, lines that remained even when he squeezed his eyes closed.

"Pasha?" he yelled. "Xavier?"

But no one answered him. He was completely alone.

THE
TURNOUT

SEREBRO
MOUNTAIN RANGE

TWENTY-TWO

Eerie was shifting uncomfortably beside Lumin, as if something was pinging at her magick. He didn't want to know what was happening in Serebro. He couldn't do anything about it.

He had just reached the main decision point in this trip, and he was dithering.

His troop needed to get to the Academy. They would walk down the last bit of the mountain, but the return would be trickier. He had already primed Eerie to open a portal, getting everyone back here, to the carriages.

There were two problems with that. The first was that he had no idea where they would portal out of the Academy. The second was the drivers. They would have to wait with their horses.

He doubted they would. And they wouldn't know what to do if the troop emerged from some portal, or even from a few yards down the road, carrying artifacts.

He had designed two hand signals that he would use with Hardin, the leader of the six Infantry members of this troop. One signal would tell Hardin to prepare his team for a walk. The other would tell Hardin to get rid of the drivers.

The air seemed to be drying out. The two Weather Sprites were leaning against each other, as if they were suffering some of the same problems that Eerie was.

Lumin took one last look at the lights below him. There were a lot of people in that valley, more than he expected. A lot of buildings as well. This really shouldn't be a one-time visit, but he had no idea how to get into and out of this place more than once.

Maybe he would tell Rugar that any Fey invasion needed to conquer the Academy first. Gray and Veil had both said there was almost no Qavnerian military here, and the ones who were stationed nearby were either professors who had left their military careers or very young cadets, finishing up one part of their education before they got sent to parts of the Protectorate where, Gray said, there was often a lot of unrest.

If Lumin were a different person, he would send someone to investigate the unrest. That might be something else that Rugar could exploit when (or if) he decided to invade Dorovich.

But Lumin was tiring of this assignment. It was bigger than he expected, and the Academy below was just one example. He wanted to report to Rugar now.

Maybe Lumin would, after this particular mission was over. Because they weren't going to be able to eradicate magick from Dorovich. It was too embedded. And they weren't going to be able to fully understand it, because the Qavnerian Protectorate had tried to destroy it.

It might take decades to understand this place, at least well enough to be successful here. Rugar's dreams of conquest might just be that: dreams.

Lumin needed to stop looking at that valley. He was seeing it as one large unit instead of—

Eerie let out a small yelp and grabbed his arm so tightly that it pinched. Then she lost her balance and sank to her knees, nearly yanking him with her.

The Weather Sprites yelped at the same time, and bent over, hands to their heads.

The horses spooked, and the drivers ran toward them, working to keep them under control.

Lumin couldn't do anything about that. Eerie's grasp had grown even tighter. She was holding onto him as if he was the only thing solid in her world.

He had to crouch down beside her to keep her from pulling him over. She was moaning. He couldn't look at his troop right now, or do anything for his Weather Sprites.

He didn't even know what was wrong. This time, he wasn't getting a Vision or even a feeling.

He half-expected her to start spewing blood. He wasn't sure that was what had happened to Hadley, but he was certain something had. He didn't know if in the beginning, it had looked like this.

Eerie was making strange sounds that he was slowly beginning to realize were words. Something about powers and links and disturbances. He probably should have leaned closer, but he felt as if he was too close already. He didn't want whatever was happening to her to happen to him.

And now, Calla was beside him. He wasn't sure how she had gotten there, but he hadn't been monitoring anyone else. She put her hands on Eerie's shoulders, forcing her upright, then touched her face.

"You're here," Calla said. "You're all right."

Tears were running down Eerie's face. She had stopped talking, though. She took a deep breath and seemed calmer.

"What about the Sprites?" Lumin asked.

"Thread has them," Calla said curtly.

Thread's healing magick wasn't as strong as Calla's, so the fact that Thread was caring for them either meant that Calla didn't think they were in as much trouble as Eerie or that the Domestics believed saving the Enchanter was the most important thing they could do.

"What is it?" Lumin asked. "What happened?"

Eerie turned her head. For a moment, her expression was almost slack. Then her eyes found his. He watched with surprise as they focused.

It was almost as if she was returning to herself.

She licked her lips, then with the back of her free hand, wiped her face. She still gripped Lumin's arm, as if he was the only one who could keep her steady.

"The wards," she said.

He waited. So did Calla, who had stopped working on Eerie and leaned back to listen.

"They're gone," Eerie whispered.

"Which wards?" he asked. There were two sets. The ones around their current residence, which was, at the moment, empty, and the ones around the old residence, including the artifacts.

"The old..."

She shook her head.

"You don't have to say anything." Calla shot him a look, one that was filled with fury. She clearly felt like he was interfering with whatever she was trying to do to help Eerie.

But Eerie ignored her.

"The artifacts," Eerie said. "They're gone."

"Stolen?" Lumin asked.

Calla shot him a second look, this time with eyes wide, as if to say, *Shut up*. He ignored that.

"No..." Eerie's voice trailed off. "Magick..."

Her fingers dug even deeper into his arm. He waited. He had a lot of questions, but he didn't dare prompt, not with Calla's glare and Eerie's lack of focus.

Eerie blinked hard, frowned, and then a tear trailed down one cheek.

"They have an Enchanter," she said.

"In Trinovante. We know," Lumin said. "We encountered her—"

"No." Eerie's voice rose. "A different one. Maybe even— I don't know."

Lumin made himself breathe. He could see his breath. It had gotten that cold.

Two Enchanters. One in Trinovante, one in Serebro. He would have thought they were the same person, but that wasn't what Eerie just said.

Two Enchanters with a lot of power.

"Was this deliberate?" he asked, not sure what *this* even was.

"Give her a minute," Calla snapped.

"We might not have a minute," Lumin said. "If I don't know what's happening, then I can't take any kind of action."

Eerie's fingers loosened. "It's..." She didn't seem to have the words. She raised a single finger, which was probably the equivalent of saying, *Just a minute.*

If she felt they had a minute, then they might be all right.

"Hey, there." Albert's voice drifted over from the carriages. "Yer spookin' the horses."

Fury rose inside Lumin. He didn't want to deal with the Qavnerian drivers at the moment.

He didn't respond.

Eerie removed her hand from his arm, and he resisted the urge to massage the skin. It throbbed where she had dug her fingers in.

"Enchanter," she said again, softer this time. "At least one."

He waited. So did Calla, as if, perhaps, what Eerie had to say would help Calla calm her.

"Their magick hit the wards, and it caused...I don't know. But the artifacts, they're gone now."

"Taken?" Lumin repeated.

"There was an explosion." Eerie closed her eyes, then abruptly opened them as if she didn't like what happened when she did that.

"You Saw it?" Part of him felt jealous. Enchanters rarely

had Visions, and if they were party to any Vision, it was almost always an Open Vision.

"No," Eerie said. "No. Not a Vision. I felt it. The fingers in my magick, the wards dissolving, the magick leaching, and then—oh."

That last was an exhalation, almost as if she was releasing an internal poison.

Calla leaned closer, ready to do...something...to help with the healing.

"If I had been there," Eerie said, "I would have died."

Her tone was not matter-of-fact, which surprised him. Usually she described harrowing things flatly, as if they had had no impact on her. This apparently hurt.

"Because of the magick?" he asked.

"Because of the power. It should have killed whoever did this." She glanced at Calla, who was still waiting, but for what Lumin didn't know.

"Maybe it did," Lumin said.

"No one died," Eerie said. "I would have known."

She sat down, as if her knees ached. Calla moved closer, but Eerie waved her off.

"We're outclassed, Lumin," Eerie said. "Their Enchanter. This one, he's Black King quality."

Lumin knew what she meant. Some Enchanters were so powerful, they would only work with the Black Family. Eerie was not that good, and Hadley hadn't been either.

No one who had come to Dorovich had that kind of magick.

"We lost all of our artifacts?" he asked.

She nodded. "If we'd been there, we might all have died."

"So you think the attack was deliberate?" he asked.

"No," she said, "that's what scares me. This was an accident. They didn't know we were there."

Calla's gaze met his. He could feel her fear. Or maybe it was his own.

"What'll they do if they find us?" Calla asked.

"The same thing that happened in Trinovante," Eerie said. "Or maybe worse."

She touched the sore spot on Lumin's arm.

"We have to leave," she said.

"Now?" he asked.

She waved a hand at the valley around them. "Not here. Dorovich. We have to leave."

He nodded. "I've been thinking the same thing. Can we finish tonight?"

"And do what? Steal those artifacts? There's nowhere to put them," Eerie said.

"The Enchanter is in Serebro," Lumin said. "There are none here, right?"

"How would I know?" Eerie asked. "I can't sense them. We're not Linked."

He glanced at that valley. The lights flickered as if they were winking at him slyly.

He had two Doppelgängers and a Spy in that valley. He could leave them, he supposed, but what would it gain anyone?

It would be better to find out the information about the Academy, maybe take important items, like maps—if, indeed, they showed magick the way that Gray suspected, and then figure out how to get back to Nye.

A few maps, a lot of reports, that would make for a successful mission. Rugar wouldn't want to hear everything they had to say, but their report would save lives.

If they retreated now, everything would be guesswork. Lumin wasn't sure they had enough time to do more than guess, but going to the Academy would at least give them a chance at knowledge.

And then his breath caught as the implications of what Eerie said hit him.

"We know there are artifacts in that valley," he said, shifting slightly. He wasn't used to crouching this long. "Can you mingle your magick with them? Make them ignite?'

Calla was shaking her head. "Do you know how many people are down there?" she asked. "And some of them are ours."

Lumin felt a surge of irritation. This was why Visionaries never planned battles around Domestics. She couldn't be a part of any destruction anyway or she would lose her magick.

"You can leave," he said.

"I don't think—"

"*Leave,*" he said.

Calla touched Eerie's arm. "I'll be over there." Calla nodded toward the carriages. Or maybe the Sprites.

Lumin didn't follow the movement. He didn't want to know where she was.

"Mayhap ye can help w'the horses," Albert said. He was clearly listening, although Lumin didn't know how. There must have been some kind of echo in this turnout.

Calla looked startled. Eerie didn't seem to notice. She was staring into the valley.

"Go to the Sprites," Lumin said. He would deal with the drivers in a moment.

Calla nodded, and stood up, touching Eerie's arm one more time.

Then Calla walked behind the carriages, so that she didn't go near the drivers. She clearly didn't want to help them with anything.

Eerie shook her head once, then frowned, as if she was having some kind of internal discussion.

"The artifacts," she said quietly. "That wasn't me."

"I know," Lumin said. "It was the intersection of the magick. If you can create something like that—"

"No," she said so curtly that he wanted to snap at her. No one talked to a Leader that way. At least not a real Leader. "It wasn't me."

It took him a moment—again—to figure out what she was saying. "The intersection of the magicks didn't cause this?" he asked. "But that was what you said."

"Oh, it caused something," she said. "That's why I could feel it."

She threaded her fingers together, then pulled them apart, as if she couldn't keep still.

"Lumin, I don't think this was an accident after all."

He was beginning to get whiplash. "You said it was."

"But the more I think about it," she said, "the more I think I was wrong."

Lumin almost sat on the ground, then realized it was still

wet from all the rain. He put two fingers down just to keep himself balanced.

"What was it, then?" he asked.

"I think, maybe, it was deliberate," she said.

"Deliberate how?" he asked.

"That the intersection of the magick started something —and the person who started it didn't stop it."

This wasn't Lumin's kind of magick and he had never finished all of the Leadership training he could have taken. He should have known exactly how all the other magick in his troop worked. The Black King most certainly did.

"Meaning what?" Lumin asked.

"I think that they wanted me to die," she said quietly.

"An assassination attempt?" he asked.

"Not as deliberate," she said. "Like a fire that could be contained but was allowed to get out of control."

"So they knew we're here," he said.

"It was probably hard to miss with the wards," she said.

He nodded. He figured it was only a matter of time before the Dorovicians realized that there were Fey among them.

"It doesn't matter," he said.

"That they figured us out?" she asked.

"Well, they didn't really," he said. "We're still here. They took advantage of an opportunity. Maybe we can too."

"What do you mean?" she asked.

"We now know those artifacts can work together to create some kind of explosion."

She looked away from the valley, but didn't look at him. Instead, she bowed her head.

"Just because we know you can do something doesn't mean we'll know how to do it," she said.

"Right now," he said, "it shouldn't stop us from trying."

She raised her head. Her gaze met his. Finally, she was completely back in her eyes. The expression, flat and determined, was much more terrifying than anything he had ever seen from her.

"You're right," she said. "We need to remove as much of their magick as we can. And we need to do it tonight."

THE
TURNOUT

SEREBRO
MOUNTAIN RANGE

CHAPTER
TWENTY-THREE

Cole tried again. "Pasha? Xavier?"

Cole's voice echoed around him, as if he were in an empty room made of marble. Sweat ran down one side of his face—at least, he hoped it was sweat. The chill air seemed to be gone, replaced by humid air.

He was sitting on that hard path, his eyes still adjusting after he somehow popped that bright light with his finger. His fingertip ached, as if he had touched something hot.

But it hadn't felt that way when he poked at it...or had it? Had he simply not registered the pain? That wouldn't surprise him, after everything that had just happened.

He had never been in an explosion before. He'd read about them in his history classes, the way that they disoriented the person who had survived it, but he didn't believe he was disoriented.

Except that he wasn't sure where the street was or if the

building was behind him. He knew he hadn't imagined that bright light because it still hurt his eyes.

His ears rang, and for the first time, he wondered if he couldn't hear Volkovich or Xavier because his own ears were reacting to the explosion, rather than the fact that he was alone.

Alone, and blinded, almost literally, by that light. And then unable to hear.

He blinked. The squiggles from the light were easing, but he still couldn't see clearly. Maybe he was inside that full dark again. He had no idea.

He decided to try again.

"Pasha?" he yelled. "Xavier?"

"This way," Volkovich's voice sounded faint, but Cole wasn't sure if that was because Volkovich was far away or because Cole's hearing was still compromised.

This way was a particularly useless answer. Especially since Cole didn't know where he was, let alone where anyone else was.

He blinked again, willing his vision to work. He turned slightly, and finally saw the conveyance. It was parked in the middle of the empty—and dry—road.

Neither man was inside.

"Where are you?" he asked.

"This way," Volkovich repeated unhelpfully.

Cole swiveled his head around and gasped. The building had been destroyed. The walls had caved in on themselves. The roof was gone. The door had landed, intact, only a few feet from him.

If he had been closer, that door would have hit him, and he would have died.

Lights still flared in his vision, but not as badly. Cole could identify them now as flashes, caused by the explosion.

He made himself concentrate and look beyond them.

Volkovich was picking his way across a debris field, his white-blond hair reflecting light from a partially full moon. Cole looked up. Dark clouds floated across that moon, making it and the stars visible for a few moments before covering them again.

"Are you all right?" Volkovich asked as he reached Cole's side.

"I don't know," Cole said. Nothing hurt as badly as it had a few moments ago, but he knew enough about serious injury to know that sometimes it took awhile for the pain to register.

Volkovich squatted beside him, face ruddy with either the cold or some kind of emotional reaction. He brushed dust and dirt and particles off Cole's clothing.

"Run your hands through your hair," Volkovich said.

Cole did. Wood bits and some unidentifiable substance fell on his arms and shoulders.

Volkovich continued to brush him off.

"Can you stand?" he asked.

Cole had no idea.

"I'll try," he said. He leaned over, braced himself with his left hand, and then pushed upward.

He bent halfway, then stood awkwardly, as if he had suddenly aged fifty years. But his lightheadedness was gone, his legs felt sturdy enough now that he was standing on them, and he could breathe.

His hands and arms were shaking, but he couldn't tell if that was because of the incident or because the air had grown ice-cold again.

"You look all right," Volkovich said. "That was close."

"What was it?" Cole asked.

"Some kind of explosion," Volkovich said.

The man was stunningly unhelpful. Cole had figured that part out on his own. He was about to say that when Volkovich added, "It was a trap."

Cole felt like someone had punched him.

"You sent me in, knowing it was a trap?" he asked. A fury was building inside him now, along with some growing pain. He didn't think he was badly injured, but he didn't know. The bruises were revealing themselves.

"No, no," Volkovich said. "We didn't know anything."

It sounded like a lie. If Cole could have walked away, he would have. If he could have, he would have taken the conveyance and driven off, leaving both of them.

Cole made himself take a deep breath. He wasn't thinking as clearly as he could have been. He knew it.

He wasn't going to tell himself to calm down, though. He didn't feel as if he needed to be calm. He had nearly died.

"You knew something," he said. "You expected something."

Volkovich glanced over his shoulder, maybe at Xavier. Cole couldn't see Xavier anywhere, though. Then Volkovich shifted slightly.

"We thought there might be trouble, yes," Volkovich said softly. "But it would have been more dangerous for us."

"More dangerous than nearly getting blown up?" Cole asked. Now that fury filled his voice. He tightened his aching hands into fists.

"Maybe," Volkovich said.

"Maybe isn't an answer," Cole snapped.

Volkovich took a deep breath, then released it. His breath was also fogged up. That warmth from earlier was gone.

"You didn't get blown up, though," Volkovich said.

"I beg to differ," Cole said.

"Really," Volkovich said. "You're here and in one piece."

Cole resisted the urge to pat his arms and legs to actually check. He did touch that sweat on the side of his face, though, and pulled his hand back.

Not sweat. Blood.

He held out his fingers like a child would. "I'm bleeding."

"I'd be surprised if you weren't," Volkovich said. "But you're not bleeding much. Head wounds are the worst, and this is just a trickle."

"I'm *bleeding*," Cole repeated.

"Yes," Volkovich said. "You're injured, but not badly, and you're not dead."

He sounded like a man who desperately needed to sell something.

Cole narrowed his eyes and as he did, he noted that the flashing had finally stopped.

"Xavier was able to protect you," Volkovich said. "That

was what we had counted on. He acted quickly enough and you survived."

Cole shook his head and felt a dizziness he hadn't expected. He should have expected it, given the fact that he now had a headache.

"Quickly enough," Cole repeated. "And if he hadn't, I would have died, and you would have been at fault."

"No," Volkovich said, and then rocked back on his heels. "Maybe. I'm not sure what good warning you would have done."

"It would have stopped me from walking up this damn path," Cole said.

"We didn't know that an explosion would come of your trip up this path," Volkovich said. "If anything, we expected someone to open a door, see you, and then shut it again."

Cole grunted, not convinced. He also wasn't thinking as clearly as he wanted to. That dizziness was easing, but it didn't help.

"Where is Xavier?" he asked.

Volkovich waved his hand toward the building—or what remained of it.

Cole squinted and realize that what he had thought were some remaining squiggles were actually those strange words on Xavier's robe, floating in the darkness as if they had gotten a mind of their own.

"What's he doing?" Cole asked.

Volkovich gave Cole a cautious look, as if he didn't trust Cole.

"You might as well tell me," Cole said tiredly. "I nearly died. I deserve to know."

Volkovich nodded, just once, as if he had had a conversation with himself.

"He's...um...making sure there's no more magic." Volkovich's voice became nearly inaudible on that last word.

"Magic." Cole felt a rush of fury. Of course, magic. He had suspected as much, but he hadn't acted on it. Nor had he asked about it.

He looked at the building, or what was left of it. The words floated through it and around it and above it, and not in any mind of man-shape, but as if they were operating on their own.

If there was magic, then that wasn't a trick of the eye. That was what was actually going on.

"That's why you wanted Xavier," Cole said. "Because he knows magic."

Volkovich let out a small involuntary chuckle. "No one knows magic. Either you have it or you don't. You learn how to use it."

"Forgive me," Cole said sarcastically. "He knows how to use magic."

"Yes," Volkovich said.

"And that's why you wanted him along," Cole said.

"Yes," Volkovich said.

"And you wanted me because I don't know anything about magic," Cole said.

Volkovich shook his head quickly, another single movement. "Not exactly."

"Then tell me, *exactly*," Cole said. "Because I don't appreciate being the sacrifice."

"You weren't a sacrifice," Volkovich said. "You weren't

meant to be. We expected a trap. We didn't expect the entire building to destruct."

"You could have warned me," Cole said.

"You wouldn't have believed us," Volkovich said.

Cole wasn't sure if that was true. He might have fought them, though. He might have stepped away from the trip to this building to recover the maps.

The maps. If they had been inside, they were gone now.

The words continued floating around the remains of the building. Small squiggles that looked more like images floated as well. There appeared to be more of them.

Cole squinted. Those squiggles looked like the ones that had imprinted on his eyes after the silver light disappeared.

"That light," he said, not taking his gaze off the building. "That silver light. It was something that Xavier did."

"Yes," Volkovich said. "He put a shield around you as you were walking away."

"Why not as I went to the building?" Cole asked.

"Because," Volkovich said. "We had no idea if anyone was inside."

"So?" Cole asked.

"So, someone with a great deal of magic can harness loose magic and turn it on the creator."

"*Loose* magic," Cole said. "What's that?"

Volkovich waved a hand. "I'll explain more later. Right now, we need to focus."

As if Cole's brain would allow anything close to a focus. The silver words and squiggles were threading themselves through the remains of the walls.

"Do we need to help him?" Cole asked.

"No," Volkovich said. "The Fe—people we're thought we would find here are long gone."

Cole frowned. Volkovich and Xavier had known who the people were that they were coming to meet, and they had said nothing. Not in the Regents' meeting, not as they drove here.

"But these people left some kind of magic behind," Cole said as he tried to understand it.

"Yes," Volkovich said. "Unexpectedly."

"No." Cole understood that much. "If it was unexpected, you both would have come with me to the door."

Volkovich's eyes skittered away from him. "Later," Volkovich said. "We'll talk about this later."

A thin silver light formed over the entire row of buildings. It looked like a tent had gone up over them, but Cole could still see through it. Bits of the light formed a small stick (or maybe it was a large stick—he couldn't tell because he was too far away) and poked at the debris. There were sticks forming all along the walls of that tent, touching parts of the remaining buildings and then backing away.

Then, suddenly, the light went out.

Squiggles remained, just like before, only this time, they seemed to have a kind of logic. Cole felt like, if he tried, he could actually make out what those squiggles were.

It took a moment for the squiggles to fade and Cole's eyes to adjust. Moonlight touched everything. The light was thin, but it was clear enough—except when more clouds passed.

He braced a hand on the path. The ground was ice cold,

but not damp. If he was careful, he could stand up. He could walk to the remains of that building and—

Then Xavier squeezed out of the broken door frame.

He looked no different. His robe looked clean and pressed. It had a faint silver glow, but there didn't appear to be any decorations on it at all.

He strode up the path as if there was no debris, as if nothing had happened. That irritated Cole even more.

"Let's go," Xavier said tightly. He wasn't speaking to Cole. He didn't even look at Cole.

Xavier was talking to Volkovich.

"They're gone?" Volkovich asked.

"They've been gone for at least a week," Xavier said. "They left nothing behind."

"How can you tell that?" Cole asked. "You didn't have time to search everything."

Xavier turned toward him, as if he hadn't expected Cole to speak. Xavier's impassive gaze ran up and down his body. "You look better than I expected."

"What?" Cole asked, that fury underneath everything. "You expected me to look worse?"

"Had you been anyone else," Xavier said, "you would have died."

His voice was calm. He seemed untouched by the explosion, the cold night, the damage.

Cole was bruised and battered. His pants were still stuck to his legs, and his shoes were so wet that his feet felt like blocks of ice. He had a headache and his ears still rang ever so slightly.

"Thanks for letting me know that death was a possibility," Cole said.

"You wouldn't have participated if you had known," Xavier said.

Cole threaded his hands together so that he wouldn't grab Xavier by the shoulder and shake him. Or maybe even punch him.

"Then why not bring someone else, if we're all expendable but you," Cole snapped.

Volkovich shook his head slightly, but Xavier didn't see it.

"You can drive a conveyance," Xavier said. "We might have had to leave quickly."

Cole let out a small laugh. "You hadn't thought it through, then, had you?" he asked. "If I was expendable, who would have driven you back?"

"We didn't expect you to die," Volkovich said quietly. "But we knew it might have happened—to all of us."

Either that *to all of us* was a placating gift or it was the truth. Something in the way that Volkovich said it made Cole think it was the truth.

"What are these people that you thought would be here?" he asked. "Murderers? Some kind of criminal that you've seen before?"

"Old enemies," Volkovich said.

"Of whom?" Cole asked. He was cold, he was tired, and he really didn't want to coax a conversation out of these men, but he would do so if he had to.

"Of Dorovich," Volkovich said.

Dorovich? How could a continent have old enemies?

"It's too complicated," Xavier said to Volkovich quietly, as if he didn't want Cole to hear.

Cole shot him an angry glare, that seemed to have no effect at all on Xavier. But Volkovich winced a little.

"Dorovich?" Cole asked. "The entire continent? People who lived in a tiny rowhouse on a dead end street in Serebro are threats to the entire continent?"

"Yes," Volkovich said quietly.

"Not here," Xavier said, a little louder. "There's still residual magic."

Cole glared at him. "Residual magic," he said. "We had purges to get rid of magic. Was it because of these people?"

"I'm not discussing history in the cold," Xavier said and walked toward the conveyance, leaving Cole alone with Volkovich.

"Either it's history or they're a grave and present danger to all of us," Cole said. "Which is it?"

"Both," Volkovich said. "We might've been lucky that they weren't here."

"If there's some kind of threat to the continent," Cole said, shivering slightly—although he knew that was from the cold, not the conversation, "how come I don't know about it? How come no one does?"

"That is a result of the Purges," Volkovich said. "You didn't learn about ancient history in school."

Cole had had enough. He stopped twice because the dizziness got bad. He wasn't going to continue this conversation. It was frustrating.

He wanted to say that it made his head hurt, but that

wasn't accurate. His head already hurt. He actually wasn't sure he could drive, but he had to.

He wanted to get back to the Academy.

Then he paused as he stood completely upright. He wanted to get back to the Academy, but he could stay here. His family had an apartment here. He could drive to the damn thing and leave these two in the lurch.

They probably had homes here too.

He wiped a hand on his forehead, feeling the blood. It had dried, giving credence to Volkovich's claim that the wound—whatever it was—wasn't as bad as the blood might have made it seem.

Volkovich waited at Cole's side, as if providing support, just in case Cole might fall over.

He wasn't going to give them the satisfaction.

He walked back to the conveyance, trying not to pick his steps too carefully. But he had to be cautious, because there was debris everywhere. Bits of wood, burning embers of cloth or paper or something stronger. Some of those embers actually sparked as he walked by.

Xavier was sitting the back of the conveyance, hands folded on his lap. He looked like a man ready to be ferried anywhere, not a man who thought there still might be a threat in the neighborhood.

Cole didn't say anything to him, but simply climbed into the conveyance. The wood on the sides of the door was wet, but the street was now completely dry. The air smelled faintly of damp. Fog was rolling in from the sea, white wisps of chill that would make the night even colder.

Cole was not looking forward to the ride home.

Volkovich joined them and got into the conveyance.

"You're going to tell us all what's going on," Cole said. "I want to know before the rest of the Regents, but you're going to tell them tomorrow. You're going to tell me tonight. You owe it to me."

"We owe you nothing," Xavier said.

Cole turned in his seat. It took all of his strength not to shove Xavier out of the conveyance.

"I don't owe you a ride back, either, after the way you treated me," Cole said. "But I'm going to do it. You will tell me what this is about, or I swear, I'll—"

"You'll what?" Volkovich spoke this time. "You have no clout here. You're a new Regent, and a young man. You know nothing about what's going on, so you can't inform anyone, if there was someone to inform. The Board is the highest authority in academia. The government doesn't understand what happens in academia, so long as whatever it does does not spill into the rest of the culture."

"Like the Purges," Cole said.

"Like the Purges," Volkovich agreed.

"Which clearly failed," Cole said.

Xavier raised his head ever so slightly. Cole finally had his attention.

"The Purge Arbitrators still exist," Cole said. "I could tell them what happened here tonight. I could tell them about the power that Xavier displayed, power you enabled, Pasha. I could tell them that a magical threat has arisen, and you're keeping the news of it hidden."

"You wouldn't," Xavier said quietly.

"Try me," Cole said. "I have nothing to lose."

"You have everything to lose," Volkovich said. "We all do. If the Fey come back—"

"The Fey? Those mysterious creatures that attacked us hundreds of years ago?" Cole asked.

"They're not mysterious," Xavier said. "They're well known in the rest of the world."

Cole remembered something like that, but his brain wasn't working as quickly as usual.

"Why do we care about them?" he asked. "You're acting like you're afraid of them."

"You would be too, if you understood," Volkovich said.

"If I understood," Cole said with biting fury, "I might not have gone to that door."

"Maybe," Xavier said. "But we needed to know."

"Why?" Cole asked. "Clearly we defeated these people. They might be elsewhere, but they're not here."

"Oh, they're clearly here now," Xavier said. "And we need to worry about that, because they're trying to take over the world."

"So?" Cole asked.

"So," Xavier said, "they need Dorovich in order to succeed."

Cole stared at him. "We defeated them."

"Hundreds of years ago," Xavier said. "They retreated. But they're here now. And that means they have a plan."

"A plan you're afraid of," Cole said.

"Their Black King is a brilliant man. If he wants Dorovich, he'll get it."

Cole shook his head, and that increased the dizziness again. "If this powerful Black King has sent them here," he said, "why are they hiding in a rowhouse? If they have magic, why aren't they using it? Why haven't we heard about this?"

"I don't know," Xavier said. "Maybe they're being smart this time. Maybe they're sending some people in advance of troops."

"We'd stop troops," Cole said.

"You know this how?" Volkovich said.

Cole swallowed. He didn't dare say that his mother had worked with the Qavnerian Protectorate, designing some of its military programs. She had not been allowed to discuss her work, not even with family, and she had broken that last admonition.

He rubbed a hand over his face. Some of the blood had dried and was now flaking off.

"We should stay here tonight," he said.

"No." Xavier was firm. "We have to return to the Academy."

"I'm not sure I can drive," Cole said.

That comment was met with silence. Maybe that was acquiescence. Maybe it wasn't. He wasn't sure.

"You have homes here, right?" he asked.

"We need to get back." Xavier spoke with authority.

"We will," Cole said. "In the morning. If nothing else, you two can send for a carriage."

"There's a meeting in the morning," Volkovich said.

"So, we'll be late," Cole said. "Or we leave really early."

He didn't want to face the darkness and the chill and all of the concentration it took to drive over that mountain road.

"And leave Chaban in charge?" Volkovich asked.

Cole shook his head again, and then silently cursed himself. He had to stop making that movement. It made him incredibly dizzy.

He took a deep breath, hoping the dizziness would ease.

"He won't be in charge," Cole said. "Not after Zubiri gets through with him. They're at his house now. I'm sure they're finding even more incriminating material."

"And do you trust them to do the right thing?" This from Volkovich. His tone had started to match Xavier's.

Cole wanted to bow his head, but he knew moving it would make matters worse.

"To be honest," he said, "I don't know who to trust right now."

Xavier let out a laugh. It sounded relieved.

"Finally," he said, as if he were speaking to Volkovich alone. "We're getting through."

Cole gripped the steering sticks, mostly to hold himself level. "Because I don't trust anyone?"

"Precisely," Xavier said. "We can't go through these next few days blindly."

"What happens these next few days?" Cole asked.

"I'm not sure," Xavier said, "but I have a hunch it will be monumental."

PART FIVE
THE MAN WITH NO FACE

LAW BUILDING

LER
L

REGENTS
LODGING HOUSE

MEDICAL

SCIENCES

CAMPUS
MEDICAL UNIT

ANATOMY

CHAPTER
TWENTY-FOUR

The rain had stopped hours ago, but the air was so cold it was frosty. Ludmilla still wore her heavy rain coat over her cable-knit sweater, but the clothing was not warm enough. Part of the problem was the wind, which teased her hair and cut through her pants as if they were made of gossamer.

Long-time practice from dealing with the mountain road between the Academy and Serebro proper made her bring two extra changes of clothing, including one more heavy sweater, but she didn't want to don any of it.

She had a feeling she'd be at the Academy longer than she wanted to, and she needed to keep her clothing options open. She had left her extra bag at the lodging shortly after she had arrived on campus, but she hadn't thought she would need them.

Now that she knew she would, she felt the trepidation she usually felt in a new environment. Sure, she had spent years on this campus, but the Regents lodging house was new. As courteous as its housemistress had been, it still felt like Ludmilla had been an inconvenience.

She hadn't let anyone know she was going to stay at the lodging house because she hadn't planned to. They were supposed to have a room prepared for her no matter what her plans, but apparently "prepared" and "ready" were too different things.

She had dropped off her bag, but she had done that before the first meeting as well, and then had not used the room in the lodging house. Apparently the housemistress had expected the same behavior from her.

Ludmilla hadn't minded; she had expected to do the same until the disastrous meeting that had gone on all afternoon.

Then she returned to the lodging house and let the housemistress know she was going to stay. That resulted in a flurry of activity. The housemistress had told her that she would need an hour or more to get the room ready "as befits a Regent."

So Ludmilla had gotten herself dinner at her favorite campus commissary, only to discover that Regents were treated differently. She couldn't blend in with the students and professors. She was fawned over and handled as if she were some kind of royalty, when all she wanted was a bowl of hot black bean soup (one of that commissary's specialties), some molasses bread, and large mug of tea.

She had gotten all of that, and a complimentary chocolate cookie, which she had eaten out of obligation. She had gone back to the lodging to find her room ready for her—

although the room wasn't a room. It was a suite. There were three rooms—a sitting room, a working office, and a bedroom with a bed piled high with pillows. There was also a private bathroom with gold pipes and hot and cold running water—a luxury she didn't even have in the family apartment in Serebro.

A fire burned brightly in the large sitting room fireplace. The suite had two other fireplaces, both smaller, and neither with fires burning, although everything was prepped. All she had to do was strike one of the long matches and light the brown paper that had been placed underneath one of the logs. The paper and the kindling would do the rest—or so the headmistress had told her.

As inviting as the place was, Ludmilla was too restless to stay. The meeting had disturbed her on so many levels that she could hardly think. She missed her father profoundly. She simultaneously wanted to ask his forgiveness and to find out everything he knew about the Regents.

She also wanted to return to the family home in Trinovante and find the maps her father had kept, along with all of the papers he'd put in his private safe. She hadn't opened it after his death, even though she was the only one with the combination.

In fact, she had learned in a roundabout way that she was the only one in the family who knew where the safe was. It had been hidden behind a fake wall, and not even her mother had known the wall was hollow.

Ludmilla hadn't told anyone either. She hadn't even mentioned the safe. One of her brothers had noted that their father's home office had a strange shape, and another brother had mentioned that their father had insisted on walls that seemed too close to him, for reasons not even their mother had understood.

At least Ludmilla had been smart enough not to blurt anything about the fake wall. Her siblings had been upset enough at her for the depth of her inheritance, even though all of them had received property as well. Just not the main properties. Her brothers had all received small homes in remote areas around the Protectorate and her sister had gotten the pretty little house on the Hidden River, just south of Isara.

Ludmilla's father had also given them enough money to maintain the properties, but that hadn't been enough for any of them. Not that she blamed them; she had gotten the bulk of the family wealth, not just in property but in money as well. They had received scraps.

Her father had tried to explain it in the will, apparently knowing that the financial divisions would cause a real division among his surviving children, but that hadn't been enough—even though, apparently, his father had done the same thing.

All that had done was explain why the rest of the Odenkirks had been estranged from her father, something that history was probably going to repeat, now that she owned almost everything, and her siblings owned—according to her eldest brother—*next to nothing*.

Ludmilla wanted to talk with both of her parents about that, but her mother had died before her father, leaving him bereft. His death, while unexpected, had not really been a surprise.

Just the inheritance had.

With Ludmilla's mind jumping all over the place and her nerves frayed, she finally decided to do something useful. In that awful meeting, someone had mentioned checking the bylaws, and oddly enough, Ludmilla knew where they were.

As a child, she had come to meetings with her father, and he had taken her to the library in the Regents Tower. The librarian used to watch over her, but didn't really seem to care what Ludmilla looked at—except the books about the Purges and all of the bylaws.

One of the many things her father had left her had been a wad of keys that were labeled *Regents Tower*. She had brought them with her to both meetings. The first time, she had worried that she might not be able to get inside. She had been under the impression that everyone had keys; maybe her father had told her that or maybe not. She was uncertain.

Reginald had the door open, however, and she hadn't had to worry about it.

The second time—this time—she brought them in an excess of caution.

And now she finally had a use for them.

She kept the keys in the right pocket of her coat—a pocket that buttoned closed, even though it was not closed right now. She had her right hand shoved into that pocket, and she gripped the keys tightly.

As she walked across campus, it felt as if everyone knew she had the keys and knew where she was going. The path she walked along was well lit; lightstone lanterns had been placed on poles at regular intervals, creating gigantic squares of light that illuminated everything around them.

Above the lanterns, light and dark gray clouds floated by as if they were in a hurry to get to Serebro. If the clouds acted like they usually did, they would gather around the mountains, making travel through them difficult.

She had no idea if any of the other Regents had decided to take the trip across the mountains to return to their own housing in Serebro. It was amazing how little she actually knew about her fellow Regents.

Maybe that was something she would demand changed, should the Board remain together.

She shook her head slightly. Maybe the bylaws would tell her what it really would take to disband the Board. Maybe they would tell her what the separated documents were all about.

Or maybe the bylaws would remain silent on all of that.

Despite the hour, the campus remained heavily populated. Students scurried to their dorms or into academic halls. Lectures on a variety of topics always took place after the dinner hour. There was also at least one class per department that met at night.

The initial rationale was that members of the community might want to take classes, and later classes would enable that, but the trip over the mountains precluded a lot of Serebro residents from casually taking classes.

Still, the schedule remained, and it made the campus at night seem as vibrant as the campus by day.

Despite the cold, Ludmilla did not mind the short walk from the lodging house to Regents Tower. The walk took her from the so-called newer part of campus to the Old Campus.

The newer part of campus wasn't really that new. If she remembered her history right, it was at least five hundred years old. The Old Campus was at least double that, maybe more. The foundation of the Academy had been that fortress built in a valley between the Serebro Mountain Range and the Coastal Mountain Range.

Every time she approached the Regents Tower, she felt like she could sense the ancient fortress, even though most of it was gone. The tower's walls, though, looked old and were moss-covered. The tower was square, just like the tower on the Old Library, only this tower didn't have the dozen additions that had been built onto the library.

This tower stood alone.

Lights remained on inside the tower. A series of windows just above the middle of the tower were brightly lit. That was the meeting room.

She frowned at it, wondering if the group that Packingham had chosen was still grilling Chaban. If so, Ludmilla didn't want to be a part of that.

Above that level, there was darkness.

She hesitated for just a minute. Maybe she didn't want to go to the Regents Library. She certainly didn't want to be part of all of the drama that had unfolded toward the meeting's end. Not anymore, anyway. Once she had gotten outside of the room, she figured the others could handle it.

She discovered that she needed the rest. The drama had exhausted her, perhaps because she had been dealing with family drama for the past few months as well.

But there would be more regent drama in the morning, and it would be better if she was informed about the bylaws and the rules. She would feel like she was on more certain footing.

She squeezed the keys, feeling the teeth bite into the soft skin of her palm. Somehow, holding those keys felt encouraging.

She glanced up at the windows one last time. The library was on the same floor as the meeting room, and she couldn't tell from this angle if the lights in the library were on or not.

This late at night there would be no librarian in the Regents Library, but that was probably for the better. Ludmilla could take as much time as she needed to investigate everything before her.

She squared her shoulders and crossed the tiny bridge that led to the main doors. That tiny bridge was one reason why everyone believed there had been a moat around the tower when there hadn't been one.

Although it looked like there was one now. The rain had filled in a natural depression in the land, making the entire area one big puddle. Smaller puddles fed into the larger one. If she hadn't been wearing her boots, walking would have been treacherous.

The path on the other side of the bridge was wet and slick, shiny black in the glow of the lightstone lanterns. A light hung over the large double doors that led into the Regents Tower.

The doors were almost two stories tall and made of heavy wood. They were plain, except for the diamond-shaped glass panes near the top. The panes had no design either, which was unusual for anything in Qavner.

Most places would have had decorative stained glass or

some kind of carving. But the plainness of the tower was one of its features and something, according to the School of Architecture, that was a feature of that Blue Isle style.

She gripped one of the handles and pulled, expecting the door to be locked. But it wasn't, which surprised her. Most buildings without classrooms on campus were usually locked after the dinner hour.

Maybe there were still regents inside. Or maybe, because of the emergency meeting, the door was supposed to remain open all night.

She kept her grip on her keys, however, and slipped inside. Light came on as she moved through the entry toward the massive staircase.

This entire area had been built to impress—with a ceiling so high up that she couldn't see it from this part of the entry.

There were no seats here, although some very plain wood tables lined the walls. Those tables had been in the building since she was a girl, if not longer.

She used to come here with her father when he had meetings, often over the protestations of her mother. Ludmilla's father would deposit her in the library. She would read while he tended to serious matters—or so she thought.

Now she wondered if he had put up with as much infighting as she had seen at today's meeting.

Somehow, she couldn't imagine her even-tempered father in the middle of any of it.

She mounted the stairs because she hated using the strange lift at night. The lift had been put in a century ago as an experiment, and sometimes, her father had said, the experiment failed.

She put her free hand on the highly polished railing. Everything was square here, just like the tower itself. The stairs went up at angles—a dozen steps, landing, turn, a dozen more. She had counted them as a child because the staircase would have seemed insurmountable otherwise.

On her two previous visits, she had been glad for that accounting, because she had felt late to both of them, even though she had been ridiculously early this afternoon.

A mezzanine surrounded the staircase on the second level, open to the floor below. Doors led into large rooms off the mezzanine, but Ludmilla had no idea what those rooms were. She had never thought to ask.

The meeting room was on the eighth floor, but the floors were only counted above the mezzanine, so in actuality, it was even higher up. The stairs got narrower the higher she went. In all of her years of coming here with here with her father, she had never given the floors between the mezzanine and the meeting room much thought. Now, she wondered what they were and why there was so much distance between the entrance and the meeting area.

Some of that was the result of climbing these stairs for the second time in the same day.

She was winded when she reached the eighth floor. A tiny hallway branched off the stairs, leading to the reception area. She walked through that hallway, her boots clicking on the stone floor.

Reginald had been standing when she had arrived that afternoon, as if he was waiting for her. And now, after Cole had mentioned in passing that the reception area was a natural echo chamber, she understood how Reginald always knew someone was coming.

She was more cautious about that this time. She was just more cautious in general. She felt like she had aged years in the space of a few hours.

Lights were still on in the reception area, but the fire in the large stone fireplace had burned to embers. Reginald's small desk was covered with papers that she hadn't seen before. Even though the rain had stopped, the window above his desk was still fogged up, with moisture on the sides. His chair was pushed back and at an angle, as if he had been interrupted in the middle of work.

Cole had sent Reginald home—or rather, to that place he went when he wasn't working, whatever that was. Either Reginald had been doing some work when he was summarily dismissed or he had returned.

Ludmilla's stomach lurched. She would bet that he had returned.

She glanced down the hall between the reception area and the meeting room. The meeting room door was open, and two voices echoed faintly. If she strained, she could make out what they were saying.

She glanced at the other part of the hallway, which veered to the right and led to the library. She could just go past and no one would be the wiser. But she couldn't do that. She would always wonder what was going on in that meeting room. Were they still grilling Chaban, hours later? Or had something else changed?

She couldn't creep to the door, because of the way that

sound carried, but she walked lightly so that her heels didn't click.

As she got closer, she realized the voices were male and female. She recognized Reginald's.

She peered inside. He was taking dishes off the long table, talking to Mrs. Halmann.

"...actually made me leave," Reginald was saying. "They seemed to believe that they needed extreme privacy today."

He had his back to the door, but Ludmilla made sure she was to one side anyway. Not that she really had to watch. Cole had been right: this entire outside area was an echo chamber.

"Aye, and with somethin' in the mornin'," Mrs. Halmann said, "I dinna have much time t'think about a menu."

She was holding a canvas duffel and carefully putting the remaining food in different parts of it. Ludmilla frowned. She had never thought about all the leftover food on campus. Did it get set aside? Given to someone in need? Taken home by the staff?

She had never seen it thrown away.

Mrs. Halmann couldn't see Ludmilla either, but Ludmilla kept an eye on both of them just in case.

"I wouldn't worry about the menu." Reginald was stacking used cups on a nearby table. "They're probably going to be too preoccupied to think about food. They seem more contentious than usual. I'm quite worried about it actually."

"Somethin's been up fer a while," Mrs. Halmann said. "I canna put my finger on it, but 'tis somethin' bad."

She set the canvas duffel down and picked up another.

"I don't think there's ever anything good with this group," Reginald said. Then he laughed. "You and I should be in charge."

"Ah, laddie," Mrs. Halmann said, putting a hand on his arm. "But we are."

She turned as she said that, suddenly facing the door. Ludmilla stepped back, hoping she hadn't been seen. She slid toward the other side of the hall, making sure that her heels didn't touch the ground.

She moved as silently as she could, not that it would matter if the other two left the room. They would see the lightstone fixtures flaring to life as she made her way toward the library.

She hoped that the lights would remain on for a very short time, otherwise Reginald and Mrs. Halmann would know that someone else was on the floor.

Ludmilla clutched her keys, hoping that she had one to the library. As she got farther from the main doors to the meeting room, she stopped trying to be as quiet. She still eased her heels down, but she made sure they didn't clack.

The lightstone lamp above the library door did not flare on. In fact, this part of the hallway was unusually dark. There was no other light near the door. The closest ones were still one, but their light seemed thin.

Ludmilla glanced over her shoulder, suddenly feeling nervous, as if she really didn't belong. She made herself take a deep breath, hoping it would calm her. She was a Regent now, free to do what she wanted in Regents Tower. Or, at least, that was what she would say if she were caught.

Then she smiled at herself. *Caught*. A word the guilty used.

The door in front of her was a smaller version of the exterior doors. It was made of very old wood, with only grooved planks for decoration. There wasn't even a little window near the top, like there was on the exterior doors.

She pulled the keys out of the pocket of her coat. Before she tried any of them, though she tugged on the metal door handle. It burned her palm, which startled her. She pulled her hand away, and looked down.

It was hard to see her skin in the darkness. Some of the lights farther down the hall had gone out. She tilted her aching palm toward them, but saw nothing.

Maybe that burning feeling was just a figment of her imagination, a bit of guilt. Still, she pulled down her sleeve, and used the fabric of her coat like a glove.

She grabbed the handle, and pushed.

The door was unlocked, which surprised her. She slipped the keys back into her pocket and slid inside the library, hoping for working lightstone lamps, because she had forgotten to bring any light with her.

A sliver from the hallway and the diffuse light from the arched windows on the far side of the room was the only light so far. She kept one hand on the door. If no lights came on, she would have to leave.

She was just about to, when an overhead light flared on, sending grayish white light all over the room.

She gasped in surprise.

The room—her beloved library where she had spent so many great moments of her childhood—was empty.

Well, not entirely empty. The long oak tables remained, covered in dust now. Chairs were pushed against them haphazardly. The floor was covered in enough dust that footprints from previous visitors were clearly etched in it.

Dust motes floated in the air, disturbed by Ludmilla herself. She eased the door closed, mostly because she was still acting on an old plan rather than out of any sense of preservation.

The shelves remained as well, but they were empty. There were little black scar marks in the shape of books, as if some of the books had dripped knowledge into the shelves themselves. The librarian's desk remained too, empty, the surface mottled from time and age. The shelves behind it were also empty. They sagged into each other, as if they were holding each other up.

She walked farther into the room, feeling lost. This place had been home to her. She had always thought about it when she had been a student here. Every day that she walked by, she had thought about entering the Regents Tower and asking for a special dispensation to study in that library.

Not to take any of the books—not even to look at them, really—but to sit in her favorite seat near those arched windows, and learn whatever it was that her professors had deemed important on that particular day.

She raised her hands to her chest, clutching them against her breastbone. The ache was profound, and sadness caught in her throat. Her eyes pricked with unshed tears.

Part of this, she knew, was about her father, about everything she had lost when she had lost him, but part of it was also about this place. This place had been safety for her, protected, filled with knowledge and light and a kind woman in charge of it all.

And now it was abandoned, a ghost of itself.

She hadn't realized just how much she had been looking forward to coming here after that contentious meeting. She had needed the comfort, and she had thought she would find it here.

Of course, she hadn't. That wasn't how this trip was going. That wasn't how the meeting was going.

Nothing was like she had imagined it.

She wondered if her father had known that this place had been denuded. It looked like it had clearly been done while he was still alive.

But he might not have had any reason to come here once she had grown up and no longer traveled with him.

Maybe he had approved this. Maybe he hadn't known.

Yet another thing she couldn't ask him.

She blinked and a tear escaped. She wiped at it furiously.

She had learned this after her mother's death: grief assaulted you at unexpected times. Its mission seemed to be to keep you off balance, to make you a lesser version of yourself.

Ludmilla had thought she was ready for grief again once her father died, thought she had understood it and knew how to ride its waves. But her father's death was different. The waves were deeper and longer and tinged with guilt.

She hadn't done what he wanted, and that bothered her so much that if she had the ability to turn time backwards, she would.

Something popped behind her, making her jump. She

turned, saw that the door was moving. It almost seemed stuck. Then it slammed open, and Reginald stood there.

His bald head reflected the pale light. His weirdly round eyes looked sunken into his face. His lips, always pursed in disapproval, seemed even more tightly squeezed together than usual.

"Who gave you permission to come here?" he snapped.

Ludmilla let her hands drop, resisting the urge to wipe the tear track off her face.

"I don't need permission," she said in the most arch tone she had. "I'm a Regent. I can go where I please within this tower."

"No one comes here," he said. "If you got locked in, no one would know you were here or would come to your rescue."

She almost grabbed her keys and waved them at him. But she didn't. He didn't need to know that she had a set.

"The door was open," she said.

He was still standing near the door. "Exploring the tower is not a good idea."

"I'm not exploring," she said. "I don't need to. I spent years here as a child. I am, however, surprised that the library is gone."

Reginald's posture actually softened. Had she frightened him? It certainly seemed that way.

She wasn't sure if that was out of concern for her, or because he had truly been worried that someone had broken into the tower.

"The library hasn't been here for years," he said.

"What happened to it?" she asked.

"The Board decided to move its contents to the Old Library." Something about the way he said it made her suspicious.

Or maybe the suspicion had come from that meeting earlier.

"The Board or Devin Chaban?" she asked.

Reginald's pale eyebrows went up. "I was told that it was the Board. I organized the move. It was quite extensive."

Ludmilla wasn't going to lose track of her question. "Told by whom?"

Reginald glanced at the windows, as if they held an answer. Then he shrugged one shoulder, almost as if he was pretending he didn't know.

"Devin told you, didn't he?" Ludmilla asked. "And the board hadn't been in session when he did so."

Reginald shrugged that same shoulder. "It's not my job to question him. The orders are the orders."

Ludmilla frowned. Had Reginald been spying on the board to find out if Chaban's orders were legitimate? Or did the two of them work together?

"What happened to the librarian?" Ludmilla asked. She had never known the librarian's name, only her title.

"She...retired." There was an entire story in that gap.

"At the same time?" Ludmilla asked.

He nodded, a small movement, almost furtive. "She wasn't happy about the move. She said..."

He stopped, shook his head, then held up his hands as if what he had been about to say didn't matter.

"She said what?" Ludmilla asked.

"That the Regents library was in the tower for a reason. The materials shouldn't be in the Old Library."

"Because students could access them?" Ludmilla asked.

"Students can't get near them. The Old Library had to clear out a room just for the materials," Reginald said. "It's locked and only the Regents can use it."

She felt cold. "Did everyone receive a key?"

"I don't know," Reginald said. "I wasn't in charge of that."

"But you were in charge of the move," she said.

"Yes," he said.

She didn't like this, particularly after the discussion earlier. There was a lot of material that needed to kept separately. If she had to guess, she would have thought that the materials in this library shouldn't have been near items in the Old Library.

"Did the librarian say why they shouldn't be near the items in the Library?" Ludmilla asked.

"She said she couldn't tell me. She wanted to meet with the Board, but it never got scheduled."

Ludmilla let out a small breath. She would have to inform the others of this.

"Was the Board told about the librarian's concerns?" Ludmilla asked.

"I don't know," Reginald said a bit too quickly.

Ludmilla gave him a disbelieving glance. "You don't know? Of course you know. You keep track of everything. That's why you listen in, isn't it? To know what's going on?"

His cheeks flushed. Again, he shrugged that one shoulder.

"I never heard the chairman inform anyone about the librarian," he said.

Clearly he had chosen his words carefully.

"What about someone else? Did anyone tell the Board about these changes?" Ludmilla asked.

"I..." Reginald closed his eyes for a moment, then opened them again. "I did. I told Horace Rogov."

That surprised Ludmilla. "Anyone else?"

"Augustus Kirilli." Reginald looked down. "He said he would look into it."

"And that was years ago," Ludmilla said.

Reginald nodded.

"Not near his death," she said again, for clarification.

"That's right," Reginald said. "You don't think they're tied together, do you?"

Ludmilla was surprised he even asked her. She was new, and he had treated her with such contempt. But now he seemed scared. Maybe he hadn't thought any connection between the loss of the Regents Library and the murder of Augustus Kirilli. Maybe Reginald thought he was in danger.

Or maybe, he was just looking for a new ally after a very bad day.

"You moved everything, didn't you?" Ludmilla asked. "You saw it all."

"No," Reginald said. "The librarian moved some. I had brought in a few trustworthy people whom she heavily supervised."

The words hung for a moment. It almost felt like he had been about to add some names. So Ludmilla dove in.

"Who else?" she asked.

396

Reginald closed his eyes again. It was almost as if doing that made him draw some inner strength.

When he opened them, he looked even more uncomfortable than he had a moment ago.

He bit his lower lip, clearly unwilling to say anything.

Ludmilla didn't have time for games. "Devin Chaban, right?"

"Yes," Reginald said.

"On his own or with others?" she asked.

"I don't know," Reginald said. "He didn't work at the same time we did."

Ludmilla let out a small sigh. "Did my father know about this?"

Reginald opened his hands, as if saying none of this was his fault. "He found out when everyone else did."

"When was that?" Ludmilla asked.

"After it was done," Reginald said, almost in a whisper.

"How long after it was done?" Ludmilla asked.

"A month, two? I don't really remember the timing." Reginald brought his hands back together and then twisted them, as if he couldn't figure out what to do with them. "It was so tiring, moving everything."

Ludmilla didn't care how tired Reginald was or what excuses he had for anything. She turned away from him, and walked over to her favorite window. It overlooked the Old Library. She could almost imagine what this all looked like when they were matching towers in the same fortress.

The Old Library was lit from within, looking almost festive in the gloom. A ground fog was slowly creeping along the edges of campus, white against the lightstone lamps.

"Do you have a key to the room in the Old Library?" Ludmilla asked. She could see Reginald reflected in the wavy glass. He looked smaller than he had earlier in the day.

"I—yes. I never gave it back." He looked down, almost as if he were ashamed.

She couldn't really guess at his emotions, though. He was someone she didn't understand, and laying on her interpretations might make her completely misunderstand what was really going on.

She turned. He was watching her out of the corner of one eye. Maybe it was all an act after all.

"You will give me your key," she said.

"I'm not supposed to give up my keys to anyone," he said.

"I'm not anyone." She walked back to him, standing as tall as she could. She was no longer going to be a timid new Regent. She had power on this campus. She needed to use it.

She put her palm out.

"Your key," she repeated.

He swallowed. "I don't...you could ask the librarian at the Old Library. Regents are supposed to have access at all times."

"And if that doesn't work," she said, "then I won't be able to do the research I was assigned."

She didn't say who assigned the research. Reginald didn't need to know she had assigned it to herself.

"The key," she said for the third time. "I'm not going to ask again."

He dug into the pocket of his suit jacket. He removed two separate wads of keys, and thumbed through them.

The sight of all those keys sent a chill through Ludmilla. She didn't have that many keys.

Did the other Regents realize how much access Reginald had to everything? Was it intentional or had Reginald just collected all of those keys like he had collected information?

He thumbed through the keys on one of the rings and finally found what he was looking for. That key was ornate, with a scrolled top and a rather elaborate set of teeth.

He detached it from the ring, then held the key out to her.

"I want it back," he said.

I'm sure you do, she nearly said, but she caught herself just in time. Instead, she nodded as she put the key in the pocket without her wad of keys.

She swept past him, then. The conversation was over, even though she wasn't sure it should have been. She had a lot more questions, but they could wait.

She needed to get to that library room, not just to see the bylaws, but also to make sure that most of the items that she had known about were there.

It bothered her that she had no real idea what had been in that room, just a child's memory of it. She wondered who else knew—someone other than Chaban.

She let herself into the hallway. The lightstone lamps eased on as she passed. This time, she didn't care about her heels.

She felt like she had been living a comfortable life until her father's death, a life that had taken very little effort on her part. She had thought that life was hard, but she had had no idea how hard life could become.

The ironic thing was that she could go back to that life. She could pretend that nothing she had heard today mattered to her. She could come to the meetings, let others handle whatever crisis was going on, and then go home as if nothing happened.

Only she wasn't built that way.

She had walked into a crisis and she needed to resolve it.

Starting tonight.

CHAPTER
TWENTY-FIVE

Jaxon began every shift by walking the interior of the campus grounds. Since the attack on Louella, he started earlier than he ever had, beginning after sundown, and he walked the outer ring as well, although he couldn't get to all of it.

The main campus was large enough that it would take hours to walk around the entire exterior, although he had done it. Since the attack, he had canceled any and all leave for his staff, made the Advanced Students who were working part-time double their hours despite upcoming exams, and tried to keep an eye on everything.

Loughty had told him the day after the attack to discuss the strange things she had found. Somehow, in the dark and confusion, he had missed an entire pile of skin.

The very thought of that made his stomach turn, even now. She had wanted to show it to him, but he hadn't let her. He didn't need something like that in his brain.

Not that the image of that skin ever entirely left. As he walked the campus, he found his mind returning to the skin over and over and over again. He had learned a lot about magic from his predecessor—the things to look for, the things to worry about.

Jaxon had always tried not to, but in the past four days, he had been unable to think of anything else.

He wore an oilskin cape over his clothing, with the hood up, and solid boots that could handle the rain. It had been raining hard for two days, and he was tired of it. He didn't like walking in the rain, he didn't like the way that it sounded—like pellets hitting the ground—and he hated the wind.

It was almost as if the weather was conspiring to steal his senses away from him, to keep him less alert than he usually was.

He made the early rounds, then stopped in the copse of trees where Louella had been attacked. It was even harder to see at the moment than it had been that night.

Even though the lightstone lanterns were lit all over campus, their light seemed diminished by the continuing storms. Light had always been poor in this little grove of trees, but it seemed worse on this night.

Still, he stopped. The trees had become a pilgrimage for him. He would stop and stare at the blood pool. It had grown black over time, and then it had hardened into something that resembled black dirt, with grass poking through.

The smell of rot had receded until the rain started, and now the smell was back, as if it lived in the very ground itself.

He hadn't asked Loughty how long that smell would last. He wasn't sure she knew.

Besides, he was avoiding her, partly because he didn't want to hear her theories. She believed that there might be Fey here, which he found odd in the extreme. He knew that the Fey had conquered countries across the Infrin Sea, and he understood that they might want to conquer countries in Dorovich one day.

But he saw no reason why they would arrive first on the campus of Serebro Academy, so far from Trinovante that everyone who traveled here complained about the distance.

Besides, when the Fey had arrived centuries ago, they had done so in Khēmía, on the other side of the continent. He saw no reason why they wouldn't do so again.

He considered Loughty's little theory about the Fey to be ridiculous, even though it bothered him. All of the talk of magic bothered him, just like the fact that no one had found Louella's attacker. That person seemed to have vanished into thin air.

Louella had had little to say about him. Only that the attack had happened quickly. She had been overpowered, and then she fell, hitting her head. She was unable to remember anything after that.

She didn't even recall screaming.

She never looked at Jaxon when she talked to him, and he had the sense that she wished the entire incident would be forgotten.

He wasn't going to forget any of it. He was the one in charge of the security for the entire campus, and that someone who had attacked Louella could just as easily attack the other women on campus. Maybe even the men, since the medical team had told him there had been no obvious evidence of sexual assault.

Not, the doctor in charge had said, *that it means assault didn't happen. It's just there's no obvious trauma in her private regions.*

Jaxon had dismissed that information. Louella was clearly traumatized and that happened with an assault. She had been unconscious for most of it, so no one knew—not even the victim—what had been done to her.

Still, he stood over that blood pool—which, oddly—hadn't expanded in the severe rains. The additional water hadn't made the blood pool all over the grass. The blood remained one solid mass of goo, stinking its way through campus.

That alone made him believe what Loughty had said—*not* the parts about the Fey, but the parts about someone practicing magic.

She had given him some references on the subject, and he had spent time in the student library, reading during his off hours. Since the attack, he hadn't been sleeping much, not that he had slept well before. Since his wife died, he'd been restless, unable to stay still.

This attack only made that restlessness worse.

His reading convinced him that Loughty had been right: magic did use bodily fluids for many things. Some types of magic—*evil* types, one of the books said—used body parts as well.

Some of the books even cited Fey magic as a reference.

All of this talk about magic put him on edge. He hadn't figured out how to think about any of it.

He didn't want to approach the Administration, especially while the Regents were in session. They had taken the Purges much too seriously back in the day, and he didn't want this incident to start a whole new round of Purges.

Maybe he was making a mistake, but he didn't think so.

Too many people had died for no reason in those Purges. He didn't want to be the one to start them all up again, especially if Loughty's assumptions about the magic were incorrect.

Jaxon clasped his hands behind his back, and studied that weird blood pool. Her assumptions weren't incorrect. He knew it and she knew it, and he wasn't sure what to do about it.

Loughty and her suspicions of magic wouldn't leave his head. The idea that body parts were somehow used for magic also wouldn't leave his head.

He had mentioned that to one of his guards, who had pointed out that the body parts were left behind.

But Jaxon realized it was only the blood, bones, and skin that was still here. The rest of it—all of that internal stuff—had completely disappeared.

He shuddered and turned away from the blood pool. Shadows moved across the path near the Regents Tower. He blinked. It was hard to see if the shadows were actual people because of the dark night, the dampness in the air, and the unusual dimness of the lights.

But he couldn't tell. The Regents had broken for dinner,

so none of them should have remained in the Tower, but he wasn't certain of that either. He wasn't given their schedule.

The only reason he knew that the meeting had ended was that some of them were wondering loudly how bad the dinner would be as they headed back to their lodging.

He was insulted for the chefs, some of the best in Qavner. He just chalked it all up to more insensitivities from the Regents, who didn't seem to understand that the staff of the Academy wasn't there to serve them.

Still, he needed to see what those shadows were. They seemed to move along the side of the building, away from the paths.

He stepped out of the copse of trees near one of the lightstone lanterns, and the shadows disappeared.

A trick of the ever-changing light, then. Something about where he had been standing had caused him to see something that wasn't there.

He shook his head a little, more unnerved than he wanted to admit. He made himself take a few deep breaths, feeling the cold air as it went deep into his lungs.

He still had a lot of walking to do. He wasn't anywhere near finishing his rounds.

He didn't look forward to it, though. A grayish-white fog was moving across the campus, almost like someone had directed it to cover the ground up to knee-height.

These weather conditions—the cold, the extreme dampness, the water pooling in unusual places because of the days of rain—often created ground fog throughout the campus. He just usually didn't see it form.

He had no idea it did so as if it was sprinting toward a

destination, rather than emerging from the ground all at once.

He straightened his shoulders and continued forward. He was going to stop reading about magic and the faraway Fey. He wasn't going to talk with Loughty unless he had to.

He needed to get a grip on himself. He was letting other people's fancies influence him—and he didn't need that.

The head of security for the Serebro Academy had to be grounded in reality, not flights of the imagination. He had to see things for what they were, not what everyone feared them to be.

With new resolve, he headed toward the Campus Security Building to greet that night's staff. And then he would finish his rounds. Quietly. Observing.

Just like he was supposed to.

LINGUISTICS

ARCHEOLOGY

HISTORY

REGENTS

TOWER

OLD

LIBRARY

ADV. STUDENT
WING

MAIN
ENTRANCE

CLOCK
TOWER

MEDICAL

SCIENCES

CHAPTER
TWENTY-SIX

She felt like a failure.

Shyly stood outside the Old Library on the Coastal Mountain side. It was sheltered here from the wind that constantly blew over those mountains. For some reason, the wind would go around this part of the gigantic building and nearly knock students over as they tried to enter the Student Wing.

There were nooks and crannies built into the building, designs she half recognized from old castles that she had seen in L'Nacin, even though this design was plainer. There had clearly been kitchens in this building because some of the walls had permanent soot stains, and in one area, the floor canted downward, probably because a heavy stove had rested on it in days gone by.

The complete opposite side of the building was too visible to the main part of campus. Besides, there was too much light directly from lightstone lanterns as well as lamps attached to the building.

She always kept her head down when she was near lightstone, just in case the rumors she heard about that strange light would somehow reveal her as a Doppelgänger or, worse, completely destroy her.

She was still relying on rumors because she hadn't had a lot of time to find out about the artifacts, materials, and books stored on this campus. The intelligence that Gray had gotten was correct, but incomplete.

Shyly had combed Louella's memories and saw that the books on magick actually filled half a wing of this library, but were not accessible to her. She did not have enough seniority. It would take her years to get to the right level of seniority to be able to go into those sections of the library at will—and even then, someone would have to die for her to get access.

All she knew was where those items were located. She didn't even know which items were where.

She twisted her hands together, trying to warm them up. She was dressing the way that Louella dressed for work, which wasn't nearly warm enough for Shyly.

Shyly had learned in her years with host bodies that half of things that seemed body-specific, such as reacting to temperature, were really personality-specific.

Louella didn't seem to feel cold much at all. Shyly had been so cold the past couple of days that she didn't think she would ever get warm.

A movement caught her eye. It was near the trees,

outside of the pools of light from the lightstone lanterns on the paths.

The movement didn't look like it belonged to a student or someone used to campus. Someone used to campus would stride along the paths, not caring about the lights.

The shadow moved with purpose. It seemed to be deliberately avoiding the light. She smiled.

That shadow had to be Gray. He had sent a message to her through one of the students, suggesting a time for a meeting tonight. She had sent a message back through the same student, who happened to live in Serebro and didn't mind receiving the extra coin, choosing this place for the meeting.

Gray seemed like half a person. He could shift his appearance just enough to make himself unnoticeable— mostly invisible, he would say—or to make his features unmemorable. Sometimes he could change his face to resemble someone else's, which only worked if that person was male and had the same general build.

Those were all useful skills for a Spy, enough to allow him to gather information while interacting with people. Some Spies —those who were more accomplished than Gray or had more magic—could actually influence their targets, making them talk or getting them to show the Spy something incredibly secret.

Shyly didn't know if Gray lacked those skills, but to her knowledge, he had never used them. Not that she had quizzed him on his activities here in Qavner. So far, he had proven to be the most effective member of their team. He had gathered information, rented them housing in Serebro, and helped them acquire artifacts that had littered one of the row houses in their first living quarters.

Those artifacts had made her nervous; they felt like they were giving off magick that she couldn't even see. She had luxury of being able to stay away from all of them, so she had.

Her work hadn't really started until a few days ago, and even then, she hadn't done it well.

Perdue had found her and chastised her for leaving skin behind. As if she had had a choice. That idiot Louella had screamed long enough and loud enough to draw attention to the attack.

Shyly had barely had enough time to complete the transfer before security started showing up. By then, she had been disoriented with her transition into the new host, and she couldn't even make up plausible lies.

Now she was saddled with the idea that she had been so traumatized that she couldn't talk about the incident. Generally, that was a good thing, but it didn't allow her to clean up her own mess.

Perdu couldn't do it either, since he had assumed the persona of some very fussy professor from Razbitay, a useless host if there ever was one. She had urged Perdu to take someone new—maybe the Head Librarian, or the head of the Thaumaturgical Department.

But Perdu had argued that the timing was wrong for that. *The last thing we want,* he had said, *is for security to find more blood and bones littered across the grounds.*

Shyly wanted to poke at him, to say, *You wouldn't allow that, though, would you?* but she didn't. Because they both knew that this place made finding a private place for such a transfer hard, if not impossible.

So she acquiesced, realizing in that moment that she was the only one who could make the upcoming job that Lumin had planned even halfway successful.

The shadow did resolve itself into the shape of a squarish middle-aged man. He wore a long overcoat and galoshes, which were necessary on the soggy ground. The rain from the past few days had actually created a thin moat around the Old Library, remnants, Croninshield had said, of its history as the largest fortress in Dorovich.

There were footbridges over the ditch that surrounded the entire large building, taking the place of actual bridges that had existed long before the campus was built. Shyly knew things like that because they interested Louella, whose memories were as messy as her apartment. Bits and pieces of unimportant facts, often acquired from books, lived inside her memories as if they had really happened to her, a fact that annoyed Shyly more than she could say.

She had devised a method to deal with those little memories, but it wasn't an effective one. She couldn't really speak about anything, because she wasn't sure how Louella acquired the information. So Shyly simply did not share tidbits or personal information, which was, apparently, a large enough change that one of her coworkers had looked at her with compassion.

That attack really messed with you, didn't it, hon? the coworker had said. *I'm here to talk if you want. But it is okay to participate in conversations just like you used to. I miss the random esoteric facts.*

Shyly had nodded and given what she hoped was a wan half-smile. *I miss saying them,* she had said, and left it at that.

"Louella," the man said, his voice watery and indistinct. She could barely see his face. "Do you have the information on the Hidden River that I had asked for?"

Gray's code phrase. Spies often used them because Spies were rarely recognizable to anyone, including their Fey compatriots.

"I do," Shyly said. "It's inside. I can take you to it, if you want."

That was her response code phrase, something they had set up when the team decided that she would take over a librarian. The meetings could be set using a Qavnerian assistant, but the code phrases could not.

Gray had two set responses. If he said he wanted her to take him to the "information on the Hidden River," it meant he needed a tour of the library. If he needed that, then Lumin's plan would wait a week or more. Somehow, she would have to figure out a way to sneak the entire team inside—not just to the stacks of the Student Wing, but into the back areas, the areas she had been able to go.

"I'm afraid I don't have time for that," Gray said. "I'm meeting friends later."

Her breath caught. That was his second coded response. It meant that the attack would happen, and it would happen soon.

"I'm sorry to hear that," she said, and actually meant the code phrase. "It would be better if I took you inside."

He shook his head. "I don't know if you know," he said,

"but there's been trouble in Trinovante. The Old Families were attacked."

Now he had deviated from the code phrases, but he clearly still worried about being overheard. She wasn't sure exactly what he was trying to tell her.

Attacks on the Old Families had been planned. The Trinovante troop had decided to get what artifacts they could through good old-fashioned theft. Some of the other troops didn't have the right kind of members to do a more finessed theft, such as the one they were trying here.

The other troops didn't have Doppelgängers and a couple only had one Spy. Without the proper kind of information gathering, the other troops often had to resort to brute force attacks.

Gray straightened. She couldn't read his expression, which was no real surprise, but she had a sense that he was upset.

"Some of the attackers were caught," he said, his voice shaking. "Others died."

"Died?" she breathed. She knew that they were all taking risks, but she hadn't expected anyone who had come to Dorovich to die. The Fey simply had too many advantages over these people, most of whom had forgotten their magick and didn't believe they needed it.

"I would have thought you knew," Gray said.

She shook her head. She'd been spending the past two weeks preparing for her takeover of Louella. Shyly had been in Serebro, then on campus in her other identity, never listening to much more than local campus gossip and trying to figure out who Perdu had taken over.

She had never figured that part out. He had had to reveal himself to her in the library, in front of Louella's colleagues, which had been awkward at best.

"Who died?" she asked.

"Almost everyone," Gray said, his voice low and serious.

"What?" She spoke a little too loudly. "Everyone?"

"Almost," he said.

"How is that even possible?"

He waved a hand, reminding her to be quiet.

She let out a breath. She had almost joined the Trinovante troop when they were putting troops together in Nye. At first, she had believed that being in one of the major cities on Dorovich would be a good use of her talents.

But then, she had learned that the Dorovicians kept information in schools and academies, that a lot of their power was based in esoteric knowledge systems, and she figured that learning those systems was better.

Besides, Lumin had been putting together the best team. Somehow he had gotten early picks of all of the people who were traveling to Dorovich, so his Enchanter had more experience than others, his Spies had actually served in hostile territory, his Infantry included people known for both brute strength and emotional control.

She had decided she belonged here. She was glad she did, but she was also rocked by the news. She had known everyone on that team.

The night's chill had grown. Not just because the air was getting colder and she was not properly dressed for it, but because the news was literally making her shiver.

"Has...um...." She didn't know how to ask the question

she wanted to ask, especially if someone was overhearing the discussion. She doubted that anyone was, but she had to be careful. "Have there been similar situations in Serebro?"

She hoped Gray understood the question. She wanted to know if others on their team had died.

"Most of the Old Families were attacked in Trinovante," he said. "Not many of them have real homes in Serebro."

Which wasn't true. Those who were on the Board of Regents had multiple homes in the Serebro area. One of Louella's colleagues in the library complained about that— about the rich bastards who ran all the schools throughout the Protectorate.

Apparently, they were here, on campus, tonight.

Shyly supposed she had better tell Gray that, just in case it was pertinent.

"So, no attacks here?" she asked, needing the clarification. She had spent nearly a year with this troop, what with the travel to Dorovich from Nye and then as they prepped for their work in Qavner.

She didn't want to lose any of them.

"Not yet, no," Gray said, lowering his voice even more. "But we believe it's only a matter of time."

"How could this happen?" Shyly asked. "They don't... we've studied them. They don't..."

Have the right kind of magick. Have magick at all. They're pacifists, who had no idea what to do in a war.

She could have said all of those things, but only some of them would have been true.

She had thought—all of the Fey who had come to Dorovich had thought—that the Dorovicians didn't have the right kind of magick to defeat Fey who were determined and unimpaired by other experiences.

The histories of the Fey suggested, although she didn't know if the suggestions were true, that the trip through the Fey's Place of Power to the one here on Dorovich had been so destructive that no one who made the journey had the same kind of magick they had had when they left.

And those were the Fey who survived. Most of the troop hadn't lived through that trip into the Place of Power, which was why no one had done it since.

But as for the warlike attitudes of the Dorovicians, she had learned that wasn't true at all. There were always skirmishes and wars here, and the Qavnerians, in particular, were brutal about it.

Long ago, they had used their ruthlessness to conquer countries outside their borders. Then they, rather like the Fey, had set up governments to keep those countries under the thumb of the Protectorate.

Any country that rose against the Protectorate was subject to actions that would make some Fey blanch. The Qavnerians had no problem destroying entire communities of people if those people rebelled against them.

Putting down rebellions was a particularly Qavnerian art form, and one that Shyly was just beginning to understand.

The mental argument she was having with herself was both a feature of being in a new host body and part of her. Gray apparently knew that, because he watched her—seemingly without any sign of impatience.

"I would think," she said slowly, "that they would need... um...you know..."

She waved a hand at herself and then at Gray, hoping he understood. She really didn't want to use the word *magick* out here, even though she couldn't see anyone watching them.

"...abilities that I didn't think, *we* didn't think, they had," she finally finished, feeling like she hadn't expressed herself quite well enough.

"Apparently they have them," he said. "And the abilities are quite destructive. Lumin Saw..."

Gray stopped himself, shook his head, and then raised both hands as if he didn't want to talk anymore.

She was glad he didn't. An anxiety she hadn't felt since the night before she attacked Louella was filling her. And if Shyly wasn't careful, the anxiety would eat her alive and make her completely ineffective.

"What do we do?" she asked, her voice as low as Gray's.

"You tell me where the materials are," he said. "I'll let the troop know."

That was blunter than she had expected. She had, apparently, gotten used to the elliptical sentences and speaking in code.

She moved a little closer to him so that she could speak as softly as possible.

"I don't know where everything is," she said. "Apparently, there's a hierarchy here, even in the library staff. I picked the wrong librarian. She doesn't have access to the right places."

"So pick the right one," he said.

"There's no time," she said. "I'm not battlefield trained.

It's taken me days to adjust to this one. Another one would—"

How did she explain this to someone who didn't transfer their entire consciousness into someone else?

"—would make me lose myself and my sense of purpose," she finished.

He let out a bitter half-laugh. "Screw yourself and your sense of purpose. I've known Dop—people like you who have changed three times in one day."

"And they're trained for it," she said. "It's a rigorous training that I have not had. Not all of us survive it."

Which was why she had hadn't even volunteered for that kind of service.

Gray cursed and looked to his right. A ground fog was scuttling toward them as if it were one of the Qavnerians strange windstone vehicles.

Shyly recognized that kind of fog. It was Weather-Sprite created.

She knew the Sprites had been playing with the weather in Serebro for nearly a month, but the fact that they had moved their work to the Academy meant the attack truly was imminent.

Lumin wouldn't let his Sprites loose on this enclosed place without a plan that he needed executed almost immediately.

Gray crossed his arms. "So what don't you know? Maybe you were more thorough than you thought."

"This place—" and she waved her right hand at the Old Library "—was once a major fortress. It has a gigantic footprint, one I haven't yet explored fully. And, as a fortress that has existed for a thousand years and been repurposed a dozen times over the centuries, it has dozens of rooms that I haven't seen, that no one sees except those in charge."

"You know where the rooms are, though," Gray said.

She shook her head. "There are staircases to nowhere, blocked-off areas, old platforms that are rotting away. Because there are also a lot of students here, the staff has erected barriers to some of the more dangerous areas. The last thing they want to do is tell one of the Old Families that one of their precious children fell to his death through some rotted floor."

Gray cursed again and took a step backwards. "We came here tonight thinking you would have the information for us. We need it."

We came, not *I* came. *We.* The attack was tonight.

"I know vaguely where things are," she said. "I know which doors will lead you into the right wing. I know where the artifacts seized during the Purges are stored, ostensibly to keep them out of the hands of the out-of-control magickal, but really to consolidate power in these Academies."

"Vaguely," Gray said, and there was a viciousness in his tone. "We need to know exactly."

"I'm aware of that," she said. "You need to give me more time."

"Haven't you been paying attention?" he asked. "There *is* no more time."

She raised her hands, opening them in frustration. "None of this is as simple as you all seem to think it is," she said. "This isn't the only library on campus."

"I figured as much," Gray snarled, "since it's called the *Old* Library."

She shook her head. "It should be called the *main* library. Because that's what it is. It's the library everyone uses and it has the largest amount of space. But there are department-specific libraries all over campus, and that includes libraries housed in the Alchemy and Thaumaturgical Departments. There are books and artifacts there, not to mention some things of ours—"

And by *ours*, she meant *the Fey*, although she wasn't sure Gray understood that.

"—housed in the Archeology Departments, the Art History Departments, the History Department—"

"Stop," he snapped. "You've made your point."

He put a hand over his mouth. The hand became watery, just like his voice was. Shyly could see the fingers and the general shape of the hand, but the detail, like the size of his knuckles, the color of the skin, the wrinkles and scars, those were all gone.

She wrapped her arms around herself. The cold had gotten nearly unbearable. Ground fog swirled around her feet, engulfing them and making them even colder.

The white fog started climbing up the side of the building, as if following a mission to reach the top.

"There's too much for us to take with our small troop," he said, "is that what you're saying?"

She nodded. "I think so. I mean, if we go slowly, over many months, we can figure out what the important items are and take those, maybe use some...you know...designed by Eerie to slowly destroy everything else—"

"We don't have months," Gray hissed. "I *told* you that."

She nodded. "Our mission—"

"Was designed on another continent by someone who had never been here," he said. "We had no idea—"

"Then maybe we should just go back there and tell him," she said. "Maybe we should take our time. Because haste..."

She almost recited a Qavnerian proverb about the way that haste compounded problems.

This morning, she would have been happy that she had absorbed enough of Louella to make a casual reference to something Qavnerian, but everything had changed since the morning.

Everything.

The fog really was climbing up the side of the building, distracting her. She wanted to slap it, send a message through it to the Sprites that they were being too obvious.

But she wasn't sure that was true. They were being obvious to her.

"We're not going back," Gray said. "We're going to complete our mission."

"How?" she asked.

"Well," he said, "we can't take it all."

Then he gave her a smile, a smile she could actually see. She could see his entire face, just for that moment, and his face looked completely feral.

The expression made her heart race.

"I said that," she said. "We don't have the personnel."

"We can't take it all," he repeated, slowly, as if she were stupid, "so we're going to have to destroy it."

LINGUISTICS

ARCHEOLOGY

HISTORY

REGENTS

TOWER

OLD

LIBRARY

ADV. STUDENT
WING

MAIN
ENTRANCE

CLOCK
TOWER

MEDICAL

SCIENCES

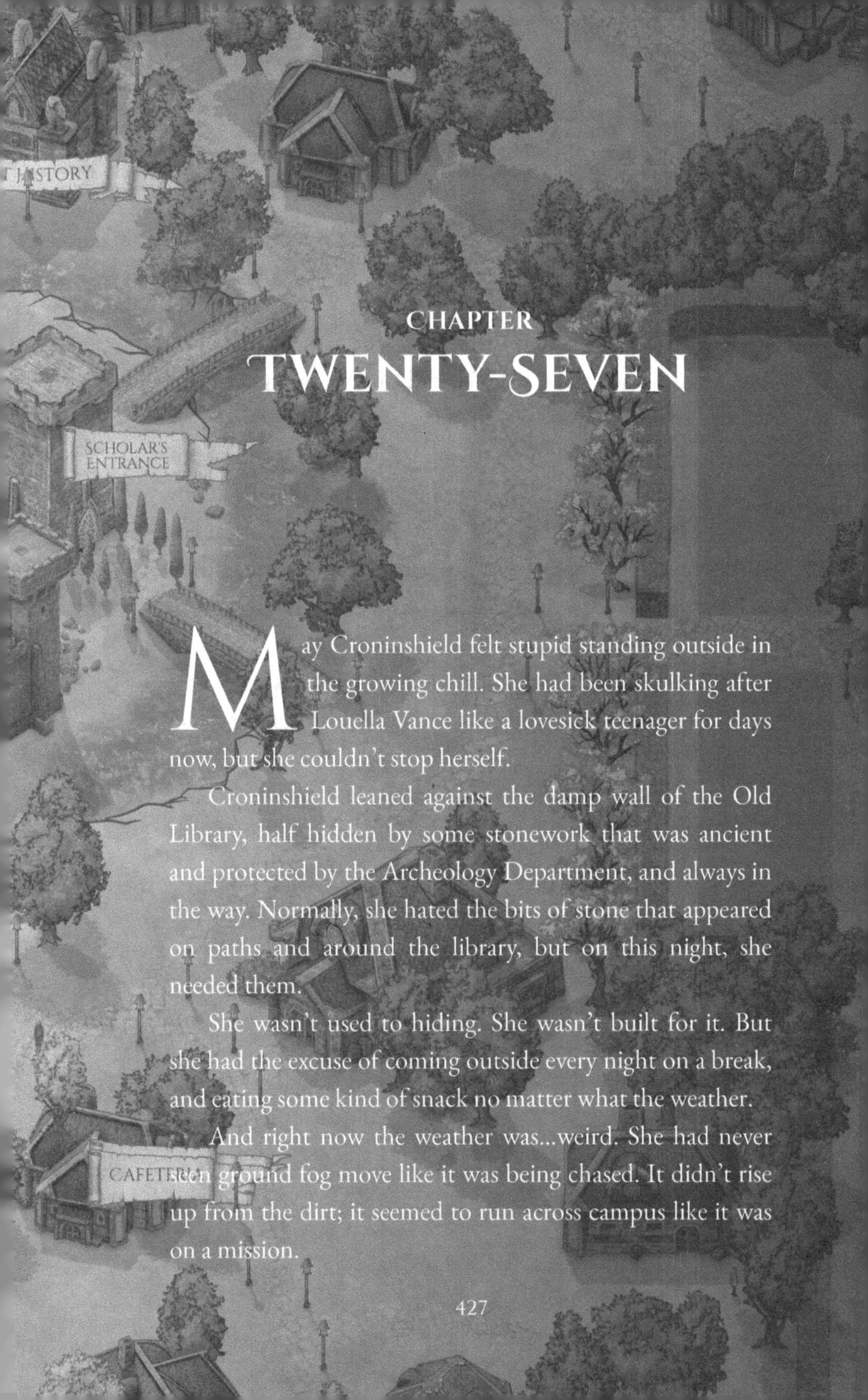

CHAPTER
TWENTY-SEVEN

May Croninshield felt stupid standing outside in the growing chill. She had been skulking after Louella Vance like a lovesick teenager for days now, but she couldn't stop herself.

Croninshield leaned against the damp wall of the Old Library, half hidden by some stonework that was ancient and protected by the Archeology Department, and always in the way. Normally, she hated the bits of stone that appeared on paths and around the library, but on this night, she needed them.

She wasn't used to hiding. She wasn't built for it. But she had the excuse of coming outside every night on a break, and eating some kind of snack no matter what the weather.

And right now the weather was...weird. She had never seen ground fog move like it was being chased. It didn't rise up from the dirt; it seemed to run across campus like it was on a mission.

The air wasn't the right kind of damp, either, for ground fog. The rain had stopped, but it was still threatening and could restart at any moment. The standing water all over campus had become little lakes.

Ground fog did use rain and lingering damp to create itself, but usually the day after a big storm. And not when there was wind. Croninshield had always thought major winds and ground fog were enemies.

The wind was coming and going this night, as the clouds thickened and thinned. That put her on an even higher alert.

The books she had been reading about the historical Fey battles mentioned weird weather before some of the battles, as if the very skies themselves had conspired with the Fey.

She had asked Sauer if he knew about the Fey affecting the weather, and he said that magic can do whatever it wants within reason. She called that a non-answer, and he had laughed.

You want me to know everything, he had said. *If I could, I'd have you talk to some of my Advanced Students. But they're in Nye, studying the Fey and working on their theses. What I know is what the historical record says, and the historical record mentions weather events unlike any that the locals had seen before.*

She had seen a lot of rain, so much as she wanted to think the past few days had been unusual, they hadn't. But this ground fog. It didn't act like regular ground fog at all.

She had initially come outside at her regular door, the one that overlooked the bridge and the copse of trees. She was early, because she wanted to have a snack before Louella arrived.

Louella was due an hour from now. So Croninshield had been surprised when she saw Louella in a summery white dress walking with purpose toward the Old Library.

She had gone around the copse of trees—which was expected, given what had happened to her there—and then had gone to the somewhat hidden side of the Advanced Student Wing of the Old Library, the part without a lot of windows, very few doors, and not a lot of visibility from other parts of campus.

Of course Croninshield had followed, even though she really didn't have a ready-made excuse for doing so. She skulked as best she could, pulling her ratty sweater around herself against the chill, and clutching the remains of the brioche she had snagged for her snack.

Instead of taking one of the paths, she had crossed the grounds, knowing that they were slightly raised here, so she hadn't expected to step in as many ice-cold puddles as she had.

Her feet were now soaked. She would have to change when she got back inside, or she'd have to go home to get more clothing, which irritated her. She hadn't planned for any of this, but she couldn't put someone else on it.

She had a feeling that Louella was up to no good.

Croninshield hadn't seen anything untoward in Louella's behavior since she returned from the attack. If anything, Louella had been more timid, hesitant in ways that anyone might have been. Sometimes she seemed to recede into herself, as if she didn't want to attract any attention at all.

Most of her movements seemed slow. She used to be

quick to grab a book, quick to ask a question, quick to make a quip.

She did none of those things now. If she did take a book from a student or a staffer, she stared at it for a moment as if she didn't know what it was.

If there hadn't been any blood or bone, Croninshield would have thought Louella was simply reacting to the trauma of her attack. But Sauer had made Croninshield nervous. The idea that Louella was no longer Louella stuck in Croninshield's mind, even though something like that was nigh unbelievable.

Croninshield had been considering backing away from the severe stalking she had been doing for the past few days. What she had seen Louella do differently had been tiny things, insignificant things. She hadn't tried to explore parts of the library where she didn't belong. She had recognized everyone on staff. And she had done her job as competently as she always had.

But this, tonight, crossing the campus with purpose, and then the attack of the ground fog, put Croninshield on alert.

That, and the man with no face.

It didn't matter how much she squinted, how hard she concentrated, how dangerously close she got, she couldn't see the face of the man who had approached Louella just before the ground fog took over everything.

Croninshield hadn't even really seen him until she heard voices—and she had been staring at Louella the whole time.

The wind came up as the man got closer, and Croninshield had only been able to hear parts of the discussion. Something about a book, and going inside the library.

But why wouldn't they already be inside? Why have a conversation in this weather? It made no sense, if what they were talking about was on the up-and-up.

Croninshield wished she could get closer, but she didn't dare. And it really bothered her that no matter what she did, she couldn't see that man's face.

Even his voice sounded off—watery, as if it were coming from some kind of deep, dark hole.

Her reading had not mentioned people without faces. At first, she thought her inability to see his face was simply because of the growing darkness and the diffuse light from the humidity in the air.

But he had walked toward Louella carefully, avoiding all lightstone lanterns. He had put his head down when it seemed like light from a lantern would touch him.

And there were no lightstone lamps or lanterns anywhere near their meeting site.

That couldn't be a coincidence. One thing Croninshield did know from her research into those old Fey battles was that many things she took for granted—from lightstone to windstone to ironwood—seemed to have an adverse effect on the Fey.

A lot of the artifacts stored inside the Old Library and the now-closed Thaumaturgical Museum of Magical History had been created in response to the Fey threat. Many of those artifacts were very old.

Some of them turned into other things, with incredible abilities to alter the world around them, and the alteration threatened people. Each country on Dorovich seemed to have developed its own magical artifacts to counter the Fey spells—particularly in Khēmía, where the Fey had somehow arrived in great numbers, and the first battles were waged.

Many of the artifacts were later banned, because their powers could be turned on Qavnerians, particularly those who wanted power over the entire continent.

Croninshield didn't like any of what she had read, and she didn't like what she was seeing now.

Louella stepped closer to the man with no face. They were almost head to head, their bodies so close there was very little space between them.

Croninshield felt a surge of anger—although she wasn't sure if it was at Louella or at herself. Croninshield had been thinking of giving Louella the benefit of the doubt—that all of Louella's behavior had been caused by trauma from the attack.

But someone who had been injured, maybe even intimately assaulted, someone who had barely survived some kind of violent attack, wouldn't get that close to anyone for any reason.

Croninshield clung tightly to her ratty sweater, wishing she could make herself even smaller. She didn't want either of them to notice her watching them.

She leaned against the stone and turned a little sideways. She could still see them out of the corner of her eye, standing too close and talking quietly, but she hoped they couldn't see her at all.

In case they did, she picked at the remains of her brioche. It was dry and tasteless without something to drink, which was why she had stopped eating it in the first place.

The ground fog had almost entirely engulfed her and her stone, also (perhaps) keeping her from being seen.

She was frightened and not frightened, angry but resolved, and still a little doubtful. The whole idea of someone taking over someone else seemed impossible to her, despite the evidence she had seen in the last few days.

The evidence was tiny when looked at individually, but in a group...it was still hard to swallow.

But so were a lot of the magic properties she had read about as well. And the other things she had seen in her family, even as a child.

She was going to have to go back inside, but she wasn't sure if she should wait until Louella's meeting with the man with no face ended or if she should just saunter away now, as if she had seen nothing.

Croninshield did want to get out of the fog and back inside.

She also needed to talk to Sauer. He would know what was happening. He would also know what to do.

She hoped, anyway.

She would have to send someone to him because she couldn't leave work now.

He would have to come to the Old Library. She wasn't sure how to word her request. Maybe...*regarding what we had discussed?* Or...*I've seen some strange things in the past few days?* Or a simple...*I think we have a problem.*

She would make the decision by the time she got inside the Old Library. She also had to decide who to send to find him.

She'd need someone reliable, someone she could trust.

And after what she had just seen with Louella, Cronin-shield wasn't sure she could trust anyone.

She shivered. Her feet were blocks of ice. Drops of water from the fog were seeping into her hair and sweater.

Maybe she should get Sauer herself, then stop at home and change clothes. But she had extras here in her office. She would change here.

Because she would get just as wet coming back to the Old Library. And she really wanted out of this fog.

It didn't feel safe here.

Nothing did.

Then she squared her shoulders, admonishing herself.

Safety was overrated. She had a job to do. And she would do it as best as possible, given what she understood at the moment.

Which wasn't a lot.

PART SIX
MIDNIGHT ON
THE OLD CAMPUS

THE
TURNOUT

SEREBRO
MOUNTAIN RANGE

CHAPTER
TWENTY-EIGHT

The drive up the mountain was the worst Cole had ever experienced. The conveyance worked fine, but he was cold and occasionally dizzy. He didn't trust his own eyes at times, slowing down for shadows in the road.

At least he wasn't the kind of exhausted that would make him fall asleep while driving. He had his fury against Xavier and Volkovich at failing to tell him everything, even though he knew, in his heart of hearts, that Xavier had saved his life.

The drive also seemed to take longer than usual. Maybe Cole had been driving more slowly than normal. It wouldn't surprise him, given his limitations on this night. His entire body ached, almost as if he were coming down with a flu, even though he knew he wasn't.

If he had the time—and he probably didn't—he would

see a medic before going to the meeting in the morning. He had no idea what kind of damage that explosion had done.

Xavier and Volkovich were not forthcoming. After that burst of conversation before they left the row houses, neither man spoke unless spoken to. They didn't converse with each other either. The ride was silent, except for the whistle of the wind in the windstone vents.

When they started down the Academy side of the mountain, the sky lightened a little. It wasn't anywhere near dawn. It took a few corners and the thinning trees for Cole to figure out what he was seeing.

The moon's thin light seemed almost as rich as sunlight as it peeked through branches. That didn't mean that the moon was full—far from it. What it meant was the drive up the mountain had been so dark that any bit of light looked like the middle of the day.

His shoulders ached, and his fingers sometimes slipped on the steering sticks. He kept wishing the conveyance was farther along the road than it was, because that comfortable bed and warm fire in the Regents Lodging were calling to him.

He needed to stop and assess. He needed to rest his brain and his body. The idea that a group of Fey—the enemy from hundreds of years ago—had returned to Dorovich seemed incredible to him. Yet the two men riding with him seemed convinced.

The evening's events were making Cole reassess everything he had learned about magic. He wanted to learn more, and he wasn't sure he could absorb any of it.

The trees thinned even more and then started to clear entirely as the road began its steepest descent. Around the next corner was a turnout. He would stop there, shake out his shoulders, maybe smell a bit of pine in the air, and hope it cleared out his sinuses.

He took the curve slowly, and then stopped when he saw vehicles in the turnout. They looked odd, almost as if they were trying to move without going anywhere.

"What the...?" he muttered.

He drove to the edge of the turnout, so that he could pull over without leaving the conveyance in the middle of the road.

"Why are we stopping?" Volkovich asked.

Cole ignored him.

He got out of the conveyance and wobbled just a little, his legs unsteady, his back aching, his stomach a bit more queasy than he would have liked or expected.

The carriages bobbled even more. As he walked closer to them, he saw the two horses in front of each carriage tied to nearby trees. There were eight horses in all, and they seemed panicked.

Their ears were back. Their eyes so wide that the whites reflected what little light there was. One of the horses snorted and that led another to squeal in what could only be described as terror.

He hated horses. He'd stopped riding them when they bucked him as a child. He tried not to ride in carriages if he could avoid it. When he reached his full growth, he had learned to drive windstone vehicles, almost in self-defense.

He didn't see anyone around the horses, and no one

came out as that horse squealed. These horses and their very expensive carriages had been left behind.

He recognized the insignia on the carriages. These were part of a fleet of rental carriages run by the Academy.

Cole pivoted and returned to the conveyance. Neither Xavier nor Volkovich got out.

He pulled open the door.

"One of you better be good with horses," he snapped. "I'm not and these are in trouble."

Xavier didn't say a word. Volkovich sighed audibly, then pushed open the door on the other side of the conveyance.

"You wouldn't have any kind of food, would you?" he asked.

Cole didn't even deign to answer that. Of course he didn't. He had driven to Serebro in a hurry at their orders, and he had figured that they would get food somewhere if they needed it.

He waved a hand at the horses. "They're tied to trees."

"They're *what?*" Volkovich said. "If they lose their footing..."

Cole understood that at least. The accident would have been spectacular and terrible for the horses. They might have strangled or fallen down the hillside. The carriages would have tumbled and rolled.

Xavier grunted and that was when Cole realized that Xavier had fallen asleep. That fact made the fury Cole had barely been able to maintain rise again. He needed to deal with these carriages, not with the fury he felt at this entire day, which just seemed to get worse and worse.

"What's wrong?" Xavier said, half mumbling.

"Come see for yourself," Cole snapped as he helped Volkovich out of the conveyance. Volkovich was moving as slowly as Cole, which made Cole wonder for the very first time if that explosion had had an effect on Volkovich too.

Volkovich walked over to the carriages, and cursed audibly.

"I'll need your help," he said to Cole.

"Horses and I don't get along," he said.

"Horses?" Xavier asked. He sat up and peered forward, then got out of the conveyance as if someone had pushed him.

He staggered forward, looking exhausted as well. His robe, so brightly illuminated in Serebro, had gray markings instead of white ones.

"I've never seen anything like this," he said, more to himself than to Cole.

"Whoever tied these animals up didn't care if they survived," Volkovich said. He started to reach for them when Xavier said, "Stop!"

Volkovich didn't move.

Xavier waved a hand—tiredly, it seemed to Cole—and a shadowy grayness appeared around the carriages. They hadn't tipped over because they appeared to be in some kind of gigantic box.

"Don't tell me," Cole said. "More magic."

"Yes," Xavier said, stepping back. "And badly done too by someone without a lot of power."

"Fey?" Volkovich asked.

"It would seem so." Xavier stepped closer but didn't touch anything. He moved his hands, as if he was drawing pictures in the air. This time, though, Cole couldn't see any words moving or light appearing around that box.

"We have to do something," Volkovich said. "Those horses are in distress."

Xavier didn't seem to notice. Cole walked around the entire turnout, looking at the ground for clues. He saw scuff marks and what appeared to be footprints.

There wasn't enough light to see it all clearly, not even with the beams from the lightstone lamps on the front of the conveyance.

Xavier brought his hands down. "I believe this was done by the same person who put up the wards."

Cole froze. "So we're facing another explosion."

"No, I don't think so," Xavier said. "I think they stored these carriages for themselves."

"Where are they then?" Volkovich sounded scared.

"I would guess, given the insignia, that they're heading to the Academy," Xavier said. "They're not here. I checked."

Xavier hadn't moved from that handful of steps he had taken from the conveyance.

"How did you check?" Cole asked.

"I have a sense of a handful of them," Xavier said. "I will be able to track them, if we need that. I'm not sure I want to use any more energy, though. The events in Serebro exhausted me."

Cole frowned. He still didn't understand any of this, and he needed to. His inclination was to find some books and have them explain what was going on, since Volkovich and Xavier hadn't told him anything.

But that wouldn't help him now.

"I can take this apart," Xavier said. "With no explosion."

He sounded hesitant, though.

"And then what?" Cole asked. "I have no idea how to handle horses."

"I do," Volkovich said quietly.

"Besides," Cole said. "It looks like these Fey people plan to return here."

"They do," Xavier said, "or they wouldn't have left this mess. And when I get rid of it, there is a chance that they'll know what I've done."

"So we leave this for someone else, then," Cole said.

"Who?" Volkovich asked. "Very few people have Xavier's skills, which means we leave this alone for the Fey who nearly killed you."

Cole's irritation rose again. That wasn't entirely how they had explained the explosion to him. It hadn't been fully the fault of those Fey.

But Volkovich had a point. If Xavier didn't get rid of this, then those Fey will have the carriages waiting for them.

"I doubt they drove these carriages up here themselves," Cole said.

"I wonder why they left them here," Volkovich said.

"It makes sense if they're sneaking onto campus." Xavier rubbed his hands together. "I'm going to free these horses."

"Let me find the drivers first," Cole said. "They have to be around here."

"Or maybe they're trapped inside the carriages," Volkovich said. "Maybe some magic made it impossible for them to get into those driver's seats."

"No," Xavier said. "There are no people inside those

carriages. Besides, they would be calming the horses if they could. See what you can find, Cole."

As if Xavier was in charge. Maybe he was, given what was happening.

"How big is that box thing?" Cole asked. "How much room do I have so that I don't touch it?"

"You can see it now, correct?" Xavier asked.

"Yes," Cole said.

"Avoid what you can see, and you'll be just fine."

Cole hoped he was right. He wouldn't be able to survive another explosion like the one that occurred in Serebro. It hurt to move, but he forced himself to.

He walked around the light from the lightstone lamps. They revealed only the mucked-up dirt and hoofprints. He walked back into the road and looked it up and down, seeing nothing but road and trees in one direction, and the curvy downhill road in the other.

Light rose behind him, which he assumed was Xavier doing whatever Xavier did.

Then Cole saw a lot of scuff marks behind the conveyance. He had probably parked on several more. He walked over to them, carefully, his heart pounding, worried that he might be making himself some kind of target for these people who scared his companions.

Behind him, the horses snorted. One of the horses squealed. Light flared around him, but he didn't turn around. He kept walking.

The smell of sap grew, along with a bit of pine. It all smelled fresh.

He stopped near the edge of the road and waited for his

eyes to adjust to the ever-changing light.

Then he saw the broken branches on some nearby trees, the snapped sections of shrubs whose make he couldn't name. The scuff marks he'd been following continued downward.

His heart was beating so hard that it was almost painful. He was holding his breath, which he knew was *not* helpful.

He reached the edge, where the turnout began, just as the shrubs and the trees thinned. Then, because he was still dizzy and didn't entirely trust his balance, he put a hand on the trunk of a nearby pine.

The bark bit into his palm. The tree was actually cold, something he wasn't sure he'd ever felt before.

He leaned over, and looked, waiting again for his eyes to adjust.

When they did, he saw what he half suspected. The body of a man about fifteen feet down, splayed on his back, neck at an impossible angle, empty eyes staring up at him.

The man wore the brownish uniform of a carriage driver, and even looked vaguely familiar. It was hard to tell from this distance, and with that kind of trauma.

Below him, another man, also splayed, also in brown, face to the sky, clearly dead.

"I found them," Cole said. "They won't be driving the carriages any time soon."

He was surprised at how calm he sounded. He didn't feel calm. He had somehow separated from himself—from the pain, the dizziness, the strangeness. It was as if he was observing himself, a tall, lean man with dried blood on his face, looking down the mountainside as if nothing disturbed him at all.

No one responded to him. He turned around, saw Xavier, with his hands raised, his robe now glowing gold—that same color Cole had seen in the bubble back at the rowhouses.

Xavier held a long golden stick in his hands. It looked almost like a spear, only it kept reshaping itself. It almost looked like it was moving and growing as he held it, with drops of light falling off of it and dissolving on the ground below.

Volkovich had moved onto the road itself, but he had his back to any possible traffic coming downhill.

"Pasha," Cole said. "Come stand by me."

Again, calm. Volkovich glanced over at him, as if he hadn't heard what Cole had said.

Cole beckoned him, and Volkovich picked his way across the road, to the very edge.

"I found the drivers," Cole repeated, and pointed down.

"Down there?" Volkovich asked without looking. "Can we help them up?"

"No," Cole said. "They're dead."

Volkovich's shoulders slumped. Apparently he had not expected that.

"I'm not sure what any of this means," he said.

"I think we stop worrying about what it means," Cole said, "and we figure out how to deal with the carriages. You know horses. Can you drive one of those carriages to the Academy?"

"Yes," Volkovich said without hesitation. "Both Xavier

and I can. We used to bring our own carriages to meetings before it got—oh, I don't know. Unseemly, I guess—to do so."

Cole didn't ask why driving a carriage would be unseemly.

"We're going to have to notify someone about the drivers," Volkovich said. "They'll have families."

"Yes," Cole said. "They will."

Still calm. Almost as if someone had put a jar over him. He couldn't feel anything.

"We'll let campus security know," he said.

"They can't do anything!" Volkovich sounded distressed.

"They will know who to contact. I suspect someone will have to go into Serebro and talk to the constabulary." Cole didn't know, though. He had never discovered a dead body before, certainly not one that had been clearly murdered.

"We have to get out of here," Volkovich said. "These Fey, they'll be back. I'm not sure Xavier will have the stamina to attack all of them."

"I thought you have magic," Cole said.

"Some. Not any useful magic, though," Volkovich said. "You have some too."

Cole shook his head, then staggered sideways. That damn dizziness.

It brought him back into himself, shattered that glass-jar feeling, made him almost ill.

"It's loose magic," Volkovich said. "You'll need training."

He seemed unperturbed by Cole's sudden loss of balance. Maybe they were coping as best as they could, seeing what they could change, ignoring the rest. It would make sense.

"I'm not going to get training tonight," Cole said.

"Clearly."

Cole had to get away from the edge. He was afraid he might tumble down the mountainside. He could almost see himself landing on those bodies.

He shuddered.

He waited a moment, until his balance returned, and then he picked his way carefully back to the road, making sure to look in case a vehicle was heading toward him.

Xavier was using that golden spear to poke at the darkness around the horses. The dark rectangle would move as he poked it, but it didn't shatter.

"I need you both here," he said. "Those horses might get even crazier when I destroy this thing."

Volkovich made a sound, almost like a protest. Cole wasn't sure what he could do with horses, but he would try.

He walked over to Xavier, followed by Volkovich. Xavier's robe glowed as golden as the spear. Words floated around him, almost like they were communicating something that Cole couldn't read.

"Are you ready?" Xavier asked.

Cole wasn't. He could feel himself tensing. "Will there be another explosion?"

"I hope not," Xavier said. "This doesn't look powerful enough to cause an explosion."

I hope not wasn't the kind of reassurance that Cole wanted. He wanted a full-throated *No, not at all.*

He stood back, trying to find that glass jar again. But it

was gone. He was shivering and he knew it wasn't from the cold.

He was terrified.

"Well," Xavier said in a surprisingly level voice. "Here we go."

And then he stabbed the rectangle.

REGENTS

TOWER

ADV. STUDENT
WING

MA
ENTR

CLOCK
TOWER

CHAPTER
TWENTY-NINE

Ludmilla scurried along the wide path that lead from the Regents Tower to the Old Library. She hadn't walked this way since she had been a student, which seemed longer ago tonight than it had that morning. She felt older, not necessarily wiser, but more disillusioned.

And determined.

The night air was colder than it had been just a few hours earlier. A pure white ground fog looked like a live thing as it moved across the grounds. In some areas, it undulated, as if it were water, not fog.

It did not reflect the light from the lightstone lanterns that were placed at regular intervals along the main paths. One of the security guards at the Regents Lodging House had told her to be careful if she was going to be out late, because there had been an attack on campus the week before.

Ludmilla had thanked him and then mentally dismissed

his words. She knew how to be watchful on campus. She had lived through a particularly violent time during her years at the Academy. A ring of thieves had worked the dormitories and had attacked anyone who caught them in the act.

She had taken some classes from the physical education department designed to help students learn how to defend themselves. Much of it was just attitude. If she looked strong as she walked, anyone who wanted to take advantage of her would chose a less difficult target.

Or, at least, that was how the theory went.

She'd never had a chance to test it, because the ring of thieves broke up after a few months and most of them were caught.

But she remembered the lessons: walk with confidence, act like you knew where you were going, and make it clear that you were the one in control.

She didn't feel like she was in control. She felt buffeted by the day's events. But undaunted. Maybe that was the definition of being in control.

She didn't entirely know.

The ground fog was thick ahead of her, almost up to her waist. She couldn't see the path leading to the Old Library. She had to go by the pools of light from the lanterns, and from the footbridge that rose out of the fog like an afterthought.

The fog was particularly thick near the copse of trees on the far side of the path. The fog looked more like a snow pile, the kind whipped up by a particularly harsh wind and shoved against the side of a building.

But there was no building in that little grove, just some intersecting paths, if her memory was correct.

Students scurried through the fog as if they were swimming upstream. None of them looked happy. All of them seemed to be in a hurry to get to their destinations.

Just like she was.

She couldn't help but feeling that there was something very wrong out here. Not just because of the meeting or the strange encounter she had had with Reginald or any one of the other myriad things that had happened this day, but something in the fog.

The fog felt unnatural. It jangled her nerves, and made her hands tingle. She wanted to grab the fog and gather it, the way that she would gather batting that was leaking out of a particularly thick quilt.

It took most of her control to prevent herself from touching the fog with her fingers. So far, the fog had only brushed against her clothing, but a part of her that rarely made its presence known admonished her to keep the fog away from her bare skin.

Even if she hadn't had that mental admonition, she would have done everything she could to keep the fog from touching her directly. Something about the fog really bothered her.

She hurried along the path, the fog swirling around her, as if it was trying to figure out who she was.

As she came up to the footbridge, she realized there was water in what, in her day, the students used to call the moat. A lot of water that looked somewhat fresh, instead of stagnant with some kind of algae growing on it.

The water looked like it had bubbled out of an underground spring, which wasn't possible. This amount of water had to have come from the rain.

Ludmilla climbed up the footbridge and stopped at the top, out of the fog. Her breath was coming in short gasps. She had to regulate it, which she did by breathing slowly.

Students kept walking past her. Others made their way through the growing fog.

Off in the distance, she thought she saw a man hurrying away from the Old Library. Then she blinked and he was gone.

A shiver ran through her. She would have attributed that shiver to the cold, but it might've been the man. He looked... watery. And she wasn't sure how that was possible.

She made herself turn away from that strange man, but turning made her see the fog anew.

It didn't gather in some areas—like the sides of some of the buildings. But just south of where she had seen the man, shadows moved. They were vaguely human-shaped and stopped moving when her gaze rested on them, almost as if they could feel her staring at them.

They looked as unnatural as the fog. Shadows usually didn't freeze when they saw movement. And it was usually easy to see how the shadows had formed.

These shadows were far from the lightstone lanterns and did not have the squarish shapes that would come from a nearby wall or building or even a lamppost itself. She couldn't see what created them. There was no obvious light hitting some kind of block that would result in a shadow.

She shivered again.

Maybe she should return to the Regents Lodging, and give up on finding the bylaws. Maybe she needed sleep more than she needed answers.

But she knew that she would toss and turn in that sumptuous bed they had provided. She wasn't tired. She was overwhelmed.

She had to get to the library. It had the answers she wanted—she hoped, anyway.

The campus was eerily quietly. The fog had dampened the sound of footsteps. If someone happened to come up behind her, she wouldn't have been able to hear him.

That thought alone got her to move.

She really didn't want to plunge into the fog again, but she had to. She needed to get to the library and out of this strange damp night.

The Old Library usually looked inviting at this time of night. As a student, she had spent a lot of late nights in the Old Library. As a new student, she had thought it would be empty at night, but it never was. Students studied around the clock, and the librarians worked the entire time.

The Old Library had been one of the liveliest places on campus after dark. She had always loved that about it.

In her memory, the Old Library would be a beacon of light against a blue night sky. Students would go to and fro, always carrying books, always laughing.

But she knew that memory was false. She had rarely looked at the library after her early days on campus, and by exams, no one laughed as they carried books from place to place. The Old Library could be a place of tension.

On this night, it seemed like a shadow of its former self.

Instead of lights against a blue night sky, the Old Library looked tired and shopworn, the lights barely visible in the gloom from the day's rain.

Even the white fog surrounding the moat and the path didn't reflect the light. The fog looked like it was trying to devour the walls of the Library, creeping upward like an out-of-control plant.

She shoved her hands inside the pockets of her coat and raised her chin just a little. She had the sense that, if she didn't hurry, the fog would get so deep that it would touch every part of her, something she didn't want to happen.

So she started to walk quickly off the footbridge before changing her mind. She didn't dare move that fast. What if she slipped and fell? Disappearing under that fog almost seemed like disappearing underwater. Part of her wondered if she would even be able to breathe underneath it.

She picked her way down the footbridge, and felt her feet slip on more than one occasion. She let out a small sigh of relief when she was no longer walking on a decline. Her feet hit the main path, sending the fog swirling around her again, and she had to do everything in her power to keep from running to the double doors.

The lightstone lamps above them seemed bright as day. The fog had not gathered near the doorway. In fact, the fog had not ventured close to the doors at all. It formed a half circle at the edge of the light pool from the lamps, almost as if they were giving off a heat that melted the fog.

Not that lightstone ever gave off heat. Or that some kind of heat could melt fog.

She shook her head, trying to pull the fantastical

thoughts from it. But she couldn't shake the feeling that the fog did not like light from those lamps. Nor could she shake the feeling that the fog actually had opinions.

Part of her truly believed that the fog was alive.

Despite the damp path, she hurried through the last few yards of fog, heading toward that well-lit half circle of light. When she hit it, she let out a sigh of relief.

She had been terrified in that fog. It took all of her strength not to turn around and see what the fog was doing. If it had been a person, she would have turned, would have seen exactly how close it was.

But it was not a person. It was fog. No matter how strange it was, it wasn't alive and it couldn't hurt her. She couldn't drown in it.

Still, she stepped deeper into the light and felt some of the anxiety that had filled her on the way here melt away.

She let out a sigh of relief, then grabbed the handles of one of the oversized doors, and pulled.

The door opened, revealing even more glorious light.

She stepped inside, and shivered again, only this time, it felt like she had shaken off the chill from that fog. She moved laterally away from the door, so that she could just stand for a moment without being in anyone's way.

The Student Wing of the Old Library had once housed the kitchens and major dining hall for the fortress. The layout of the dining hall was evident to anyone who knew the history of the place.

This hall had arched ceilings and a wide, wide floor, which, even now, was covered with tables. Only they weren't attached to each other. They were separated from each other. A few of them were pushed up against the walls, leaving room for the doors that opened every few yards.

None of these walls had books or bookshelves. Instead, they were covered with tapestries on the lower part of the walls, and artifacts on the upper part.

At the opposite side of the hall from where she stood now was a dais where rulers of this particular part of Qavner had been served their meals. The dais had once only been in the middle of the floor, but when this wing had been converted to a library, it had been extended so that it ran from wall to wall.

Students had to take a small series of steps up to the dais, where a long desk stood between them and the back rooms. She had never known what was in those rooms—more books? Special books? Papers pertinent to the library?—and as a student she hadn't asked.

Now, she wondered if that Regents Library that Reginald had told her about had been moved to one of those rooms, and if so, how hard it would be for her to get inside that room.

Students graced many of the tables ahead of her. Most of the students were working, bent over books before them as if the books held the secrets of life.

Some of the students were standing near their tables, talking with other students. The ceiling rose several stories above them. The arch, with its crisscrossing wooden beams, seemed to absorb sound. The conversations became muted, part of the general sound of the hall, rather than something she could eavesdrop on.

She knew from personal experience that if she sat two

tables away from a group of talkers, she wouldn't be able to hear the details of their conversations. It was one of the many things she liked about this library.

She also knew that when she got to the dais in front of her, no one who was standing a few yards from her on the same dais would be able to hear any of her requests.

The flooring here was marble, pulled from quarries in the Coastal Mountain Range. This marble was completely local, but it had threads of lightstone throughout. That meant this part of the library was never really dark—and probably never had been, even when this section was part of the fortress.

The light from the floor helped a lot, because the high ceilings seemed to make the light diffuse. There were light-stone lamps on the walls, but the lamps didn't seem to give off a lot of light.

There were individual lamps at regular intervals on the tables as well, but every student knew that sitting between the lamps meant reading would be exponentially more difficult the farther from the lamps the chair was.

The chairs between the lamps were usually empty, unless it was exam time, when even the worst students showed up and tried to pretend they hadn't skipped as many classes as they had.

She unbuttoned her coat, and resisted the urge to remove it. Even though she was standing close to the doors, the air was warmer here than it had been outside.

She actually felt comfortable. And, like she always had in this gigantic hall, she felt at home.

Now, though, she was seeing it with different eyes. Most

of the rooms on either side of the hall led to the regular stacks. As a student, she had often gone into the stacks and just browsed, marveling at both the wealth of knowledge and the number of books inside just this part of the library.

Thousands of books, by her guess, although she had no definite count. And the lightstone lamps in those stacks came on only when someone touched the lamps at the edge of each towering bookshelf.

The ceilings weren't as high in the stacks, but they still went up more than a story. The shelves on the walls in the stacks went all the way to the ceiling, although the other shelves went up only three-quarters of the way. There were ladders on wheels that anyone could use at their own peril.

She had only done so a few times.

She knew that those stacks weren't where the Regents Library was. There were rooms beyond the stacks, though. She remembered seeing doors, and hearing that some of them led to still-standing kitchen storage, not to mention other corridors that went to doors on different sides of the building.

There was some kind of courtyard in the middle that she had only seen once.

None of which mattered to her at the moment. But it sure felt good to bask in the library proper.

She doubted the Regents Library was on this level, unless it was behind the dais. Surely, it wouldn't be that close to a door. There had to be too many artifacts and materials that had to be protected.

Although this part of the library was pretty cavalier about some artifacts. That had always bothered her, since her family had taught her to be very cautious around the artifacts stored in her childhood homes.

Most of the Academy's artifacts were decorative, from paintings of the Academy to maps of the grounds. Some walls even had current displays, showing work from students. High up, out of reach, were some weaponry, such as swords and knives with hearts along the hilts. The swords fascinated her, because she never thought of hearts as something appropriate for weapons.

There was also a display of shields, many with familial crests. Her father had once tried to point out the Odenkirk crest, but it was up near the top of the wall, and nearly hidden in shadows.

Still, on this evening, she glanced at it, wishing she could see it more clearly, wishing that it would give her some strength.

She squared her shoulders and plunged into the central aisle, the only place in this entire hall where there was enough room for students to walk two abreast in either direction.

It took nearly fifteen minutes to walk from the student entrance to the librarians' desks. Behind them were nearly a dozen ten-foot tall tapestries. She had seen those tapestries throughout her entire student career, but she had never really registered them.

They created a map of the Protectorate, following the Hidden River as it made its way along the middle of the continent. The countries that had either fended off the Protectorate or had removed themselves from the Protectorate years ago were outlined, but not filled in, while all of the others were a riot of color that seemed to befit their nature, from the dark greens, grays, and browns of Qavner to the bright golds and yellows of Khēmía.

The Hidden River changed color from tapestry to tapestry as well, often following its ancient name changes. It went from a bright blue in Khēmía to the gray-brown river that had provided the foundation for Trinovante.

Ludmilla frowned at it, thinking about the discussion of the maps earlier in the day. There were maps all over Qavner, often used as decoration. Mapmaking was considered as much an art as a science here, and mapmakers were revered. There were several courses in mapmaking at the Academy, including some that were very exclusive.

She made her way up the stairs to one of the librarians. The woman stood near an open door at the back. She looked tired, her hair escaping from the bun on the top of her head. She wore a wildly inappropriate dress, a floaty one that looked better suited to a warm summer day than a strangely foggy middle of the night.

Ludmilla stopped in front of the desk and politely waited. The librarian didn't seem to notice her at first, although that might have been a ploy. Ludmilla had seen librarians use it in the past to keep students from inter-rupting.

Eventually, the student would move on to another librarian, and if there had been any nearby, Ludmilla might have done that.

But she had some time, anyway. She could wait.

Besides, she wasn't entirely sure this librarian saw her. The librarian was engrossed in a map that she had unfolded along her desktop. The map was of the library itself.

Ludmilla was familiar with that map. Every dormitory had a version of it near the entry. There were other maps as well, all of them depicting campus buildings.

The depictions were woefully incomplete, designed mostly for students who had never been on campus before, and who needed some kind of aid.

This map, for example, had a lot of blank spots and unmarked areas where other libraries and study rooms were. Ludmilla had become familiar with many of those over her years here. She also knew that there were many parts of the library that no one but the librarians and a few select Scholars saw.

She was about to clear her throat to get the librarian's attention, when the librarian looked up.

The librarian had old eyes, much older than the rest of her face. She stared at Ludmilla for a moment, as if trying to place her.

When that obviously failed, the librarian said, "May I help you?" in a tone that suggested she didn't want to help at all.

"Yes, thank you," Ludmilla said, and took a step closer, because she didn't want to speak too loudly. There weren't a lot of people nearby, but still. She didn't need to everyone to know her business.

An older woman looked up as Ludmilla stepped closer. She had silver hair that looked damp, and a rounded face, filled with lines and folds that somehow accented her dark eyes. She wore a long sweater over a matching skirt, thick stockings, and boots. The sweater was baggy and out of shape. It took Ludmilla a moment to realize that the sweater had pockets that were clearly stuffed full.

That older woman looked a bit familiar. She had probably been working in the libraries since Ludmilla had been a student here.

"I...um..." Ludmilla spoke slowly in the face of the young librarian's obvious disinterest. "I used to be a student here—"

The librarian's eyes hooded, as if she was bracing herself for complete stupidity. She probably got a lot of that from the younger students.

"—and I spent a lot of time in the library." Ludmilla silently berated herself. The librarian didn't need to know that either. "But I'm not sure I can find what I'm looking for on my own."

"What are you looking for?" If anything, the librarian's tone got drier. It was almost a shove backwards.

"Um, well, you see, I'm a Regent now, and I'm—"

"Oh." The librarian's eyes brightened. Apparently Regents were important to everyone on campus, even librarians who handled regular students.

"—looking for the Regents Library," Ludmilla said, lowering her voice just a little. "I'm told that it was moved here...?"

The librarian frowned, almost like she had to think about each word that Ludmilla had said, almost like Ludmilla was speaking a foreign language.

"Yes," the librarian said. "Yes, it was."

She glanced at her map as if it held the answers. Ludmilla put a hand on the map. It crinkled as it flattened.

"I know it's not depicted on there," Ludmilla said, beginning to realize she had approached the wrong person. "I'm familiar with that map. It's posted at every dorm on campus."

The librarian's cheeks grew flushed. "Of course it is. Yes. I was just checking something else before I put it away."

That was such an obvious lie that Ludmilla frowned. She'd never had a librarian lie to her—to her knowledge anyway.

Ludmilla looked around the back, trying to find someone else to help her. She didn't like this librarian at all.

The librarian folded the map back up and set it aside. Then she smiled, another look that didn't meet her eyes.

"Let me find the keys and I'll be right back," she said.

Ludmilla waited until the librarian stepped away, a little stunned that she hadn't mentioned to the librarian that she already had a key.

The librarian should have known that very few people had keys to the Regents Library. Ludmilla doubted they were handed out willy-nilly. She had a hunch this particular librarian wasn't cleared to use the key to the Regents Library.

Ludmilla caught the gaze of the older woman. If anyone knew anything about the library, it would be the older woman. Ludmilla felt confident about that.

She decided to let the other librarian continue her futile search for the key, and walked to a part of the desk closer to the older woman.

"Excuse me," Ludmilla. "I'm one of the Regents, and I need some assistance."

The woman looked almost panicked when she heard Ludmilla's introduction. She glanced toward the tapestries, where the other librarian was talking to one of their colleagues.

Then the older woman said in a loud, stentorian voice, "Louella. You can return to your post. I'll help this woman."

The librarian in the floaty dress—Louella, apparently, who had a name that didn't suit her at all—gave the older woman a look of pure hatred. Ludmilla felt a shiver run through her. That look was completely out of place. Ludmilla couldn't remember ever seeing anyone look at another colleague that way, particularly somewhere like a library.

The older woman's eyes narrowed, then she firmly turned her back on the younger librarian.

The older woman approached the desk, and gave Ludmilla a kind but curious smile.

"Louella's not supposed to leave the desk right now," the older woman said. "My name is May Croninshield. I run the library. How may I help you?"

"I was told that the Regents Library had been moved to this building," Ludmilla said.

Croninshield's right eyebrow twitched. Otherwise, her expression remained unchanged. But she had had some kind of emotional reaction to Ludmilla's comment.

"You mentioned you're a Regent," Croninshield said, "but I don't believe we've met."

Her comment implied that she had met all of the Regents.

"We probably did," Ludmilla said. "I was a student here. But this past year I just took my father's seat. His name was Franklin Odenkirk."

"Ahh." Croninshield's smile changed. It actually became warm. "I remember your father. And, unless I'm remembering incorrectly, you're the young girl who used to trail him and sit near the arched windows in the Regents Library when it was in the Regents Tower. You didn't seem to mind that meetings took forever."

Ludmilla frowned. She had remembered a librarian, but not this woman. Or perhaps Ludmilla's childhood memory wasn't as clear as she thought.

Croninshield caught the expression and apparently understood what it meant. "I don't think you knew, but your father needed special permission so that he could leave you in the library. We were happy to give it."

"Oh," Ludmilla said. "I was very surprised and saddened to learn that the library had moved."

"There's been a lot of changes since Devin Chaban became chairman of the board." Croninshield's tone implied that she wasn't happy with those changes either. "I oversaw the transfer of materials to the new Regents Library space. Are you looking for a particular item?"

Ludmilla lowered her voice even more. "I need to review the bylaws."

This time, both of Croninshield's eyebrows went up. "I don't believe anyone has done that in a generation or more. You do realize that the bylaws are not in a single book...?"

Ludmilla didn't officially know that, but part of her sensed it. "It doesn't surprise me."

"I can't remove more than one book from that library," Croninshield said.

"I understand," Louella said. "I don't mind reading in the library."

Croninshield tilted her head for a moment as if she were trying to figure Ludmilla out.

Ludmilla liked the woman and somehow trusted her, but not enough to admit that she wanted the bylaws because that day's meetings had gone so badly awry.

"You know," Croninshield said. "I remember the day your father brought you to this library. You couldn't have been more than twelve."

"Ten, actually," Ludmilla said. And then, because she had a hunch it was expected of her, she added a small detail. "That was the day that my father pointed out the Odenkirk Family Crest on the wall. I see that you haven't moved it. It's still too high up for most people to notice."

Croninshield's lips moved in a tight little smile. "He used to say that it comforted him to have the crest in the student library."

"But also that he was happy no one but the family could see it," Ludmilla said. Her father used to say that all the time.

Croninshield let out a small breath, as if she was relieved to hear Ludmilla say that.

"I will have to take you to the library myself," Croninshield said.

Ludmilla shifted slightly. "You don't need to interrupt

your work. If you give me directions, I can find it. I have my father's keys."

Even though Reginald had been the one to give her the key to the library. She didn't have to tell Croninshield that.

Croninshield let out a small laugh. "I'd love to give you directions," she said. "But that presumes that the library is easy to find. It is not. You could be wandering the building for days."

She tightened her baggy sweater, then looked over her shoulder. The strange younger librarian—Louella—was still watching them.

"Come to the far side of the desk—" Croninshield waved a hand to Ludmilla's right. "—and I'll take you the shortest route."

"Thank you," Ludmilla said, and followed instructions. She knew that the desktop lifted at strategic points on the dais. She'd seen it in the past. So she walked to the far side, feeling like she was being watched.

She probably was, by both Croninshield and the strange librarian. The entire evening felt a little off. But what should she have expected, especially given that no one else seemed to know that Chaban had tampered with the Regents Library too.

When this was over, she would tell Cole and maybe a few others. Or maybe she would wait until she was done examining the bylaws.

Because she might find something in those that would change everything.

Even though, at the moment, she had no idea what, exactly, that would be.

SCHOLAR'S
ENTRANCE

OLD

LIBRARY

CE

CAFETERIA

CHAPTER
THIRTY

May Croninshield had made her step away from the desk. In all of Louella's memory, there didn't seem to be any other moment like that one.

Shyly could possibly blame the head librarian's curtness on the fact that the woman in front of the desk had been a Regent that Shyly didn't recognize, but as far as she could tell, no one else had realized it either.

She was standing near the tapestries, whose magic was so subtle it had taken her nearly a day to realize the images moved. Not because the tapestries moved—which they did, whenever someone walked past—but because something triggered the images to change ever so slightly.

Magickal change always had a purpose—that was one of the first lessons any Fey child learned—but that purpose might not be immediately obvious. Once Shyly had actually

471

shown up at the library, she knew she had to spend more time studying what was around her.

Lumin's desire to have information quickly was getting in the way of completing this mission properly. She had tried to tell Gray that before her work shift started, and he was having none of it.

But the arrival of the Regent was a case in point. Regents ran the schools and, according to most, controlled the way that knowledge was handled throughout the Protectorate. Every Fey knew that knowledge was a commodity like everything else.

Whoever had the most knowledge had the most power.

Although that wasn't entirely playing out in Qavner, since librarians seemed to have a great deal of knowledge and they were only in charge of the books and items in their various libraries.

Shyly had had no idea there was a Regents Library in this building. If she had known that, she would have sent the troop there first. Because if the Regents were in charge of knowledge, then it stood to reason that their library was filled with secrets, the kind that the Fey needed.

Shyly watched Croninshield talk with the Regent. The Regent seemed awfully deferential for someone who wielded that much power. She was taller than many in Qavner, though, and she had upswept features that suggested Fey and magick in her lineage.

Despite what she had told Gray, Shyly would risk another transfer if she were alone with that Regent. It was too big an opportunity to miss.

Maybe an opportunity she could take even now. Maybe

if she followed Croninshield and the Regent to the library, Shyly could take the Regent then. The things she would learn...

Would be useless by the time the evening was over, at least if Lumin had his way.

Shyly wasn't certain how Lumin planned to acquire everything on this campus, unless he abandoned the mission. Gray's suggestion that they destroy it all warred with Shyly's Fey instincts and the remnants of Louella that remained inside her.

Louella would have been appalled at all of the destruction. Shyly understood the reasons for it, but she too felt like it might be too much.

If only they could easily contact Rugar. But he had not come to Dorovich. These troops were finders of fact for a future invasion. They weren't there to start a war now.

Although, she now knew, no one in Dorovich would think of Fey behind any attack. If anything, the Qavnerians would blame other malcontents inside their Protectorate— or the countries that had so far refused to join.

The problem everyone in Dorovich seemed to have was that they rarely looked outside their own continent—either in trade or in governance or with magick.

Maybe it wouldn't hurt to become the Regent. Shyly would gain a great deal of knowledge and some power inside of Qavner. She would have to stay here after whatever it was the Lumin planned, but if these troops were successful, having a Fey as Regent would certainly help Rugar conquer Qavner, if not the Protectorate, and Dorovich itself.

The Regent was nodding and almost smiling at Croninshield. Louella had no idea what kind of person would smile at Croninshield. The woman was a problem, curt and diffi-cult. Surely, the Regent would notice that.

Shyly stayed back, letting herself be half hidden by these annoying tapestries. One of the other librarians gave her a sideways glance, one she understood without checking her Louella memories. That librarian wanted her to get back to work.

If Shyly spent the next hour or so correctly, she wouldn't need to get back to work. She wouldn't need to fight at all inside this tiny fiefdom. She would move toward a greater power.

She would have to plan better, though, than she had when she had taken over Louella.

But, Shyly knew, there were a lot of nooks and crannies inside this building, not to mention walls so thick that no one would be able to hear screaming—if the Regent's last act was a scream.

Shyly would probably even be able to find a good place to hide the bones. The blood pool, she wouldn't be able to do anything about, but if she picked the right location for the transfer, no one would notice that until it dried.

She was still tired from the last transfer, but she could get through another. And then she would have to find another little unused room in this building to recover. She might not be able to communicate to Lumin before he started whatever he had planned.

But the Old Library itself should protect her, if she found the right room.

She would have to follow Croninshield and the Regent,

though, which would be tricky. Because Shyly wasn't supposed to leave this front area right now.

And she couldn't anticipate, since she still had no idea where the damn Regents Library was. It wasn't on any of the library maps that she had seen.

The fact that the Regent had caught her with the wrong kind of map, that stung. Shyly thought she had been past those small telling errors, but apparently not.

However, if she managed to take over the Regent, none of this would matter. Shyly would have to look at the next few hours as an opportunity, not as something that she might get caught at.

Croninshield and the Regent were now both walking toward the far wall. They were mirroring each other, so that probably meant Croninshield was going to take the Regent through some back passages.

Shyly had no idea how she would keep up with them. She needed to follow, only without drawing too much attention to herself.

Skulking around wasn't usually a Doppelgänger trait, though. She didn't have much training in it. Once a Doppelgänger had overtaken their subject, they could move forward with impunity.

Or so the training said.

It wasn't designed for moments like this one.

Shyly headed back to the desk, saw a pimply-faced male student heading up to the desk, clutching a piece of paper. Usually that meant he had a list of books that someone had assigned him.

She had helped five students just like him the day before,

and it had taken forever. Louella had had patience with those kids, asking them about their reading and what they liked about their studies.

Shyly just wanted them to go away.

And now, she really needed that kid to go away. So she pivoted, ignoring one of her colleagues who said, "Hey, Louella! Someone at your desk!" and hurried toward the other side of the tapestry, away from where she had stood before.

She saw Croninshield lifting the desktop for the Regent, who smiled her thanks. Then they walked toward the back of that part of the dais, side by side, conversing about something.

"Hey, Louella!" Another colleague, a man whose name she couldn't immediately access, touched her arm.

She emitted a squeak and moved away from him. She hadn't realized he was coming.

He flushed, and drew his hand back.

"Sorry," he said, and she realized he had thought she didn't want to be touched because of what the staff had started to call "the attack." She'd let that assumption stand.

She moved away as if he had hurt her, then made her lower lip tremble. Finally she fled toward the side of the dais where she had last seen Croninshield and the Regent.

Maybe no one would come after Shyly if they thought she was in emotional distress. This was a pretty buttoned-up culture, after all.

She pushed her way around some smaller desks, made herself bang into a chair, pretending she didn't see it, and then bowed her head just enough to look like someone who was crying.

Through the corner of her eye, she saw that Croninshield was holding a door for the Regent. They were still talking.

The Regent passed through the door, and Croninshield followed.

The door was easing closed. Shyly hurried. She recognized that door. She had tried it the past two nights and it had always been locked.

She arrived beside it just in time to slide her hand between the door and the jamb.

Then she pushed the door open just enough to slip through.

The back area was dark, but she heard voices in the distance, and recognized one as Croninshield's. Shyly eased the door closed so that it wouldn't bang shut.

The voices faded, but there was still no light. She could see shapes that she couldn't identify, things that had to be something other than tables and chairs and desks and shelves.

She had no idea where there were no lights in here, but it irritated her. Maybe this was one of those places inside the Old Library that didn't have wall lamps. Maybe there had been a lantern, and maybe Croninshield had taken it.

One of the many strange things about the lightstone lanterns was that they had no discernable odor, unlike an oil lamp. Shyly couldn't follow the smell.

She pushed forward as best she could, hands in front of her, cursing the fact that she was so far behind already. She thought she heard more conversation, and footsteps on marble, but she wasn't sure.

And she had to move slowly, because the worst thing she could do would be to bang into a table and send something crashing.

Her hands found the edge of a chair she hadn't been able to see, and another and then another. The chairs were randomly scattered, which led her to believe she wasn't in the proper aisle in this room full of things.

She wished she could see what the things were. Maybe they were what she was supposed to be looking for.

Not that she dared focus on that right now. She needed to catch up to Croninshield and that regent. If the rest of this back area was as deserted as this room, it would be an absolute gift for Shyly.

She would be able to take over the Regent and no one would be the wiser...if she could figure out what to do with Croninshield.

And that might not be as easy as it seemed.

THE
TURNOUT

SEREBRO
MOUNTAIN RANGE

THIRTY-ONE

The sleeves on Xavier's robe fell back toward his shoulders as he stabbed the rectangle around those carriages. His arms were thick and muscled, and the muscles rippled as he shoved that golden spear into the shadowy darkness.

The horses were all moving now, their eyes rolling in their heads. Some were snorting. One continued to squeal. Two tried to rear up, but they couldn't. Still, their panic made the others shift.

If they all got free at the same time, this would be awful. Cole wasn't sure what to do, but he knew he couldn't stand next to those carriages or the horses themselves.

Xavier was too close, but Cole couldn't do anything about that. He could, however, move Volkovich back.

Cole grabbed Volkovich's arm and tried to pull him away, but Volkovich shook him off.

"We need to get out of the way," Cole said.

"We need to calm those horses," Volkovich responded.

"Horses hate me," Cole said.

Volkovich peered at him sideways and then cursed.

Xavier was still stabbing at the rectangle. It was as if he was trying to pierce really thick fabric, and couldn't do it. Finally his entire body glowed golden. The spear became part of him—or so it seemed—and he launched himself forward with such power that the entire rectangle changed color.

It glowed golden as well, the color moving along it as if each drop of color also possessed a spear tip. The rectangle was wobbling, losing its shape. Maybe it wouldn't blow up after all. Maybe it would dissolve.

Inside the rectangle, the horses were all snorting or chuffing and bucking, the carriages rocking. Volkovich shook Cole off and hurried to Xavier's side, almost as if offering moral support.

Cole didn't want to think about what he would do if they both got injured as that thing exploded. It was large enough to hold the carriages and the horses. So that explosion might be much bigger than the one he had experienced in Serebro.

He wondered if anyone could see the golden rectangle from the Academy below. The golden glow was certainly lighting up the trees and the road ahead.

Fortunately, he didn't see anyone coming up that road.

He was threading his hands together, uncertain what to do with them. What to do with any of this.

The screams of the horses hurt his ears. The light was

blinding. His dizziness was returning, almost as if the screams were making it stronger.

And then the rectangle popped, the way a bubble would.

It was there one moment, gone the next, only little bits of it floating in the air.

The stench of horse flesh mixed with horse manure and horse urine was so strong that his eyes watered. Apparently sound could penetrate that bubble, but the bubble had held in smell.

Cole wasn't sure how that worked.

He wiped at his watering eyes, and staggered forward. Xavier was swaying on his feet, the spear gone. Volkovich held up his hands, facing the snorting, bucking horses.

The carriages rocked so hard they seemed unsteady on their wheels. Any more movement, and they would either fall into the road or roll down the mountainside.

Volkovich didn't move, though. He kept his palms pointed outward, and as Cole approached, he realized that Volkovich was chanting in a sing-song voice.

The horses seemed to hear him too. They stopped bucking. The four closest to the road turned their heads toward Volkovich. Their teeth were still bared, their ears still flattened, but their eyes weren't as wild.

They planted their hooves on the dirt. The horses on the other side were still fighting the carriage restraints, but they had stopped bucking too.

Xavier staggered slightly, but managed to avoid Volkovich.

Cole realized in that moment that it was Volkovich who

was calming the horses, with that chant, that tone, maybe even something with his hands.

Volkovich made a clucking sound that even Cole found soothing. He hurried to Xavier, put hands on his arms, and said, "I've got you."

And when Xavier heard that, he collapsed.

It took all of Cole's strength to hold Xavier upright. Cole managed to half-walk, half-drag Xavier toward the conveyance.

The horses were still making little sounds of distress, but calmness seemed to be working its way through them.

Cole opened one of the doors on the conveyance, and helped Xavier inside. Xavier put a hand to his head.

"I'm out of practice," he said. "I don't have the stamina for this."

"At least it didn't explode," Cole said.

Xavier raised his eyes to Cole, as if unable to believe that Cole had said that.

"Bubbles don't explode," Xavier said tiredly. "They pop. And fortunately, no one had put something lethal inside that thing. They didn't expect us. They built that bubble to keep the horses and carriages contained and not for any other reason."

Cole shivered. So, apparently, this could have been worse. He glanced at the carriages now. They had stopped rocking. The horses' ears were flicking, almost like there were bugs attacking them. But the horses had stopped moving. They weren't even shifting from hoof to hoof.

Cole turned his attention back to Xavier. Xavier still had

his hand on his forehead. He looked both exhausted and maybe just a bit frightened.

Cole was unsettled too. He wasn't sure what they'd do after Volkovich finished with the animals.

"They'll know I did it," Xavier said quietly.

Cole had barely heard him. "Those Fey people?"

"The one who made the bubble, yes," Xavier said. "They'll be coming here."

Cole exhaled. The night was so cold he could see his breath. Not even the warmth from that bubble—a warmth coated in stench—had made a difference out here.

"But those Fey people," Cole said, "they didn't show up at the explosion in Serebro."

He was protesting not because he needed more information, but because he didn't want another problem. The night had been filled with impossibilities—the *day* had been filled with impossibilities—and he was already tired of them.

He wanted to go home and pretend none of this had happened.

Xavier wiped his hand over his face. His eyes had sunken into their sockets. He looked as exhausted as Cole felt.

"I'm not sure they meant to return to that place," Xavier said. "Up here, they had the horses and carriages corralled so that they could take them back to Serebro."

He blinked, rubbed his forehead as if it ached, and then muttered, "The books must be right."

"What books?" Cole asked.

Xavier waved a hand, almost in dismissal. "The books. On the Fey. And magic."

Cole wasn't aware of any, but that meant nothing. He hadn't believed in this kind of magic either, until tonight.

He glanced again at Volkovich. Volkovich hadn't moved. He was still chanting, palms still out. But the horses' ears had stopped twitching. The horses—all eight of them—were looking at him as if they expected something from him.

Pretty soon, someone would have to take charge. And that would probably be Cole. But for now, he needed to keep Xavier awake.

"What were the books right about?" Cole asked.

"Windstone," he said. "Lightstone. Ironwood. It's supposed to hurt Fey. If they were like us, and wanted to get to the Academy, one of these conveyances would have been better."

Xavier patted the conveyance as if it was a friend. Then he leaned his head on the door panel.

Cole couldn't argue with Xavier's logic. Bringing a windstone vehicle up the mountain was easier than a carriage. Windstone vehicles didn't spook at any sound. They purred along, and provided light forward and aft. They traveled quicker than any carriage.

Plus, it would have been easy to leave a windstone vehicle on the side of the road. Locking the vehicle would have protected it. No one would have thought anything out of the ordinary if they saw a windstone vehicle roadside. People often slept in their vehicles, especially after driving too far.

The horses were silent. So was Volkovich.

He had finally moved. He made his way to the horse that had been tied to a sturdy tree. He reached the lead horse on

the side of the road, and had his head pressed near the horse's.

That posture scared Cole. If the horses got spooked again, they could kill Volkovich. But Cole couldn't say anything about it. He didn't want to startle anyone.

Xavier leaned out of the conveyance and looked at Volkovich. Then Xavier leaned back, adjusting his robe, which had gone completely dark.

"It's all right," he said. "That's part of his magic. Children and animals. He can calm them."

Cole frowned. He hadn't heard of that either. But then, he was beginning to realize just how little he knew about magic and its types.

"He can make them do his bidding?" Cole asked.

Xavier barked out an involuntary laugh. "None of us can do that," he said.

Cole sideways glanced at Volkovich. The horse had actually moved closer to him. It seemed like the others were trying to move as well. They were acting like toddlers who wanted whatever Volkovich had.

Xavier ran a hand over his face again, then sighed. "I don't want to do this," he said, "but we're going to have to. We'll have to leave as soon as we can. The people who trapped those horses will come back. They might already be coming here."

He sounded exhausted. Cole understood that. This day and night felt like it had gone on forever. He was becoming used to the dizziness and the headache.

He wondered if he could get used to the lack of sleep.

"I don't want to yell at Pasha," Cole said. "It might disturb those horses and he just got them calmed."

Xavier's lips quirked slightly, as if he found Cole's comment amusing. "I meant that you'll need to inform him that we don't have much time, if any," Xavier said.

Cole shook his head. "I don't want to go over there. I shouldn't get near the horses. I'll only upset them."

Xavier looked exasperated. "Just because you don't like them—"

"It's not that I don't like horses," Cole said, even though he did dislike them. They were large and smelly and they didn't care who they hurt or what they trampled on. He disliked their long faces, their wild eyes, and the way that they looked at him, as if he was some kind of enemy. "It's just that horses don't like me."

Xavier tilted his head. "Really?"

"Yes," Cole said, feeling impatient. "They don't like me at all."

"And they never have?" Xavier asked.

"They never have," Cole said. "Not that it's important."

He had gotten so much ribbing throughout his life about the fact that horses loathed him. As a young boy, he'd been coaxed onto horses continually, and he finally learned to say no. He hated their lurching, their attempts at shaking him off, or, just as bad, biting him with those big nasty yellow teeth.

"It is important," Xavier said. "Because you can drive a conveyance."

"Yes, I can," Cole snapped. "Which is why you and

Pasha will have to take the carriages. We can't leave them here. We're going to have to take them to the Academy."

Xavier nodded and waved a hand as if that part of the conversation made him impatient.

"You've always been able to drive windstone vehicles, though, am I correct?" Xavier asked. "And I will wager that your family wanted you to adjust lightstone lamps or perhaps move something made of ironwood. Maybe even fix their windstone vehicles?"

Cole frowned at him. No one had ever asked him those three things together. "Yes. Why?"

"Because we are beginning to learn about your magic, my boy," Xavier said. "Yours is mechanical. You can make and run gadgets, can't you?"

Of course he could. But he figured anyone could, if they put their mind to it. Gadgets were designed so that everyone could use them.

He used to think that people like Xavier who avoided gadgets simply weren't trying hard enough.

Perhaps that assumption had been wrong.

"Yes," Cole said. "I prefer gadgets."

"And they prefer you."

That seemed like an odd thing to say. Gadgets didn't prefer anything.

"I don't see why this is important, especially since you just told me that we need to leave quickly."

"Hmm." Xavier's small smile had returned. "Your magic is becoming clear."

"I don't have magic," Cole said.

"Not like I do," Xavier said. "But all magic is different, and yours is focused on ironwood, windstone, lightstone."

He tapped a finger against his lips, clearly thinking.

"Did you see any lightstone near that row house?"

"No," Cole said. "Just an oil lantern hanging off one of the doors. You're not going to try to pin that explosion on me, are you?"

"No." Xavier sounded distracted. "No. But there's something—"

"I don't think it matters," Cole said. "Especially if we need to leave here now."

He wasn't sure what to do with these two. They made pronouncements and then ignored them.

He glanced at Volkovich. He was standing in the middle of all the horses now. The horses in the front of the carriages were looking back at him. The others had moved their muzzles toward him, as if they wanted to be petted like dogs.

"We do need to leave," Xavier said, as if the idea was new to him. He pulled himself out of the conveyance. He was moving with more ease than he had a few moments ago, almost as if the news of Cole's possible magic buoyed him up. "I will get Pasha, and we will take the carriages down the mountain. You will follow in the conveyance."

"It's my experience that following carriages is never a good idea," Cole said. Especially if the horses were nervous or had physical problems. Driving in the dark after carriages often meant driving through piles of dung, which would get inside the vents and send a stench through the entire conveyance.

"In this instance, we have no choice," Xavier said. "If we get attacked on the road, we might need you."

Cole's shoulders tensed. Xavier was right. If the people who had put a bubble around those carriages wanted to come after him, they probably wouldn't want to come near the conveyance—if Xavier was to be believed.

But they might try to attack the carriages again.

"All right," Cole said. "But enough talking. We'll figure out all the magic later. Let's just get off this mountain, okay?"

Xavier smiled. Some of the letters on his robe glowed a slight grayish-white, almost as if they were gaining power from somewhere.

"All right," he said. "Let's go."

STORAGE
BUILDINGS

CHAPTER
THIRTY-TWO

The road finally bottomed out into a sea of houses. Lumin hadn't expected that. From that turnout, it had appeared that the valley was filled with Academy buildings, even though he had known there was housing for the professors and staff. He had somehow figured that housing would be inside Academy buildings, not these standalone boxes that all looked the same.

They appeared to be built at the same time—rectangular and single story. They had an L shape, with a tiny garden or patio in the center of the L. Lights were on inside many of the houses, but none in the patios or gardens, probably because the weather had been so awful the last few days.

The Weather Sprites had eased up on the rain. They had started a ground fog that would envelop the entire campus within the hour. The team could maneuver through it. The Sprites would eventually give them their own bubbles, so that they could see—more or less. If they needed to, anyway.

Lumin hoped they would be near the Old Library by then.

But the houses, and the distance, confounded him. He had been told that the valley housing the Serebro Academy was big, but he hadn't realized how big. He had thought they would get to the Academy when they reached the bottom of the mountain road.

Maybe they hadn't reached it entirely yet. They were still going down ever so slightly. It wasn't as cold down here, but the air was still damp and smelled faintly of burning wood.

He didn't like the lightstone lanterns that illuminated the street corners. After all these months in Qavner, the team understood lightstone, but it could still be a problem if someone stood beneath the light too long.

Eerie had tried to find a way to protect them all from it, but she wasn't a Spell Warder. She couldn't come up with anything that worked really well. Just a tiny sheen of armor that protected them a little. Lumin didn't even let her use it on this trip, because he figured they would need all the energy they could get to make it through the mission.

The houses were not on a grid. The streets curved and meandered. He could see the towers of the Academy ahead, and so he moved as quickly as he could.

The neighborhood was mostly silent, except for the occasional thread of music, usually a keyboard instrument. He didn't know musical instruments well enough to be able to tell the difference between them all, and he wasn't willing to learn it, figuring it was one of those unimportant Qavnerian details.

The longer he'd been here, though, the more he

wondered if those details were unimportant. Qavnerians seemed to weaponize everything they touched, from sculpture to lamps to pens. Or, at least, they had, back when they accepted magick as part of their normal lives.

The vestiges of those days were causing him problems, because there was no easy way to understand what, exactly, Qavnerians could do. Half of them didn't know either.

He made sure the team stayed low as they passed all of the different houses. He tried to steer his people toward the darker homes, the ones farthest from those lightstone lanterns.

The matching houses area ended near a group of fields. The fields had fences and markers, along with bleachers on one side. He'd heard that Qavnerians played sport, but he had never seen evidence of it before.

The only reason he recognized this at all was because of the Nyeians. They too had entire fields and parks dedicated to various sporting events. He had never tried to understand the sports, but he had been told they existed to teach teamwork and prep some students for military life.

He had laughed at that. Military life prepped people for military life. Understanding that was why the Fey had the strongest military in the entire world. They didn't make fighting into a game. From the very beginning, the Fey were taught how serious it was.

Those fields were serious too. His team would be vulnerable as they crossed. They wouldn't be able to go all the way down the road, because the lightstone lanterns proliferated in those fields. Obviously, someone had pointed out how dangerous the darkness could be. Or maybe, the Qavnerians just liked an abundance of light.

Beyond the fields, the old buildings of the Academy loomed. They had been built at different times and different heights, but they seemed a lot more welcoming than these houses.

The ground fog originated on campus, not back here. The white tendrils were hugging the edges of some brown buildings, but he couldn't tell what they were.

The Sprites had worked with the Spies to map the path of the ground fog. It would grow as the team got to work.

But first they had to cross the fields. As Lumin stepped out of the protection of the houses, he heard a gasp. He turned, saw Eerie stumble, and then grab Hardin's arm.

Lumin stopped. A few of the Infantry went farther, though, and formed a ring around the team, protecting it from anything physical that might come at them. He went back to Eerie, who still swayed as if she couldn't keep her balance.

"They found the carriages," she said, sounding breathless.

"Who?" Lumin asked. "The Enchanter you mentioned?"

"I don't know," she said. "I can't See anything."

He wanted to snap, *Of course you can't*, because she wasn't a Visionary. He was the Visionary. But he hadn't Seen anything either. Just the fields and the Academy ahead.

The future, not the present, and certainly not far away.

"Then how do you know?" he asked.

She blinked, a tear running down her face. He had never

seen that, not in all the years they had known each other. She swiped angrily at the tear.

"The protective bubble," she said. "Someone shattered it."

"The horses couldn't have done that?" he asked.

The look she gave him was withering. "I built that bubble to keep them in," she said. "Horses can't destroy something like that. Neither can someone without magick."

"But it wasn't that Enchanter," he said, trying to clarify. The idea of a Qavnerian Enchanter following them chilled him more than this night air did.

"I. Don't. Know." She was angry now, which was better than scared. "But they know we're nearby. And I don't like that at all."

Neither did he. Someone with magick freed those carriages, which caused him two problems. The fact that someone with magick knew there were Fey nearby and there was now no obvious escape route. Either Eerie would have to portal them back to that mountaintop, and they would have to walk (or wait until her magick gave her enough strength to portal them short distances all the way to Serebro) or they would have to steal carriages here.

Maybe the Doppelgängers could help with that. Maybe they could find someone who could take one of the Academy's carriages and get them all out of here.

He cursed, wishing he had thought of a backup plan before now. But he hadn't expected someone to find the carriages. He had thought that the lateness of the hour and the remoteness of that mountain road would protect them.

He had also figured that the drivers might wait for them. But the explosion in Serebro had destroyed that.

The drivers, he realized, had been his first plan. His second had been storing the carriages.

He just hadn't realized that he needed a third.

"Are you going to be all right?" he asked Eerie.

She glared at him, then let go of Hardin's arm. "These last few hours have been harder than I wanted," she said.

Lumin waited. She hadn't answered his question.

She straightened her back, towering over half of the Infantry, and him as well.

"I will be fine, provided that these Qavnerians don't tamper with my magick again."

They weren't really tampering with her magick, Lumin wanted to say. They were discovering it and destroying it.

He didn't have the kind of magick to know just how painful that was, but he suspected it hurt a lot.

He glanced at the rest of the team. The Domestics shifted from foot to foot, uncomfortably. They did not like being part of any action that might result in someone's death, but he needed them. If the injuries got any worse than what he expected, his knowledge of field medicine wouldn't be enough.

He couldn't tell how the Infantry was feeling, which was just as it should be.

And the Weather Sprites seemed more concerned with their growing ground fog than with any discussion that Eerie was having with him.

Which meant that they hadn't felt anything impinge on their magick.

He turned to Veil, who lurked behind the entire group. As usual, Veil's face seemed blurred. Stante, the other Spy, had his back to the group. He appeared to be looking at the houses, although for what reason Lumin couldn't fathom.

"I need you to locate the Academy's carriages," Lumin said to Veil. "We're going to need two to get out of here. Or maybe just a cart that can take us back to Serebro. It's going to be tricky. We'll be moving quickly at that point, and we're going to have to convince whoever to take us."

"Or we steal the carriages," Hardin said, speaking for the first time. "If we are destroying their magick, like you proposed, then they will be running toward the destruction. No one will be thinking of carriages."

Lumin hoped Hardin was right. But Hardin had gone on a lot of raids over the years. He had seen the patterns.

"Finding us might be difficult." Lumin continued talking to Veil. "You're going to have to let us know where to meet you."

"I'll take one of the Domestics," he said.

Lumin nearly protested, but ultimately didn't. Instead, he said, looking at Stante, "Take one with you as well."

Stante nodded. He rarely spoke, and when he did, his voice was whispery and raw. It obviously never sounded that way to any Qavnerian targets, but that was always how it seemed to Lumin.

He had to figure that Stante was saving his magickal energy as well. He wasn't as talented a Spy as Gray, and he wasn't as canny as Veil. Maybe Stante would be able to do something with the carriages, though.

Lumin hoped so, because he didn't want to think about the secondary plans.

He glanced at Eerie. She was disentangling her arm from Hardin's, and standing on her own. She wobbled more than Lumin liked.

"You ready?" he asked her.

She nodded.

It was already a long night.

LINGUISTICS

ARCHEOLOGY

HISTORY

REGENTS

TOWER

OLD

LIBRARY

ADV. STUDENT
WING

MAIN
ENTRANCE

CLOCK
TOWER

MEDICAL
SCIENCES

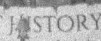

CHAPTER
THIRTY-THREE

Croninshield stopped just past what she always called the junk room. It was filled with books that needed repair or filing or maybe even culling. The chairs were never pushed against the tables, but always left wherever someone had abandoned one. It was a difficult room to navigate even when one was familiar with it.

It would be harder when one wasn't.

To make matters more difficult, Croninshield was not activating the lightstone lamps attached to the wall. Louella's interest in this Odenkirk Regent was disturbing enough that Croninshield was taking no chances.

She stopped midroom, and said, "Follow me closely. Once we leave here, I'll grab a lantern."

"All right." The regent—Ludmilla—seemed a lot more accommodating than most of them. But she had been accommodating from childhood.

503

Croninshield hadn't been lying when she said she remembered this woman as a child. Ludmilla Odenkirk had been unnaturally tall for her age. Most people had mistaken her for a young woman when, in fact, she hadn't yet reached the age of ten.

Her father had worried about her because, he said, *She's tremendously smart about books and hasn't yet learned enough about people.*

This adult woman, though, seemed to know a lot more about people than her childhood self. She seemed calm, but Croninshield could sense a nervous energy beneath that calmness.

And Ludmilla wanted the bylaws, which meant she wasn't happy with what she had experienced with the other Regents. Rather than blithely going along with all they were doing, she was going to check the rules, which made her a kindred spirit.

Besides, Franklin Odenkirk was one of the few regents that had treated Croninshield—and all the other staff at the Academy—very well. As if they were people.

So many of the Regents, wealthy children of even wealthier parents, seemed to believe that the staff were their servants, and nothing more.

"Once I get the lantern," Croninshield said, "I will be walking faster than I am now."

She didn't know what excuse she could use for walking quickly. *I usually walk very fast* would probably do. But *I think you might be in danger* might not.

Might be in danger. Croninshield shook her head at the understatement. If she hadn't stepped in, would Louella have pulled Ludmilla Odenkirk, *a regent*, into one of the back nooks and performed some kind of magic on her? Like that not-herself magic that Croninshield had been unwilling to believe?

Apparently, a part of her did believe it, because she had scurried to Ludmilla's side and had gotten her away from Louella.

And judging by the way that Louella had watched them, Louella was resentful of it.

Croninshield didn't want to contemplate what might have happened had a Fey managed to take over one of the Regents, either as a person or maybe even just exert some kind of mental control.

The very idea made her skin crawl.

"It's all right," Ludmilla said, her voice deep and still calm. "I don't mind walking fast."

Croninshield felt a sense of relief. She didn't want to explain herself much more than she already had.

She wended her way around the chairs, navigating them with her hands forward. Behind her, she thought she heard a door close. She moved a little quicker and was happy to see that Ludmilla kept up.

They reached the far door. Croninshield scanned the tables, and saw what she had been looking for. A group of lightstone lanterns that had been set aside because they were built oddly.

She had remembered them from a year ago when one of the librarians, maybe even Louella, had found them in a closed and locked back room. If the lantern was grabbed incorrectly, the shadowed glass around the lightstone slid into the ironwood base and the light became so bright it was almost blinding.

Rather than try to explain these lanterns to the students working the library, Croninshield had decided to keep the lights in the junk room, in case someone needed something very bright.

In over a year, no one had.

She grabbed one now.

"I'm not going to activate it yet," Croninshield said softly. Again, she felt like she needed to add an explanation, but she wasn't sure what that explanation could logically be.

She didn't know Ludmilla Odenkirk well enough to explain anything to her.

Croninshield walked to the door. She waited beside it as Ludmilla joined her, and then opened the door, sending too much light into the junk room.

Croninshield thought she saw a hand around the door to the library proper, but she wasn't sure. From this distance, though, it looked as though that door hadn't closed properly.

Croninshield almost pushed Ludmilla out of the junk room, then followed and yanked the door closed behind them.

Normally, Croninshield would have taken the main corridor up to a wider flight of stairs. It was slightly out of the way, but it would have made for an easier trip to the Regents Library.

Right now, though, she didn't want an easy trip. Louella had never been to the Regents Library—most of the librarians had not—and Croninshield wanted to keep it that way. She didn't want to make it easy for Louella to find.

Croninshield turned sharply to the right, and pushed open a nearly invisible door.

"Stairs immediately," she said, and almost shoved Ludmilla through.

Ludmilla started down, picking her way much too carefully. As long as the door to this corridor was open, some light from lightstone lamps from the main hallway filtered in. Once the door closed, though, they would be in total darkness.

When Croninshield closed that door, she would have to activate the lightstone lantern. And that might give Louella a clue as to where they had gone.

Croninshield went as far down the stairs as she could while holding the door open with her fingers. The stairs curved and became half-stairs, making them very dangerous. Ludmilla stopped partway down, looking up.

"How far do these go?" she asked.

"Another few feet," Croninshield said. "Stay to the right."

If they could get down the stairs without lights, then they would be heading in the correct direction. Even if Louella did follow them into this stairwell, she would get confused when she reached the bottom. What she would find was a long hallway filled with doors.

She might not even know that from that hallway she would need to go up.

"It's going to get dark," Croninshield said. "Use the wall to brace yourself."

"Something has frightened you, hasn't it?" Ludmilla asked.

"We're being followed," Croninshield said.

"Surely, someone in the library wouldn't be a problem." Ludmilla's voice was traveling down the stairs. Otherwise, she was being unbelievably quiet.

Croninshield actually appreciated the naïveté, because it was actually based on a love for the library.

"I'm pretty sure this person isn't affiliated with the library," Croninshield said.

She was trying to follow her own advice, keeping one hand on the wall, and tapping her way down the stairs with the front of a shoe before putting her foot down. It *was* slow going, which irritated her.

So far, though, she didn't hear the door above them open.

"I'm at the bottom," Ludmilla said.

"I'm almost there," Croninshield said.

Her free hand clutched the lantern. She could probably turn it on now. The stairs had curved their way down, and she doubted anyone would be able to see the light through the door.

Besides, she couldn't remember how to open that door.

Finally, there was no stair below her to tap. The wall widened, and she staggered a little. She hadn't realized she had been using the wall as support.

Still no sound above them.

She decided to risk the light.

"Brace yourself," she said. "I'm going to activate my lantern."

She held it low, then fumbled along the side for the panel that would depress ever so slightly. She wished she could control the light's intensity without moving panels around, but knew she couldn't.

Her fingers finally found the panel, and it moved inward. The light flared, nearly blinding her, because she had been looking down.

She looked up, blinked hard, and waited for her vision to settle.

They were in a small antechamber as old as the building itself. It had probably been a servant's staircase back when the Old Library was a fortress. The walls were made of uneven stone, which was crumbling. Far up the side that she (fortunately) hadn't touched, the stone was covered with a black goo, probably some kind of mold.

The air here didn't smell damp, though, so if that was mold, it probably came from an ancient leak.

The door ahead of them was made of wood. Croninshield nodded toward it.

"Open that slowly," she said.

Like so many parts of the Old Library, this hallway was inaccessible from most parts of the building. The hallway ended at the only other staircase here, but that staircase—which would take them up several flights—wasn't accessible from the part of the building where Croninshield had left Louella.

Ludmilla found the latch, and shoved the door forward, but it didn't move.

"It appears to be stuck," she said.

Of course it was. Hardly anyone ever used this staircase.

Croninshield set the lantern down, which shifted the light and the reflections. The walls seemed closer than they had a moment ago.

"Let me," she said. "There's a trick to some of these doors."

Especially when they hadn't been used for a while. She didn't add that part. She knew this would seem unusual enough for a regent. Ludmilla probably thought she was crazy.

But she was the one who wanted to see the bylaws, and it all felt important, so Croninshield was going to honor that.

Ludmilla moved away from the door and, without prompting, did not stand near the lantern. She folded her hands together, the posture of someone who had decided to wait patiently for whatever it was that was going to happen.

Croninshield grabbed the iron handle, still warm from Ludmilla's hand. Croninshield depressed the latch, and shoved the door with her shoulder at the same time.

The door shook, but didn't open. She pushed harder on the latch, and shoved with all of her strength.

The door opened with a loud pop. Then it swung around hard. It would have carried Croninshield with it, but she had released the latch. The door continued until it hit a wall with a bang that echoed down the corridor.

Croninshield cursed silently. So much for a secret entry into the hallway.

She hoped the noise wouldn't carry upward.

She turned to grab her lantern, but Ludmilla was already bent over, picking it up. The light moved, and traveled halfway up the stairs, casting shadows that moved.

Croninshield didn't like that. She also didn't like the way that the light seemed to move upward on its own, almost illogically.

She shook herself. She was starting to believe all kinds of things that her usually common-sense self would have laughed at a month ago.

Croninshield took the lantern from Ludmilla, not saying anything about her concerns. Part of Croninshield thought that maybe, once she got the lantern away from Ludmilla, the light would behave, but it didn't. It still clung to the walls as if the walls were made of lightstone.

But Croninshield knew where all the lightstone walls were in this huge old building, because lightstone often faded books, and she knew there wasn't any here.

The light seemed to be climbing the stairs.

Ludmilla started toward the door, but Croninshield caught her arm.

"Let me go first," she said. She didn't expect any problems, but there might be.

Ludmilla frowned, but stepped aside. She looked up the stairs too, as if the light bothered her as well.

Croninshield stepped into the hallway. It was longer than she remembered, and cooler. Lightstone lamps flared on as she moved, each above a different door.

Her boss's boss, decades ago, had had the lamps installed, because these old hallways were dark. Croninshield had no idea how the lamps seemed to know that someone was in the hallway, but she wasn't technically inclined.

Besides, she had never asked.

There were maybe a dozen doors. The hallway was wide,

and now quite bright. She normally would have shuttered her lantern, but she didn't, because she knew the stairwell on the other side of the hall would also be dark.

"Is the Regents Library behind one of these doors?" Ludmilla asked.

"No," Croninshield said as she grabbed the edge of this stairwell's door. "This is the oldest part of the building. We'll be going through six different towers to get there."

"Six...?" Ludmilla frowned at her. "There aren't six towers on this building."

"Oh, but there are," Croninshield said. "They're small and not visible from the outside. Some of them are parts of other buildings that got subsumed into the ancient fortress. So we'll be going through some interesting passages to get to the library. Still want to see those bylaws?"

Ludmilla's jaw was set. She looked determined.

"Now more than ever," she said.

"All right." Croninshield closed the door, and wished she knew how to lock it. "Here we go."

LINGUISTICS

ARCHEOLOGY

HISTORY

REGENTS
TOWER

OLD
LIBRARY

ADV. STUDENT
WING

MAIN
ENTRANCE

CLOCK
TOWER

MEDICAL
SCIENCES

SCHOLAR'S
ENTRANCE

CHAPTER
THIRTY-FOUR

S hyly's eyes finally adjusted to the extreme darkness in that room filled with things. She knew she wasn't that far behind Croninshield and the Regent, but she was far enough. Shyly could see shapes, wishing she could see more, but non-magickal eyes never really worked properly.

Shyly could see better in the darkness than Louella ever could because Doppelgängers had just enough magick to be able to see the edges of things. They needed that skill to track their quarry. It was one reason why she had been able to find and trap Louella in that grouping of trees.

Shyly had been able to avoid the lightstone lamps on the path, and ignore the shadows. Louella had stepped into a pool of darkness, and Shyly had been able to see her better. CAFETERIA But adjusting to this new body had been hard, and slower than Shyly liked. She knew she hadn't lost her abilities, but she also knew they were working differently here in the Protectorate.

She wasn't sure why. She had heard that Doppelgängers had more trouble adjusting as they grew older, but she didn't think of herself as old. She had never been particularly skilled, not like some, which was why she stayed off the battlefield as much as possible.

Maybe if she measured her abilities, they hadn't changed at all. She just needed them to kick in faster on this campus, and they hadn't.

It might not be because she was older, either. It might because there was so much residual magick in this place.

And the Old Library was one of the worse offenders for loose magick. Coming in here for the first time as Louella had actually frightened her, not because Shyly had to pose as Louella, but because the air fairly tingled with magick Shyly couldn't completely identify.

As in this damn room. It was filled with books and chairs and tables, all strewn about haphazardly. She had no idea if Croninshield had come this way to slow Shyly down or if this was truly the way to the Regents Library.

Shyly hated the fact that Louella didn't know. There was so much that Louella didn't know. Too much, really. Shyly always felt like she was playing catch-up on things she had expected to know immediately.

When the Regent showed up, Shyly had thought that taking her as a host might be the smart thing to do. Regents were supposedly the ones in charge of all of the knowledge in the Protectorate, and that included magickal knowledge.

Shyly had seen it as a big opportunity. But as she waited

and watched, she started to realize that the person with the knowledge was May Croninshield. Croninshield knew where everything was in this building, and that included magickal items—even if she couldn't identify them as magick.

Shyly wished she had thought of that earlier. She had already had more than one chance to take over Croninshield.

Shyly reached the last table before the door. That table was covered with lanterns. Louella remembered putting them on the table because the student staff members wouldn't be able to figure out how to operate them. But the memory was as vague as some of Louella's other memories.

Shyly had no idea why the staff wouldn't know how to use them, unless maybe they were oil lamps. The library seemed to prefer lightstone, which meant she was always avoiding some lamp or asking someone to turn it on. The overhead lights were too far away and diffuse to bother her (much), but the ones that were close made her feel as if she was going to leave this new skin.

If the lanterns before her were oil lanterns, Shyly could take one and see in some of the dark corners that Croninshield would have to walk through. Shyly reached for the nearest lantern, and brushed her fingers against it.

It flared brightly, as light as the sun.

The light stabbed at her face. Instinctively, she covered her eyes with arm. Her fingers burned from touching that lantern, and so did the skin on her arm.

The burn was sharp and painful.

She ducked under the table to get away from that light, keeping her eyes covered.

The light flowed around the table, poking, as if it was searching for her. She could sense it more than she could see it, although it seemed to seep past the makeshift defenses she had set up for herself.

She brought her arm down, because she had to get out of here, and to get out of here, she had to be able to see.

The light was moving like water, seeping around the edges of the table, dripping onto the floor where she had stood a moment ago.

So she half crouched and crab-walked to the edge of the table. The door's outline had to be maybe three feet from her.

If she moved fast, she could cover that three feet quickly. She hoped the door would open quickly. If she had to fight it, the light might find her.

Before she could think any more about it, she braced herself, her sore fingers throbbing on the cool floor, her body still in that crouch. She made herself take a deep breath, then launched herself at the door, using Louella's weak legs to push herself upward.

She grabbed the door handle mostly because she needed to prevent herself from slamming into the door's wood.

The handle burned as well. She yelped and nearly pulled her hand off it, but she didn't dare.

Something in her mind whispered that the handle was made of iron. Doppelgängers could handle iron, but they paid a price for it.

Not usually one that burned, though.

She tugged the handle downward, and miraculously the

door banged open. She slid into the hallway, then closed that door tightly and leaned on it, heart pounding.

Her arm and hand throbbed. She looked down at them. They were red, with tiny welts rising across the skin. She touched the redness. It was warm. She'd seen this in Nye. The very pale Nyeians had this reaction to the sun.

But Louella hadn't been pale, and the lightstone lantern didn't give off sunshine.

Shyly shook her arm, wished the pain away, and knew it wouldn't be that easy. She had never touched a lightstone lantern before, not in her other guise, not in this one either. She had thought she might disable the lightstones in Louella's apartment, but she hadn't had to. They didn't automatically activate. She could choose to use them, and she hadn't.

Shyly took a deep breath and steadied herself. She was in a wide hallway that neither she nor Louella had ever seen before. Louella, at least, had an inkling of where this hallway led. It led to one of the interior towers.

The fortress had engulfed a number of buildings. There had been some kind of ancient war, something that fascinated Louella. The war hadn't had anything to do with the Fey, but it had a lot to do with those mountain ranges and with the river that went around this part of Qavner, and this little valley.

Someone—Louella knew who, but Shyly didn't really care—had decided to build a fortress around the buildings, making them all part of some giant complex. The fortress was old, some of the buildings were older, and whoever had built this had decided to attach them all, one to another.

She suspected she was in one of those other buildings now.

This hallway was better called a corridor. It was wide. It had some lightstone lamps farther down the corridor, near some doors that looked like they were made of the same wood as this door had been. Which might mean that the door handles were also made of iron.

This place might be a lot more dangerous than she realized.

But if she could get to Croninshield and the Regent, then Shyly could figure out what was safe and what wasn't.

The problem was that Shyly couldn't see them. Anywhere. Quite a distance ahead of her—she wasn't sure how far. The corridor was repetitive: There was a staircase. The staircase was wide. It went to an upper floor and a lower floor.

If the Regent and Croninshield had already gotten to the staircase, then she had no idea which way they would have gone. Louella had known that there were small secret rooms on the lower levels of this fortress, particularly near the Scholars wing, but Shyly wasn't sure something called "The Regents Library" would be in a small room.

She wasn't even sure why there was a Regents library in this building. It had once been in the Regents Tower, which seemed logical to her that it remain there.

Louella's memories were frustratingly silent on a variety of important things. She had been a mental pack rat and Shyly was beginning to find that more and more useless.

The fingers on her right hand hurt so badly that she could barely move them. She glanced at them. The tips were bright red with white in the center. A real burn, then, and one she would have to medicate at some point.

But first, she needed to find Croninshield and the Regent. They couldn't be far.

Shyly pushed herself off the door and started down the corridor, weaving just a little before she mentally admonished herself. She didn't have time to be weak. She was here to gather knowledge, information, and artifacts, and she hoped that something called the Regents Library would have artifacts.

She was going to have to figure out how to get through that corridor without stepping into any more light given off by the lightstone lamps. She had a feeling she might be overly sensitive to them at the moment.

She was looking at the first one, which was above a door to her right, when something popped behind her. She whirled, expected to see maybe an exploded lamp or some kind of threat that she couldn't quite imagine.

Then something banged so hard that it hurt her ears. Yet something told her the bang was muffled, and would have been louder if she were closer to it.

She walked back toward the door she had just left, and then realized she had missed a small door. The door was recessed and shaded, almost as if it had been designed to be invisible.

This was how Croninshield and the Regent had disappeared so quickly. They had gone through this door.

She reached for the door handle, then stopped. It didn't look like iron. It looked slightly different. Pockmarked in a way that iron never could be.

But Gray had showed them pockmarked iron before, kicking it toward them when he found it among the artifacts that were stored in the rowhouse.

This is ironwood, he had said. *It's dangerous to us. We don't dare touch it. I saw someone in the Isara group grab one, and his hand melted.*

She had thought Gray had been exaggerating at the time, but now she believed him, given how much her fingertips throbbed.

She cast about for something she could use to open that door, but she didn't see anything.

So, she grabbed the hem of the ridiculous skirt she wore, and ripped it. Then she wrapped the fabric around her bad hand, figuring there was no reason to injure the other hand.

The fabric scratched at her skin, and she bit her lower lip at the pain. Then she willed herself to ignore it, just like she always ignored the bumps and bruises on any new body she would take whenever she found a new host.

She quickly wrapped her hand around the door handle, and pulled the door open. She could feel heat through the fabric. She braced the door with her right foot and peered down.

Stairs that looked treacherous. And no lights at all. The stairs became half stairs as they curved downward.

She wondered for a brief moment whether or not she could run to the stairs at the end of the hall and go down. Those stairs were open, and probably led to the same place.

But it was the *probably* that was the problem. With this fortress being composed of so many buildings, she wasn't sure if stairs that far away would lead her completely astray.

She'd have to go down these stairs in the dark.

Before she started down them, though, she looked at the walls. If they were ironwood, she wasn't going to go.

She wouldn't tell anyone about the missed opportunity, either. She would just pretend that it hadn't happened.

But she didn't want to be that person, if she could avoid it.

She pushed the door open farther, so more light flooded into that stairwell.

The walls looked like stone. Regular stone, not ironwood.

She was going to find the Regent and Croninshield.

And then she was going to hurt them.

STORAGE
BUILDINGS

CHAPTER
THIRTY-FIVE

Gray stood in semi-darkness near one of the old storage buildings on the northeast part of campus. Lumin recognized Gray by his general body shape—squat, not tall, a little thinner than most in Qavner, and a tad blurry.

Gray's features were blurry as well, which to anyone else might appear like a trick of the light.

Gray had set up this meeting place when he learned that the team was coming. He had been very specific. He had said that there were ancient storage buildings near the empty fields.

When Gray had designated that meeting place, he had assumed that the ancient storage buildings would have arti-facts, but it turned out that they were filled with practical things, like old chairs and desks and blankets and bed frames.

Even after Gray had learned that the storage buildings

525

wouldn't make their mission easier, he kept the meeting here, because, he said, no one would be lurking nearby.

Spies were generally very good at finding places where they wouldn't be noticed.

Lumin wanted to run to Gray's side. Lumin was ridiculously pleased to see him. Now Lumin wouldn't be trying to figure out this vast campus on his own.

Lumin mentally shook himself. He had been more distressed than he realized by the explosions and the loss of the carriages. Somehow, he had thought this entire evening would go smoothly, and he was beginning to realize it would not.

He had been told, years ago, by one of the other Visionaries that he didn't have the makings of a good Leader.

You're too rigid, the man had said. *You seem to think everything will happen as you Saw it, rather than allowing yourself to flow with the changes in the field.*

Lumin tried to shake off the thought. It was doing him no good right now. He was in the middle of this, and he had to see it through.

Although none of that changed the relief he felt at the sight of Gray. And the mild exasperation Lumin felt because he couldn't read Gray's reaction to seeing the team.

They were most of the way across the field, with only a few yards to go. Lumin picked up the pace, and as he did, he put a hand on Eerie's arm.

He had kept her beside him throughout this entire trek through the housing and the fields. He was extremely worried about her. Her mood had been strange since the two different breaches, and he wanted her calm.

Much of this mission depended on her, particularly now that they had decided to destroy almost every artifact they could find.

The ground was spongy beneath Lumin's feet. He almost felt that if he ran, his feet would get caught in the muck.

He knew some of that was because of the constant rain over the past few days. But he also felt like even the ground was unfamiliar here, unfamiliar and hard to navigate.

Gray shifted slightly as they got closer. Then he came forward to edge of a path that Lumin hadn't even realized was there. The ground fog seemed thinner around Gray, which was both odd and good.

Lumin wondered if the Weather Sprites had cleared this area just a bit. Or if the ground fog was all moving toward the old part of campus. It looked that way.

Lumin did not want to ask the Sprites. He didn't need more details in his head. Whatever was going to happen now was set, because he couldn't change his planning any more than he already had.

He left the field, letting go of Eerie's arm. She looked at him as if losing his physical support left her bereft.

He approached Gray. Gray's face became just a little more solid. He looked vaguely Fey now, with upswept eyebrows and a pointed chin. But there was enough softness to make him seem Qavnerian as well.

"It's been a difficult night," Lumin said, and started into an explanation without going through any of the usual preliminaries. He explained the explosion and ended with the loss of the carriages. Then he said, "I'll be sending Veil and Stante to get us a way home."

Gray glanced in their direction. Lumin wished he could read Gray's expression, but clearly he couldn't. He had no real idea what Gray thought of the plan.

"After we're done here, I'll tell you the best place to steal a carriage," Gray said.

He didn't sound perturbed or upset by the change in plans. He seemed calmer than Lumin wanted him to be.

Lumin almost said, *Tell them,* meaning Veil and Stante. Then Lumin realized the rest of the team would have to know where the carriage was, so that they would have a rendezvous point.

His head was starting to swim from all the details. He was half tempted to cancel all of this, but he couldn't. Not after the explosion and the carriages.

If the team waited another few days, the Qavnerians might be ready for them. Maybe not ready magickally, but physically.

He didn't have enough people to take on dozens of armed Qavnerians, especially if Eerie was not at her best.

"We don't have a lot of time," Gray was saying. "I need to talk with you about the artifacts."

He apparently had seen Lumin's indecision, and decided to take control on his own. Lumin's cheeks heated. He didn't need that kind of assistance from a Spy.

Then Lumin reminded himself that he needed as much assistance as he could get right now. This attack, in this strange country, was new to all of them.

"All right," Lumin said.

"There are too many of them," Gray said. "The artifacts are scattered all over this campus, and there are not hundreds. There are thousands. I'm not sure if we'll ever find all of them. I think we're going to have to do what we can to destroy them, and—"

"I already thought of that," Lumin said, deliberately cutting him off. "Eerie and I believe we can harness the energy of those artifacts and destroy them in a way that's similar to what happened at the apartment."

"You think?" Gray asked. "Will you have to be near them to do this?"

"No," Lumin said. "We weren't near the apartment."

Gray looked skeptical. "I understand that," he said. "But someone magickal was."

Lumin almost shrugged, feeling slightly irritated. Gray was probably right. So Lumin wasn't going to argue. "Do you know where most of the artifacts are stored?"

"I know where the major groupings are," Gray said, "but let me be honest with you. The woman Shyly took over is mostly useless. Some lower-level librarian who only knows about some of the items here. I think Perdu could have found them on his own if we had given him more time."

Was there judgement in that statement? Lumin didn't know. He couldn't really tell.

He had to shake that off. He had to work with everyone on this team, no matter what they thought of him. Because of the events of the past few days, and particularly the events of this night, he didn't have a chance to try this again, maybe plan it better.

He was going to have to do what he could.

And then, when it was all over, he would head back to Nye and report to Rugar. There would be no sense in staying on Dorovich after this.

"Well," Lumin said, "we don't have the time to give him. We're going to do what we can with what we have."

Gray sighed and looked over his shoulder. Lumin followed his gaze. The white ground fog illuminated the buildings more than he liked, reflecting light from the campus itself.

Two large towers rose out of that fog, but other stone buildings rose up as well. And beyond them, even more buildings, all of various ages.

He couldn't get to all of the artifacts. He probably couldn't even get to most of them.

He needed to alter his strategy one more time.

"We're going to have to split into three teams," he said.

"What?" Gray asked. "Now? I thought we had a plan."

And who is the rigid one here? Lumin almost said, then realized he was fighting with an old nemesis in his head. Gray hadn't called him rigid.

"We did, and it's not viable," Lumin said. "We need a at least two carriages to get us out of here. We're going to need to destroy the biggest caches of artifacts but, once we destroy one, the people on this campus will be on alert."

"They have security," Gray said, "but it's not always effective."

Lumin didn't care what Gray thought was effective or not. They were going to have to move quickly.

"We're also going to need to get our hands on their

maps," Lumin said. "We're going to take the maps out of here, and nothing else."

Besides, he didn't know how dangerous the other artifacts were. They had sapped the team's strength at those apartments. If he picked up the wrong artifact, then that might hurt everyone on the team.

"Do you know where the maps are?" Lumin asked. "Are they with the other artifacts?"

For a moment, Gray's face became solid. His skin was literally gray. Lumin had never seen anything like that. His eyebrows looked like cuts in his forehead. His ears were plastered to the side of his head, their tips pointing to the sky.

"No," he said, with surprise. "They're not. There are map rooms in both the Old Library and in the Thaumaturgical Department. Perdu told me about the one in the Thaumaturgical Department. I have a vague idea where it is."

"And the one in the library?" Lumin asked. He was beginning to feel a sense of urgency that he hadn't felt before.

"Shyly says there's a map room on the ground floor, but that the ground floor is quite large. She said that the map room is in the Scholars Wing."

"I assume you know where that is," Lumin said.

"I know where the Scholars Wing is," Gray said, "but not how to get in or where that map room is. I'll go ahead and find Shyly. She'll get us in there."

There he was, making plans as if he was running this mission.

"No," Lumin said. "Three teams, remember? I think we do this differently."

He gestured at his team. They had been standing farther behind him so that they could give him and Gray privacy.

He stared at them for a moment—six Infantry, three Spies, two Weather Sprites, two Domestics, and one Enchanter. A great team for blending in and finding out information.

A terrible team for leading an assault on a place this large.

He had initially thought that the Domestics—Calla in particular—could be with the team as they picked up the artifacts. She could help if anyone got hurt.

But it looked like there would be more than hurt involved here, and that might destroy the Domestics' magick entirely.

"Calla, Thread," he said, "you will commandeer our carriages. Take Stante with you. He will be the one who will find them. You will be the ones to handle the horses and to make sure everything is ready when the rest of us arrive."

Calla twisted her hands together. She glanced at Thread, as if Thread was in charge instead of Lumin.

"We don't even know where we're going," Calla said. "We can't—"

"Gray will tell you in a minute," Lumin said. "We have changed our plans, and we need you elsewhere."

He let the words hang for a moment, hoping Thread and Calla would understand. Calla opened her mouth to protest, but Thread put a hand on her arm.

"We will be ready for you," Thread said quietly. She clearly understood.

Lumin paused for a moment, thinking about this. He

had no battlefield magick skills. Eerie was their secret weapon. But she was exhausted. The Spies could do very little, and the Weather Sprites...

He turned to Arid, who had been watching more closely than Eune, the other Sprite. Eune had enveloped herself in the ground fog, so that only her head poked through. It looked like she was wearing a fluffy white cloak that trailed into the distance.

"I need you and Eune to go with the Domestics," he said to Arid. "Change the fog slightly. I want it to envelop both the Old Library and the Thaumaturgical Wing of whatever building it's in."

Arid started to shake her head, but Lumin held up a hand.

"I know you have no idea where the Thaumaturgical Wing is. Gray will tell us all where we're heading in a moment."

"I can also tell you," Veil said, his voice watery. Lumin didn't even spare him a glance.

"I'll get to you in a minute," he said. He didn't need another Spy messing up the works, not right now. This was too chancy as it was.

"So we're not stealing?" Hardin asked, taking a step forward. The five other Infantry formed a modified V behind him.

"We are," Lumin said, "but not like we planned. Give me a moment."

He took a deep breath, thinking. He needed two Eeries, and he couldn't have that.

This entire mission was taxing his abilities.

He put a hand on Eerie's arm. She jumped, which was precisely not what he needed. He wanted someone solid and comfortable, and ready to do battle.

"Would you be able to destroy artifacts from a distance?" Lumin asked.

"I would have to know what they are," she said. "And where they are exactly."

"A map won't help?" he asked.

She shook her head. "These artifacts aren't our magick, Lumin. I can't just send out a magickal feeler and find them. Everything here is different—"

"I understand," he said, even though he didn't, not completely.

He turned back to Gray, who was watching him avidly. Gray's eyes were sharp in his blurring face. His appearance was almost off-putting. Lumin felt like he was seeing a pair of eyes floating in a pool of brackish water.

"Which building has the most artifacts?" Lumin asked.

"I assume it's the library," Gray said.

"You don't know?" Lumin asked.

"I haven't seen most of these," Gray said. "But the Old Library is bigger than the Alchemy, Science, and Thaumaturgy building."

"All right," Lumin said, and started to turn toward the Infantry.

"But," Gray said, "quantity isn't the key question. You'd want to know where the most powerful artifacts are."

"Yes," Lumin said, not quite able to keep the sarcasm from his voice. "I would."

"And that I don't know for certain. I have a guess, though."

Lumin shifted, his frustration making him restless.

"I think," Gray said, "that the most powerful ones would be in the AST building. I get a sense that the professors in there jealously guard their secrets, and wouldn't want the root of their power to be in another building."

"But that's a guess," Lumin snapped.

"Yes." Gray sounded calm. "An educated one."

Lumin didn't like any of this. But he had gotten them into a mess that he needed some kind of way out of.

He had the glimmers of a new plan forming in his mind. He didn't like the plan, but he had to make do.

He had to remember his priorities: he needed to do things that would help Rugar in a future invasion of Dorovich. Information, mostly. That would be the maps. Destruction of the artifacts was secondary.

To get information back to Rugar would require getting the team out of here alive.

"Lumin?" Hardin said. "We can't stand here all night."

Lumin wanted to whirl on him, face him, tell him that he had no idea how hard this was, except that Hardin probably did know. As the head of a small troop of Infantry, he had to have a bit of leadership ability. He probably was incredibly decisive, maybe even stupidly decisive.

"Here's what we're going to do," Lumin said, sounding more confident than he felt. "Three Infantry—and I don't care which ones—will go with Gray into the...what did you call it? Alchemy Building?"

"Alchemy, Science, and Thaumaturgy Building," Gray

said as Lumin silently cursed himself for making the name of the damn building a question at all. Someone like Rugar never would have. It showed a lack of confidence.

Lumin decided to ignore the comment, and continue.

"Hardin," Lumin said, "you and the remaining two on your team will go with Veil to the Old Library. Both teams will find the maps first. Then you'll take what you can, just like we had planned."

Hardin nodded, his face as close to expressionless as it could possibly get.

"Gray and Veil," Lumin said, "after you get to the Map rooms, you will locate the remaining artifacts in the building."

Veil raised a hand, as if he was about to flag an objection, but this time, Lumin didn't want anyone to speak. So he continued.

"I realize that neither of you knows exactly what you're looking for. I trust you to find it."

Neither man moved, except they seemed to blur more. Lumin wondered if they could control that blurriness at will.

"I realize," he said, "that Veil will have the more difficult task, given the size of the Old Library."

Veil nodded his head. The blur left an afterimage as he moved, making it look like his skull was liquid.

Lumin didn't like any of this.

"I want you to give yourself a time limit," Lumin said. "You will have more time than Gray, because Eerie and I will go to the Thaumaturgical building first."

He didn't care about the name of the stupid building any more.

"Once Eerie knows where those artifacts are, she will do whatever she does so that we can destroy them." This time, Lumin waved a hand. "Then we will come to the Old Library."

He was keeping himself beside Eerie, partly to guard her but also to make sure she came through. She was a lot more frail than he wanted her to be.

"By then," he said to Veil, "I trust you will have found Shyly. Enlist her in your mission to find these artifacts. We don't need to get all of them, but enough to make some kind of dent."

"Maybe we should just take the maps and leave," Veil said quietly.

Lumin frowned. It was a good option, maybe even a better option. Or it would have been if the Qavnerians hadn't demolished the Trinovante cell and destroyed Eerie's spells just this evening.

"Yeah, I would have loved to do that," Lumin said. "But someone here in Serebro, some powerful Dorovician Enchanter, knows that there are Fey about. We have no idea if the maps are protected or spelled so that they can be tracked. We're going to need to keep that Enchanter busy, and that will require some kind of disaster here on this campus."

He had everyone's attention now.

"It'll be more of a diversion than anything else," he said.

Eerie glanced sideways at him. He hadn't discussed this with her at all. On the mountain, he had said he wanted to destroy everything. He could feel both her surprise and disappointment.

She had been so angry earlier that she probably wanted revenge as much as he did.

But revenge wouldn't help them, not right now. Now, he had to focus on getting the team in and out of this campus with minimal interaction with the locals.

"Questions?" he asked. He didn't plan to answer most of them, because he didn't have answers. But he wanted to know where his team was mentally.

No one spoke. Maybe they understood that he really didn't want questions, or maybe they just wanted to get on with it. Maybe they felt the strain of the night as much as he did.

"All right then," he said. "Gray, give out the directions. Veil, you don't need them, so take your group to the Old Library."

Veil nodded.

Lumin kept his hand on Eerie's arm. "You and I will wait until Gray is done."

"I don't like waiting," she said.

"I know," he said, and left it at that.

THE
TURNOUT

SEREBRO
MOUNTAIN RANGE

CHAPTER

THIRTY-SIX

The trip down the mountain should have taken maybe a half an hour, but it was taking much longer than that. At least Cole was in the conveyance now, although he had to focus to keep it going as slowly as possible.

The conveyance did not like traveling at a horse's pace, particularly the pace of the traumatized horses on those carriages. One set of horses didn't even want to leave, not without their usual driver—at least according to Volkovich.

Cole had to trust that Volkovich knew what he was talking about, because it seemed strange that horses could be so emotional and flighty.

Cole wished he wasn't following them. He had to continually massage the conveyance. At this speed, the vents weren't getting enough wind. He was also veering all over the road. Any time he saw a pile of something or even a shadow, he thought maybe it was horse dung. That would screw up the conveyance almost as much as a lack of wind.

They weren't traveling in the trees any longer. The lights from the conveyance illuminated the back of the nearest carriage—the wheels turning so (damn slowly) in front of him, the carriage's body swaying from side to side.

He could catch a glimpse of the horses' legs and hooves moving in unison. He couldn't see much from the carriage in front, but he had to hope that it was heading down the mountain the same way.

Xavier was driving the first carriage. Getting him onto the driver's bench took some work, particularly since the letters decorating his robe were alternating between red, white, and gray flares. The white and red flares bothered the horses.

Volkovich said he had wished he had blinders for them. Instead, he made sure that their heads faced forward, and, he said, all three men had to hope that nothing would distract the horses. Volkovich felt that they were very fragile right now.

"Fragile" was a reason that windstone vehicles— conveyances—were so much better than horse-drawn carriages. Any mechanical conveyance powered by wind-stone did not shy unexpectedly. Conveyances didn't spook at a shadow in the road.

Nor did conveyances have an emotional reaction when they saw their drivers murdered.

Cole shuddered just a little. The headache he'd had since the explosion remained, mostly a dull throb in the back of his head. His muscles were seizing up, and the bruises were sorting themselves out into the ones that would give him grief for the next week and the ones he could ignore.

The biggest problem was his hands. The palms were sore. He hadn't noticed it on the drive to the top of the mountain, but the pain was becoming more pronounced now. He might have done something while he waited for Volkovich and Xavier to resolve the magic on that turnout or maybe Cole had been so numb on the first part of the trip that he hadn't even noticed.

This day felt like it had been months long. Everything he knew and understood was being challenged. And now, there was an enemy lurking that he hadn't even realized existed, let alone thought that it might threaten the places he loved. Xavier seemed to have an idea what to do about it all—or maybe Xavier just knew how to respond.

Cole wasn't quite sure what could be done, if anything. And now that he was alone and had time to think, he also found himself contemplating that Regents meeting. All of the revelations about Chaban, about forcing families out, and taking the artifacts.

Clearly Chaban had been selling those artifacts to these Fey people. Chaban had led everyone to believe it was about money, but what if it had been about something more?

Cole needed to talk with Zubiri. Maybe they had gotten more out of Chaban. Maybe there was some kind of plan here that none of the Regents were aware of.

Still, Cole needed more information. He wasn't sure how to get it. He also needed to figure out exactly what happened to some of the older Regents, the ones who died. Everyone knew that Augustus Kirilli had been murdered, but not how. And Cole was beginning to think that detail was extremely important.

His aching head was swimming, and to make matters worse, every few yards, the conveyance protested the speed by chugging. He'd only heard conveyances chug a few times before this. Either their vents hadn't been properly cleaned or the conveyance was going too slow.

He wouldn't be able to keep up this pace much longer. In fact, the conveyance might stall completely if he didn't take action.

He pulled over to the side of the road. There wasn't a turnout, but he wasn't deep in the trees either. He shut off the conveyance and sat there for a long moment, letting the carriages get farther ahead. That way he could follow them at a minimum speed.

At the moment, though, he needed to move his body. He got out of the conveyance and walked to the edge of the road.

There was a precipitous drop. He could still see the valley beyond. There were fewer lights than there had been when he had looked, before they found the bodies. There was also a whiteness spreading across the middle of campus.

He had seen something like that before, usually on foggy winter nights as he traveled to the Academy either for a board meeting or as a student. Fog seemed to accumulate in that valley after heavy rains, like the ones they'd had recently.

But the fog was never white. In those instances, the fog was always a grayish color. It would undulate like water in a pond as it rested over the Academy.

This white fog didn't move like fog. It was traveling

forward, as if there was a harsh wind behind it. But wind usually dissipated fog, didn't it?

The fog spiraled around the center of campus, and seemed to be thickest near the towers of the ancient fortress.

Or maybe he was seeing that wrong from this angle. Maybe he was seeing magic in everything.

Part of him cursed whoever it was that started the Purges. Whoever thought burying all of that knowledge was a good thing to do. He swayed a little from dizziness and lack of sleep.

He was going to have to figure out how to keep moving forward, despite all that had happened to him, because he had a hunch this was not over.

He had a feeling this was only the beginning.

LIN

ALCHEMY, SCIENCE
& THAUMATURGY

GOVERNMENT

R
T

LAW BUILDING

WHISTLER
HALL

CHAPTER

THIRTY-SEVEN

Wolfgang Sauer leaned back in his chair and rubbed his eyes. He was exhausted. He had been in his office for most of the day, except for the two hours he spent teaching students who were panicked about their upcoming exams and the hour he had taken for the overly large dinner he had eaten in one of the dining halls.

He hated this part of the semester. Students suddenly forgot all interest they had in their classes and only wanted to know what was on the upcoming tests.

Tests, he would boom at them, *aren't about regurgitating knowledge. They are about* absorbing *knowledge.*

No one seemed to understand that. And as he gave that speech today in two different classes, he couldn't help but think about the conversation he'd had with May Croninshield a few days ago.

Ever since she had come to his office to discuss what she

had found at the site of Louella Vance's attack, he had felt unsettled. Whenever he felt unsettled in his life, he would dig through information until he found some kind of answer, something that would calm his mind.

He had been digging in old tomes and through some scrolls, written by people who had survived those ancient Fey attacks, and all that had done was leave him with more questions.

Although one of his old professors, a man who had been crushed by and ultimately died in the Purges, had claimed that he believed the Fey never used books because they had altered their magic to absorb bodies and minds.

Books didn't tell them how to do magic. The Fey were *born* knowing how to do magic.

Yet one of Sauer's other professors in this very department, so many years ago, believed that Qavnerians were born with magic as well. They had just never had the right training to use it.

Sauer shuddered, trying not to follow the thread of that memory. Because that professor—like so many others—had been accused of poisoning minds, forcing them to absorb knowledge they didn't want.

All Sauer's Thaumaturgy professors, every single one of them, had either been murdered in the Purges or had died broken and alone.

Sauer had started teaching the History of Magic as a young man, as a rebel, trying to prove to the government and the Board and everyone at the Academy that magic was at the heart of Qavner.

He'd been arrested and beaten and thrown into cells so filthy that a little bit of dirt no longer bothered him. He trained himself, experimented with magic when he could, and did his absolute best to "poison young minds" with an understanding of magic, if not a desire to pursue it on their own.

How he had gotten this old, he had no idea. And set in his ways. At least he had kept himself physically active, except on days like today when he spent most of the day in this damn office, warded and protected, filled with books on spellcasting that he had once feared the Academy would destroy, as well as artifacts that spoke to him—literally spoke to him.

He needed to keep them at his side, and the office was the safest place to do that, in a building that had magic embedded in its walls.

That was why, despite several attempts by the Academy, the Alchemy, Science and Thaumaturgical Departments could not move from here.

What the Academy didn't seem to realize was that the building itself always grew to accommodate them. He had paintings of the building from the Academy's earliest days. That small building, the hut as some called it, had been the entire department. There were no stairs or stories or separate wings. Just a small building with a wide room that the three departments had to fight over when someone was going to lecture, and three tiny storage areas for equipment from each department.

Somehow, and he'd never been able to chase the records to see how, the separate wings had grown out of those storage areas. He liked to think of the building as a live thing which grew according to need.

It had certainly acted like a live thing when a previous Chancellor had mandated that the departments move to a different, smaller building during the Purges. That had made the fear worse, because students moved the contents of the AST building to their new home during the day, and the items all moved back to the building *by themselves* at night.

That Sauer had still had a job after that surprised him. He would have thought that the previous Chancellor would shut all three departments down. To this day, Sauer was surprised that he was still alive after that incident.

That particular Chancellor's predecessor might have killed every single professor in all three departments to "save" the Academy from all of that magic.

Sauer wiped a meaty hand over his face. Remembering the past was not going to help him—not the recent past, anyway. The parts of the past that might help were shrouded in tradition and legend and ancient memories.

He had books here that recounted the Fey invasion centuries ago, books handwritten by elderly participants who wanted to write down their memories before the end of long and eventful lives.

Previous scholars dismissed a lot of this information, calling it "fanciful." As a young man, Sauer had wanted to write his thesis on the "fanciful" information, maybe research it to see if there was evidence of all of that fancy in Khēmía and in other places where the battles were actively fought.

He'd had the support of Constance Kirilli Sabry, who

had come to the Academy to teach Khēmían studies after her Khēmían husband was murdered under mysterious circumstances. She had survived the Purges by virtue of her Kirilli name and the fact that her brother, Arthur, had been a member of the Board of Regents.

Professor Sabry believed that understanding the events of the Fey invasion from the perspective of Khēmía, working with the Khēmíans, was the only way to know what had really happened.

But the Purges, which had waxed and waned depending on who ran the Protectorate, had been on an upswing, and Sauer's advisor wouldn't sign off on his thesis topic.

I'm just trying to save your life, Wolfie, his advisor had said, using the nickname that Sauer had used during his years as an Advanced Student. *Find something that won't draw as much attention to your* other *abilities.*

His other abilities. The fact that he could make wards. He could handle books and maps that almost no one else could touch without feeling a jolt of power or a burn as if they had touched a live flame. The fact that he could bring some of the artifacts to startling life, as well as bits of art. Some sculptures changed position when he touched them. Some pieces of art redrew themselves as if they hadn't liked the image on their canvas.

Abilities he had to hide during the early years of the Purges, and couldn't really flaunt even now.

Abilities that some, in the books he'd been reading, claimed were valuable for doing things like fighting the Fey.

He stood, shoving his chair away with the back of his

knees. The chair banged against the bookcase behind him, and he had to turn to make sure no books fell down.

None had. Everything behind his desk that was precariously balanced remained precariously balanced.

His hands were shaking, and not from exhaustion, even though he was tired.

He felt a sense of unease so profound that his entire body hummed. The night was a strange one. He had hated the rain over the past few days. It had felt unnatural, and then, when it stopped, he thought about the accounts he'd read of a battle in the Khēmían city of Mantopk where days of rain were followed by a Fey attack so violent that half the town lost their lives.

Then, as he walked back from dinner, he had seen tendrils of ground fog that looked more ghostly than fog-like. This ground fog had been white and it had poked at things, like a person trying to understand what they were seeing.

He'd actually avoided it, hurrying toward the main door of the AST building so that he could stay ahead of the fog.

Some of the accounts that he had read had claimed that the Fey could control the weather. He remembered first reading those accounts as a young man and scoffing, thinking that no one controlled the weather.

But now, given his unease and the strange weather as well as those bones, he was beginning to wonder.

Bones, weather, a blood pool.

He didn't like any of it.

He paced to the office door and checked the wards. He

had refreshed them after May Croninshield's visit, but he wasn't sure that was enough.

He was beginning to wonder if he should have warded the doors to the entire building. But if he had done that, then he would have had to let everyone else on staff know what he had done. There were others who might make competing wards, and that would benefit no one.

He walked back to his desk. Really, what he was doing wasn't actual pacing or walking. The office was too small and narrow. And it was feeling stuffy. He usually didn't mind the heat; in fact, he had welcomed it.

He had spent six years of his career as a Practical Intern, teaching at a branch of the Academy in Khēmía that was later closed due to unrest in that part of the Protectorate. He had learned there that he adored hot weather and sunshine. The weather here, so close to the Infrin Sea, where it was gray and rainy often, where the air never really warmed enough to make him feel hot, felt like a place he had been sent for torture rather than enjoyment.

Still, he loved his students. He loved surprising them. He loved teaching them, except when they were focused on exams.

And he didn't do what his old professors had done to him—beg him and his classmates to remain silent about the content of the classes. That request, to him, made it seem like they had been ashamed of what they were teaching.

He wasn't ashamed at all. He considered it essential.

Maybe tonight more than ever.

He stopped pacing, and glanced at his shelf. Some of the books glowed, a phenomenon he had seen before. He never really knew what that meant, but he had learned to take the books off the shelf when it occurred.

He did so now, one book at a time.

The first book was written in Pahrucees. He had spent some time in Pahrucii when he'd been flirting with a different dissertation topic, and had felt uncomfortable, as if he were being watched at all times.

Maybe he was. To this day, Pahrucii had managed to stay out of the Protectorate, often through violent rebellious means. Sauer had never felt comfortable there, more so on the day he found this book. It had followed him around a bookstore, literally.

Every time he turned around, the book was on a nearby table or chair. Finally the proprietor had told him, in broken Qavnerian, that the book clearly wanted to belong to him. Sauer had protested that he did not read Pahrucees, but the proprietor had insisted.

Sauer had purchased the book, and only when he brought it back to his tiny bedsit did he realize that it was filled with maps—one of which was glowing right now.

He placed the book on top of several others on his desk. The book fell open to the glowing map. It was near the center of the book, and took up two pages. It looked hand-drawn. It also appeared to be a map of the Academy. He did not remember ever seeing a map of Qavner in this book, let alone a map of the Academy, but then, he hadn't looked too closely.

He never learned to read Pahrucees, so the book had remained a rather terrifying curiosity. He had thought that perhaps he'd bring it to the Linguistics Department for translation, but every time he had put it in his bag to take elsewhere, it wouldn't remain in the bag.

He, of course, gave himself the usual explanations—he didn't remember removing it from the bag or he had put it in the wrong bag or he had only *thought* of taking it to Linguistics; he hadn't really started to do so.

But now, faced with the glowing map of the Academy, he wondered how much and how long he had been deluding himself.

He glanced back at the shelf, wondering what other information awaited him there, but he saw no more glowing books. Part of him felt like it was a conspiracy of books— that they wanted him to look at this one first.

So he did.

And at first, he didn't believe what he was seeing. The map looked like it had been drawn that morning in the Pahrucii style, with light pens and an almost feathery touch, but still drawn recently.

Too many details hadn't existed when the book found Sauer, let alone when the book had been printed.

The map started in the Serebro Mountain Range, near the end of the trees, as the road made its way into housing for staff and professors who wanted a standalone home rather than something in one of the old buildings on campus.

There were footprints on the road, tiny ones that were a ghostly gray or a strange copper. Then the footprints trailed through the neighborhood, past the fields, and stopped at the edge of campus proper. There, they gathered as if they belonged to a group.

The group crowded into a circle, and then, as he stared at it, split into three parts. Three walked toward what he called the functional end of campus, where the physical plant was housed, where the vehicles parked, and where the barns hugged the Coastal Mountain Range.

One of the barns was near the vehicle park in the Vehicle Department, because that barn provided the horses for any carriages that the Academy let their staff use.

The hair was rising on the back of Sauer's neck. He clamped a hand on it, trying to control it, but the feeling—the eerie feeling—remained.

Three sets of footprints, in gold, were heading toward that part of campus.

Eight sets of footprints, also gold, started toward the center of campus. Two more sets moved more slowly, as if they weren't part of those groups.

Then the map shifted and changed. All he could see now was the Old Library, as clearly as if someone had drawn it using the photographic process created in the Science Department before the Purges. This book was much, much, much older than that. There was no way that anyone from Pahrucii would have seen the Academy or the Old Library, or even this part of Qavner, given the reluctance, particularly during the worst of the Purges, to allow anyone other than Qavnerians attend the Academy.

Sauer let out a breath. He knew what he was seeing—in part anyway. He just had to accept it.

This map was telling him something.

So, he watched as it kept changing, passing the copse of trees where Louella had been attacked (and sure enough, as he looked at it, he saw a silvery puddle glistening on the dark image), then the bridge and finally the Students Entrance.

There were no footprints here, nothing moving except the perspective itself.

He couldn't help himself though; he pinched his arm, and winced at the pain, an old trick taught to him by Professor Sabry to make sure he wasn't dreaming.

He wasn't.

He was seeing this in real time, although he didn't know what it meant.

The image kept moving through doors, past the tables, up to the dais, the librarians' desks. There it wobbled, and he braced himself, because watching this was making him dizzy.

Then the map altered itself again, and became an architect's rendering, an outline of every single space in that part of the Old Library. Once again, there were footprints, two different groups this time.

The first was near the back, a single pair of footprints that had faded to a bloody pink. The other set consisted of two pairs, both faded yellow. Those two went toward a different room behind the dais on the right side that he hadn't known existed. After a moment, the pink ones appeared.

He had to squint because the footprints were changing as he watched. The yellow ones remained ahead, and seemed to go down a narrow flight of stairs, then into a corridor, where they turned bright gold.

Behind them, the pink footprints hit that extra room and then circled in confusion. For a moment, he thought that was all he would see.

Then the pink appeared outside of that room, and went down a different hallway, before turning back. The bloody pink footprints were inside the stairs now—he knew it was now—and they were heading toward the gold ones.

He twisted his hands together. He had no idea why the map was showing him this. He was too far away from the footprints to make any kind of difference. He didn't have an ability to change locations at a whim or send what few magical abilities he had ahead of himself.

Nor was there anyone else in this building whom he could send to warn...whomever.

He had no idea what he was watching.

Until the image shifted yet again. A straight map, showing only the Old Library part of campus. The pink footprints decorated the copse of trees. They were everywhere, back and forth, and around, but they hadn't arrived there from anywhere.

Instead, there were one set of green footprints that appeared to be decorated with white flowers, and another set of dark purple prints that followed them.

He traced the prints, then watched them intersect, turn black and disappear for a half moment.

When they reappeared, the blood pool sparkled with silver and red highlights among the trees.

His breath caught.

This map was showing him magic. Or maybe it was showing him people using magic.

Here. On campus.

His heart started pounding.

He knew what he had seen in the copse of trees wasn't

happening now. He could tell that from the blood pool and what he had known about what had occurred days ago.

"Show me now," he said, wishing he knew how to say it in Pahrucees. "Show me what's happening right now."

The map blanked out, and for a moment, he thought he had broken it. Or maybe he had been dreaming after all, and he was sitting in his desk.

He reached for the loose skin to pinch under his right arm when the map fuzzed back, showing the entire campus.

Pink footprints in one of the old buildings that housed visiting professors. Gray and copper footprints marching along campus. Now they formed four sets—a group that was heading toward the Old Library, another group of two that was moving very slowly, a group still going toward the barns, and a fourth group that had just veered away from the first.

The group heading toward the Old Library and the fourth group looked similar. They each had three sets of ghostly gray footprints and one set of copper prints. The twosome, that separate group, was all copper, as was the group heading to the barns.

The colors had to mean something, but what, he couldn't figure out. He wasn't sure if he should ask the map.

He certainly shouldn't before he had finished examining it. There were other colors and markings along the map itself.

Then there was a silver sparkling group that didn't make footprints at all. The silver sparkles looked like wheel tracks, making their way down the last of the mountain into the foothills.

And the prints inside the Old Library, stationary in those positions he had seen them last.

There were other starlike sparkles all over campus. Tiny sparkles that winked in and out in silver, gold and fading yellow. But nothing pink or red or copper or that odd gray.

Nothing except the four groups, and the two pink prints, one in the visiting professors' building and one in the Old Library.

He glanced at the Old Library again, his heart pounding. He had assumed those bloody pink prints were stationary, but now he wasn't sure.

Maybe those bloody pink prints were farther along the rendering of stairs.

He put his hands over his mouth, not sure what to say or do. As he watched, the fourth grouping, the one that had veered off, had turned on what he thought of as the private path, one that would bring that group—four sets of footprints—to the AST building.

To him.

As far as he knew, he was alone here.

That strange feeling—the hair rising on the back of his head—repeated. But the feeling had a charged vibe to it, as if there was more than fear powering it.

He made himself pull his hands away from his face, and he resisted the urge to cover the back of his neck with his right hand again.

He needed to feel that emotion. He stared at the fourth grouping, moving along the path.

They were definitely coming toward the AST building.

He had resources. He had just never thought of them as resources. Before, all they had been were research tools.

But this map, even though it was in a book written in Pahrucees, was communicating with him.

"I need to know who else is in the building," he said to the map. It didn't move. The images he saw were the footprints, moving in several different directions.

Even the tiny starlike sparkles appeared to be gone.

Had he screwed this up? He didn't want to. He needed some kind of assistance, or he was going to have to barricade himself into this room. He wasn't a military leader of any kind. He had spent his mandatory year in the Qavnerian military shelving books in their library.

What he knew about military tactics had come from books. He loved reading about wars, not fighting in them. And even then, he had scanned over the parts about tactics. He hadn't thought that important. Tactics were for people on the frontlines, and necessary only in the moment.

He really had never cared if an army had turned west, or if some person had figured out how to use a spear properly. Or when someone had gotten a lucky shot with their pistol.

And now, here he was. Alone, with footprints coming his way.

Although he hadn't tried everything.

"Map, please," he said, keeping his voice low, as if the owners of those footprints had already come into the building. "Show me where the magical people are inside the Alchemy, Science, and Thaumaturgy Building."

The map didn't move. The image continued its strange glimmering show, footprints heading in different directions.

Then something banged beside him.

Sauer's heart damn near came out of his chest. He let out a tiny yelp and turned, expecting someone to have breached all the wards in the hallway and the lock on his door to slam it open.

Instead, a book had fallen off one of the shelves, although *fallen* was a strange word to use. It couldn't have landed in the center of the floor the way it had, if it had actually fallen.

It seemed to have leapt as close to him as possible.

And it didn't land closed, either. It was open. He took one tentative step toward it, and saw that it was open to a two-page tipped-in illustration.

He let out the breath he hadn't realized he had been holding. His entire body was vibrating, from adrenaline and a growing fear, and that charged sense that was moving from the back of his neck down his spine.

He crouched near the book, afraid to touch it.

So he looked up at the shelf, to see if he could identify what the book was.

Sure enough, he knew exactly what the book was. It was one of his favorite books in a special edition.

The History of Alchemy, Thaumaturgy, Science, and Magic at Serebro Academy.

He sometimes assigned that book to his students, but not in this edition. Their edition had a few black-and-white drawings of the more famous graduates, scholars, and professors (at least at the time the book was written).

But the edition before him, the special edition, had color plates that were hand-tipped in, as well as several maps that he could have pulled out of the book if he wanted to.

The book also had architectural renderings of the AST Building at various points in its existence. Many of those renderings were drawn after the fact, after, as one of his professors said, the building grew on its own. There were also drawings of various "rooms of note" which, again, were considered so back in the time the book was published.

The illustration was a map. It was one of those maps of the building that had been drawn with great care, years ago. Only it included labels now for places like his office—labeled *Sauer's Office*—and he hadn't even attended the Academy when this book had been written.

That tingly feeling on the back of his neck was growing worse and worse. He had to remind himself to breathe.

The map showed the building as if it were being disassembled by floor, each floor floating in a different direction from the other, with some space in between each floor for labels.

The rendering, done this way, made it easier to view the floors. It almost made them look like blocks he could remove from the image, and get a better picture of what was inside.

He crouched, not willing to pick up the book.

The map was separating itself into the three departments. If he squinted at them, he saw six other sets of footprints. Two were ivory with silver edges. Two were almost black, also with silver edges, and two were sparkly silver, as if they were lit from within.

He didn't see his footprints at all.

He stared at those prints, wanting to ask the maps if

what he was seeing was true. But that was just a delaying tactic. He knew what he was seeing was true.

There were six people in this building besides him. He knew where they all were at this moment. Maybe if he took the book with him, he would be able to track them through the building.

But he'd have to take both books, because he wanted to see what those other footprints were doing.

His knees and thighs ached. He hadn't crouched like this in years. He wobbled his way up.

The closest set of footprints, an ivory pair with silver lining, was just down the hall. Probably Hester Fenwick, who taught the language of magic in all of its forms. Fenwick hated mornings, and preferred to work late into the night.

Sauer had encountered her ending her day several times as he was just starting his.

She was a thin little woman with a smattering of white fuzz on the top of her head, and a vague manner that belied the sharpness in her eyes. She'd dressed him down on more than one occasion.

She was not the ally he would have chosen with Fey magic on the loose.

But, as one of his military history professors had once said, heroes don't get to choose their moment. Their moment chooses them. And the hero was the person who rose to the moment instead of running from it.

"I'll be right back," he said to the books, and hoped that was even remotely true.

LINGUISTICS

ARCHEOLOGY

HISTORY

REGENTS
TOWER

OLD
LIBRARY

ADV. STUDENT
WING

MAIN
ENTRANCE

CLOCK
TOWER

MEDICAL
SCIENCES

CHAPTER
THIRTY-EIGHT

Croninshield was halfway down the corridor when she thought she heard something. A scraping? A scrabbling?

She couldn't quite identify the sound, and it made her nervous.

She turned back toward the stairwell that she and Ludmilla Odenkirk had just gone down.

They had remembered to close that door after it had banged open, but Croninshield knew from long experience that once a door like that had been opened, it would be easier to open a second time.

The dozen or so other doors in the corridor would probably stick just as badly. No one came down here unless they needed something, and most of what was here was either unused classrooms from the Academy's early days, or storage for items of everything from books to pens to chairs. Most were in terrible condition, but it was a tenet of the library that nothing got thrown away. It could all be valuable one day.

Some of the items hidden away here had once been in other rooms. This corridor was considered one of the most remote, so items that were stored behind these doors were thought of as nearly useless.

"Everything all right?" Ludmilla asked.

Croninshield gripped the lantern tightly. "I don't know," she said.

She couldn't hear the scrabbling any longer. Maybe it was just a rat or a mouse, some kind of creature that she would probably need to get the janitorial staff to eradicate.

She had long argued for cats throughout the Old Library, but they presented their own problems, marking their territory and unsanitary bathroom habits if they couldn't find an exit.

"You said there were stairs ahead," Ludmilla said.

"Yes." Croninshield knew that was her cue to turn around, but something else was bothering her. She frowned, unable to put her finger on it.

The chilly damp air smelled faintly of mildew, which was a librarian's nightmare, but that was an old problem, something that she had been battling since she started to work here.

So what bothered her wasn't temperature or smell. It might have been that scrabbling noise, but if she and Ludmilla hurried, then that wouldn't be an issue either.

No. What bothered her was the light.

The light from the lightstone lamps on the walls wasn't illuminating the space around the lamps. The light was traveling back toward the doorway that she and Ludmilla had just come through.

Croninshield had never seen light act like that.

She lifted her lantern ever so slightly. Its light was trailing back to that door as well.

It was a warning. It had to be.

She pivoted, caught Ludmilla by the arm, and said, "We have to hurry."

Then Croninshield started walking as quickly as she could, making Ludmilla keep up with her. As they passed lamps on the wall, the lights that hadn't been on activated. Those that had been on flared slightly, as if in greeting.

"What's going on?" Ludmilla asked.

"If I knew," Croninshield said, "I would tell you."

The door behind them banged open. The sound resonated throughout the hallway.

Croninshield's heart rate increased too.

The lamps flared and rotated on the walls, moving the bulk of their light toward that door. Something moaned.

Croninshield turned toward the sound.

Louella staggered forward, hands up, as if the light hurt her eyes. She looked odd, almost blurry, like her body was losing definition.

The light appeared to be hurting her.

Croninshield remembered that the Fey had hated light-stone. Some of the battlefield accounts claimed that one single lightstone lantern defeated an entire Fey troop.

Croninshield raised the lantern, then adjusted the hood so that all of the light poured out of one side. She made sure that side faced Louella, and then walked swiftly back toward the door.

"Wait!" Ludmilla said. "Wait, don't you think we should leave?"

Croninshield didn't answer her. Instead, Croninshield focused on Louella, who seemed to lose more and more definition.

Louella let out another moan, but it cut off. Her body vibrated into two.

The first was the body itself, which looked just like Louella, only as if she was losing control of her limbs.

The other was a tall, slender woman, with coal-black hair, a narrow chin, uplifted cheekbones that matched her uplifted eyebrows, and ears that came to a sharp point.

Her eyes—the new woman's eyes—met Croninshield's. Croninshield couldn't read what she saw—anger? Fear? Pain?—and then the dark-haired woman floated upward toward the ceiling.

The body collapsed as if it had lost its spine, falling in a heap onto the floor.

Behind Croninshield, Ludmilla gasped. She started to walk toward whatever it was, but, using her free arm, Croninshield blocked her. Ludmilla stopped, hand over her mouth.

Croninshield said, "Stay here," and then walked forward, holding the lantern before her like a beacon.

The light from the lantern focused on the floating woman. The other light from all of the lightstone lamps was tilting upward too. The floating woman was bathed in light. As the light grew brighter, she grew dimmer.

"Stop," she said, her voice weak and watery. "You're hurting me."

Croninshield lowered the lantern. "I'll stop if you tell me how to revive Louella."

The floating woman looked down, then shook her head. "You can't. There is no Louella anymore."

"Because this lantern killed her?" Croninshield was asking the question out of fear, and knew it, but she couldn't stop it.

"No," the floating woman said, "she died days ago."

"You killed her." Croninshield wasn't asking a question at all. "What are you?"

"My people call me a Doppelgänger," the floating woman said, her voice growing ever fainter.

"What are your people?" Ludmilla asked. Croninshield wanted to shush her. Croninshield wanted to be in charge of the questions.

"The Fey. I'm Fey." The floating woman waved a hand, as if she was trying to block the light still pouring from the lamps. "If you shut off those lights, I'll tell you about my people."

It sounded so tempting, until one considered the body lying at the floating woman's feet.

"No," Croninshield said, and raised the lantern again. Louella, dead? She had been a sweet girl with a lot of potential. That attack in the copse of trees hadn't been an assault. It had been a murder.

Croninshield marched toward the floating woman, holding the lantern ever higher. As Croninshield got closer, the light seemed to flare brighter. She felt like she was walking in a ray of sunlight so powerful that it could burn anything it touched.

The floating woman was growing more and more transparent.

"Please," she said, her voice almost a whisper. "Stop. I'll cooperate. I'll help you. I'll—"

"You murdered one of my colleagues," Croninshield said. "There's no guarantee you won't do it again."

"I'll tell you why we're here," the floating woman said.

Croninshield lowered the lantern just a little, wondering if she was far enough away from the floating woman to protect herself.

"Tell me first, and then I'll make sure you're protected," she said.

"Please," Ludmilla said from behind her. "Don't do that. I don't think you can trust her."

No kidding, Croninshield nearly said, but didn't. Instead, she said to the floating woman, "You have ten seconds to talk."

"We—my team and I," the floating woman said, speaking rapidly, her voice barely above a whisper. "We're one of several advance teams. We're scouting this continent for magic. We're supposed to destroy it."

"And?" Croninshield asked, because that couldn't be all of it. That wasn't enough to murder an innocent like Louella.

"And report back to the Black King's son, so that he can mount an attack on this place."

"Oh, dear," Ludmilla said.

"Why?" Croninshield asked.

The woman floated a foot closer. "That's what we do," she said, and then whooshed toward Croninshield so fast that Croninshield's eyes barely tracked her.

Images floated across Croninshield's brain—the bones, the blood, the stranger in Louella's eyes.

That was no stranger—not now. That was the floating woman, whose eyes were focused on Croninshield's right now.

Croninshield raised the lantern to protect her face, turning the light outward.

A scream reverberated around the hallway, loud and whispery at the same time. Croninshield ducked, and hoped Ludmilla was smart enough to do the same.

Croninshield couldn't see the floating woman. Croninshield couldn't see anything because the light was so bright.

It felt like Croninshield was looking into the sun, like the sun had come all the way down to this hallway, to burn through everyone who was here.

Only the light wasn't hot. It was cool, and soothing, and it surrounded her like a shroud.

The scream faded, and slowly the light faded too.

Croninshield blinked. She saw patterns every time she closed her eyes—lamps, lanterns, the door, that floating woman.

But as the brightness eased, she couldn't see the actual floating woman. The light coming from the lamps was fading too. It appeared to be normal now, just lights coming from a fixture.

The lightstone lantern was lighter than it had been. She

couldn't help herself; she peered inside the lantern. The lightstone seemed too small for the space.

Usually lightstone filled the inside of any lantern. This one didn't.

Almost as if it had been diminished.

Ludmilla came up beside her, standing close enough to Croninshield that Croninshield could hear her shallow breathing. Maybe even her heart beating—or perhaps that was Croninshield's heart.

Croninshield stepped to the left, away from Ludmilla. Standing near someone right now felt wrong.

"What just happened?" Ludmilla asked.

"I don't know," Croninshield said, although maybe she did know. Maybe she didn't want to admit she knew. "Is it gone, that creature? Or is it still lurking?"

She didn't want to call it a woman, even though it clearly had been. But women didn't float. They didn't take over other people. They didn't scream when light had been turned on them.

"I hope it's not lurking," Ludmilla said, which wasn't reassuring at all. "The lights think it's gone."

There was that. The lights had returned to what passed for normal. They hadn't been normal since Croninshield turned on the lantern at the bottom of the stairs.

She turned. "Let me see your eyes," she said.

Ludmilla frowned, but cooperated. Her eyes looked like they had before, not that Croninshield had known her well. But Croninshield had seen enough of her to recognize that floating woman in her face, right?

Or maybe Croninshield had seen the floating woman enough to recognize her. Right?

It was enough to make anyone paranoid.

"She didn't disappear into me, did she?" Croninshield asked.

"She separated into pieces," Ludmilla said. "Like a dark wispy cloud in a strong wind."

Croninshield nodded, even though she didn't entirely understand. "Maybe that creature could turn invisible. Maybe it's lurking."

Ludmilla let out a shaky breath. She seemed as unsettled as Croninshield was.

"Let's continue," Croninshield said.

"But the body...?" Ludmilla asked.

"It will wait for us," Croninshield said. "And honestly, I don't want to get near it right now. What if the creature is in there, still?"

"Cover it with light from the lantern, maybe?" Ludmilla said. "Maybe we can—"

"What? Deal with it right now?" Croninshield said. "I think we keep moving. I think we have to get out of here, and there are only two ways to do it. Either we go back the way we came, or we go up the stairs at the end of the hall."

Ludmilla let out a startled breath. "All right, then," she said. "The stairs at the end of the hall it is."

She started that way, then peered over her shoulder.

"It doesn't feel right to leave someone's body down here," she said.

And she was right: it didn't. But Croninshield wasn't going to go near the thing.

"I think we have to switch our mindset," she said. "I think we need to consider ourselves to be at war."

"Even in war, bodies get removed," Ludmilla said.

"When the battle is over." Croninshield gave what remained of Louella one last glance. "Only when the battle is over."

"Then we should do something," Ludmilla said. "Because this battle is over."

Croninshield shook her head.

"No, it's not over," she said. "What we've been through? I think it's just the beginning."

"You think this is going to be a war?" Ludmilla asked.

"You heard her," Croninshield said. "She said that she was a Fey, and they wanted to attack this place."

"And she did," Ludmilla said.

"I don't think she meant the Old Library or even the Academy," Croninshield said. "I think she meant Dorovich."

"Why would they want Dorovich?" Ludmilla asked.

"I don't know," Croninshield said, "but we're not going to figure it out in this hallway."

Ludmilla nodded. One short movement, almost military in its precision.

"You're right," she said. "Let's go somewhere safe."

Croninshield wished they could. But she had a feeling that safety was something they wouldn't see again for a very, very long time.

SCHOLAR'S
ENTRANCE

OLD

LIBRARY

CE

CAFETERIA

THIRTY-NINE

Hardin adjusted his pack over his right shoulder. The pack was more irritating when it was mostly empty than it was when it was full. He had a few tools in there, but mostly, he was supposed to use the pack for loot. He'd stored some other bags inside of it so that he would be able to carry as much as possible out of the Old Library.

He felt comfortable with that part of the plan, even though much of it had changed. He also had a variety of different-sized knives and one crowbar in his belt. That felt lighter than usual too. He often carried even more tools than that around his waist, including the slingshot that Lumin had mandated for each Infantry member.

Hardin thought slingshots were stupid, but he went along with it, just like he had done for most of Lumin's strange plans.

Hardin was leading his small group through the old part

of campus. Unlike Lumin, apparently, Hardin had studied the maps they had found, even though many of those maps had unnerved him. Therefore, he knew where they were going.

The campus was dotted with small groupings of plants and trees. Sometimes the paths went through those groupings. Sometimes they went around. When the paths went around, Hardin led the group through the trees, knowing that the campus gardeners did not like undergrowth.

Everything here was manicured within an inch of its life, which made some parts of this journey predictable. Sometimes he preferred a lot more undergrowth, but this was a campus, which was like the grounds of any other large complex. It had a design, which meant that he could use the design to move the group into position rather stealthily.

Not that he needed stealth, at least at the moment. None of the Qavnerians knew that the Fey were in their midst. That would not last, now that the carriages were discovered and there was some mysterious explosion back in Serebro.

But it was hard for these people to spread news, so they wouldn't be able to alert others. And even if they did, what could they say? They had no idea how many Fey were in this advance team or what their purpose was.

He knew that some might know of the attack in Trinovante, but that was even farther away. Part of him applauded Lumin's decision to take action now.

Another part of Hardin believed that Lumin should have waited until the Trinovante situation settled down. After all, no one had known that there was a Serebro team, just like no one knew about the other teams.

But Hardin wasn't in charge of this team. Infantry members rarely were. He didn't have any Vision at all. If this were simply an Infantry troop composed of six members, he would definitely lead them. But he couldn't, not with a Visionary around, even a Visionary without any real military experience whatsoever.

Hardin set his irritation aside. He was pleased, at least, that Lumin recognized which Infantry members should head to the most important target—the Old Library. Hardin had brought a good team on this mission to Dorovich, but some of his team were more experienced than others.

Without realizing it, perhaps, Lumin had assigned the two best to accompany Hardin. Oylae had been at Hardin's side since the battle of Salztal, one of the most decisive in conquering Nye. They'd both been young and newly trained, and they yet hadn't gotten in trouble for failing to follow orders.

He didn't regret that moment, the one that had brought him and Oylae here. His "failure" to follow orders at a later uprising in L'Nacin had saved dozens of Fey lives as well as prevented the slaughter of innocent L'Nacin children.

He fought like crazy when he had military objectives and a military target. That uprising hadn't been an uprising at all, but a joyous parade that celebrated L'Nacin culture. Rugar might have wanted the joy extinguished to keep the L'Nacin under control, but Hardin didn't want that kind of slaughter on his conscience.

His troop had later thanked him. They hadn't wanted it either.

Oylae had gotten in trouble for backing him up. They

remained a team, if a disgraced one. She was with him now, moving sideways and back, constantly surveying the scene. She wasn't that tall, but she was muscular, stronger than Hardin himself. She could also move quickly, so that when she was along, he always felt that he had an extra layer of protection.

He needed it on this night. The ground fog provided some, but it seemed to be acting strangely. It should have covered the entire area in a one- to two-foot-high layer, but it didn't. It blew toward the Old Library, which it was supposed to surround, granted, but not as if the fog wanted to capture it.

He also suspected that some of the fog was heading toward the Alchemy building as well. The fog's movement led him to believe that it was attracted to some kind of magick here, something that his people hadn't identified yet.

He and the other Infantry member in this little troop, Daeloi, had discussed the strangeness of the magick in Dorovich. Daeloi didn't have any magick like most Infantry, but he studied it, the way that Hardin did. They had to know how to fight it without having any magick themselves. Even Fey magick.

Sometimes, Hardin believed, that Infantry like him and Daeloi knew more about magick than people like Lumin. Lumin seemed to think he understood it all until he realized he didn't; the magickless, like Hardin and Daeloi, knew they understood very little about it, so they became a different kind of expert. They understood how most magick worked, and when they didn't, they often volunteered to hold or test it.

Most outside magick—like the kind they had encountered in Dorovich—had repercussions for other magick users, but not for the non-magickal. Which was why he and the other members of the Infantry could recover so many Dorovician magickal artifacts, without realizing that they were going to have an impact on the magickal among them.

There was only one of the magickal in this group. Veil, one of three Spies that Lumin had brought along. Lumin truly had not thought this mission through. He needed more Infantry and fewer Spies and Doppelgängers. As far as Hardin was concerned, the Doppelgängers had been more than useless, unable to figure out where the artifacts were stored on this campus, even though the place radiated magick as if those strange lightstone lamps illuminated each piece.

The lightstone lamps were another matter. They were something else he had to avoid, not just for Veil, but for his people. The lightstone seemed to sap something from inside every Fey, not just the ones with magick.

So far, he had managed to lead this group away from all of the standing lightstone lamps that illuminated the path, but he knew that would become a problem once they were inside the Old Library. And of course, Veil had no map of where the lamps were inside that Old Library.

His only comment about the lamps was that in most parts of the Old Library, the lightstone lamps were placed too high to be much of an issue.

Hardin glanced at Veil, who was walking slightly behind him. Veil's face had solidified into a roundish older man's face, with light brown skin and thin little lips. The eyes were dark, but that was normal for Qavnerians. The hair was close-cropped and grayish.

Veil's appearance made Hardin think that Veil was using an actual template of someone known to him, something that Spies often did. Hardin hoped that Veil was cautious enough to make certain that whoever he had based his look upon wouldn't be anywhere near the Old Library tonight, or maybe even campus.

They finally reached a copse of trees not too far from the Old Library. Hardin could see a stone footbridge over what Gray had called a moat, even though the maps never called it that.

On this night, that description seemed accurate, though, only the dip in the ground looked like it was filled with ground fog. In fact, the bridge itself rose out of the fog like a bridge incongruously out of a flooded river.

Hardin took a deep breath. The air tasted of salt and fish, probably from the nearby Infrin Sea.

He put his hands on his hips and stared at the building. It was three times larger than he had thought, based on the maps he had looked at. He knew if they went in on the student side, they had a long arched hallway to walk through, filled with tables and books and studying students. Then there was a dais toward the back, which probably had some librarians at it.

He would assume that the lightstone lamps were on the high walls, but he didn't know for sure, and asking Veil felt fruitless.

Hardin wished he had the ability to conjure up one of the maps. But he didn't. He closed his eyes for a half-second, remembering one of the library maps that the team had already liberated.

One of the map rooms was in the Scholars Wing. This was a room that scholars could visit, as long as they were supervised. Given the team's short mission, that might be the best place to start.

"Correct me if I'm wrong," he said to Veil, "but the Scholars Entrance is on the right side of the building in the middle."

Veil looked at him, dark eyes almost blank. "You do realize how far 'in the middle' is, right?"

Hardin felt a surge of irritation. "Do you have a different suggestion?"

"I don't think we can get into the Scholars Wing. You need to be connected to the Academy, as a professor or a known researcher." Veil tilted his head. His voice sounded higher and a bit nasal, and it seemed like Fey words didn't quite fit into it.

"Do you have a different suggestion?" Hardin asked.

"I thought maybe we would go into the student section and fan out," he said.

Which was why Spies rarely led troops. Hardin felt his irritation rise. "We're to get the maps. The most accessible maps are in the Scholar Wing, am I right?"

"I don't know about accessible," Veil said. "They're not really accessible at all. Let's just go and ask Shyly to get us to the maps."

The Doppelgänger with such a low status that she couldn't complete her mission. Hardin almost spat out his contempt, but knew it would have little to do.

"There is a map room on the first level of this building, in the Scholars Wing, right?" he repeated.

"For what good it'll do us," Veil said. "I think Shyly—"

"We're not going to talk with Shyly," Hardin growled. "We're not going to talk with anyone. You go in the Student Wing here—which is what's in front of us, right?"

"If you know all of this, why are you asking me?" Veil asked.

Good point. Hardin had thought Veil would be useful. Apparently not.

"You go into the Student Wing," Hardin repeated, "and you find Shyly. Figure out where other map rooms are, if there are map rooms. If not, we need the exact location of the artifact rooms for Eerie."

"Gray already got what he could," Veil said.

Hardin had had enough. It was clear now that this little Spy was terrified to be in the middle of the mission.

"You will go in and find Shyly," Hardin repeated. "You will locate artifact and map areas, regardless of what Gray has done. You will leave with that information, and you will tell Eerie. Are we clear?"

"I'm not going with you three?" Veil asked. His voice went up even higher, the way a person's voice did when they had good news that they really didn't want to acknowledge as good news.

"Yes," Hardin said. "We're going to play to our skills tonight. You would be a liability for us."

He already was, but Hardin didn't add that. Veil was giving them nothing and costing them time they didn't have.

"All right," Veil said. "She's probably going to be annoyed because she gave this information to Gray already."

As if the team needed to worry about what an incompetent Doppelgänger thought. Hardin did not say that either.

"It is better to have too much information than too little," Hardin said, and didn't add that they already had too little information, and that was a problem. "Now, get out of here."

Veil gave him a startled look, almost frightened. His face rippled, as if he had suddenly lost a grip on his image.

"Go," Hardin said, making a shooing motion with his hand.

Veil glanced at the others, as if he expected them to defend him. Against what? Orders he didn't believe in? Or was he worried about scurrying across campus on his own?

Ultimately, Hardin didn't care. He raised his eyebrows at Veil. If Hardin had to tell him to leave one more time, Hardin would bodily chuck Veil onto the nearest path.

But Veil turned and walked through the ground fog toward the stone bridge. It took him a moment to gain his confidence back. For the first few steps, he looked like a terrified man, taking small steps, hunched against the cold.

Gradually, though, he stood up straight and headed for the bridge.

At that point, Hardin no longer cared. He turned to his team.

Oylae was shaking her head as she watched Veil cross the bridge. Then she seemed to realize that Hardin was looking at her. She grinned at him, an almost feral look.

"That's one sorry excuse for a Fey," she said.

"I couldn't agree more." Daeloi had his arms crossed. He wore his pack over both shoulders although his had to be as light as Hardin's. "How much do you want to wager that he will not have any constructive news from Shyly after we've finished securing the maps?"

"No wager," Oylae said. She glanced at Hardin. "You know the best way into that Scholars Wing?"

"I don't know the best anything," he said. "Only what I saw on those maps we stole a few months ago. But what I can remember of them has been accurate so far. I will continue to rely on them, which means, we head around this moat thing toward our right. We should see a door rather like the one we see here, and that's the one we use."

Or so he hoped. He had no idea what the door looked like. It had been marked with words in Qavnerian, which he'd had to parse out. He had found all of the entrances to this building, and several others on campus when he had learned that was why Lumin wanted to be in Serebro.

Apparently, Lumin had thought that the Serebro Academy was in Serebro proper. Their so-called Visionary leader hadn't said a word about his disappointment or concerns when he had learned that the Academy was many miles away, over mountains.

Now, though, Hardin wished he had shared those maps with the rest of the Infantry. It would have been nice to get their reactions, as well as their opinions.

Stupid him, he had trusted the Spies and Doppelgängers to do their jobs, forgetting that he was in a group of screw-ups, ones who could be sacrificed if their missions went awry. Maybe, if Rugar had wanted real intelligence from

Dorovich, he should have sent people who could have gotten the job done.

If he wanted magick destroyed, he should have authorized a small fighting force.

This hybrid mission was doing no one any good at all.

"All right," Hardin said. "You all follow me."

He was going to take them around that moat, past some more trees, and keep them off the paths. He would keep an eye out for the door that he needed.

Part of him hoped that door would be locked. Another part hoped that it would be surrounded by lamps, so that he could smash them.

Then he would smash his way inside.

He'd been so frustrated for so long that he wanted break everything he saw. And this night might give him a chance to do that.

LIN

ALCHEMY, SCIENCE
& THAUMATURGY

GOVERNMENT

RE
T

LAW BUILDING

WHISTLER
HALL

CHAPTER

FORTY

The moment Wolfgang Sauer left his office, he felt like he had walked into the hallway naked. The feeling was so strong that he actually checked to see if he was wearing clothes.

Then he realized where it had come from.

In his office, he had been surrounded by books on magic, and books that *had* magic, no matter how much he wanted to deny it. He had also placed wards inside his office to protect himself, and a few more outside the door to make sure no one could open it without his permission.

Now, as he stood in the hallway, which was so much colder than his office that goosebumps rose on his skin, he felt like he'd left all of his defenses behind, even though he had warded the hallway as well.

The wards here, though, weren't as powerful or as specific as the ones he had created for himself. These were generic wards, meant to filter out people with "bad intentions," a ward he'd had to tweak a dozen times because once in a while it filtered out angry students who came to complain about a grade.

The hallway looked longer than usual, which was a feature of his exhaustion. It had looked that way to him in the past, usually late at night when he was so tired all he could think of was returning to his suite in the oldest building for professors. Maybe, though, the hallway stretched out at night.

The AST building certainly had a mind of its own. It formed rooms and wings at will, even though, according to the book he had left open on his floor, it had done so over months as if someone were actually building the wing, instead of having it form, say, overnight.

He let out a small sigh. He couldn't solve all of the mysteries of the AST building in one night. He couldn't solve anything right now.

He wanted to go back into that office and check where the fourth set of footprints was. Had those footprints veered onto the secondary path leading to the AST building?

He shook his head slightly. One thing at a time. The first thing was to convince Hester Fenwick to find the others while he monitored everything.

It actually took an effort to make himself walk down that hallway, past the closed doors. The ceiling felt lower than normal too. The lights on the wall were a little dim—and lightstone lamps were never dim.

He suddenly wondered if he was reacting to something

else—some other kind of force or spell that was holding him back. He had no idea. Maybe the building was trying to protect him.

He didn't think that the owners of those footprints even knew he existed, so it probably wasn't them.

But it might have been the books. They might want him to remain with them.

"I'll be right back," he said, and immediately felt ridiculous. Who talked aloud to books? But after he spoke, he felt lighter, as if something that had had a grip on him was actually letting go.

He made himself hurry forward.

Hester Fenwick had been a professor longer than he had, and she had been given one of the larger offices on the floor. Or maybe she had demanded it. People didn't usually refuse Fenwick anything.

He reached the door that led to her office, saw yarn all over the front of it, woven in lovely patterns that were almost hypnotic. Those were new.

He also recognized what they were. Rudimentary wards, made by someone who had no idea how to make a ward. The pattern had probably come from a book.

He wondered if Fenwick was feeling the strange energy of the evening as well.

He made a fist to knock on the door, then stopped himself. He needed to be cautious, even around rudimentary wards. Sometimes rudimentary wards worked differently than expected. Sometimes they worked better. And sometimes, they injured the wrong person.

"Hester," he said as loudly as he could without shouting. "It's Wolfgang. I need to talk to you."

He heard shuffling in the room. The shuffling confirmed what he had figured out from the map: the silver-lined ivory footprints were hers.

"Just a minute." Her voice sounded querulous, which was odd, since she always spoke with great authority.

He heard more shuffling. He shifted from foot to foot, then glanced to the right, so that he could see his door. Nothing had changed in the back end of the hallway.

Then he looked to the left. So far, no one appearing that way, either. He suspected he would hear footsteps on the stairs.

He hoped he would, anyway.

He suddenly felt the lack of that book, and the map. He needed to track that fourth set of footprints.

Then the door opened. Hester Fenwick stood before him, wearing a black floor-length sweater over a black long-sleeved cotton shirt, and a black skirt that barely covered her black button-up boots. All that black made her face, normally a bit brownish, look pale and yellow.

Or maybe it was the very obvious stress that had her biting her lower lip.

"Wolfgang?" she asked. "What's going on?"

He wasn't sure how to answer that because he wasn't sure exactly what she was asking. Was she asking why he was at her door? Or had something made her put up the wards?

"I need you to come to my office now," he said.

She leaned her head back, and raised one of her barely there eyebrows.

He had no idea what she was assuming, but he didn't like the expression.

"I have some books I have to show you," he said.

"Now?" she asked.

"Yes." He hoped the curtness of his tone conveyed his concern.

"Let me grab my bag," she said, and closed the door in his face.

She was moving more slowly than he wanted her to. He wanted her to have the same urgency he did, even though she had none of the same information.

There was more shuffling, then the door opened again. She held a shoulder-length black suede bag with patchwork all across its surface and fringe along the bottom. She was groping inside the bag, then pulled out a fistful of keys in something like triumph.

"We need to hurry, Hester," he said gently.

"I am hurrying," she said, and made a shooing gesture with her right hand. *That* was the Fenwick he knew, and that made him feel better.

She locked the door, and then led the way to his office. He watched her walk, sweater trailing behind her. She put the bag over her shoulder, and the fringe tapped her leg.

He half-expected to see silver-lined ivory footprints trailing behind her, but there were none.

She reached his door, and reached for the knob.

"No," he said. "Let me."

He hadn't disabled any of the wards, and he wasn't sure what would happen. Not that they were designed to hurt someone like her, but still. There were too many strange things happening for him to trust anything.

He stepped around her, opened his door, and felt a rush of charged warm air escape. It almost felt like the air during a lightning storm in the Forbidden Valley, not something he'd ever experienced here, though. The ocean protected this area, or so some of the scientists said.

Protected. That was an interesting word.

He slipped through the door ahead of her, half embarrassed at the mess. He had left books on the side of his desk, on a chair—and then there was that book, still open on the floor.

Fenwick took it all in without changing her expression, as if she had seen something like this before.

But she couldn't have, could she? After all, the book open on his desk glowed golden, as if it was welcoming him back.

"What's going on?" she asked again.

"Come with me." He skirted the book on the floor and went to his desk. The map was glowing along the edges. The actual map itself still showed the various sets of footprints, sparkling stars, and lines.

Everything looked different.

She joined him. "What is that?" she asked, then gasped. "Did those...?" She shook her head, as if rejecting the very question she was asking.

So he asked it for her. "Did the image on the map just change? Is that what you were going to say?"

"Yes," she whispered.

"It did," he said. "And that's what I need to talk with you about."

She let out a large sigh, and said, "I knew it. I knew something was happening on campus tonight. I just knew it."

He thanked whatever gods there were that she seemed open to what he was about to tell her. Because he knew it would sound strange—and he needed to convince her as quickly as possible.

LINGUISTICS

ARCHEOLOGY

HISTORY

REGENTS

TOWER

OLD

LIBRARY

ADV. STUDENT
WING

MAIN
ENTRANCE

CLOCK
TOWER

MEDICAL

SCIENCES

CHAPTER
FORTY-ONE

Ludmilla was relieved to reach the stairs at the other end of that enclosed hallway. The stairs were wide and well lit. They veered in two directions. One went down into darkness, the other up into a lighter area. She hoped there would be lightstone lamps along the way—lamps that hadn't yet lit up in their presence.

She was beginning to think of lightstone as some kind of blessing.

May Croninshield was behind her, constantly checking to see if that woman—that creature—that Fey thing—was following them. Ludmilla had no idea if they'd know. The Fey thing (and what else could she call it, really? It wasn't quite human, was it? It hadn't seemed that way) had shredded under the light, the shreds dissipating as if they were feathers on the wind.

But someone could reassemble those feathers, right?

Make them into something else? Maybe that Fey thing could reassemble itself.

Maybe it was waiting on this staircase, having flown here over the light.

That thought stopped Ludmilla. She had thought of herself as a courageous woman, but she really hadn't done anything as Croninshield fought that Fey thing.

At least Ludmilla hadn't stood there and screamed.

She was shaking. This whole day had been odd and stressful. She wanted nothing more than to talk with her father, and she couldn't.

But she had a hunch that he wouldn't have known what to do either. He had loved Serebro Academy. He had loved his work as a Regent, and he had loved the libraries here.

He had disliked much of what he had seen in the Protectorate, but when he talked politics, he talked about Protectorate issues, not some vague threat of magic from a people who lived an ocean away.

She knew about these Fey, but she didn't know a lot. She hadn't thought it important. She had no idea why one would take over the body of a librarian, of all people.

But Ludmilla had spoken to that woman, treated her like a person, thought of her as an equal, even though she had acted a bit odd. Ludmilla rubbed her hands over her arms, feeling gooseflesh. It wasn't really cold in this corridor, but she was reacting as if it were.

The lamps had returned to normal as well, giving off pools of light only around a limited area, instead of moving like a river toward that back staircase.

All the fighting, all the Purges, all the squelching of

magic—she was beginning to think that it had been a very bad idea. Had it come from a Fey creature masquerading as a real person? Was that the impetus, years ago, for the fear and terror that had taken over the Protectorate?

She didn't know. History had not been her favorite subject. It had always seemed so sanitized, so irrelevant to her life.

She glanced at Croninshield, who had acted with authority, wielding that lantern like an actual weapon. The conversation she'd had with the Fey creature, the way that she had stood her ground...who knew that an unassuming older woman with graying hair had such personal power.

Croninshield didn't even look winded right now. She had asked if the Fey creature was lurking nearby, so she was unsettled, but she hadn't really acted like a woman afraid.

They were headed toward the Regents Library because that was what they had planned. The bylaws seemed so unimportant at the moment. The events of the meeting felt very far away.

But someone—something—had gone wrong with the Regents too. That and the presence of these Fey creatures couldn't be a coincidence, could it? Ludmilla didn't know.

She was deeply out of her depth.

She reached the edge of the very wide staircase and stood by the thick wooden railing. It should have been polished, but the wood looked like no one had touched it in years. The stairs themselves were clean, though, and very wide. They were made of a stone she didn't recognize, maybe some kind of marble, and they dipped in the middle, where clearly countless feet had worn the stone down.

All of that made these stairs—this section—very old. Which was what Croninshield had said. They were in an ancient part of the fortress now.

Croninshield was walking slowly. She completed a half circle every time she took a few steps, looking around to see if someone was following them.

She even looked up, which meant that she too was worried that the Fey creature would reassemble.

She finally reached Ludmilla's side.

"Going to the Regents Library seems strange now," Ludmilla said. "Is there someone we can report this to? Security maybe?"

Croninshield's mouth opened just a little. She seemed to have a notion of who to contact, and then she shook her head just once.

"I'm not sure what we should do," she said. "It's late at night, so the administration isn't in their offices. The security team is small. I suppose we could go to them. It just feels right to go to the Regents Library. Safe."

She had a point. Ludmilla hadn't thought of it that way, but the destination did feel safe, and not just because it had been where they were going before this horrid thing happened. The Regents Library felt protected. It felt like a place she needed to be.

"There's magic in that library, isn't there?" she asked.

Croninshield looked at her sideways, a frown creasing her forehead. Ludmilla could see her having a war with herself about answering.

Damn the Purges. They made talking about magic almost impossible.

"I don't know," Croninshield finally said.

It sounded like a lie. She had to know. She helped move the library.

"You don't know or won't say?" Ludmilla asked.

"I don't know for a fact," Croninshield said. "But I do know this: if there is magic in that library, we won't know how to access it. I mean, I don't know. Do you?"

Ludmilla felt her shoulders sink. She didn't know. She had no idea what to do if someone magical came after her.

Like that creature.

"You know how to deal with that Fey creature," Ludmilla said.

"I'm not sure that's accurate," Croninshield said. "The lightstone knew what to do. I was just holding it."

"And you targeted it," Ludmilla said. "You saved us."

"This time." Croninshield gave her a small smile. "Let's get to the library. Let's pull the bylaws and you can look up whatever it was that you wanted to see. Maybe by then, we will have figured out who we can talk with about that body."

That sounded sensible on the surface, but it wasn't. Not really.

"What if there are more of them?" Ludmilla asked. "How can we trust anyone?"

Croninshield gave her a sharp glare. "I hadn't thought of that until just now. Thank you for that."

The sarcasm was strong.

"I mean, it doesn't make sense for there to be just one Fey creature, right? Don't they run in packs?" Ludmilla realized how ridiculous the question sounded, but she really didn't know.

"They're not really creatures," Croninshield said. "They're military. They work in groups when it's advantageous. I'm sure they send scouts too."

Scouts. That actually made sense.

"You think this creature was a scout?" Ludmilla asked.

"Why else would they overtake a librarian?" Croninshield asked. "If they wanted someone who would help them attack a country, wouldn't they overtake a leader of some kind, someone who could facilitate their invasion?"

That seemed logical. Ludmilla felt a shiver run through her. How many of these creatures were there? How could she trust anyone anymore?

"How do we know they haven't?" Ludmilla asked.

Croninshield let out a small sound of disgust. "Talking with you is not making me feel better."

"I don't think it's my job to make you feel better," Ludmilla said.

Croninshield let out a reluctant laugh, as if she didn't want to laugh, and it had just emerged from her unbidden.

"Point taken," she said.

She glanced up the stairs. So did Ludmilla. She could see a landing, and then the stairs continuing upward. Apparently that was where she and Croninshield were going to go.

Ludmilla glanced down the stairs. "Where do those go?"

"Dungeons," Croninshield said.

Ludmilla looked at her in shock. "What?"

"This is a former fortress, remember? There are dungeons down there. It's the only part of the fortress that we haven't remodeled into library rooms." Croninshield shivered. "They're damp and they feel...awful." Then she shook her head. "Sorry to be so nonspecific."

It wasn't nonspecific. It was specific in the same way that the Regents Library felt safe to both of them.

Apparently, there were things that they agreed on—things that worked by feel rather than by thought.

"I hate to be the one to say this." Ludmilla put a hand on the rail. "But maybe we'll have need of dungeons again."

"In a library?" Croninshield asked.

Ludmilla extended her hand toward the crumpled body by the other staircase. "Right now, I think we have to accept —as you said—that this is a place of war. That means bodies in a library. It means keeping prisoners, if we take prisoners, in a place designed for them."

"Taking prisoners," Croninshield repeated. "I don't think we're capable."

"When you got up this morning, did you think you were capable of killing someone?" Ludmilla asked.

"I didn't." Croninshield spoke quickly, as if the thought hurt her. "The light killed them."

Ludmilla could have said, *But you were directing that lantern*, only she felt it wasn't constructive.

Instead, she put a foot on the first step. "You know," she said, deliberately changing the subject. "Right now, you and I are the only people we can trust in this building."

Croninshield looked at her in shock. "What do you—? Oh." Croninshield took a deep shuddery breath. "I like that even less. I trusted everyone in this building when I got up this morning."

The call \back to the earlier phrase felt important.

Maybe it was. Their world had changed a lot since they woke up.

Ludmilla had a hunch it was going to change even more before they fell asleep again.

"Well, then. To the Regents Library," she said.

"To the Regents Library," Croninshield said. "And safety."

If safety even existed anymore, which Ludmilla now doubted. But this time, she didn't express it.

She had been making Croninshield uncomfortable enough.

CHAPTER
FORTY-TWO

The walk through the campus's interior had gone much more slowly than Jaxon liked. Part of the problem was that he had insisted each campus security office have a partner. His, Lochlin Norvel, was a good man, but prone to stopping and investigating the smallest thing.

Jaxon wanted to finish the campus walk first, and then scout for trouble.

Norvel had stopped already, peering through the trees as if he had seen something suspicious. Norvel was a solid man with a florid face and a look of perpetual dissatisfaction, even though he was more or less upbeat whenever he was on the job.

His silver uniform never really fit properly, and he walked as if his feet hurt. But he could be sensible in a crisis, and Jaxon valued that.

He and Norvel had finally reached the copse of trees

near the Old Library. That copse of trees made Jaxon's heart stutter every single time. He couldn't quite get that blood pool out of his head. Everything had been strange on this campus since then—although, he was willing to acknowledge—some of that might have been his attitude.

His attitude, his mood, was foul and had been for days. As each shift wore on, he felt more and more grim. He probably wouldn't have minded Norvel's attention to detail on other occasions—maybe even applauded it. But now, it felt like a time waster.

And, if Jaxon was honest with himself, he wasn't sure why he cared about time being wasted. It was almost as if he was on some kind of clock that he didn't even realize existed.

"Did you see that?" Norvel asked, waving his hand toward the Old Library.

Jaxon swiveled in the direction that Norvel was pointing. Jaxon wanted to grab Norvel's hand and pull it down, half afraid that someone would see it—would see them.

They were hard to miss. Both of them wore their uniforms tonight, and the silver was catching the light from every lightstone lamp they passed. Norvel also wore a cap. Jaxon hated the caps, because they prevented him from seeing anything clearly, so he didn't wear his.

Norvel's cap almost glowed in the weird white light from the ground fog. The fog felt almost alive in this copse, as if it was drawing power from the ground. Jaxon didn't want to be here any longer than he had to.

"See what?" Jaxon asked.

"Over there." Norvel lowered his voice. "By that side of the Old Library."

He waved his right hand, indicating something that he thought Jaxon could see. Jaxon nearly grabbed the offending hand a second time, but then figured the best way to get Norvel to stop was to look where the man wanted him to look.

Jaxon frowned, wishing that the lightstone lamp wasn't giving off so much light. Between the brightness of the lightstone lamps—all over campus, if he was being honest—and the strange whiteness of the fog, the glare was interfering with his usually sharp vision.

He didn't see anything on that side of the Old Library.

He frowned, making himself concentrate. And then he saw it. Movement. Movement that made the ground fog shudder just a bit, the way that water did when someone was moving through it slowly, trying not to disturb the surface tension.

"I count three people," Norvel said.

"Four," Jaxon said. He could barely see the fourth, but there was a space for him—at least he assumed that person was male. The person almost seemed to be made of fog himself, which, on this night, Jaxon wasn't going to discount.

He wished he knew more about these Fey, but he didn't. He knew they had shapeshifters and control of beasts, and maybe some control of the elements too, from all that he had read.

Maybe they could make nearly invisible people as well.

"They're moving with purpose," Norvel said.

He was right. They were in a kind of military formation,

following a leader and advancing forward with some kind of stealth.

They had already passed the door leading to the student entrance. The paths on the scholars' side of the Old Library weren't used as much, especially at night.

Jaxon had petitioned the Administration for more light-stone lamps on that side of the building. He had also told the librarians in the Scholars Wing to place signs everywhere, warning Scholars to take a more populated route home at night.

That side of the Old Library was just too dark, even with the strange white ground fog.

"Come on," Jaxon said quietly to Norvel. "Let's see what they're doing."

It would also get him and Norvel out of this copse of trees. It seemed that Jaxon ended up there more than he wanted to. Twice tonight already, almost as if something was drawing him to the place.

He shook that feeling off. He almost thought of pulling out his pistol, but he didn't. For all he knew, what Norvel had seen were students engaged in an end-of-term prank.

He did take his nightstick out of his belt, and as he did, Norvel did the same.

"You're thinking they're a threat?" Norvel asked.

"I'm thinking we need to be prepared for whatever we see," Jaxon said.

Norvel nodded.

They walked together along the path. As they did, Jaxon thought he saw a shape on the other side of the stone bridge. It looked very similar to the person made of fog.

He had to squint to see that shape, and even then, it seemed blurry.

He tapped Norvel on the arm and headed across the stone bridge, behind a male student who was scurrying toward the student entrance. The gray foglike shape put its head down as it came up the bridge.

Jaxon tried to get a good look at it, but still couldn't quite see it. A man, maybe. A woman? Slight, anyway, and hunched, as if it didn't want to be noticed.

Norvel didn't seem to notice it at all. Jaxon wanted to tap him again, but couldn't, not without calling attention to the gesture.

The male student almost walked into the shape made of fog, but the shape veered slightly. The male student didn't seem able to see the shape either.

The hairs rose on the back of Jaxon's neck. He was cold, yes, from the fog and the general chill of the night, but he was also unnerved. He wanted to turn around and follow that gray shape, but he had a different mission.

"Do you still see them?" he asked Norvel, without looking away from the fog-shaped person.

"Yeah. They're heading toward the Scholars Entrance." Norvel's voice shook.

Those people were the threat. Maybe the foglike shape meant absolutely nothing. Maybe it wasn't as important as he had thought.

The night was darker than he expected. He wasn't sure if that was the strange ground fog or if there was something off about the lightstone streetlamps.

The ground fog rose up before them, almost like waves

on a violent sea. Or hands rising toward the night sky, trying to block Jaxon's passage.

He willed that image away. He wasn't a fanciful man, although he'd been feeling like one of late.

Fancy wasn't going to help him here. Being strong and prepared was. Braced for whatever was going to come his way—but no overreaction.

That was the other reason he had brought Norvel. Norvel was not the kind of man who ever overreacted, even when he was threatened.

Jaxon could barely see where he was going. But he kept himself focused. He stopped looking at the fog-shaped person, and started looking for that distinctive military movement.

When he saw it, he continued forward, trying not to let his newly discovered imagination convince him that he was seeing something worse.

THE
TURNOUT

SEREBRO
MOUNTAIN RANGE

CHAPTER

FORTY-THREE

ole reached the rolling foothills at the base of the Serebro Mountain Range. The neighborhood spread out before him, filled with single family homes for professors and staff. They had small yards and the illusion of autonomy, even though half of the neighborhood was owned by the Academy itself.

He had to go slowly down the winding road that led to the barns and the physical plant. He'd driven this road fast only once, and he had nearly hit a child who was running across it, chasing a ball.

The reason so many professors and adjuncts lived here was to raise their family as separately as possible from the Academy. That meant there were dogs and cats here, as well as children. Children might have been in bed by now, but the pets had full run of the entire neighborhood. Cole had seen cats all over this area, mostly reflections from their eyes, looking like tiny eerie lamps in the dark.

Or like the strange symbols on Xavier's magic robe.

Cole still wasn't sure what those were or what they meant. He hadn't asked yet, either.

He had gotten far enough behind the carriages that he couldn't see them. That made him feel better. He'd been able to travel down the last part of the road at a good speed, one that worked for the conveyance as well as for him.

The fresh air had cleared his head a little, making the headache recede just enough to make him less woozy. He would move like an old man when he got out of the conveyance, though, because his beleaguered muscles were seizing up. As he tugged on the steering sticks, his right arm had gotten tighter and tighter.

He was wincing in pain now each time he moved it. He wasn't sure how much longer he'd be able to drive this thing effectively.

He was glad they were nearly done. He needed to get back to his room, and close his eyes, even if it was only for a few hours.

The conveyance went over one more rise. The fields spread out before him—wasted space, Eustace had once called them in his lucid period. He'd been among the Regents who had argued against the fields, saying they were dangerous, although he had never been able to explain why.

Now, though, Cole thought about that every single time he had traveled over them. He had no idea how fields, which were used for picnics and family gatherings and games, could be dangerous.

He didn't even know it now, after the night he'd had. But the thought remained, existing in his mind in Eustace's querulous voice, fighting a battle he had lost a long long time ago.

Cole turned sharply to the left, and then squinted. Something rose out of the fog. Not just one something, but two. Carriages. Again. And next to one of them, Xavier's robe, flaring large yellow letters that actually spelled words Cole could read.

They read: *Cole. Stop.*

He blinked, wondering if he had made that up. But the image didn't disappear with the blink. So he pulled the conveyance in behind the carriages, staying back far enough to avoid the horse stench, and got out.

The ground fog was now waist-deep. Or maybe it had always been waist-deep. It had seemed shallower when viewed from the mountain road.

It wasn't cold either, not like he'd expected. He'd walked through ground fog all of his life, and it had always made his legs colder than the rest of him.

Tonight, it did not. It didn't even make his already-sore muscles seize even more.

He walked around the nearest carriage. The horses were frighteningly quiet, but they were in position, heads down. The other carriage was parked ahead of this one. Volkovich stood alongside both of them, arms out, as if he were holding the horses in position.

The yellow light from Xavier's robe cast shadows along the field behind him. For a moment, Cole didn't see Xavier at all, and worried that Xavier's robe was here, but Xavier wasn't.

Then the robe moved, and Xavier's bald head reflected

the light. He took a step toward Cole as the yellow lights of the robe vanished, leaving shadowy images of the letters.

Cole couldn't talk to both men. Volkovich was on one side of the carriages and Xavier was on the other.

Cole went to Xavier first, since Xavier was the one who had sent the message.

"What's going on?" Cole asked, barely able to resist adding *now*. If he added the word *now*, his irritation would show, and his headache would get worse all over again.

"Pasha says there are three Fey near the barns," Xavier said.

"How does he know?" Cole asked. And why didn't Xavier know, the man with all the magic? Oh, Cole's mood was a lot more foul than he had realized when he had stopped the conveyance.

"He says they're scaring the horses," Xavier said.

"And you say?" Cole asked.

"I've been sensing something all night. We've been following these people." Xavier waved a hand toward the fields. "They stood over there for some time, and then split up."

Cole didn't ask how Xavier knew that. Cole wasn't sure he would understand even if Xavier told him.

"I want to go to the barns," Xavier said, "but Pasha says it's not safe for the horses."

"So you want me to go," Cole said drily, almost angrily. He couldn't do more, and he didn't want to be an unwilling sacrifice all over again. He was tired—and, if he was being honest with himself—he was scared.

"Yes, I do," Xavier said. "With me. We leave Pasha with the horses."

"What about the horses in the barns?" Cole asked. "Is it unsafe for them to have us show up?"

He was trying to hold back the sarcasm, but he wasn't succeeding. He had to calm himself down, and he wasn't sure how.

"Oh." Xavier gave him a small, half-hearted smile. "When I said horses, I meant these. They've been traumatized by the Fey. We don't need the distraction."

Of course we don't. This time Cole caught the sentence before it escaped.

"What do you propose we do?" he asked.

"I have the sense that the powerful ones are not with these," Xavier said.

"Meaning what?" Cole asked.

"Meaning that you and I might be able to stop them," Xavier said.

"Or we'll end up like those drivers," Cole said.

"I won't let that happen," Xavier said.

Cole looked at him. Xavier clearly believed what he said, but Cole wasn't sure. This was a man who had let him walk into a trap that had literally exploded in his face.

But, if Volkovich was to be believed, Xavier was also the man who had put some kind of protective barrier around Cole, and saved his life.

"What do you think we can do?" Cole asked, moderating his tone. "I don't have any weapons. There aren't any in the conveyance. I have no idea if there are any in the carriages."

"There's a pistol under the driver's bench of mine," Xavier said. "Alongside a whip that angered Pasha. He said no horse should ever be whipped."

Cole wasn't sure if he agreed. But the pistol was good news. "Does the pistol have bullets?"

"I have no idea," Xavier said. "A pistol is not my weapon."

It really wasn't Cole's either. The pistol was an uncertain weapon, one that was hard to aim and even harder to use effectively. He preferred swords or, in a tight situation, a knife.

If course, he had neither, not now that he needed one.

"Does Pasha's carriage have weapons as well?"

"You'll have to ask him," Xavier said.

Cole didn't want to. He felt like one of the children he'd been trying to avoid. He didn't want to do any of this. He wanted to go back to his suite. He wanted sleep.

He wanted this day to never have happened.

But it had, and it looked like it was still happening.

"I will," Cole said. "After you tell me your plan."

"All right," Xavier said. "See if you can find any holes in it."

And then he started to talk.

ALCHEMY, SCIENCE & THAUMATURGY

GOVERNMENT

LIN

RE

T

LAW BUILDING

WHISTLER HALL

CHAPTER
FORTY-FOUR

Shamra liked the ground fog. It swirled around her feet and legs, making her feel like she was floating. She could sense the magick in it, even though the Weather Sprites claimed that was not possible.

Shamra knew it was all possible. Sensing magick was part of the magick of a certain kind of Visionary. She believed herself to be that kind of Visionary, even though she had failed dozens of tests for it.

Still, she had some leadership skills—acknowledged by all of her superiors—and she knew that eventually, her kind of magick would become recognized by the leadership of the Fey.

Until then, she would serve her little Infantry unit with honor. That was all she could do, especially since the last Spell Warder she had tangled with in Nye had recommended that she be forced to stay away from anyone with real magick.

He had been an ass, and she had told him that. Apparently, one did not tell Spell Warders they were idiots to their faces.

Which was why she was here, at this Academy that seemed like less of a school to her than it was some kind of town dedicated to learning. There were strange practices here in Qavner, and she understood very few of them.

She had had little interest in those practices as well, until she had learned that the Trinovante team had been all but wiped out by some Qavnerian magick. The very idea shocked her. There were Infantry in that team, good people whom she had known, and she found it hard to believe that they would fall for some kind of magickal trick.

They had to have been overpowered by some greater force.

So she was on alert as she walked swiftly down this path. Hardin had put her in charge of this little fighting unit. He expected results from her and she would give it.

Right now, though, she was letting Gray the Spy believe that he ran everything. He had gotten them through several different tree groupings, along a few less traveled paths, avoiding lightstone, and over a small rise, leading to an unassuming building. That building appeared to be made of ancient stone—not any of the magickal stone she had encountered in Qavner, but standard riverstone—and it only had one very small door.

The unit stopped on the path. There were no students around them, and no professors. The hideous lightstone lamps that dotted campus were sparse here.

The door looked old and plain and small. Shamra would

have to bend over as she went through it, and even then, she would have to be cautious about the pack on her back.

She was carrying a lot of weapons, more than Hardin wanted her to. She had knives strapped to both legs, their hilts easily reachable. She wore two more knives on each hip, and inside her pack, she carried some clubs and batons that could transform themselves into swords with the simple toss of a case. She also had a slingshot—they all did—although she doubted she would ever use it.

She would have to dump some of the weapons from the pack once the unit reached the so-called map room, but if the maps were anything like the ones she had seen from the artifacts that Lumin had gathered, she might be able to squeeze everything into place.

The other two members of this little troop were just behind her, and they had weapons as well. No one really trusted Hardin's plans. He had brought a crowbar in his pack, and her tiny group had snickered at that. A knife, particularly one with just a touch of magick, could open any door with less force and a lot more finesse.

Gray held out an arm, stopping them all. He didn't even know the proper signals for commanding a small unit like this one. She would mention that as she took over—if she even needed to.

The man seemed decidedly uncomfortable with his position in front of the group.

"All right," he said quietly. "This building is called the Alchemy, Science, and Thaumaturgy Building. There are many, many stories connected to it, all of them indicating powerful magick housed inside."

Aziza, standing next to Shamra, shifted. Aziza hated talking before a mission. She was short and wide, almost the size of a Red Cap, but she used that smallness to her advantage.

Shamra had seen Aziza strike down opponents by destroying their knees first, putting them in extreme pain and knocking them off their feet. Then she would cut their throats and move on as if it was all in a day's work.

"We will have to be very careful inside," Gray said. "I have taken two different tours of the place, and was loathe to touch anything. Everything seems to be warded or dusted with just enough power. I was afraid that if I wasn't strategic, the magick inside would have revealed my true self."

Medwyn, the only other man in this group, grunted. He was the strongest Infantry member on this entire team. He could lift four times his body weight without any assistance from magick at all. And, more importantly, he could walk with that weight for miles.

He trained to lift things, something the regular Infantry in Nye thought ridiculous. But Shamra was happy to have him on her team. He had once grabbed two unconscious Foot Soldiers and carried them for two days under his arms to get them back to a Shadowlands.

He could break doors with his fist, destroy a wall with a double punch and not scrape a knuckle.

His body was as hard as his hands. He had more muscles than Shamra had ever seen on a Fey.

His problem, like all of theirs really, was his attitude. He didn't always follow orders.

In a situation like this, she did not mind at all.

"If you're scared to be inside this place," Medwyn said to Gray, "then you should stay outside. Tell us where to find those maps. We will handle the problems from there."

Not only did he not follow orders, but he also did not follow the chain of command. Another reason he was here on Dorovich, and another reason he wasn't with Hardin. Hardin didn't like Medwyn much either.

"I can't tell you where to find the maps," Gray said. "They're—"

"If you can't tell us, why are we following you?" Medwyn said, raising his voice.

Gray cringed.

Shamra rolled her eyes, and shook her head slightly. She wasn't happy with that revelation either.

"I thought you said you knew where the maps were," she said.

"I do," he said. "But this place is deceptive. I think the entire building is made of magick. It will change when you walk in it. I'm convinced that if you're not a sanctioned guest, the place will turn on you."

"You better tell me that you're a sanctioned guest," Medwyn said.

Or what? Shamra wondered, although she kept quiet.

Aziza had stepped slightly forward. She had craned her neck, peering at the building.

"Is the fog different there?" she asked, and pointed.

Shamra looked. The fog around the building was gray, not white, and it seemed to be threaded with a bit of black. She had no idea what that meant.

"The building was surrounded by fog when I was here before," Gray said. "Not from our Sprites."

He spoke definitively as if that was proving his case about magick.

"Could that be a problem?" Aziza asked.

No one answered her, not even Medwyn. Shamra had no idea. She knew very little about Fey magick outside of her own battlefield expertise. She certainly didn't know much about the powers of Weather Sprites.

"There's only one way to find out," Shamra said. "We go inside."

"Even though it's all magick that we don't understand and there's some kind of fog battle going on outside?" Aziza asked.

"Those are our orders," Shamra said. And she wasn't about to screw that up, not even on a small command like this one.

Medwyn grunted again. Gray squared his shoulders. His entire body looked like it was made of fog—the kind that was flowing around the outside of that strange building, not the white ground fog.

Shamra didn't wait for Gray or the others. She started down the small hill, going deeper into the white ground fog. It had risen to her waist now, and seemed to flow in two different directions—toward the building and back from it.

The movement reminded her of water battering against a barrier in the middle of a storm.

She swallowed against a dry throat. Maybe this wasn't the best idea after all. Maybe Lumin had been wrong; maybe they should have retreated from this place and sent a message to Rugar that this part of Dorovich had more magick than expected.

Then she heard herself. Shamra didn't think of herself as coward, and she was thinking like one. Just because she was coming upon a situation she didn't understand, she was thinking of retreat.

The very idea made her angry. She waded through the ground fog toward that door.

Then she looked over her shoulder. The others were watching her, and not following.

"Come on," she said with as much force as she dared. "We're going in."

After a brief second, Aziza came down the hill, followed by Medwyn, with Gray bringing up the rear.

So much for him being a leader.

But she shouldn't have expected that from a Spy. They weren't supposed to lead other people. They used people to a single end.

She beckoned him. "Gray, you need to show us how to get in."

He cleared his throat and nodded nervously. She half expected him to say, *Through the door, obviously*, but he didn't.

She strode down that path, feeling a bit of pushback from the ground fog, as if it really was water. Up close, the two different kinds of fog seemed to be in their own battle. A grayish blackish fog pushed down on the white ground fog. In some places the white was growing dirty, the way that fresh snow changed into something dingy and off-color after a few days in the dirt.

But there was a trail of white ground fog on either side of the door, almost like the ground fog itself was holding a line for the troops. When soldiers held a line, they battled behind them, and protected whoever had to get through.

She smiled, respecting that.

And then she looked at the door.

She had been wrong about it. It wasn't made of old wood. It glowed, like she had never seen a door do before. Someone had carved a design in it—a heart, which was larger than she expected, a crown that was also large, and a broadsword that rotated outward as she approached.

Outward. The tip toward her.

More swords appeared, all rotating toward her, as if a small army stood behind them, challenging her to attack.

"Is there another way in?" she asked Gray.

He had stopped beside her. He was shaking his head. "I don't remember swords," he said.

"Of course there's another way in," Medwyn said, and waded into the fog conflict as if he didn't see it.

Maybe he didn't. Maybe a person needed just a small touch of magick to see it.

Maybe they needed that to see the swords too. Did that mean the swords weren't real?

Shamra didn't want to touch them to find out.

Aziza and Gray stood beside her. They all watched Medwyn stride through that multicolored ground fog.

It surrounded him. The grayish blackish fog climbed up his arms and legs like serpents trying to strangle him. He didn't seem to notice.

He grabbed one of the stones in the wall, and yanked.

The entire front of the building shuddered, but nothing happened.

He yanked again, and then the stone came loose.

The entire wall shuddered, and the stones fell as if he had taken the most important rock out of a rock pile. The falling stones clattered loudly, echoing in the windless night.

Then a lamp above the door flared, and Shamra ducked to avoid the light. It rotated, pointing itself at Medwyn. He staggered backwards as if the light was composed of swords.

He gave it a prodigious frown, one that, if he had magick, would have destroyed everything in its path. Then he grabbed a small rock off the pile, one that fit solidly in his meaty hand, and chucked the rock like a ball at the lamp.

The rock hit with startling force, and the lamp shattered. Another rock fell out of it, tumbling to the ground.

That rock was strewn with light, the way that some rocks were strewn with gold. The light seemed to be orienting itself, but Medwyn threw more rocks at it, burying it.

Then he waved a hand at the wall.

"Let's go in," he said.

Shamra let out a tiny laugh of disbelief. She never would have thought of destroying a wall to enter a building. Already, she could see some of the rocks moving, as if they were trying to rebuild the wall. Medwyn stepped through, grabbed another rock, and threw it at something inside.

Shamra could only assume he had been throwing the rock at another lightstone lamp.

He peeked his massive head out of the hole he had made in the wall. "Hurry," he said.

She didn't need to be told twice. The grayish blackish fog poured inside the building as if it was going to attack Medwyn. The white ground fog reformed its two lines away from the door, and at the opening instead.

Shamra waved a hand at Aziza. "Go," Shamra said.

Aziza ran down the path that the white ground fog had cleared and stepped into the opening. Medwyn was no longer anywhere to be seen, but Shamra could hear the sounds of shattering.

Aziza was bent over, reaching into her pack. She had a club she could use against the lightstone lamps. The entire team did. Hardin had insisted on it.

Gray was still hesitating, literally swaying side to side, as if in the grip of some kind of terror.

"We need you in there," Shamra snapped. "Go."

"That light..." he said. "It'll reveal me."

"Let it," she said. "*Go.*"

Then she shoved him forward, although as she did, she wondered just how useful he would be. Yes, he claimed to know where the maps were, but she also knew that terrified people on a team could destroy an entire mission.

He hobbled his way down the incline as if his feet hurt him, hunching away from the fog—both types—as if it scared him more than the sounds of shattering glass coming from inside the building.

Shamra started a 360-rotation, making sure no one else was near them. The white ground fog was so thick that it looked like a flood of white. It reflected some of the campus's light, but it also seemed to absorb some of the lightstone light. That absorption didn't seem to have any effect on the fog at all.

But there was no one else around—not that she could see.

Which was good, because she didn't want campus security to follow this team. Gray had told them all about it, back when Lumin was planning this entire mission. *Campus security*, Gray had said, *isn't that big, but it can be annoying*.

He had never explained that, though, and Shamra hadn't thought to ask. She had no idea how anyone would contact them. She suspected the security would only go after things it could see.

Right now, she doubted anyone could see through this ground fog.

Buildings rose in the distance, but in the odd opalescent light, they seemed farther away than she knew they were.

She nodded to herself, finished her spin, and then followed her troop down that slight incline into the building.

The building looked bigger than it had a moment ago, and the rocks were rising on their own. The opening that Medwyn had made was half the size it had initially been.

She pushed through and stepped inside, noting a startling darkness.

"I damaged the lights," Medwyn said. "But I don't know for how long. The damn things are stubborn."

"Like you," Aziza said.

"I hope you know where you're going, Gray," Shamra said.

"Me, too," Gray said under his breath. "Me too."

ALCHEMY, SCIENCE & THAUMATURGY

LIN

RE
T

GOVERNMENT

LAW BUILDING

WHISTLER
HALL

CHAPTER
FORTY-FIVE

S auer hated the smell of the Science wing in the AST Building. The wing smelled of sulfur half the time and the rest of the time, it had a chemical odor that made his nose twitch. Sometimes he could feel the smell as if it had coated him.

Not to mention that the Science wing was dark. It had lightstone lamps everywhere, like the rest of the building, but most of the time the lamps were shut off. In a few places, they'd been disabled.

The head of the Science Department claimed that lightstone had a terrible impact on the experiments that the staff conducted. Sauer had never probed deeper than that. He didn't want to know what kind of experiments they ran in the Science Department, and he didn't want to be part of them.

He didn't even like the way that some people described them—as technology that would improve lives.

After all, it had been the Science Department here at the Academy that had developed all the different versions of the lightstone lamps that they mostly refused to use, even though the lamps would have illuminated the hallways better than the oil lamps that were provided on various tables around the wing.

Oswald Erling had taken it upon himself to carry one of the oil lamps. He also held a lightstone lantern in his left hand, and had somehow kept it from turning on.

Erling was one of the many footprint people (as Sauer was mentally labeling them) that Sauer and Fenwick had found scattered throughout the building. Erling's prints had shown up on the map as black with silver edges, and Sauer couldn't help but think that those prints were a sign of something.

He had never liked Erling, who was a Professor of Alchemy. Erling was a man shaped like a spindle. He liked to wear shirts with horizontal stripes, that made him seem rounder across the middle than he actually was.

Now, carrying two lamps—one out in front of him, and the other at his side—caused him to resemble the prow of a ship from one of those ancient portraits housed in the Academy's History Gallery.

Sauer had never liked those paintings, and he certainly didn't like oil lamps. The light from them flickered unsteadily, as if it couldn't decide whether it wanted to share its bounty or not.

He wanted to force Erling to use the lightstone lamp, but Sauer wasn't really in charge of this group. He was just the one who organized it.

The group was a mishmash of prickly personalities. There was Fenwick, of course, who trailed all of them. She had both map books under her arms, although the Pahrucii book that housed the moving footprints from the outsiders would occasionally slip from her grasp and slap Sauer in the back until he opened it to the proper page.

He would carry it for a while, then hand it back to Fenwick, who took it begrudgingly. Most of her focus had been on the History of Alchemy, Science and Thaumaturgy book with the architectural renderings of the AST building. She had used it to direct Sauer to the location of the five other footprints he had seen.

That had led Sauer to Erling, in the Alchemy Department, as well as Bruno Thane, who was at least a man that Sauer could get a drink with. They'd often commiserate in one of the alehouses in Serebro, when they could escape campus.

Somehow Sauer hadn't been surprised that Thane was one of the owners of the footprints he had seen. Like Fenwick's, Thane's footprints had been ivory outlined in silver. Which was rather like Thane himself.

He was a toothpick of a man, a bit too pale, and he preferred to wear glittery clothing, which did not help on this night. If the group wanted to shut off the lights and fade into the background, it would be difficult with Thane among them.

His overcoat, belted over a pair of dark pants, was all silver glitter. It even caught the flickering light of the oil lamp, which made it seem like the glitter had a life of its own.

Then there was Frida Wystan. She didn't glitter at all—at least in person. If anything, she was hard to see and even harder to remember. A tiny woman who preferred to wear a gray that made her blend into the stone walls, she never said a word and would hardly meet anyone's eyes.

Her hair was gray and bristly. Her skin was dark in good light, but here, it looked as gray as her clothing. Her eyebrows swept upward, though, and so did her cheekbones. But she was missing the pointed ears that most of Sauer's other compatriots had.

Sauer kept glancing at her, though, half expecting her to come alive with brightness. Her footprints on the architectural renderings were sparkly silver, as if they were the only part of her that had any life at all.

It bothered him that the maps had led him to three people in the Alchemy department. He had often thought of Alchemy and Science as bastard children of the Thaumaturgy department. But, as far as he could tell, he and Fenwick were the only two from Thaumaturgy.

Of course, the prints only showed the people in the AST Building. It might have simply been a function of which departments worked late at night and which ones worked early in the morning.

The other person they had found so far was Maud Kenelm here in Science. She had been teaching as long as Sauer had, and showed the wear as much as he did. Her face was lined so much that it was sometimes hard to make out her tiny features, and the slender girl he remembered from school had become a large, imposing woman whose body finally matched her large, imposing presence.

She was the one who insisted—at the top of her deep booming voice—that they follow the rules of the Department.

You have no idea what your silly lightstone reliance might activate here in the department, she had said, as if lightstone lanterns were something that Sauer had invented. *If we're going to be stealthy, the last thing we want to do is set off some kind of chain reaction.*

Whatever that meant. He had acquiesced, partly because he wasn't used to being in charge of his colleagues, and partly because he didn't want to fight with anyone.

He particularly didn't want to fight with someone who had black silver-lined footprints. Something about the black ones with silver lining put him off.

Or maybe he thought it was off because he just didn't like the two people he had found with those prints. He had no idea what his would have looked like in the book—individual prints actually vanished when someone was in his proximity.

Now, they were down to one set of footprints, which was (of course) at the end of the laboratory section of the Science Wing. Those prints were one of the sparkly silver sets.

The sharp, pointed smells that assaulted Sauer's nose whenever he entered the department were stronger here, overlaid with that rotten eggs scent of too much sulfur.

He had no idea how anyone could work here without getting a massive headache. He had one now, although he suspected it came from trying to suppress his emotions and manage the strange personalities around him.

No one in the group had weapons. All of them had been intrigued by the prints—both sets, the ones that were heading to the various places on campus, and the ones that belonged to each person here in the building. None of the people he had gathered had been able to see their own prints, just like he couldn't, although Kenelm had wanted to experiment, to see if she could make the book "reveal its secrets."

He had kept that book away from her, and loudly ordered Fenwick to make sure that only he and she could handle the books. Then he had turned to the group, as if feeling abashed by his forcefulness (he wasn't) and said, *They're from my personal collection. They're collectible.*

As if that really mattered. But these were scholars with a reverence for books. None of them questioned that statement. In fact, it made them back off.

The remaining set of prints were—of course—at the very end of the laboratory hallway. The smells grew stronger here, more astringent, making him want to sneeze. The astringency wasn't a cleaning smell. It was as if the scent of lemons had been magnified three hundred times, and given a dangerous edge.

He didn't like it, but he wasn't about to let everyone else move forward without him.

Still, he let Kenelm go to the final lab's door first. To his surprise, she pulled out a set of keys and unlocked the door. Then she slammed it open—deliberately, he thought—so that whoever was inside would know that she had arrived.

"Stand aside," Kenelm boomed.

Sauer wasn't sure if that command was for his little

group or the person inside, but he pushed his people out of the way, as if they were children following his command.

As he did, orange-red smoke poured out of the room, followed by a trail of bright blue smoke that had sparkles that rivaled the sparkles of the silver footprints. The orange-red smoke was the source of the lemon smell, but that dangerous edge seemed to come from the bright blue smoke.

Sauer's eyes were watering. He wanted to wipe the stench off himself, and as he reached up, he saw something clear and glittery form around him.

He glanced to one side, saw Frida Wystan's hands raised, releasing what looked like a clear bubble on top of a coating of sea foam. The bubble enveloped the entire little group, except for Kenelm, who had gone inside the room.

Once the bubble closed, the stench was gone. Sauer knew better than to wipe his eyes, although he wanted to.

"Thank you," he said to Wystan.

"I hate the Science Department," she said through gritted teeth. "They're so *reckless*."

The orange-red smoke roiled down the corridor as if on a mission. The blue smoke trailed, apparently gobbling up the remnants of the orange-red smoke.

This wasn't anything that Sauer understood, but he always felt that way about the experiments in Science.

A bit of blue dripped off the bubble. Wystan blew on her hands, and the exterior of the bubble cleared up. The blue smoke scum vanished.

She snapped the fingers on her left hand, and the bubble disappeared.

The lingering smell of lemons filled the corridor, but it no longer felt dangerous.

"What was that?" Fenwick asked, sounding startled. She juggled the books under her arm, as if they were starting to slip.

"Probably some technology we'll be using in a few years," Erling said, his voice rich with sarcasm.

Sauer had a slight headache from the smell. He noted that no one really answered Fenwick's question.

He wasn't going to press it, though. He wished they were obtaining their last set of footprints somewhere else, though, because he was worried that the group would want to stay in this lab. They needed to find somewhere else to have a little meeting, even though he wasn't sure what the upshot of any kind of meeting would be.

The four who were outside the door all looked at him, as if expecting him to make some kind of decision about what to do next. There really was only one decision—go into that lab and have the same version of the conversation he'd been having ever since he started on this little quest.

The books brought us here. See? Look. See these prints? I'm sure they mean something magic. I suspect they're Fey.

Others, chiming in: *We're all worried about this. We've sensed something. We know something is off.*

The last person: *Why me? Or how did you know where I was?*

Only the problem here, if Sauer understood what was happening, was that with the discovery of the last person, there would be no more footsteps in the history book.

He squared his shoulders, bracing himself. In his experience, everyone in Science was annoying and filled with too many questions.

He nodded at his little group, though, and took one step forward. Fenwick was at his side, as she had been since they started this little quest. It felt odd to have that woman as his cohort.

Sauer peered around the door. The lab was filled with flickering light from small flames enclosed under glass. He couldn't see the fuel, but he did realize that the flames were not in regular lanterns.

The room was large enough to fit two long marble tables, as well as a shorter one toward the back. There were stools pushed up to the tables, and a chalkboard along the back wall.

A larger flame rose from the table farthest back. There appeared to be a small divot in the table from which the flames rose. Behind the divot, Grimbold Harewald stood, goggles covering half of his face.

He was recognizable by his shock of white hair, which normally exploded around his head. Right now, though, he had tied it into four separate short ponytails that rose from the top of his head like giant mushrooms.

The parts of his face that were visible glistened with sweat from the flames before him. On either side of him, glass jars sat on top of metal stands, with a small flame burning underneath. The contents of at least two of those jars boiled.

Sauer's nose was still reeling from the lemon smell. If the boiling jars had any odor, he couldn't smell it, not yet.

Harewald pointed a gloved finger at all of them. "How dare you!" he yelled.

Kenelm, who stood just to the left, was shaking her head. "I should have told you to stay out," she said. "He's being unreasonable."

"See how you would feel if someone ruined two months of meticulous experimentation," he snapped.

"Recreate it," she said.

"As if that's easy," he said. "You don't understand—"

"No," Sauer said. "You don't. We're under threat, and we need you at our side. It's—"

Something slammed into his back so hard that it knocked the wind out of him. He had to put one hand on the marble table before him just to keep from falling to his knees.

"Sorry, Wolfgang," Fenwick said. "It got away from me. It wants you."

Somehow he managed to turn in time to see the book she had been trying to corral wriggle out of her hand and fly toward him. Open.

It slammed on the table beside him, and the pages shuffled.

"What the hell is this?" Harewald asked.

"I'll explain in a minute," Kenelm said. "Just shut up for once."

But he didn't sound angry any longer. He sounded almost intrigued.

Sauer didn't look at Harewald, though. Sauer's gaze had fallen on the book on the floor, the book that had hit him first, which was also open, the map floating above it.

646

All of the gold footprints had moved to different parts of the map. The three that were heading toward the stables had arrived at the very edge of the stables complex. The four sets that were heading toward the Old Library had moved to the center of the building, where the Scholars Entrance was.

The bloody pink footprints inside the Old Library were gone, but the faded yellow ones were moving through the building at a good clip. They seemed brighter than they had earlier. Or maybe he was misremembering their color.

Two sets of gold footprints stood at the juncture in the path between the Old Library and the AST building.

But ones that should have been near the AST Building weren't near it. They appeared to be inside it.

Something poked at his already sore back. He turned. The history book was poking him, the way a child would, as if it was trying to get his attention.

He damn near snapped, *What now?* but he caught himself just in time. Fenwick had come to his side.

She was reaching down for the map on the floor, when he said, "Just leave it."

He turned toward the History book, and it slid back on the table, as if it was trying to get its balance.

Everyone else just watched, including Harewald, who had moved away from his little potion fire to see what was going on.

The pages of the history volume shuffled as if they were in a harsh wind. Then the book opened wide, and the architectural renderings reappeared—the ones that had led him here.

Only they folded together and jutted out only the rendering of the very front of the building.

A wall was gone. It glowed black, as if a gaping hole had appeared there.

Sauer bent over and picked up the Pahrucii book, setting it beside the history book. He had a hunch he knew what he would see. He suspected the four sets of gold footprints would be next to that wall.

What he didn't expect was the way that the map and the architectural rendering rose in the air, meeting in the middle, and then resolving into a new map, one with all of the specificity of the Pahrucii map and the minute detail of architectural rendering.

"Great lightstone," Harewald said, using a very old oath as he came up beside Fenwick. "Those are the Fey maps."

"What?" Thane asked. "They're maps drawn in the Protectorate. Sauer has the verification—"

"No, no," Harewald said. "That's not what I mean. Maps were drawn in a special way for centuries by mapmakers—you know, before Purges—to show where the Fey were on Dorovich."

"We're not Fey," Erling said, without sarcasm this time.

"Unless we're all part Fey," Kenelm said.

Sauer wasn't going to comment on that. It was his understanding that many of the people with magic in Dorovich had some Fey blood in their past.

"Fey maps," Sauer said to Harewald. "I had forgotten about them. But you're right, at least about the Pahrucii map. This other is in a book on the history of the Academy. It didn't show those gold prints until a few minutes ago."

"Then what was it showing you?" Harewald asked.

"Where we all were," Thane said. "You'd know if you weren't the last."

"I don't think that matters," Sauer said. "What these maps are showing us is that the Fey have breached the building, and it will only be a matter of time before they find us."

"And then what?" Erling asked.

Sauer looked at him in surprise. He would have thought that Erling would understand—that they all would understand—just how much danger even one Fey put them all in.

"Well," Sauer said, trying to control his own sarcasm. "I guess we determine what *then what* means. I think the books want us to deal with them."

"And how do we do that?" Erling asked.

"Together," Fenwick said. "They're not going to expect us to have skills, isn't that right, Wolfgang? I say we show them."

"And how do we know that this isn't a trap? The beginning of a new Purge?" Erling asked.

Everyone looked at him as if he had lost his mind.

"My grandparents were slaughtered in the Purges," he said, extending his hands outward, as if they could explain for him. "I don't want to die like that."

"This is not that kind of test," Sauer said. Normally he would be sympathetic to that position, since the Purges were awful. "This is a deeper, older one. And we only have a few minutes to figure out how to stop it."

CHAPTER
FORTY-SIX

The door to the Scholars Entrance was almost pretty, in an old-fashioned, ceremonial sort of way. Hardin had seen a dozen different entrances like this in fortresses all over Galinas, the bulk of them in L'Nacin, and none of them were quite as fetching as this one.

It had strategically placed lightstone lamps around beautifully groomed trees with rounded tops, all of them taller than he was. The path was wide and covered in a pale pink flat stone that stood at sharp contrast from the greenery of the grass and shrubs and those lovely trees.

The fact that he could see the path bothered him. It should have been covered in ground fog, but the fog seemed to hang back, as if something prevented it from touching the path.

He didn't like it.

Two more lights hung over the double doors. The doors

651

bothered him. They appeared to have carvings in them, carvings that jutted out from the doors themselves.

The figures appeared to be people, carrying books. Some of the books were open, and one glistened, as if it had its own light. Maybe that was a reflection of the lights above the doors, or maybe not.

He didn't like it at all.

He hadn't expected it.

Nor had he expected the fact that the crack between the closed doors formed a large sword, resting on its hilt, the tip pointing to a crown. Above the crown, a heart floated, the same color as the path.

"Don't walk on those pink stones," he said quietly to his team.

They had gathered around him, staring at the doors just like he had. No one else was in the area, nor, he thought, could anyone see the three of them.

The doors were recessed. The entire entrance was a little hollow that seemed to create its own peaceful setting.

He was a little unnerved that when he sent Veil off, Hardin had thought that he had seen a single door embedded in the stone wall, with no lights around it whatsoever.

"Oylae," he said, "destroy the lights on the path. Daeloi, take out the lights above the door."

Neither protested what he had said, which meant they had seen the same things he had.

Oylae scurried ahead of him, bringing her pack down from her shoulder as she did so. She was moving low, head down, reaching inside.

She pulled out her slingshot, along with the rounded stones she had been collecting all over Qavner. All of his team had done that—even the ones who were currently not with him, but he wasn't sure if they carried him.

He had jettisoned the stones, because he didn't want the weight, knowing that enough of his small team would have them.

It appeared that Daeloi carried his as well. He positioned himself behind one of the trees and pointed his slingshot upward, aiming for the light closest to him.

Oylae sent a stone flying toward a light on the far side of the path. The light from these streetlamps didn't shatter, but the glass exteriors did. The lightstone itself could be knocked off its pedestal, and most of the light would get absorbed by the ground.

The stone shattered the glass as expected, then toppled the streetlamp, which fell into the ground fog as if it were falling into a river.

Oylae sent another stone after another lamp, and another, and another, and they all toppled backwards, disappearing into that fog.

Which was glowing more than it had.

Hardin didn't like that either.

Daeloi had moved around the first tree, apparently not liking his chances of hitting the light above it.

"You want to tell me what's going on?" a man asked in a deep authoritative voice. He was speaking Qavnerian, and his voice came from only a few yards from Hardin.

Hardin spun around. He hadn't heard anyone approach. That was not like him at all.

The man stood on a red stone path, which was also clear. Another man stood beside him. The man who had spoken was tall and lean, but his features were rounded, which meant that if he had Fey blood in his past, it had been diluted long ago.

He probably had no magick, but he had stealth, which irritated Hardin. Those two men in their silver uniforms, slapping nightsticks against their palms, looked like no threat at all.

Daeloi was standing ever so slowly from his position behind that tree. He still had a rock in his slingshot, only now he was aiming at the guards.

Oylae had wrapped her slingshot around her fist, making her fist into even more of a weapon.

The second man—the one who hadn't spoken—backed up just a bit. He was fumbling against his right side as if looking for something. Maybe a knife.

Hardin wasn't afraid of knives.

He lunged toward the man, the one who was clearly afraid, and that man pulled out some kind of weapon. It exploded loudly, giving off light and fire, and at that moment, Hardin realized the man held a pistol, and Hardin had been too close. Something slammed into him, hard, feeling like a fist.

He staggered backwards, even as the rock from Daeloi's slingshot sailed past him and hit the second man in the head with a sickening thud.

That man crumpled downward, most of his face gone.

Hardin couldn't catch his breath. He hadn't fallen, but that was only inertia. He would in a moment.

Oylae screamed the Fey battle cry—which Hardin wanted to tell her not to do; it might bring others—and then she launched herself at the man, apparently forgetting Hardin's order. Her feet touched the pink stones, and her cry turned into an actual scream of pain.

She stopped moving forward, instead tripping, as if her feet no longer worked.

She fell with a splat onto the pink stone and seemed to melt into it.

Hardin's knees finally gave way, but he had enough presence of mind to fall backwards, into the fog.

The first man was not screaming. He groped for his own pistol.

Hardin tried to call out a warning to Daeloi, but Hardin couldn't get any sound out. It was as if whatever hit him was debilitating him slowly, taking parts of him one at a time, making them vanish. He couldn't move at all now. He could barely see through the fog.

The man with the pistol was aiming it at Daeloi, who had grabbed another stone. The man was moving forward on that reddish pink path, not moving through fog at all. It was as if he was magick, he was floating, and yet, he didn't seem to have any magick.

Hardin tried to raise himself out of the fog, hoping it would revive him. But he couldn't. He felt foggy inside and out.

The man braced that pistol on his left arm and stopped. Fire came out of the pistol again, but this time, Hardin couldn't hear the bang. He couldn't hear anything.

The fog was moving toward him, but it was also turning golden. Like lightstone lamps did.

They had fallen into the fog. Maybe that was why he couldn't move. There was lightstone near him.

He wondered how he could push it away, but that sounded like work. He wanted to close his eyes, but he couldn't. Not that it mattered.

The world was growing dark anyway. He tried one last time to claw himself upward, to warn...who?...he couldn't remember.

He decided to let the darkness take him because there was still a part of him that was terrified of the light.

LINGUISTICS

ARCHEOLOGY

HISTORY

REGENTS
TOWER

OLD
LIBRARY

ADV. STUDENT
WING

MAIN
ENTRANCE

CLOCK
TOWER

MEDICAL
SCIENCES

CHAPTER

FORTY-SEVEN

F ey. Attack. Croninshield's mind was swimming. She was walking as fast as she could, clinging to the lightstone lantern as if it was a lifeline.

Which it was, considering what it had helped her do.

She was scurrying past a secondary tower, the last one before the Regents Library. She kept looking over her shoulder to see of Ludmilla Odenkirk was following her closely enough.

Ludmilla kept glancing over her shoulder as well. The woman looked terrified, and Croninshield didn't blame her. Croninshield would have been terrified too if she had time to be.

Fey. Attack. She wasn't even sure who she could warn. She wasn't sure if she should leave a regent alone anywhere in this building.

But the Regents Library was probably a good place to go. It had all kinds of books and maps and supplies, things that she had thought irrelevant when she'd helped move them in, and now she knew that they were anything but irrelevant.

Somehow she had never believed it would come to this. She had always kept the Fey in that made-up category, even though she had known that they existed, that they had taken over Galinas, and that some of the scholars said the Fey was saying they would take over the world.

She had thought that the stuff of legends, or maybe even something that wouldn't concern her. That an attack from the Fey might come in the future, but not now, not while she was thinking of other things.

The path she and Ludmilla were taking—and Cronin-shield couldn't think of it as anything but a path—was made of stone on top of one of the buildings that had been absorbed into the library. There were parapets on both sides, and a drop of a good three stories on one side, and two on the other.

The air smelled of mildew and dampness, as if the day's rain had made the odors worse. This place always had an unused and slightly moldy scent, though, which normally made her anxious. It also made her feel like she wasn't doing her job properly.

Not that she should be worrying about that right now. Her only job was to get Ludmilla to the Regents Library, which was taking so much longer than Croninshield ever thought it would.

She felt very vulnerable here, even though she knew hardly anyone ever came this way. This particular old building was mostly used for storage, and not just storage of books. All kinds of supplies, artwork, furniture, and records. For years, she had been meaning to have someone come clean it all out and straightened, but she had never gotten it done.

The parapets were lit with very small lightstone lamps, ones that dated from before the building was enclosed. She wondered about them now, as she scurried by, wondering what her own ancestors had been thinking.

Had they felt this mixture of confusion and fear? This overwhelmed moment after killing someone—something? She wasn't even sure what she had done.

Or maybe she was, and she didn't want to think about it.

She'd love to talk with Wolfgang Sauer about it. Maybe he knew what had happened, what had caused all of this to happen.

She shook her head slightly. She had no idea really who to report this invasion to. The government? Could she even mention anything? She'd used magic—unintentionally, sure, but magic all the same—to kill that Fey. She wasn't sure how anyone would react to it.

Ludmilla's boots scraped against the stone, just like Croninshield's did. Those—and their breathing—were the only sounds.

She didn't like that either.

If no one was following them, though, they would be safe. Because outsiders had a heck of a time finding the Regents Library. Ludmilla's father had requested that. *If we have to move the library*, he had said, sounding a bit uncertain about even that directive, *let's make certain that we move it somewhere that is difficult to locate.*

Croninshield had promised they would do that, and promised that only librarians and some of the security staff would know where the library was.

Then that Fey took over Louella.

At least Louella had been a lower-level librarian. She hadn't been promoted high enough to learn where all of the secret rooms were. She hadn't known a lot of things about the library.

But how had that Fey known that the library was one of the most important places in the Academy? That Fey had been Louella for only a few days. Croninshield had no idea how much Louella had known about the library. She had been a good employee and Croninshield would have promoted her eventually. Louella had had a magpie brain, necessary for all librarians. What had she stored? How much had she passed on?

Then Croninshield remembered the man with no face that Louella had met with.

Perhaps that Fey had passed on so much more than Croninshield ever imagined.

"How much farther do we have to go?" Ludmilla sounded winded. Croninshield empathized. She felt winded. She hadn't exercised this much in years.

But right now, the fear and the momentum from killing that Fey propelled Croninshield forward. She would deal with all of the problems this mad run toward the Regents Library might cause later, when she actually had time to think about all of the implications.

"We're almost there," Croninshield said.

"Somehow, I thought the Regents Library would be closer." Ludmilla sounded annoyed.

"It's deliberately far from everything," Croninshield said. She reached the edge of the long path and stepped into what remained of the final tower. Part of it had been destroyed long before it became part of the Old Library, lost to another historical battle that Croninshield had never bothered to look up.

The walls here were made of ironwood, though, with some lightstone threaded through it.

Croninshield waited at the top of the last set of stairs. Ludmilla caught up to her.

"This place is a maze," she said, sounding worried.

"I'll stay with you," Croninshield said. "After you look at the bylaws, we'll leave together."

"And then what?" Ludmilla asked.

Croninshield had no idea, so she pretended she hadn't heard the question. She gripped the lightstone lantern tightly, even though she didn't need it on these stairs, and started down.

Ludmilla followed, just a little too closely for Croninshield's comfort. She wondered if she would ever be comfortable having someone trail her closely again.

This staircase was short and took them to the last part of the Old Library. Croninshield went through a set of arches, and again, waited for Ludmilla to follow, which she did.

At the end of this short hallway—which was darker than the one they had just come from—was a massive wooden door.

Croninshield fumbled in her pockets for her key ring, suddenly worried that she might not be able to find it at all.

Then her fingers closed around the ring, as if it had realized it had been hiding from her needlessly.

She picked it up, keys jangling, and found the oldest key, the one with an arched top that matched the arches they had just walked through.

She resisted the temptation to put the lightstone lantern down. She might never set that thing down again. She leaned a shoulder against the door and inserted the key beneath the latch.

The door groaned just a little, as if it didn't want to do anything at this time of night, and then the key went all the way in.

She turned the key, tumblers fell, and the door eased open, nearly knocking her down.

"We're here," she said, and led the way inside.

LINGUISTICS

ARCHEOLOGY

HISTORY

REGENTS
TOWER

OLD
LIBRARY

ADV. STUDENT
WING

MAIN
ENTRANCE

CLOCK
TOWER

MEDICAL
SCIENCES

CHAPTER
FORTY-EIGHT

Medwyn led the way down the narrow little corridor, smashing lights as he went. Shamra could track his progress by the sound of tinkling glass and the sudden dimming of the lightstone lamps.

Gray was only slightly behind Medwyn, far enough back to stay away from the full beams of the lights, but close enough to give instructions.

"When we get to the intersection of three hallways," Gray said, "we need to go right."

Medwyn had just grunted a response. He seemed unable to give Gray much more than a passing consideration.

Shamra was glad that this team would be together for only a short time, because the conflict between the two of them bothered her. It didn't seem to bother Aziza, who seemed to keep her own pace. Every now and then, she would turn around and look behind them, the returning light from the reassembling lightstone lamps illuminating her dark eyes and making them glitter.

Aziza seemed confident enough. Shamra felt goosebumps grow on her arms and the back of her neck.

Something about this place bothered her, and she wasn't even one of the magickal. Gray seemed so far on edge that he actually skittered as he walked. At the moment, he didn't look like a Spy at all.

Initially, Shamra had thought that the fog had followed them inside—both types of fog. The air was chill enough and damp.

But the farther into the AST building this troop got, the warmer the air got. Weirdly, it started to smell of lemons, and she thought she heard a zapping sound, like lightning hitting a tiny branch of a tree.

She was feeling a bit woozy too, but she expected that. They were going into the heart of magickal studies for the Academy, and that probably meant there were items in this place that would have an effect on Fey magick.

That was one of many reasons Eerie had sent the Infantry in first. If something magickal that could have a sideways effect on the Infantry, then that magickal something might actually harm someone like Eerie, who was made of magick.

Once this mission was over, Shamra would warn Eerie to stay away from all of the magickal places on this campus. It simply felt too dangerous.

The lemon scent was growing. It was sharper than lemons, though, almost as if the astringency attacked the nostrils rather than teased them with scent.

Shamra's eyes had started watering.

"Anyone else smell lemons?" she asked.

"And hot metal, like the smithies on Nye," Aziza said. "It's strange."

Medwyn didn't answer. He had rounded a corner, but the sound of breaking glass had stopped.

Gray was standing right in the spot where the corridor turned. "This doesn't look familiar," he said, sounding perplexed. "I don't remember the corridor twisting and turning like this. Maybe we're going the wrong way...?"

His uncertainty irritated Shamra. *He* was the one who had scouted this place out. *He* was the one who should have known where he was going.

She was about to say so when Medwyn shouted, "Go back! Go back! Get outside!"

His voice sounded tight and constrained, as if shouting hurt his throat.

She didn't go back—she wasn't made for going back. She needed to know what was happening.

She waved a hand at Aziza—"Go," Shamra said. "Take Gray with you"— and then hurried forward.

The corridor wasn't twisty, not like Gray was saying, but it looked odd. Medwyn hadn't gotten rid of the lights. He was standing at the edge of them, one arm raised.

Behind him, a fire burned, sending out orange and red smoke that crackled and popped. She thought she saw some silver sparkling lights at the edge of the smoke, but she couldn't see the flames.

If there were flames. She didn't smell a fire either.

She took a few steps forward. She would pull Medwyn out of she had to.

He seemed to see her. He shook his head, or maybe it just seemed that way as the smoke bobbled around him.

"Gooooo!" His voice bobbled too, almost as if he were dipping in and out of a pool of water, trying to talk even though his mouth was half-submerged.

The lemon smell was so strong that it now hurt her sinuses. All the way up her nose and into her head. Her eyes were watering so much that it her cheeks were wet.

The air wasn't burning hot either, not like it would have been in a fire. That smoke—it was the cause of her unease. The crackling and popping and that zapping sound grew louder.

The smoke was enveloping Medwyn, as if he were being swallowed up by a big orange-red cloud. Then it turned silver and blue, sparking and glittering—and she thought she heard him scream.

A man like Medwyn never screamed. His pride wouldn't let him. The scream had to be involuntary.

Anyone else would have turned tail and run, but Shamra wasn't trained to run. She was trained to fight.

The orange-red cloud seemed to congeal in front of Medwyn, whom she couldn't see anymore, and she had the sense that the cloud was looking at her.

She wouldn't be able to go past it and she wouldn't be able to rescue him.

Better to save the rest of her little troop.

She turned around. She ran. It felt so odd to run, as if she were failing. But she was in charge here, and she had to report to Hardin, to Lumin; Hardin so that he could save his own people, and Lumin so he could let Rugar know that this place was not what it seemed.

She sped around the corner, feeling the orange-red stuff behind her, not warm but humid in an oily way. It was trying to catch her.

It crackled and zapped, and instead of turning lights out, it seemed to turn them on.

Then she rounded the last bit, saw Aziza and Gray in the area with the destroyed lightstone lamps. Only the lamps were on. Aziza had grabbed some kind of stick from her pack—or maybe from the floor (Shamra couldn't tell)—and was flailing at the lights, as if she were a child with no strength in her arms at all.

And Gray...Gray had a Fey face. It was older and grayish-brown, with a pointed nose and haunted eyes. His cheeks were sunken, and he was shuddering.

"Get him outside," Aziza said. "These lights are killing him."

"No, I'm fine." His voice was nasal and thick, a real voice. "They are revealing me, not killing me."

That might not have been a real difference. But Shamra didn't have time to think about it—about any of it.

"We have to leave. *Now!*" she said, hoping they would hear the command in her voice rather than the panic.

She had never thought of herself as a panicker, but she had never thought of Medwyn as a screamer either.

Aziza didn't seem to hear her, though. Aziza was gripping her stick like a club and was facing Shamra, but Aziza's gaze had alighted on something behind her.

The orange-red smoke. It was moving faster. Shamra could smell it, all lemony and metallic, the strange sizzling so close that she could feel it against the hair on her skin.

The lightstone lamps flared, growing brighter, sending direct rays toward that orange-red smoke behind her, hitting her along the way, slowing her down.

She stumbled.

"*Go!*" she said, or hoped she said. She fell to her knees. The lights seemed so bright that she couldn't see anything— and then they turned orange. Or red. Or something.

She wanted to yell *Go!* again, but couldn't. Someone screamed—Aziza?—followed by another, only that scream was prolonged. Shamra didn't think she was screaming, but she could barely hold herself upright. She could barely hold a thought.

She fell forward, grateful that the stone floor was cool. Then the oily orange smoke slipped beneath her fingers, raising her slightly, coating her skin, her eyes, stabbing her everywhere—

And she finally screamed, until she couldn't anymore.

CAMPUS
MEDICAL UNIT

ANATOMY

AGRICULTURAL

COMPLEX

CHAPTER
FORTY-NINE

Xavier was clearing a narrow path for himself and Cole through the ground fog. The path was barely wide enough for them to walk through. Cole hugged his arms as close to his sides as he could.

Xavier believed that the white ground fog was magical, and he didn't want either of them to touch it. He believed it would give away their position.

Cole wasn't sure if the magic moving the ground fog aside would give away their position, but he said nothing about that. He was aware now of how little he understood about anything. One question would not clarify, and would lead to another and then another and then another.

The two of them did not have time for questions.

They were almost to the barns.

The barns extended from this path most of the way to the foothills of the Coastal Mountain Range. The barns held all kinds of animals, including livestock for food, but those barns were closer to the mountains, so that the stench didn't permeate this part of campus.

Although it did smell of horses, even now, in the lack of wind and the growing darkness.

It took him a moment to realize that someone had destroyed the lightstone lamps along this path, so the night seemed even darker than it probably was.

Xavier trudged slightly ahead of Cole, opening that path. After nearly collapsing on the mountainside, Xavier seemed to have regained all of his energy. Or maybe he was just feeling stronger now that he had a target.

He had both whips from the carriages over his shoulders, one on each side. He had lifted them out of the carriages and grinned in the face of Volkovich's disapproval.

Anything can become a magical tool, Xavier had said, *in the right hands, anyway.*

The nearest horse skittered when it saw one of the whips. Volkovich gave Xavier an angry glare, but had said nothing. Nor had he said much as Cole rummaged through the carriages, finding a pistol in each, gunpowder, and a few extra miniballs.

The pistols were front-loaders, but to his surprise they were already primed. He wasn't willing to take them apart. He agreed with the now-dead drivers: it was better to have a weapon ready than to make one ready in the heat of battle.

Unfortunately for those drivers, they hadn't realized they were in a battle until it was too late.

Cole carried the pistols gingerly, one in each hand, because he didn't trust them shoved into his pants or the holsters he had found in the carriages as well. The holsters were specially designed to carry powder and the extra mini-balls, so he brought them along, figuring he would need them.

He kept his gaze forward, on five figures near the large carriage house. They all seemed to be of a height, tall and very thin. Xavier wouldn't have been out of place among them, or so it seemed from this distance.

They appeared to have their back to the path, which surprised Cole. He would have thought that the greatest warriors in the world would be making certain that no one was coming toward them.

Or maybe their magic—the ground fog or something— notified them of intruders.

He didn't want to ask Xavier about that either.

They seemed to be discussing something. One of them was flailing their arms as if making a grand gesture, a great point. They seemed to be arguing, and they seemed to be nervous.

There weren't a lot of hiding places near the carriage houses. The carriage houses that had actual carriages were near the front of the path. The carriage houses that held the conveyances were farther away. The more modern wind-stone vehicles were stored even farther back. Normally, Cole would have gone to them. There would be tools to repair the vehicles that he could actually use, unlike the items in a carriage house.

But they were too far away to be of any help.

His heart was pounding. He wished there were more people than him and Xavier heading toward these Fey.

Around the carriage houses, the paths became wide

roads that became carriageways where the horses could be attached to carriages and brought forward. Then they could go round the circular drive, and head onto the main road that would take them to Serebro.

Except for a short drive over the mountains to the coast, there weren't a lot of other places to travel, not from the Academy. Just Serebro and the cold rocky beaches of this part of the Infrin Sea.

"Shouldn't we take cover somewhere?" Cole asked Xavier, voice as low as he could make it and still be heard.

"Normally, I'd say yes, but they're not paying attention," Xavier said, speaking just a bit louder.

"Or maybe it just seems that way," Cole said.

Xavier shook his head. "I don't think these are fighters. Their magic seems very specific. The fog is coming from them."

Cole had no idea how Xavier knew this, but, as before, Cole wasn't going to ask. He just wanted this night to end.

"So how do you want to do this?" Cole asked. He had expected to hide behind things—unknown things—until he got close enough to shoot someone.

Xavier stopped, creating a little circle around them that held no fog at all.

"I want you to focus on those pistols. Before you shoot one, I want you to mentally choose a target, concentrate on it, and then fire. Guide the round with your mind."

Cole gave Xavier a sideways glance, wanting to ask, *Are you kidding?* and then deciding to jettison that question as well. Because he knew Xavier wasn't kidding, and he knew

Xavier believed that Cole had some kind of affinity for anything mechanical.

Cole guessed that pistols counted, then.

"I just walk up to them and start shooting?" he asked. Not that it would work. He'd get off two shots and then have to reload. There were five people in front of him, although the fog kept making one of them go in and out of focus.

"Use one of the lampposts to brace yourself," Xavier said. "As close as you need."

"And you?" Cole asked.

"I will do whatever it takes to stop them," Xavier said, which was a non-answer. Cole had been getting a lot of non-answers from Xavier.

Maybe Cole just wanted more than Xavier could give. Such as an answer to whether or not they would survive this night. What it all meant.

But this wasn't the moment for that. Cole knew it, but he'd rather dither. He was beginning to realize he wasn't a man of action. He was someone who preferred to contemplate the bigger questions.

And right now, he had no time for contemplation.

He sighed.

"All right," he said, "let's get it done."

ALCHEMY, SCIENCE & THAUMATURGY

LIN

GOVERNMENT

RE

LAW BUILDING

WHISTLER HALL

FIFTY

They were tiptoeing down the corridor, Sauer's little band of misfit professors, each holding something that they had determined might help them, although help them with what, he had no idea.

They were following the astringent lemon scent—not deliberately—but because it led toward that displaced wall. Fenwick was carrying the books, one on top of the other, the map floating in front of her.

The gold footprints in the map seemed to be fading, but that could be because Sauer's little band was moving.

He didn't ask to see anything else, not yet. The threat to the AST Building was primary.

He and Fenwick were leading the band. He held nothing, because he had no idea what kind of weapon he would need or use, although he really wanted a lightstone lantern.

There were usually several in the corridors, resting on

the side tables, and so he would snag a lantern as soon as he could.

Somehow Fenwick was managing to keep pace with Sauer, even though she wasn't looking forward.

The three Alchemy professors had spread out in the center, Thane following Sauer directly, with Wystan hugging one wall and Erling hugging the other.

Behind them, the two members of the Science Department were chattering, something about interrupted experiments and possible weaponry.

Sauer really didn't care what Harewald and Kenelm were discussing. Half the words they were using were words he didn't understand anyway.

The very idea of an experiment made his too-long hair rise. He preferred books to everything else, and maybe those were his weapons. That and his ability to persuade.

"The prints are almost gone," Fenwick said, and he could hear the ragged edge of a question in her voice. *Should we keep walking toward that broken wall, then? We're just professors, after all. What do we know?*

Since she didn't say that, though, he wasn't going to respond to it. They rounded a corner and headed into one of the shared corridors between departments.

The lightstone lamps were very bright here, almost blindingly so, and the two lanterns on the side tables seemed to be bouncing in the increased light.

Everyone knew that lanterns didn't bounce, though, so Sauer figured that was a trick of the light. Of course, books usually didn't slam into his back to get his attention either, so he couldn't really ignore this.

"Oswald," he said to Erling, "turn on your lightstone lantern and leave the oil lamp behind."

"I said we shouldn't tamper with the lightstone," Maud Kenelm said. "It has surprising properties that we don't—"

"You mean like making lanterns bounce?" Sauer asked, letting his sarcasm through. "We're going to carry the lightstone lanterns."

Since this group put him in charge, he was going to use it, and they were going to listen.

He almost smiled at himself. He wasn't usually this way with his colleagues, but he often treated his students with the same kind of ferociousness. So, if he just thought of this group as students, he would do just fine.

He grabbed one of the lightstone lanterns, and handed it to Thane, who seemed startled by the assignment.

Sauer didn't care. He needed them all to do what they could, although he as yet wasn't sure what *what they could* actually meant.

He doubted they knew either.

The lightstone lantern was surprisingly cool in his fingers. He hadn't carried one in a long time. Oil lamps always grew warm from their flames, but lightstone never did, something that he had trouble getting used to. He usually let other people deal with things like lanterns. He rarely left campus, which was always beautifully lit, so he never really had any need to carry a lamp anywhere.

The lightstone lantern was heavy, though, and he tried not to look at it, because the light kept getting brighter.

He took the corridor downward, then the small flight of

stairs, hearing his colleagues breathing behind him but otherwise being surprisingly silent.

The smell of hot metal and lemons was strong at the bottom of the staircase, so he stopped and waited for Fenwick.

Fortunately she was right behind him.

He looked at the map the books had created. It had changed again, and he couldn't see this building at all. The footprints near the library were gone, except for one set which seemed to be inside.

A different set, bloodred, had also appeared in the library, near what he guessed was the Student Wing. The pink(ish) prints, though, the ones that had been deeper in the library, were gone, although the yellow footprints seemed to be moving up and toward the center of the building.

A group of footprints had gathered near the barn, and two remained on the edge of campus, just like before.

But he couldn't see this building at all.

"Let me see the architectural maps," he said to Fenwick.

The other members of his merry band had joined him, and were crowding close. Fenwick tried to hand the Pahrucii book to Wystan, but the book wouldn't leave Fenwick's hand. Wystan tried to grab it, and the book bent in half so that she couldn't touch it.

"Oh, for the love of oranges," Sauer said, and took the Pahrucii book.

It opened in his hand to the map he had just seen, glowing golden as if it were trying to give him a message.

"I need to see this building," he snarled at it, feeling less stupid at talking to a book than he had earlier in the day.

The book still in Fenwick's hand opened. The exterior of the building appeared, as if it had been drawn in pencil.

Sauer rolled his eyes. He had no idea what kind of game the book was playing—if, indeed, books played games—but he'd had enough.

"Let's just head to that wall," he said, and was happy his voice didn't shake. That wall where they had seen all those footprints.

Someone sucked in air, and then started to cough. The air was truly foul here.

"What were you experimenting with?" Erling asked Harewald. "It's awful."

Harewald's lips thinned. "I do not share my research until it is complete," he said. "And now that I need to start over..."

He marched forward as if he were leading the group instead of Sauer.

Sauer let him. The air was starting to get that oily sensation that it had had near the lab room door. He wanted to brush off his skin. He was happier to let Harewald go first, in case the stuff adhered to him as well.

They had moved into one of the oldest sections of the building, a part of the building that was always changing. It would grow larger or shrink, and Sauer could never figure out why.

The walls were made mostly of ironwood, although some part of the walls were standard riverstone, with no real magical capability at all. The front part of the building, near the door, had always been riverstone, probably so that it could blend into the rest of the scenery in this part of campus.

That was where the wall had come down, or so he thought.

He was about to push past Harewald, when Harewald sped up.

"We need more light," he said as he walked.

Sauer frowned. There was a lot of light here, but it did seem a bit dimmer than it had at the stairwell.

Sauer opened his lantern so that it would flood the area before it with light. He had Thane and Erling do the same with their lanterns.

Then he realized that the orange-red smoke was hovering near the ceiling, roiling like thunderstorm clouds around the mountain.

Harewald actually looked panicked. He started to run.

Sauer ran to keep up with him, and then tripped, almost falling.

He nearly dropped the lightstone lantern, but managed to hang onto it. He slammed the Pahrucii book between his other hand and the wall. Threads of iron appeared like little rivers, heading in the direction that Harewald was running.

Sauer had to step to one side, bracing himself as he pulled the book back into position.

He looked down to see what had tripped him, and gasped.

A man was sprawled on the floor, his face downward, hands holding onto the stone as if it was a mountainside that could pull him upright. The man was wearing brown pants and a fawn shirt, the kind that many of the professors wore when they weren't teaching.

But his dark hair was pulled back, away from his face, which kept shifting between rounded features and pointed features. Just like the tips of his ears were rounded and then pointed and then rounded again.

That made Sauer want to touch his own ears and see what they were doing.

"Someone figure out if he's okay," he said, not wanting to delegate the job with any more specificity.

He felt a sense of urgency to catch up to Harewald.

"Erling," Sauer said, "you're with me."

"So am I," Wystan said with such fierceness that Sauer got the sense she expected him to fight with her.

He wasn't going to. He really wanted everyone to join them, but he wasn't going to give that order.

There wasn't time for the bickering.

He ran forward. The orange-red smoke cloud had draped itself over the ceiling and a quarter of the way down each wall, almost like it was part of the interior design.

The lemon scent was very strong here, but that hot metallic smell was gone, as was the popping and sizzling. He couldn't hear anything except Harewald's panicked footsteps ahead of him.

Wystan was keeping up with Sauer. Erling was maybe a step or two behind. Sauer didn't even try to figure that out.

The other three didn't appear to be talking, but how would he know? The corridor had turned just enough to block some of the sound, and maybe that orange-red smoke did as well.

Then he saw Harewald.

Harewald stood in the very center of the corridor, hands on his hips. His four white ponytails looked like tiny hands pointing to the ceiling.

There was no orange-red smoke around him. But there was a hole in the wall—a window-sized hole that even as Sauer watched, was patching itself up. Stone rose off the floor and fitted itself into place.

Harewald wasn't looking at the wall, though. He was looking down.

There were three more bodies here, very close to each other.

Sauer reached Harewald's side, and looked down.

The bodies all had red and purple faces as if something had colored their skin. Their black hair was straight and stiff, which did not look natural.

Their features were classically Fey, like the images that graced some of the artwork in the very book that Sauer carried.

They were clearly dead.

"What the hell?" Sauer asked.

Harewald tilted his head, then looked at Sauer. Harewald's expression was half frown, half bemusement.

"Well," he said, "I didn't expect this."

"Neither did I," Sauer said.

"No, no," Harewald said. "You misunderstand."

He waved a hand behind him, at the cloud of orange-red smoke.

"My experiment," he said. "I guess it worked."

CAMPUS
MEDICAL UNIT

ANATOMY

AGRICULTURAL

COMPLEX

CAMPUS
SECURITY

CHAPTER

FIFTY-ONE

Cole slipped in behind the lamppost that he and
Xavier had chosen for him. It was the closest
post to the carriage house, a post that wasn't on
the drive near the five Fey.

They still appeared to be talking. He could barely hear
their voices, which seemed odd since the night was so still.

Xavier had moved some of the ground fog on the path to
the lamp, and then around the lamp itself, but if Cole
stepped outside of that narrow circle, he would brush
the fog.

Xavier had stressed so many times that touching the fog
might alert the five Fey that Cole was paying more attention
to his feet than he probably should have. He didn't have a lot
of room here, and the lamppost did nothing to hide him.

The darkness did, though. The glass on the lantern had
been shattered, and lightstone itself looked damaged. He

wasn't sure how that had happened. There were no rocks nearby, nothing that could have hit the lamp.

But Xavier claimed that two of the Fey had somehow touched it, dismantling it at great cost to themselves. He had pointed them out. They were huddled near the other three and, it seemed, the cause of some of the consternation.

I thought they might have been healers at first, Xavier said. *But now I'm not sure.*

Cole tried not to think about the things Xavier was telling him, things Xavier couldn't really know. So far, though, Xavier had been right about pretty much everything. Except, of course, that explosion earlier in the evening, the one that had given Cole a headache that he still had, that he was trying to ignore.

He was supposed to concentrate on the pistols, though, not his own head.

He had to set one down on the ground—away from that fog (he hoped) and clutched the other one. Xavier had said that Cole should pick a target.

He couldn't shoot at the Fey that seemed to be made of fog. He had no idea what that man was—if, indeed, it was a man. He could hardly see that one.

The one he could see most clearly was a lean woman in robes, who seemed to have more fog around her feet than anyone else. The light from the fog illuminated her hair, made her seem brighter than she was, even though there was no light from lightstone anywhere nearby.

She was standing next to another person (woman?) who looked similar and had been the person who was gesturing. The little group would notice if the person who had been gesturing got hit first...and who knew what these creatures would do if they knew what was happening.

He had decided to go for surprise. So he was looking at the woman with the bright hair.

Xavier had told him more than once to lean on the lamppost, even though he didn't need to. Xavier had said, with great emphasis, that the posts were often made of iron-wood, as if that should matter to Cole.

But Xavier seemed to know what this was all about or how magic worked or maybe he just wanted Cole to think that everything was as easy as Xavier made it sound.

Not to mention the fact that this lamppost was barely within the range of the pistol. Cole wasn't the best shot in the world in the first place, and from this distance, he might actually hit one of the carriages instead of the group of Fey.

He had mentioned that to Xavier more than once, and Xavier had countered with, *Let me worry about that,* each time, so there was nothing that Cole could do except let Xavier worry about that.

Cole figured that Xavier had told Cole to focus on certain things just to calm Cole down. Maybe Xavier just wanted the distraction of a pistol—the small explosion, the little fire. Maybe that was all that Xavier would need.

For once, it wasn't Cole's job to think about such things. It was his job to fire the stupid pistols.

So he focused on the glowing head of the woman standing in fog. Her entire head, not her nose (which seemed long) or her thin lips, which didn't even look like they had ever smiled. She was frowning at the hunched women—and

Cole was now close enough to see that they were women—and had her hands on her hips.

He had never shot a person before.

His head ached even more. He made himself remember those drivers, crumpled by the side of the road, the feeling of that explosion as it blew him backwards, but that didn't bring up the rage he wanted.

Maybe rage wasn't necessary. Maybe a coldness like Xavier was evincing. Maybe that was all it took.

Or just concentrating.

Cole leaned on the cool, smooth surface of the lamp-post, realizing that yes, indeed, it was ironwood. And as he had that thought, the lightstone above him glowed just a little, like a fire whose embers were still slightly active and warm.

Great. That was all he needed. To become visible.

Then he made himself focus on his shoulder, leaning on that surface, the weight of the pistol in his right hand. The woman, with the glow around her entire body from the unnaturally white ground fog.

He raised the pistol, braced his left arm between his body and the post, and then set his right wrist on his left arm, hoping that would hold.

He focused on the pistol, the mechanism. Pull the hammer, create a spark, ignite the powder, set off a tiny explosion that would propel the miniball across that wide expanse of carriageway, until the shot hit that woman in the head.

He pulled the hammer back, keeping his gaze on the

woman instead of the pistol itself, and then released the hammer.

The pistol exploded, propelling his right arm upward more than he wanted. But he made himself focus on that miniball even though he couldn't see it.

He could imagine it, the force of that explosion pushing it forward in the cool night air, sending it toward that woman's bright head. The miniball would slam into her and send her flying into one of the hunched people—

And as he had that thought, the very thing happened. The spot he had mentally chose on her head exploded into blood and brains, the whiteness vanishing, her body staggering backwards and sideways, and falling across the two hunched women.

He didn't watch the chaos. Nor did he try to see if these Fey people turned around to see what he was going. Instead, he crouched, set down the pistol he had fired, and picked up the second one.

He stood back up, and everything had changed. The edge of a brilliantly white whip touched the lightstone lamps one at a time, including the one above him. He heard the whistle of the whip, figured it had to be coming from Xavier, but decided not to look.

The entire area was lighting up, almost as bright as daylight, and the fog was shrinking. It no longer came to Cole's waist, but had moved to his thighs.

He was still careful not to touch it.

He rose back to the same position he had been in before, shoulder and left arm against the lamppost, right wrist resting on left arm, pistol in position.

But he didn't have a target. They were all moving. The other tall woman was now crouching. He could hear shouting. That fog-person was moving around, as if it was trying to see what was going on.

The hunched people were pushing at the woman he had shot.

Focus. He had to focus. Pick a target. Not the fog-person, because he didn't know if that person was solid or not.

Instead, Cole picked the mass of squirming Fey, then realized a mass was not what he could pick as a target, especially if they moved apart.

So he focused on the woman who was struggling to push the one he had already shot away from the other two.

She was kneeling, arms underneath the wounded (dead?) woman, shoving as she went, the other two grabbing, their hands glowing. He tried not to see the glowing hands.

Instead he looked at the kneeling woman's torso, the way she was pushed forward. He couldn't get a shot of any of their heads, but that didn't matter. He could see the middle of her back as clearly as if sun was shining directly on her.

Then he realized that, in a sense, it was. All of the light-stone had been revived, and much of the light was focused on that squirming group of people. Even the fog-person was becoming solid enough to look like a man.

Cole took a deep breath. Pistol. Focus. He went through the same litany in his mind—the hammer down, spark, explosion, miniball—only ending with the woman's back.

Then he thumbed the hammer, keeping his gaze on her. The fog-man looked at Cole, nearly throwing him off, but then Cole mentally dismissed the fog-man. Even if the fog-man tried something, he wouldn't be able to stop that mini-ball—if Cole released it now.

He let the hammer go, felt the pistol's kick (different and stronger than the first one), saw that tongue of flame and a little puff of smoke, and then the miniball moving in the night air, seeming to gain speed rather than losing it (which was not possible, but Cole had seen many impossible things this night) and then it slammed into the woman's back, just like he had planned.

She collapsed on the others, and there was screaming, and he couldn't let himself care.

He crouched, set down the pistol he had just used so that it could cool, then grabbed the first pistol. He picked up the base and poured powder into the muzzle, hoping he got the mix right. He hadn't done this in years, and even then, his training had been spotty.

He had been surprised at his ability to hit a target just now, and he wondered how much it had to do with Xavier's order to focus. Xavier had said that Cole had magical abilities that centered around tech, so perhaps that was what this was.

Because Cole couldn't believe he had just gotten off two lucky shots.

The yelling and the crying continued from the area near the carriages. The area was growing brighter. The lightstone lamp above him had returned to full power. The ground fog was receding, making the smell of the ocean rise.

His hands were shaking, but not from the cold. He shoved the miniball into the muzzle, and stood.

Xavier had moved closer to the group. Both whips were extended, as if they were in mid-strike. But they weren't falling to the ground. Instead, they were covered with light. One was wrapped around a nearby lightstone streetlamp, but the other had wound itself around the leg of the fog-man.

Only now, the fog-man looked like any other person. He was solid, broad-shouldered, and slight, his hands gripping the dirt as Xavier pulled him away from the pile of injured women. One of those women was on her knees, attempting to tend to the woman that Cole had shot in the back.

The other woman was still sprawled, and it looked like part of her head was missing. The third hadn't moved off the ground.

Cole let out a shaky breath. He could aim at the man who was being pulled toward Xavier, but Xavier seemed to have that well in hand.

So Cole aimed at the woman who was helping the one who had been shot. He didn't like this. He would have tried to help someone too in similar circumstances, and an attempt to help meant that the woman was a good person, right?

He banished the thought from his head. He had to, or he couldn't continue. No good person would have murdered those drivers or set that explosion. The woman was complicit in all of that.

He resumed his position—shoulder leaning, left arm bent, right wrist braced—and he imagined the shot before he attempted it. Hammer, explosion, miniball flying—

He executed the shot before he even realized he had done

it. The miniball hit the woman squarely in her chest, pushing her backwards. He thought he heard a scream or a moan, but that might have been him.

He crouched again, set his pistol down, and grabbed the next one, not even sure if there was anyone to hit. Maybe the man that Xavier was dragging.

Cole loaded the pistol, then stood, and paused. The women were down, and not moving. The man had nearly reached Xavier, but the man seemed diminished. Almost as if he were melting from the outside in. The light around him was so bright that it was almost blinding.

Cole wanted to ask Xavier if he needed help, but couldn't. Xavier was still dragging the man toward him. Most of the lightstone lamps seemed to be focused on the man, although some of the lightstone light covered those women as well.

They were a pile of limbs and blood, seemingly no threat at all.

Cole didn't know what to do. He was about to leave the safety of the lamp when Xavier tugged on the second whip. It pulled one of the streetlamps over, close enough that the lightstone itself fell out of the case. The lightstone landed on the man that Xavier had dragged, and the man screamed.

Cole had never heard a sound that hideous in his life. The man thrashed and bucked, trying to get the lightstone off him. The lightstone flared brighter, melting its way through the man's back, until the stone stood upright, like a flag planted on the ground.

The man no longer moved. He had stopped screaming.

He had grown slighter and grayer, almost as if he were turning to ash.

Xavier dropped both whips, then staggered backwards, losing his balance, and sitting down, clearly involuntarily.

Cole was about to run toward him, then realized he held a loaded pistol. He couldn't run with that, nor did he want to leave the weapons behind.

He gathered the other pistol, slung the holsters over his shoulder, and carried the pistols—muzzles downward—toward Xavier.

When he reached Xavier's side, he set the weapons down.

The fog-man was clearly dead, just a pile of ash. The women were either dead or unconscious, and the ground fog had vanished entirely. It should have felt like a victory, but it did not.

Xavier had braced his arms behind himself. He seemed older than he had a few moments ago.

He saw Cole and chuckled. "My grandmother always said I didn't practice enough. She said natural ability would only get me so far. I thought I'd been practicing...."

"It's all right," Cole said, even though he had no idea if it was. "We got them."

"This lot," Xavier said. "There are others...."

He half-smiled, his arms buckling behind him.

"I'm so tired," he said.

Cole slipped an arm around his back. "Let me get you to Pasha."

"I'm not a horse," Xavier said. "He can't help me. I just need to rest."

"Not here," Cole said. "Not in the open."

He had no idea how many more of them there were, but he had to assume there were a lot. And he had to assume they were dangerous.

"Can you carry the pistols?" Cole asked. "Because—"

"No." Xavier gave him a wan smile. "Those are your weapons."

"I can't leave them here," Cole said.

"Then leave me," Xavier said, and leaned back even more, his weight heavy against Cole's arm.

"I won't," Cole said. "You're going to stand up. You're going to walk with me."

Because that was the only way Cole could manage Xavier and the pistols. Besides, both men needed to get out of here. Who knew if those Fey would revive? Who knew what they would do if they did?

Xavier didn't argue, which Cole took as a good sign. He slid his arm up Xavier's back, gripping him under one arm, and struggled to get him upright.

They stood, and Cole braced him, then bent over and grabbed the pistols. The empty one, he shoved into his pants, even though the metal was still warm. He gripped the other in his right hand, muzzle pointing downward.

They weren't that far from Volkovich, but it felt like they were.

Cole wanted to run in that direction, but there was no running with Xavier.

They were going to hobble, but they would get there, and Cole was going to do everything he could to make sure that Xavier would be all right.

STORAGE
BUILDINGS

CHAPTER

FIFTY-TWO

The white ground fog was drifting away, shrinking as if it had never been. Just a few minutes ago, it had been floated around Lumin's waist, a comfort that was letting him know his people had the entire mission under control.

Now the fog was mere wisps on the bare ground, remnants of itself. The entire campus had been blanketed with it not long ago, and now, he could see every detail of every building, including the ancient storage ones beside him, the ones he had initially believed would hold the artifacts he wanted.

So far, no one had reported to him and Eerie about the location of the maps. He couldn't see or feel anyone on his team, not that he ever could, but the signs weren't good. There seemed to be more light on campus, not less, and now with the fog dissipating....

Eerie grabbed his arm tightly, and shook him, as if she thought she had to wake him up.

"Our people are dead," she said, her voice flat.

"They just lost control of the fog," he said. "We've been having them influence weather for days. Magick has its limits—"

"They're dead," she repeated. "Only Veil remains. And Perdu."

Lumin looked down at her hand first, thin and bony and gripping his skin so tightly that it hurt. Then his gaze followed her arm to her face, which was pinched, eyes wide.

She was clearly terrified.

"How is that possible?" he asked. "No one even knows we're here."

"I told you," she said, "there's loose magick."

It didn't seem loose if it could take out his people. His people weren't Rugar's finest, but they could do this—find maps, report back, give him information.

"You're imagining this," he said. Surely, she had to be. Because she had been off all night.

"We need to leave," she said, not even angry that he had just said he didn't believe her. "We need to leave now."

He frowned, seeing her face in the growing light. The light was coming from the campus, as if those lightstone street lamps had become even more powerful than they already were.

At least there were no lamps near here. It was one of the reasons he had picked this spot.

No fog, growing light. He had known that lightstone was dangerous, and obviously, someone else knew it too.

Maybe they had enough information. There was more active magick here than expected, a different kind of magick, one he didn't entirely understand. It would take study, he would tell Rugar. Maybe a few more Spies to investigate but not do anything.

Eerie's grip grew tighter.

"We need to leave *now*," she said.

He blinked, heard her, decided that he believed her after all. If she was wrong, the others would trail their way back, and maybe yell at him or figure out how to return to Nye on their own.

"Can you portal us out of here?" he asked.

"Where to?" she asked. "The carriages? Can you handle those? Because I can't."

"Serebro?" he asked.

"No," she said. "Those mountains, they're a source of some of the stones that are causing us problems. I can get us to the carriages, but that might not help us."

"Well, they're away from here," he said.

"And if we get there," she said, "I'll have no energy to defend us. We can walk, Lumin. No one will think anything of it, if we walk with confidence and stay in the darker areas."

He didn't like it. He didn't like it at all. It felt like he was abandoning his people without proof.

Except, the dissipating fog—well, the lack of fog now, because it was completely gone—wasn't that proof?

With that thought came a kind of helpless fear. How could this have gone so wrong? He'd had artifacts and maps and money so that he could buy more. He should have taken those to Rugar, but instead, Lumin had thought he needed to figure out what the Academy was like, where the magick was located in Serebro.

He had overreached.

Eerie shook him again. "Lumin," she said fiercely. "We have to go."

Then she shoved him, and he staggered sideways, his arm aching where her hand had been.

"I don't care if you don't want to leave," she said. "I'm going."

And then she marched down the road they had come in on, back toward the foothills of that mountain.

Her words penetrated: Veil and Perdu. A Spy and a Doppelgänger. That was all. The others, gone.

Only four remaining, so far. A Spy and a Doppelgänger. They had a good chance of surviving on their own.

Better than Lumin and Eerie did, in fact.

He was already thinking about the report to Rugar, which wasn't going to help anyone.

Lumin and Eerie had to survive first.

Then they could talk to Rugar. Because this was not a place the Fey should come without a lot of preparation.

They had lost the last time they had come in large numbers.

They would lose again.

Eerie was right; they had to get out of here. And they had to survive.

At this moment, nothing else mattered.

They had to live long enough to make their report, to save the Fey.

SCHOLAR'S
ENTRANCE

OLD

LIBRARY

CAFETERIA

FIFTY-THREE

J axon was shaking with the cold. At least, he was telling himself that the cold was causing all of that shaking, because he was too strong a man to be shaking for any other reason.

Even though he was surrounded by four dead bodies, including a man he had trained.

Jaxon would have to talk with Norvel's wife. He had no idea how to do that.

And then, as if someone had shut off a faucet, the ground fog receded. It grew less and less, shrinking down to knee height, then ankle height, then barely shoe height within a matter of minutes, revealing both intruders, who were clearly dead.

They looked sallow in the changing light. The light-stones, which had fallen into the ground fog and might have been the source of the original yellow light, were glowing on the ground, undiminished by their fall from the lanterns.

Within minutes of the fog's disappearance, the scene outside the Scholars Entrance had changed. Instead of standing alone in a sea of yellow and white fog, Jaxon stood with four bodies, a warm pistol in his hands.

He had not expected to be here when he woke up that morning. Nor had he thought this was possible when he and Norvel followed this group.

It had looked so military, so official.

Jaxon turned, suddenly feeling very alone. What if there were more? What if they came for him?

His hands were still shaking. He should probably reload the pistol, but he didn't want to. He didn't want to carry a loaded weapon across campus.

If he was going across campus.

There might be more of these people, though. Then he realized, there were more. He had seen a man who looked foglike head into the library.

Was that another man with no face, like the one who had spoken to Louella? What were those men?

Jaxon let out a breath, which he could now see in the cool damp air. He had never experienced a night like this, not in all of his years working and running security on this campus.

Why would military folk like these try to invade the campus? Why would the Fey—if that's what they were—be so interested in this place?

And why would they go for the Scholars Entrance instead of the easier to access student entrance?

Jaxon wanted to stop, to clean up, to talk to someone in charge. But when it came to security, he was in charge.

And now he was alone, at least here.

He had no idea if others were hiding nearby. If he opened that Scholars door, he would give them what they wanted.

So he would go to the student entrance and warn the librarians. They could barricade the Scholars Wing. They could initiate protective measures that hadn't been in place in decades—not since the riots during the Purges.

Then he would find some more members of his staff and patrol the campus. He couldn't do anything else.

He glanced at the bodies, so diminished here on the grounds. That large man still seemed large, but the woman looked like a skeletal version of the person who had let out that feral yell and tried to attack him.

And the third man, he seemed smaller too. The light had pulled something out of him, something that Jaxon didn't understand.

He would have to send for the Serebro Constabulary when this night was over. And he would send someone important to bring them here, not one of his deputies.

He took a deep breath, feeling the chill air in his lungs. He didn't like leaving Norvel here with the people who killed him, but there was no choice.

Jaxon had to see what else was going on. And he needed to know what that blurry man was doing in the library.

It certainly couldn't be anything good.

ALCHEMY, SCIENCE
& THAUMATURGY

GOVERNMENT

R

LI

LAW BUILDING

WHISTLER
HALL

CHAPTER
FIFTY-FOUR

"You did not intend that," Maud Kenelm boomed from behind Sauer. He jumped.

He had been studying the three bodies before him, and hadn't heard Kenelm's approach.

He couldn't believe he hadn't been paying attention. He was crammed in this narrow hallway, with the orange-red smoke lingering on the ceiling, the smell of lemons all around him, and an ache behind his eyes.

Sauer had lost track of his own people, even though he assumed they were near him in this hallway. Harewald was just in front of him, and Erling was slightly behind.

The light from the lightstone lanterns was dimmer than it should have been, partly because of that orange-red smoke. It seemed to be everywhere. But it didn't zap or pop here, and the blue was missing.

Kenelm cleared her throat, as if she wanted some attention. Sauer turned slightly. She had her arms crossed over her massive torso, and she looked even more powerful than she had before.

But she didn't even seem to notice Sauer—or the bodies, for that matter. She was staring at Harewald.

Harewald hadn't noticed her. His head was bent. He was studying the bodies as if they were speaking to him.

At that moment, the final stone snapped into place with a loud bang. The wall was closed, again.

The air in this passageway should have crackled with magic, but it did not. Sauer had never experienced magic like this, magic that just occurred, magic that didn't call attention to itself. But the wall had taken care of itself, and the books, while they nagged, did not seem flashy in any way.

However, that orange-red smoke, it lingered, like it was watching them.

Sauer didn't want it anywhere near him.

He had no idea what had happened to these Fey intruders. He suspected the orange-red smoke or maybe lightstone or the building itself, but he didn't know, any more than he knew exactly how the wall had repaired itself.

And he called himself an expert in Thaumaturgy. He was glad his students weren't here, glad they couldn't ask questions, glad he didn't have to put on his professorial face. Glad that he didn't have to be the expert, for once, because he wasn't.

"Your experiment," Kenelm said loudly. She had taken a step closer to Harewald. "You didn't intend to have it attack Fey. You were not trying to kill Fey because we had no idea that there were Fey on campus until an hour ago."

Harewald turned around slowly. His expression had changed from bemusement to barely controlled fury.

His expression surprised Sauer. Sauer had no idea why Kenelm's words would make Harewald so angry.

"I have contracts," he snapped. "I've told you that."

"For murderous smoke?" Kenelm asked. "Who would contract for...?"

Then she stopped, as if she now knew who would contract for murderous smoke. But Sauer didn't.

"What are you talking about?" he asked.

Harewald waved a hand, trying to quiet everyone. Oddly, his movements didn't cause the orange-red smoke to bobble. It was as if it was too heavy to be moved by a slight breeze caused by someone's waving hand.

"I have a confidentiality agreement," Harewald said flatly, as if he expected everyone to understand. "And I've probably already revealed too much."

"You think the smoke killed them?" Sauer asked. He had been thinking that something about the ironwood or the lightstone had been poisonous to these four people.

Because clearly, no human actor had attacked them. There was no evidence of a fight at all.

Kenelm pushed her way past Erling and Wystan, and toed one of the bodies. It didn't respond, nor did it move from the pressure of her foot.

Then she lifted her head and raised her eyebrows ever so slightly, almost as if she was mocking Harewald.

"Your precious military contracts have all been theory so far," she said. "I'm sure they'll appreciate that your potions work in the field."

Harewald's eyes grew wide at that, as if he couldn't believe what she had just said.

"And since we are in the field," she continued, "you might want to whip up more of that stuff, so we can go after the other Fey on campus."

"No." Wystan's voice was thin but it cut through everything. "This 'potion,' as you call it, attacks anyone with Fey blood. Which is most of us standing in this hallway. You will not bring out more of this 'potion.' We can't fight on two fronts."

Apparently, Sauer was one of the few who had had no idea that Harewald had been working on weaponry. But weaponry that targeted Fey—that seemed either prescient or ridiculous.

Or it would have been ridiculous, if the Fey hadn't shown up here, in something like numbers, trying to do... what, exactly? He still couldn't quite understand why they wanted to go after the AST building.

Then he let out a small breath. Or maybe he did know why they were going after the AST building, if they knew about Harewald. Was Harewald the only one in the Science Department with contracts?

He certainly wasn't the only one who was conducting experiments at all hours.

Harewald was glaring at Kenelm. Harewald wasn't even trying to figure out what had happened to the Fey at his feet. Instead, he seemed angry at Kenelm's revelation.

Sauer hated dealing with the mess of personalities. His brain was swimming with everything he had learned this evening. Fey on campus, military contracts against the Fey originating in his building (but not his department), magic books, and people who couldn't hold their own image while lying dead on the floor.

"We need to package up this..." Now, Wystan waved her hand, this time to substitute for a word that she apparently didn't have or couldn't think of. "This...stuff. You need to bottle it again, Grimbold."

Harewald looked at her. "I have never done that outside of the lab."

"So, go get the tools you need," Wystan said. "We can't have this...stuff...hanging loose, in this building in particular. You've seen what it can do."

"You prevented it from hurting us earlier," Sauer said to Wystan. "Can't you do something?"

She narrowed her eyes. "You do know that magic has limits, right? It's like anything else physical. The more I use now, the less I can use later."

She was clearly envisioning something, warning him about something.

About what, he wasn't sure.

Or maybe he was sure, and he didn't want to think about it. She clearly thought there would be another fight ahead, and she would be at the center of it.

"We can't have this linger, from what you're saying." Sauer hated that he was the one in charge. "It sounds like a threat to all of us."

"It's not." Harewald's voice was dry. "This smoke has lost its power. That's why it hangs on the ceiling."

"You know that for certain?" Kenelm asked. "Because you've been saying it's an experiment."

"Just block it in the hallway with these bodies." Thane spoke for the first time since they all arrived. "We can't deal with them right now anyway."

"And I really don't want to touch them," Fenwick said. She clearly didn't. She was standing toward the back of the group. She hadn't even gotten close to them.

"A bottle would be easier," Wystan said.

"But do we know if these creatures stay dead?" Erling asked. His voice actually shook a little.

Everyone turned toward him, as if they couldn't believe what he had said.

Sauer had never really noticed just how paranoid Erling was. But then, Sauer had never had prolonged contact with him before. They had nodded at each other as colleagues and had done little else.

"They're human like us," Sauer said.

"They're not like us," Erling said. "They have powers—"

"What do you call this?" It was Sauer's turn to have his hand at the ceiling. "We have abilities too. We have just chosen not to use them."

Then he frowned at Harewald. Harewald backed away from the look, like students often did when Sauer looked at them the same way.

Harewald's foot hit one of the bodies, and he squeaked and stepped away.

"You didn't clarify," Sauer said. "These contracts. They're not for Fey, are they?"

"I have promised confidentiality," Harewald said. "I can't—"

"You can and will," Sauer said. "We're in an emergency.

A big one, and you designed a weapon that we might be able to use."

"It can't float freely across campus," Wystan said. "I can't imagine who might die if it did."

Harewald glanced down at one of the bodies, then back at Sauer. "I...the experiment isn't finished."

"And this was a surprise," Sauer finished for him. "A surprise that it attacked Fey or a surprise that it killed at all?"

Harewald cleared his throat, then blinked hard. He took a deep breath, coughed, and ran a hand over his mouth, as if he was trying to clean it before saying anything at all.

"Grimbold," Sauer said. "This is important. If we don't make it through the night, then your stupid confidentiality won't matter at all."

He hadn't meant to say *stupid*, but it had slipped out.

"Um," Harewald said, then glanced at Kenelm. "Um...I can say this. The military probably didn't consider the Fey an active threat to Dorovich."

"Meaning what?" Thane asked. He sounded even angrier than Kenelm. "They were going to ship this to Nye?"

Harewald looked trapped, as if he were the target of some kind of attack.

He cleared his throat again, looked from Sauer to Thane to Kenelm and then at the body on the ground.

Harewald took a deep breath. He seemed to be the only person not bothered by the lemony scent that now coated everything.

"You do know that there's unrest in Feltshyon, right? There are also rumors of dissent in Khēmía. And that there's

719

a lot of Dorovich that hasn't become part of the Protectorate."

"Oh, for the sake of all that's sane," Thane snapped. "You're saying that they were turning this on our own people?"

Harewald shook his head. "Not our people, per se. It's the *Qavnerian* Protectorate, after all. It's—"

"We're all the same," Sauer said. "We're all the same. Haven't you studied the history of magic? The cultures may change, the types of magic might change, but our priorities make the magic different, not some kind of strange assignment of traits."

"I'm a scientist," Harewald said, his voice small. "I never had to study history."

Sauer turned away, and nearly tripped on the body that had been changing with the light. The changes appeared to have stopped. The body looked like it belonged to a small man now, with mostly regular features, someone that Sauer wouldn't have noticed on the street.

That was probably the magic. To go unnoticed.

"History is the foundation of everything," Sauer said, not willing to look at any of them. Except Fenwick, of course. She had to agree with him. She had done her thesis on the history of magic in Qavner. Decades ago, but still.

"History is the foundation of Thaumaturgy," Erling said. "The rest of us don't need it. We're working in the now, not the past."

"And the now might kill us if we don't understand how it works." Sauer turned back around and faced Harewald.

"You designed this stuff to go after the people living in specific countries?"

"Um...I was working on that. I don't use people in my experiments. I use—"

"Cadavers," Kenelm said with disgust. "He uses cadavers to see what these potions will do to them. The stench in the laboratory wing can be overwhelming, which is why Grimbold works at night. Sometimes the smells are even gone by morning."

Sauer shook his head. He had to focus on the now, which he did not like. But the now was filled with Fey and dead bodies and revelations of things he would never have expected.

He looked at Wystan. "That stuff is dangerous. Let's trap it here until we have time to bottle it. That'll also protect these cadavers."

Then he peered at Harewald.

"The cadavers will become your responsibility when the night is over. I'm sure security or the Serebro Constabulary won't mind if you take custody of them. Then you can figure out what happened here."

Harewald nodded.

"We don't have time for that, so we're going to block this area off, or rather, Frida is, right, Frida?" Sauer looked at Wystan.

"If you think that's the best use of my limited powers," she said.

"I think saving lives is a good use of your powers," Sauer said.

"I don't think the smoke is harmful any longer," Harewald said. "My experiments point to a one-use."

"*I don't think. Point to,*" Sauer repeated as if Harewald was one of his dumber students. "Neither of those phrases are reassuring. *Neither* of them."

He stepped over the nearest corpse and grabbed the Pahrucii book from Fenwick. He didn't even have to open it. As he touched it, the map rose out of its pages.

The map seemed to know what he wanted.

He stared at it.

There were no golden footprints in this building. None. There had been four earlier, and they had been right here, right where he was standing.

Now, those prints were gone.

He studied the map. No one spoke around him, and he couldn't tell if they were looking at the map too or if they were doing something else.

He would worry about that in a moment. These maps— Fey maps, as someone had called them—showed him where the magic was, where the Fey were.

There had been the four around this building, and four around the Old Library, as well as one inside the library.

Now there were two inside the library—a red set of footprints and another gold set. But there were no other prints around the library, and it hadn't been that long ago that he had seen them.

Nor were there footprints at the barns.

It so unnerved him to see that the prints had disappeared that he almost confirmed with his little band that the prints had been there in the first place.

But he knew the prints had been there. He had seen them, the band had discussed them, and he had felt like he had to do something.

Besides, there were still two sets of footprints on the Academy grounds. Those prints had been near some of the storage buildings, but the prints were on the move now, heading into one of the academic housing areas that Sauer loathed.

Fleeing? That would make sense. And no one would know.

He looked at the prints in the Old Library. There were usually security guards near the library. They would notice anything amiss, and even if they didn't, there were students nearby who might be able to help if those two Fey tried something.

But the two that were heading into the neighborhood, filled with professors and spouses and innocent children— no one would know about them. No one would even notice them if the Fey did what the history books said they could do.

The Fey could hide in plain sight. That's what the first-person accounts from the attacks after the descent from Mount Vitaki told him. People were often surprised that the Fey had infiltrated businesses, homes, neighborhoods, and no one had seen them.

No one would see these two either.

He felt stronger, suddenly, as if he had acquired a purpose.

"All right," he said. "I'm going to give us a mission."

Everyone looked at him, as if startled by his words.

He gestured at the corpses on the ground.

"These maps told us about this group. We have another

group that's starting to head out of the valley. We need to catch them, and stop them."

"Why?" Erling asked. "We could let them go."

"And take their new knowledge of campus with them? How many Fey would they report to? How many would they bring back with them?"

Sauer had no idea if he was being fanciful or if he really did have a point. But the key was that he had to convince the others.

"Block this area off now," he said to Wystan, "and let's go after these Fey."

"And do what to them?" Erling asked.

Sauer narrowed his gaze. The answer seemed obvious. But he was going to say it anyway. He made sure he sounded confident, and in charge.

"Why," he said almost blithely. "We have to kill them, of course."

LINGUISTICS

ARCHEOLOGY

HISTORY

REGENTS
TOWER

OLD
LIBRARY

ADV. STUDENT
WING

MAIN
ENTRANCE

CLOCK
TOWER

MEDICAL
SCIENCES

CHAPTER
FIFTY-FIVE

The smell of old books comforted her. Paper, crumbly and ancient, had its own odor. Ludmilla stepped inside the Regents Library, just behind Croninshield, and took a deep breath of that wonderful smell.

Ludmilla hadn't realized just how much she needed it.

Croninshield was still wielding her lightstone lantern as if it were a weapon—which, after what had happened in the corridors, it apparently was.

It lit the area near the door, which had a table and another lightstone lamp. The light from the Croninshield's lantern hit that lamp, and the lamp came on all by itself.

Then the lamp's light touched another lamp on another table, and that lamp came on. Lamp after lamp after lamp turned on after the lightstone light hit them. It looked like a running chain of lamps, as if someone had designed them to come on when they were needed.

"Did you set that up?" Ludmilla whispered. It didn't feel right to speak out loud in this space.

It was the first room (or series of rooms, really) that felt like a library to her—at least since she had left the Student Wing earlier.

"No," Croninshield said, her deep voice echoing in the main room. She apparently felt no need to be quiet. "I just put lamps on tables so that someone could work here."

She didn't seem unnerved by the way that the lights had worked, though. Maybe she was past unnerved. Maybe she had moved to that numb place that threatened inside of Ludmilla.

Ludmilla was tired and overwhelmed, but also determined. She felt safe here, and she wasn't sure why. Maybe because the Regents Library had been so hard to find, or maybe because Croninshield had managed to defend them both so far.

Croninshield didn't seem to be focused on the lights. Instead, she wiped a finger on the table beside them, and held the finger up in the light. There was dust on her skin, and a deep track where her finger had been.

"How long has it been since someone worked here?" Ludmilla asked. She still couldn't bring herself to speak loudly.

"I don't think anyone has since we moved the library," Croninshield said, "although I did assign the janitorial staff to clean the rooms."

Ludmilla winced. "They're not doing a good job."

"I can see that," Croninshield snapped. Then she let out

a small laugh. "Not that it's the biggest issue we're dealing with today."

Not by a long shot. Ludmilla eased the door closed behind her and stepped deeper into the space.

The Regents Library looked different here, and yet it still looked the same as it had in the Regent's Tower. To her right was the librarian's desk, open to the main area, but with a U of shelves that were crammed with papers, monographs, and loosely bound books in need of repair.

There was a small lamp on the librarian's desk, and it illuminated an old blotter that had some writing on it. Ludmilla guessed that the blotter had been moved with all of the materials from the old location.

The chair behind the desk was pushed back as if someone had recently sat in it, but nothing about the area seemed like it had been used in a long time.

Around the main part of the room were long tables, like the ones in the Student Wing, only these appeared to be made of the reddish-brown wood that came from the Razbitay Mountain Range. They also had carvings along the side, mostly images of hearts and crowns and swords, interspersed with books.

Matching wooden chairs were pressed against each table, with a single heart carved out of the backs of the chairs. The chairs made the room seem formal, as if everything here was waiting for students to attend a class.

The lights continued to turn on, going deep into the shelving that ran along the walls.

She moved away from the door. She wanted to block it

with a chair, just to make doubly sure that she and Cronin-shield were safe, but she didn't.

Besides, a chair wouldn't stop a determined person from getting in here.

Although something in the air might. The air felt alive, like the night air after a lightning storm.

She realized, as she walked deeper into the room, that she had felt this charged air every time she'd been in the library at the other location. She had accepted—even welcomed—the feeling as a child. And now, it felt like coming home.

Croninshield walked toward the shelves behind the librarian's desk. She ran a hand over the edges, dislodging even more dust.

"This is criminal," she said, apparently referring to the dirt.

Ludmilla actually smiled. They had nearly been killed by some kind of Fey creature. They had been stalked and terror-ized, and this was what Croninshield considered criminal.

The ironic thing was that Ludmilla actually agreed. She hated seeing how filthy and abandoned this library had become.

She wondered if the abandonment had been intentional.

She walked over to the desk and peered at the blotter. It was a calendar with notations along the edges. The calendar was five years old.

Clearly no one had been up here, and no one seemed to care.

"Do you have any idea where the bylaws are?" she asked.

"Actually, I do," Croninshield said. "I helped organize all

of the books in here, and those were the only ones that didn't have an obvious place to go."

She pivoted and bent down, opening a small file cabinet that Ludmilla hadn't noticed earlier.

Then Croninshield began removing books, one at a time. The top ones were bound with string woven in and out of holes in the front and back covers—and, Ludmilla assumed, in the papers themselves.

Although, as Croninshield set the books on the desk, dust rose in the air and sparkled as the light caught it. Ludmilla resisted the urge to sneeze.

She moved closer to the desk, watching as Croninshield took even more books out of that cabinet.

But calling them books wasn't accurate. They weren't books, not really. They were papers, slipped into predesigned cases, as if someone realized that they needed to be kept safe, but there was no way to do it.

The papers' edges were ragged, and as more and more books came out, Ludmilla realized that some of them were parchment. Even older books landed on top, until the stack threatened to fall.

Croninshield stood, and wiped off her hands.

"That's it?" Ludmilla asked, then realized she made it sound like that wasn't enough. It was more than enough. There were a dozen books, maybe more.

"Oh, no," Croninshield said. "There's the last one, but it's really fragile. I suspect it's the original bylaws, the very first. I'm going to see if I can find some gloves before handling it."

She opened drawers in the desk, shaking the books on

top. Ludmilla moved even closer, putting her hands out so that the stacks didn't fall. She coughed, her eyes irritated by the growing dust storm.

Croninshield didn't seem to notice. She made a sound of satisfaction, then held up two pairs of gloves, yellowed and old and probably too big for both women.

Not that it mattered. The gloves were what mattered. Ludmilla took hers and slid them on.

They felt like silk—old silk, the kind that had been worn down into nearly nothing. Not only could she feel the impression of other hands inside these gloves, but she had a sense of the wearers. The most recent wearers had been female, with hands larger than Ludmilla's, but still too small for the gloves.

Some of the previous wearers had been male, going back a long way. How long, she couldn't tell. But what she could tell was the original wearer of the gloves had had the gloves made special, just for him.

There was an echo of him in the air, a ghostly presence, as if putting on the gloves had conjured him.

She could almost see him. He was spectral, clear, taller than she was—and she was a tall woman. His features were narrow, like hers, his nose actually hooked just a bit, and his lips were thin. They seemed thinner than they probably were because they were pressed together in disapproval.

He wore a tight suit, maybe black, with a high collar and a pocket watch dangling down the side. His trousers were baggy, and his shoes looked more like engraved boots.

She'd seen paintings of that attire in the portrait wing of

the Trinovante Gallery, but she had never actually seen anyone wearing clothing like that.

He examined the entire room as if he had never seen it before (and he probably hadn't), then he asked, *Where in the forsaken lands did you take us?*

"This is the Old Library," she said.

"What?" Croninshield asked.

Ludmilla held up a hand. She didn't want to explain to Croninshield what she was seeing. Clearly Croninshield couldn't see it at all.

There is no Old Library, the specter said. *Where are we?*

"It was a fortress once," Ludmilla said.

He gasped.

"What was that?" Croninshield asked.

Ludmilla kept that hand up, but bent the fingers so that just her index finger remained. She wanted to bring it to her lips to shush Croninshield, but thought that might be unwise. The specter might think the movement was for him.

We kept the library away from the fortress on purpose. He actually sounded panicked. *You must move it back.*

"We will," she said, and she didn't feel like she was making an empty, placating promise. "We will move it back. But not tonight. Tonight, there are Fey on the Academy grounds…"

Then she stopped herself, thinking of the right word.

Croninshield's eyes were glistening, and she had stopped talking. She wasn't looking where the specter was, but she was standing motionless, as if she finally understood what was going on.

The specter was shaking his head, as if he couldn't understand.

"...the land around the fortress," Ludmilla finished. "And inside the fortress too. My companion, May Croninshield, killed one of them, using a lightstone lantern."

The specter turned toward Croninshield. He bowed his head, almost as if he was honored to be in her presence.

A Croninshield, he said. *That is good. And you are...?*

"Ludmilla Odenkirk," she said.

An Odenkirk. The specter actually smiled. *The Old Families live on.*

Ludmilla had no idea what to say to that. But she did recognize him as a resource. She said, "Did you hear me? There are Fey about."

Yes, he said. *I'm appalled that you let them get to the heart of our lands.*

"We had no idea they were here. The one May killed looked like one of us."

The specter shook his head. *You sound surprised.*

"I am surprised," Ludmilla said.

Croninshield tilted her head just a little, as if she was trying to hear the specter's side of the conversation.

You shouldn't have been. You should know what you're facing. We wrote books, designed magic practices, established defenses. You should know what these Fey are.

Ludmilla had no idea how to explain the Purges to this specter.

Still, he said, *your companion, the Croninshield, understand the tools. Or she would not have used the lantern.*

Ludmilla didn't want to tell him that the use of the

lantern had been a mostly happy accident that Croninshield had managed to wield.

"We don't know everything," Ludmilla said. "It's been hundreds of years since the Fey came to Dorovich. Some of the protections are lost."

Or ignored. He looked around the room dramatically. *This space is good enough for now, but you will lose your magic if the materials stay here. You must move them, the sooner the better.*

"I will," Ludmilla promised again.

Good, he said, and faded.

"Wait!" she said. "Wait! I have questions!"

But he was gone.

She tugged the gloves tighter, then threaded her fingers together, but that didn't make him return.

She had no idea if anything would make him return, or if this was just a one-time thing.

"What was that?" Croninshield asked.

Ludmilla looked at her gloves, then up at Croninshield. The specter was gone, truly gone, and what Ludmilla had to say sounded crazy.

But crazier than watching something spectral emerge from a librarian's body, and die? Their entire day had been crazy.

This specter, though, it seemed different than the one that Croninshield had killed earlier. It was more ethereal. It knew things.

And it wore an ancient clothing style.

"I think," Ludmilla said quietly, voice shaking. "I think that was the original owner of the gloves."

Croninshield frowned. "Original...?"

"They were made for him," Ludmilla said. She didn't want to say that she had felt all of the previous wearers of the gloves. That really did sound crazy. "Try yours on. See what happens."

Croninshield held up her hands. She was already wearing the gloves.

"I put them on," she said. "Nothing untoward happened."

Ludmilla hadn't said this was *untoward*. "Did anything happen at all?"

"They're frayed on the inside," Croninshield said. "I had a sense that someone nearly wore them out. But anyone could sense that. They were *frayed*, after all."

Ludmilla started to rub her hand over her mouth, then remembered the gloves. Who knew what they had on the surface. And what might happen if she touched her face with them.

That thought made her slightly queasy, but she didn't pull them off.

She had never had something magical happen to her, not like this. And now, twice in one day, something happened, something inexplicable.

"He wasn't happy," she said. "He needs us to move the Regents Library back to the Tower. He said none of the books are safe here. They'll lose their..."

What did he say? *Power? Magic?* She couldn't remember the exact word. She had been so stunned to hear him talk to her, to see him at all.

"He was adamant about that, once he realized this was

the old fortress." She had to make this all sound rational. She understood his urgency. Something about this room didn't fit with the library she had loved.

"Did he say why?" Croninshield was taking her seriously. And why not, given what happened today.

"Just that the magic would dissipate over time. Power, magic, whatever." Ludmilla shrugged. "I'm not sure how accurate that was. The library has been here for five years."

"And if you're to be believed, that specter was in those gloves for generations. Time means something different to him." Croninshield looked around the room. "He wasn't like that woman who attacked us, was he?"

"If so, I would think he would have been destroyed by all this light." Ludmilla heard herself speak the logic of it all. "Plus, he knew our last names. He said the Old Families live on."

Croninshield's gaze sharpened. "The Old Families. From Trinovante and Serebro. My family has been part of this land from the beginning of recorded time."

Ludmilla had no idea if hers had around that long. She didn't know as much about her family as she should have, obviously.

"Well," she said, still feeling odd. Her hands were growing warm in the gloves. "We can't move the library right now." And she didn't want to concentrate closely on what he had said about magic and power. "Let's just look at the bylaws, all right?"

Croninshield waited just for a moment, then nodded, as if the idea made sense to her.

She removed a sheaf of papers wrapped in what

appeared to be a linen cloth. The cloth was old enough to have yellowed. The papers were almost brown with age.

The edges of the papers flaked, sending tiny pieces to the floor.

Croninshield set the linen-wrapped group on the side of the desk, away from the other books.

"Be extra careful with this," she said. "It feels like my fingers can go through all of it without a lot of pressure."

"Great," Ludmilla said. She wasn't the most graceful person at the best of times. The last thing she needed to do was destroy the original bylaws for the Board of Regents just by looking at them.

But she had wanted to do this. She had claimed it was important, and she felt even more strongly about that now, after she had seen the specter.

She hadn't been afraid of him. She realized that now. She had wanted to please him, to take away his concerns, but she hadn't been terrified of him the way she had been terrified of that strange, ghostly woman.

Ludmilla made her way to the side of the desk and peered down at the linen. It was old enough that the weave looked brittle.

"You want to sit?" Croninshield asked.

"No," Ludmilla said. "If I sit, I'll get careless."

Then she took the edge of the linen in her right thumb and forefinger, and slowly moved it away from the parchments.

The parchment had originally been brown, stained, maybe with some kind of tea to preserve it. Someone had written *Bylaws* in a flowery hand. The date below it was smudged.

Beneath that were the words, *Created, Agreed Upon, and Attested To by* with signatures below.

She scanned the names. Saw Odenkirk almost immediately. Croninshield as well. And Packingham, Wallingford, Hoodwinkle, Elin, Kirilli, and several others that sounded vaguely familiar.

Not all of those surnames were on the Board now, but, she told herself sternly, that meant nothing. Surely, some of the seats were passed to family members with different last names. Or maybe the board had grown.

She leaned forward just a bit, second-guessing her decision to forgo the chair, and started to read.

LINGUISTICS

ARCHEOLOGY

HISTORY

REGENTS
TOWER

OLD
LIBRARY

ADV. STUDENT
WING

MAIN
ENTRANCE

CLOCK
TOWER

MEDICAL
SCIENCES

CHAPTER
FIFTY-SIX

Veil walked down the center aisle of the great room in the Student Wing of the Old Library, astonished that even in the middle of the night there had to be a hundred students reading and studying at various tables.

He was in the center aisle because the lightstone lamps on the walls were on very bright, but the ones on the tables were mostly off unless a student sat near them.

He was more or less safe in the diffused light, although it made him nervous.

Most of the students sat alone. They hadn't clustered like they seemed to do in the daytime. These students looked harried and exhausted, and more than one of them had fallen asleep with their head resting on a fist bracing their cheeks.

Even more students had fallen asleep on top of their book pile, and one student was sprawled backwards in his chair, head bent backwards, mouth open. He was snoring loudly enough that he could be heard from several tables away.

The librarians didn't seem to notice him or if they did, they didn't care. Maybe this scenario was normal to them. They were behind the long desk on what could only be called a dais, shuffling books around into a pattern that seemed to make sense to them.

Veil couldn't see Shyly among them, but that didn't mean anything. He had only met her once in her new body, and that body had been very similar to the others. Youngish, eager, dark hair and features that expressed a hint of Fey.

Nothing to distinguish her from any of the other librarians, or half the students for that matter.

If Veil hadn't known that she worked all night, he would have thought her not here at all. But she had to be. She might even have been in the back.

He trudged up that aisle. This part of the library was ridiculously large, and that didn't even count the bookshelves, hinting at other book-filled rooms on either side of him. She could be anywhere.

He was trembling with a low level of fear, and he didn't want to be. It wasn't that he felt threatened by these Qavnerians, but he felt vulnerable. The feeling had started on the mountainside when those drivers had looked at him like they couldn't understand him at all. He had been adjusting his face, and it had alarmed them.

That had started an entire cascade that had led to deaths of the drivers, which he really hadn't wanted to see. He had been about to see more deaths when Hardin took pity on him and sent him into the library to find Shyly.

Veil had the sense that Hardin wanted him gone, thought maybe Veil was in the way. In some senses, he was. He didn't have the kind of important knowledge that Hardin needed. Gray had only given vague instructions about where the maps were.

That had been a change in plan anyway. They had been planning to steal everything from this Academy that had to do with magick, even though Veil had tried to say (quietly) that there was too much here.

Lumin hadn't listened. He had never listened to any of them until it was too late.

Lumin hadn't been the best leader in the world. He was a poor Visionary, and his leadership skills left a lot to be desired. Veil had never been on a mission whose primary purpose had changed so many times, some in the space of this one night.

He didn't like being so deep inside this library. He knew that something was going to happen soon, and everyone would panic. He would need an escape plan, because right now he was on his own.

Maybe Shyly knew about some exit that the librarians used.

If only he could see her.

Veil paused at the bottom of the stairs leading up to the dais when someone grabbed his arm so tightly that he yelped. Three librarians looked at him in surprise.

He tried to shake the person off, but he couldn't. Then he looked sideways.

A man he didn't recognize was holding his arm tightly. The man had a roundish face, dark skin, and a pointed beard but no mustache. The man's eyes looked familiar, though, as if Veil had seen them before. They were brown with a hint of grayish silver that almost seemed to sparkle.

"You're coming with me," the man said, and his grip grew tighter.

"Is everything all right, Professor Bascherini?" one of the librarians asked. She was leaning over the desk as if she planned to come to the man's aid if he needed her.

The man holding Veil's arm smiled. "It's fine." And then he offered no explanation at all, even though it was clear that the librarian wanted one.

Veil tightened the muscles in his arm, preparing to shake the man off. He had worried that the man was security. But he wasn't. He was some kind of professor. If he was in the Alchemy or Thaumaturgy Department, that might pose a problem.

"Oh by the Powers," the man said almost under his breath. He looked to his right and then his left, and seemed satisfied with what he saw.

What Veil saw was that no one was close enough to hear the man at all. A few students had looked up to see if there was some kind of trouble, but apparently didn't see anything awry at all, because they immediately went back to their books.

"I'm Perdu," the man whispered, still speaking Qavner- ian. "Relax. You're creating a scene."

Perdu. Veil let out a small sigh. Some Fey had the ability

to see Doppelgängers even in their host's form, but Veil wasn't one of them.

"We're going to get you out of here," Perdu said.

"But I'm supposed to find Shyly," Veil said.

"I haven't seen her for more than two hours," Perdu said.

"Hardin wants to know where the map rooms are," Veil said.

Perdu dug his fingers so deeply into Veil's arm that it was all he could do not to yelp again.

"You don't understand, do you? This place is filled with wild magick," Perdu said.

"So?" Veil asked.

"So nothing is going to go as expected. Our job now is to get out of here and tell Rugar what's going on. I'd have told Lumin that if he had thought to contact the one person whom he had embedded into this horrid place."

Lumin hadn't contacted Perdu? But Veil was under the impression that he had.

"I thought you told him to bring Shyly into the library," Veil said.

"Oh, I did," Perdu said. "I gave specific instructions that were not followed. I wanted us to take our time, do this slowly over months, not a full assault."

Veil frowned, trying to fathom this. The one person who knew how this Academy worked didn't think Lumin's plan was the right one? Had he told Lumin that?

Perdu pulled on Veil's arm, not quite yanking him forward.

"We're going to get out of here," Perdu said, "and then

we're going back to Rugar. We're going to tell him what we found."

"But we haven't found anything," Veil said.

Perdu growled deep in his throat, as if he was the most frustrated man in the entire world.

"*I* have discovered a lot. We won't be able to bring back artifacts, but we don't need them. We just need to let Rugar know this place's strengths and weaknesses. And we have to tell him there are more strengths than we expected."

Veil swallowed hard. "I'd feel better if we tell Lumin what we're doing."

"And I'd feel better if you listen to me," Perdu said. "We don't have the time to find him, save him, and get his approval."

"Save him?" Veil asked.

"You think he's going to be successful tonight?" Perdu asked.

Veil frowned. The plan had already gone sideways. The dead drivers, the walk down the mountain, the mission's goals being shaved back. That explosion that had weakened Eerie.

"How did you know we were here?" he asked quietly.

"I pay attention," Perdu said. "You people weren't exactly hiding. I came here because I figured if I could find Shyly, we might be able to head you off, but no one has seen her for hours. That doesn't bode well for any of us."

"*SSSSShhhhh.*"

Veil looked toward the source of the sound. A young woman a few tables away tapped her forefinger against her lips, looking very fierce.

"Sorry," he said to her. She gave him a final glare, then looked down at her books again, shaking her head.

Perdu barely gave her a glance. "Let's go," he said, and pushed Veil with his arm.

Veil staggered forward, tripping. But he managed to stay on his feet, partly because Perdu held him so tightly.

They had a long way to get to the door. Veil knew this didn't look normal, but fortunately, he didn't see any security, and the students were deeply preoccupied with their studies.

He tried to shake Perdu off. "I'm good," Veil said.

"You're not," Perdu said. "I'm done talking. We're just going to walk. And you're going to do exactly what I say."

STORAGE
BUILDINGS

CHAPTER

FIFTY-SEVEN

THE TURNO

They had reached the darkest part of campus, an area that had made Lumin nervous the first time he and his team had walked through it. Now it seemed even quieter.

The houses were filled with sleeping people—or so he assumed—and very few had lights in their yards. There were a handful of lightstone streetlamps, but they were on corners.

Lumin felt even more exposed than he had coming into this place. There was no ground fog, and the cold air felt as brittle as crystal. There wasn't much wind, which meant that sound would carry.

Fortunately, Eerie was moving silently beside him. She had slowed down a bit—neither of them were used to running very far—but she still moved more quickly than he would like.

The mountains seemed farther away than they had a moment ago. Some of that might have been a trick of the light. Their tops were visible now, etched against the dark sky.

The etching let him know that dawn was going break soon. It was still dark down here, in the valley, but the farther he and Eerie went, the more daylight they would encounter.

They had to get up that mountain trail. The trees along the twisty part would keep the road dark, and would give them hiding places.

He would worry about where they would end up after they got to Serebro. He wasn't even sure they had coin. He certainly didn't. Maybe Eerie could figure out a way to handle his Spy and Doppelgänger, and see if they could all meet somewhere.

Eerie grabbed his arm and she yanked him toward a small side building near one of the houses. There was a shadow behind the side building, caused by the glow of a streetlamp almost two blocks away.

"What?" he asked, as quietly as he could.

"They're coming for us," she said. "There are seven."

"They won't be able to find us," Lumin said. "We have to keep moving. That's what you said before."

"They're walking in our footsteps," she said. "Literally."

He looked at her. Her face was pinched, and she seemed exhausted. He knew he was.

"I'm going to do what you asked," she said. "We'll have to do it here."

He had asked many things. He couldn't remember what they all were. Then he realized what she meant.

A portal.

"Where will we end up?" he asked.

"That turnout. On the road. It's the only place I can envision that's close enough." She sounded panicked. She looked around the small building, as if she was waiting for someone. "This is risky. I don't know what their magick is. I don't know how safe we'll be."

"It's better than running," he said. He didn't want to say much more, because otherwise he would have said, *It has always been better than running*.

She stepped away from the building, then bent her arms at the elbows in front of her, fists bumping against each other. Slowly she opened her fists, and a light appeared.

He hadn't watched her create a portal before. It looked different than he imagined. He had thought it would work like a Visionary creating a Shadowlands, which he would have done if he could. But his Shadowlands had always ended up small—tiny little boxes that might store a piece of jewelry or a key, but not something as large as a person.

The light grew. She was creating a box, and through it, he could see the contours of the road.

The portal waivered, as if it wasn't steady, but it only took a moment for it to become large enough for him to step through.

"Go," she said.

"What about you?" he asked.

"I'm coming too," she said, "but it'll be slow."

He didn't move. He didn't want to go without her.

"*Go*," she said with force. "I don't know how long I can hold this."

So he had no choice.

He stepped through.

LINGUISTICS

ARCHEOLOGY

HISTORY

REGENTS
TOWER

OLD
LIBRARY

ADV. STUDENT
WING

MAIN
ENTRANCE

CLOCK
TOWER

MEDICAL
SCIENCES

CHAPTER
FIFTY-EIGHT

The great hall of the Student Wing in the Old Library looked astonishingly normal for the middle of the night in exam week. No one in here realized there were dead bodies outside the entrance to the Scholars Wing, and Fey all over the campus.

Jaxon holstered his pistol because it suddenly felt odd to carry it. It also felt odd to be without it. But he didn't want to harm any students.

There had to be a hundred students in here tonight, and the librarians were going about their jobs as if nothing was wrong. In here, nothing *was* wrong, at least that he could see.

The place was nearly quiet, only the occasional voice raised, a snoring student close to the door, and a low-key argument happening in one of the corners as four students seemed to disagree about what they were studying.

He scanned the great hall, looking for the blurry man, and not seeing him. His gaze caught on one of the visiting professors, a rude man from Razbitay named Bascherini. He had treated security with contempt, spoken harshly to librarians in the past, and sometimes left his students in tears.

The head of his department had actually talked with Jaxon late one evening about the various ways that they might rid themselves of this terrible man early.

And now the man was standing in the center of the library, his sharp features turned downward. He seemed to be conversing, but Jaxon couldn't see with whom.

Until he realized Bascherini was gripping a man's arm. A man who, from this distance, seemed slightly blurry.

Jaxon's heart rate spiked. He could head toward the two of them, maybe try to take the blurry man away from the professor, but there were so many students around that he was afraid to do so. He couldn't attack, couldn't use his pistols.

But he had to get that blurry man, somehow.

The Fey that were dead outside the Scholars Wing had tried to destroy the lightstone street lamps. When the fog released the lamps, the yellow light had congealed over them.

Maybe using the light would help. If nothing else, it would warn the students and the librarians that something was about to happen.

Of course, it would warn the blurry man too, but he couldn't attack more than one hundred people at once.

"Everyone!" Jaxon shouted. "I'm with campus security. I need you to turn on every light near you. Every single one."

Students looked up, startled. They reached for lamps closest to them. A few students got up and touched lamps near empty seats.

Both Bascherini and the blurry man started to run toward Jaxon and the main door, threading their way through the darker pockets of the library.

But more and more lights came on, and the blurry man's face was changing, almost melting, his legs wobbling. He clutched the side of a table, his body going from blurry to solid and back again. His skin wobbled, just like his feet had, and then he started to scream.

The students screamed as well, and some of them started to run. It was precisely the kind of stampede that Jaxon wanted to avoid.

"Everyone! Stay at your tables!" he shouted, but his voice faded with the distance and the sound of screaming.

The room had become exceptionally bright, almost as light as day, and then he realized something.

The lightstone lamps were actually aiming their light toward Bascherini.

Bascherini dove under one of the tables, but a nearby student grabbed his legs and pulled him out. Bascherini grabbed the kid's shoulders, as if he wanted to kiss the kid, but the kid shook him off.

Something rose out of Bascherini—something ghostly and white and it floated in the air for a moment.

Jaxon wanted to run toward it, to see what he could do about it. He clutched the grip on his pistol, but didn't pull it out of the holster. Too many students were running by him, all of them looking panicked. Most of them avoided him, as if he were a stone in the middle of the ocean.

None of them really came close to him, all going around.

The blurry man had fallen to his knees, and then fell backwards, his face changing as if it were creating dozens of pictures.

Bascherini's body crumpled like a suit of clothes without anyone inside it.

The wispy thing tried to float above the light, heading toward one of the students, a young woman, who smartly or unthinkingly—Jaxon couldn't tell which—grabbed the lightstone lamp in front of her and swung it at the wispy thing.

The thing—some kind of person shape? A ghost, maybe? Jaxon couldn't tell—tried to use its see-through hands to block the light from its face, but it didn't work. The light coalesced around the ghostly thing, breaking it apart.

Pieces flew upward, but even they melted and dripped down onto the tables like a cloud reluctantly releasing rain.

Students continued screaming past Jaxon, knocking over chairs in their panic. The lightstone lamps seemed to grow even brighter, almost blinding him.

He couldn't see any of the librarians. They must have left through other doors.

And suddenly there was silence. The students were no longer in this part of the building. They had left, running outside to who knew what. He hadn't seen other Fey, but that didn't mean they weren't around.

Still, there was probably safety in numbers. He hoped, anyway. And he had given the students a way to get rid of the Fey, if they remember. The lights worked for some reason.

The lights in here were fading. They hadn't gone out, but they were returning to their usual intensity.

He didn't see any librarians at all. He appeared to be alone in this unbelievably large room, with what appeared to be two bodies before him.

He finally removed his pistol from its holster and he walked forward, surprised that he wasn't afraid at all. Maybe he had moved beyond fear. Maybe he had moved into a new state, one that kept his system moving without letting him feel anything.

Maybe he had become completely numb.

Even with the dimming lights, the great hall of the Student Wing was still brighter than usual. The lamps on the walls were turned on high, although he had no idea how that had happened.

The family crests, things he rarely saw, seemed to have taken a prominent place on the walls. He hadn't realized that some of the designs had swords, and the swords appeared to be pointing outward as if defending that part of the library.

The tapestries on the back wall behind the librarians' dais seemed to be moving as well, and he couldn't quite catch the images. Maybe that was because of the unusual brightness in here.

The brightness was causing all kinds of visual hallucinations. Some of the books on the various tables appeared to be glowing, and a few seemed to have fallen open of their own accord.

He didn't look at them, though. He was keeping his gaze on the blurry man and Bascherini.

They weren't moving.

Although as he got closer to the blurry man, he realized that the man's face was moving. It kept changing, showing different faces, different images. His ears would go from round to pointed and back. His eyebrows would sweep up and then recede. His nose would get big and become small. His hair would change color from black to gray to blond to black to brown.

But he didn't appear to be breathing. His eyes remained open, and they were a cloudy black. His mouth was open as well.

However, Jaxon knew nothing about Fey magic. He didn't know if these creatures could revive themselves or if this was some kind of mimicry of death.

Light usually didn't kill anyone.

So, he stood as close as he dared to the blurry man—just out of arm's reach—and pointed his pistol at the blurry man's chest.

Then Jaxon shot it.

The blurry man's body bounced, blood exploding outward as the shot destroyed his ribcage. The blurry man's eyes did not blink, his mouth did not close, but his face stopped changing.

It settled into something with sharp, pointed features, upraised eyebrows, and pointed ears. The blurry man's hair stopped changing too, settling on an almost blue-black.

If Jaxon had to guess—and really, that was all he could do—he would have said that the blurry man was well and truly dead.

Bascherini hadn't responded to the explosive sound of the shot in anyway. He had crumpled forward, as if someone had taken the air out of him, arms spread outward, knees bent, shoes sideways.

He was face down on the floor, resting on his nose.

Jaxon hadn't seen anything like that either. He walked around one of the tables—all the way around, which took him to another aisle, and then came back, pushing in chairs as he went.

He reached Bascherini's body. It hadn't moved. So he set his still-smoking pistol on the table, just within arm's reach, and grabbed the nearest chair.

He lifted it, then poked Bascherini's back with it.

The chair pushed the clothing and skin downward, as if it was all made of cloth. There were no bones inside that body. Nothing, really, except what appeared to be a skin suit.

Bile rose in Jaxon's throat, and he had to swallow hard so that he wouldn't vomit. This wasn't a body at all. It was something else entirely, something that made him think of the bones and blood he found the night of Louella's attack.

It had to be the same kind of magic. Something he didn't entirely understand.

Whatever that ghostly thing he had seen had been, it had given Bascherini his shape and form. The skin really had been a suit.

Jaxon backed away from all of it, then, because he couldn't help himself, he primed his other pistol. He had to shoot that body, because he had to take the possibility away that it might rise up again.

He pointed the pistol, happy to see that his hand, at least, wasn't shaking at all, and shot Bascherini in the back.

The round cut a hole in the suit and pinged against the floor. There was no blood, and, from the look inside that hole, no bones either. No organs, no nothing.

He let out a shaky breath, hoping that the light and the melting ghost had meant that the thing had disappeared.

It wasn't attacking him now, though, so maybe even if it survived, it had found a way to flee.

He picked up his other pistol and backed away, heading down the aisle farthest from the bodies.

He had no idea how he would explain this night to the Serebro Constabulary. He wasn't even sure he wanted to.

Maybe he would leave that to the administration. Maybe they could figure out how to deal with all of this.

If indeed it was done. He fervently hoped it was. He wasn't sure how many more impossible things he could take in one evening.

He paused beneath one of the lightstone lamps, feeling some kind of energy from its light. It wasn't warm, like the sun, but it felt soothing somehow.

He glanced up at the wall. The family crests didn't seem as prominent as before. And maybe he had imagined the swords sticking out of them.

Maybe that had been a trick of the light.

He hoped that the light had no more tricks. That none of what he had seen had been a trick. Because he needed those two to really be dead, needed the Fey near the Scholars Entrance to be dead too.

He leaned against the wall and took a shuddery breath. He had to go outside and see how the students were faring.

After one more minute in the light.

He needed just a minute to gather himself, before he moved to something new.

ALCHEMY, SCIENCE & THAUMATURGY

GOVERNMENT

LAW BUILDING

WHISTLER HALL

LI

R

CHAPTER
FIFTY-NINE

The book led them into the darkness around the staff homes. Dozens and dozens and dozens of homes, all filled with sleeping professors and a few Practical Interns and support staff, the beating heart of Serebro Academy.

Sauer didn't like any of this.

He and the six others from the AST building were hurrying along without much of a plan. They didn't have real weapons—no pistols, no knives, not much in the way of a fighting force, although both Wystan and Kenelm said they didn't need much.

Harewald had wanted to stop in his lab to get more of that potion, but no one would let him. Harewald worried Sauer. He did seem reckless, just like Wystan had said.

They were marching along the path of the two sets of footprints that headed toward the foothills. The other two sets of footprints, the ones in the Old Library, had vanished as well, which Sauer hoped meant that someone had done something to those Fey.

He couldn't worry about it at the moment.

Weirdly, he did worry about his books. Fenwick had convinced him to leave the book about the building history in the AST Building. She had wanted him to leave it near the bodies, but he couldn't. What if someone found those? Would they confiscate his books? He couldn't let that happen.

So he ran the books up the stairs and left the book on the secretary's desk near the doors to the Thaumaturgy Department.

He had no idea what the others had done in the same moment, although he wasn't the only one who returned to the main door ten minutes later. Erling arrived last, and he was carrying a pouch. Thane had a backpack that he hadn't had earlier.

Fenwick assured Sauer, in a quiet undertone, that no one had let Harewald leave.

Sauer believed it, when he saw how close Kenelm stood to Harewald. It was almost as if she was guarding him, and keeping him from doing something stupid.

Then they had all left the AST building, and headed in the path of those prints. The prints were moving forward. Fenwick kept the Pahrucii book open to the map, and she kept saying they would never catch up.

Yet it seemed like they were catching up, especially when they hit the edge of the neighborhood.

Now, the prints had stopped near a home on the corner. The footprints weren't moving.

"We have to hurry," Sauer said, and started to run.

He couldn't remember the last time he had run. It had been years, as his knees were reminding him. They were also telling him that he hadn't weighed this much the last time he tried to move this fast.

His hair got in his face. He looked over his shoulder, saw that Kenelm was keeping up with him, as was Wystan, but the others weren't.

He didn't care. He wasn't going to let this group of Fey get away. He was going to talk them to death if he had to.

This part of the neighborhood was much too dark. Later, if he survived this, he would tell the administration that they needed a lot more light here. Lightstone street-lamps, because clearly lightstone had properties that had an effect on the Fey.

He wished he had more than the two lanterns that they had brought.

He didn't really even have those, since Erling and Thane were the ones carrying the lanterns.

Sauer probably should have grabbed one before sprinting forward. Sprinting had seemed like a good idea in the moment, but it didn't any longer. He was breathing too hard.

The exercise he still did—keeping himself strong enough to lift books and shelves—wasn't enough to enable him to run after fleeing Fey.

He would have to reassess that too—if he survived.

A light appeared ahead of him. A large light, square that seemed to grow.

It revealed a shed, and two figures standing behind it. He

turned slightly, saw that Fenwick wasn't anywhere nearby, so he couldn't ask her if this was the place where the Fey were hiding.

It seemed to be.

The square bit of light was turning into a door. He could see a tall thin woman standing near it.

She seemed to be creating the door, as if she could draw it in the air, and it would appear.

But the light didn't look stable. The door winked in and out, almost as if it were part of a light that was about to go permanently dark.

Someone else stood near the woman, someone Sauer couldn't see in the shadows.

Then that someone—a man stepped into the light—his entire body illuminated for just a moment.

He stepped through that light—that door—and it disappeared.

Sauer cursed.

"Did you see that?" Kenelm asked.

"Yes," Sauer said.

"There's someone else there," Wystan said. "We have to stop her."

Stop her from what? Sauer wanted to ask, but he didn't have enough air. They would do what they could, but they probably had to ask where she had sent that man. Because how else would they find him?

"Get me close," Wystan said.

Sauer glanced at her. She was slightly behind him and she didn't seem winded at all.

"Don't let her see me," Wystan said.

Kenelm moved next to Sauer. They were like advance troops in the paintings he had seen. Human shields who would protect Wystan.

He found that he didn't mind. She had proven that she could do things he couldn't even imagine.

He wished he wasn't breathing so loudly. That would make the person at the edge of the darkness hear them approach.

The tall thin woman stepped into the street. She raised her hands.

"You stop," Wystan said to Sauer. "I can't keep track of you."

But he didn't stop. He wasn't sure what she wanted. He did stay in front of Wystan though.

The woman's hands glowed. She seemed to be creating small balls in her hands.

Wystan halted a few yards from the woman and waved her own hands. She left a sparkle of lights that looked like some kind of bubble.

The balls from the other woman's—the Fey woman's— hands flew across the sky, leaving a light trail. The balls hit the sparkle and it bobbled.

Then the Fey woman cursed. She stepped back behind the shed, and light started to appear.

"She's making another door," Kenelm said.

That meant she was going to get away. Sauer turned around and sprinted, as best he could, to the rest of his band. At least they were closer now. He grabbed Erling's lantern, half afraid that Erling would fight him for it, but Erling released it quickly, as if he wanted nothing to do with it.

Then Sauer ran back to Wystan and Kenelm. They were pushing forward, that bubble staying ahead of them.

The bubble only extended around them slightly, so Sauer ran around it.

"Wolfgang!" Kenelm said. "Don't..."

He didn't hear the rest. He could see that Fey woman making another wobbly door. The door was so pale that it looked like an outline.

She was swaying as she worked, which looked less like the way someone made magic and more like someone about to pass out.

He hoped it was the latter, because he had no real way to go after her besides this lamp.

He approached the shed, trying and mostly failing to control his breathing. The Fey woman heard him, moved toward him, then seemed to think the better of it. She continued to move her hands, trying to draw a door.

He grabbed the lantern and opened it all the way, hoping that he had understood the properties of lightstone correctly.

The light focused and headed toward her in a single beam. Part of him felt relief—he had understood—and the other part watched, appalled, as the light surrounded her.

She screamed and batted at the light as if it were a wall. It held her tightly. Her face looked almost familiar—narrow with upswept eyebrows and high cheekbones. She looked older than he thought, and she seemed to be growing older with every passing second.

She created more light with her hands, red light this time, almost like she had flames instead of fingers, but the light did nothing. It couldn't seem to dent the prison of light he had created for her.

Wystan reached his side. So did Kenelm. Sauer was still gasping for air. Kenelm put a hand on his shoulder as if she expected that to help. He didn't shake her off. Her touch didn't help his breathing, but it was nice to know that he wasn't alone, watching an imprisoned woman fight against what looked like sunlight.

The imprisoned woman sank to her knees. Her hands stopped creating flames. She touched the light as if it was made of glass and held her in place. Then her gaze met his.

She wasn't pleading. She didn't even seem angry. She shook her head slightly, as if she couldn't believe what was happening to her.

Then she toppled forward and didn't move.

The door she'd been trying to draw remained, watery and thin, as if it was waiting for her to finish. Sauer couldn't see through it. He'd hoped it would lead to the man who escaped, but Sauer had no idea how.

Then Sauer realized that the door was fading. Its outline had become diffuse, almost as if the door itself had been drawn of smoke. The edges were no longer crisp. The watery middle wasn't waving anymore. It just seemed blurry.

Then it disappeared altogether.

The woman still hadn't moved. The light from the lantern was moving, though. It had widened, as if it was making sure there were no more Fey around.

Then it eased backwards, becoming standard light from a lantern, illuminating only the area nearby.

"I think she's dead," Wystan said. Her voice seemed louder than it should have.

That's when Sauer realized almost all of this—the woman's attack, the doorway, the way the light surrounded her, even her fall—had occurred in silence.

The only sound that had accompanied it had been his own breathing, which was finally slowing down.

Although he didn't think his heart would ever stop pounding.

"Thinking and knowing are two different things," Kenelm said, which was, if Sauer had to parse it out, a very science attitude. He liked thinking. Sometimes knowing was overrated.

"Let's give it a minute," Wystan said, but it was as if she hadn't spoken at all.

Kenelm walked toward the Fey woman.

Sauer half expected the woman to rise up and making those flame-hands again, attacking Kenelm. Maybe Wystan did too, because she took a few steps forward, her own hands raised.

There was no bubble around anyone anymore. The lantern had lost most of its light. The lightstone thought—if lightstone could think (which Sauer was beginning to wonder) that maybe, just maybe, the Fey woman was dead.

"Her footprints have vanished." The voice came from behind him, and he didn't even have to turn around to know who had spoken.

Fenwick had finally reached them. Fenwick and the other three.

"What about the other pair of prints?" Sauer asked, still

staring at the woman. The lack of footprints he was beginning to understand. She *was* dead.

"I have to show you that," Fenwick said.

But Sauer didn't turn, not yet. He watched Kenelm make her way slowly to the Fey woman. When Kenelm got close, she didn't do what he would have done. He would have grabbed something, like a stick, and poked the Fey woman with it.

But Kenelm used the toe of her boot. She prodded the Fey woman so hard that the woman flopped. It wasn't the flop of a conscious person. It really wasn't—if Sauer were honest with himself—the flop of a living person.

He let out a small sigh even before Kenelm backed away.

"She's dead," Kenelm said. "You should see her. I mean, it's hard to mistake this kind of dead."

So clinical. So matter-of-fact. That startled him. That almost disturbed him.

He didn't want to think about it, not yet, so he turned around. Fenwick still held the Pahrucii book, and it was open, and the map glowed. Only the map didn't show the campus at all.

Instead, it had changed to show the mountains.

She tapped the road. "Look," she said. "He's there."

Little gold footprints near a turnout about halfway up the mountain. Sauer even knew where that was. The footprints were heading toward Serebro.

The man was getting away.

"I have no idea how we get to him now," Thane said, sounding like the voice of reason.

"We take a conveyance," Erling said.

"We're not going to lose him," Fenwick said. "Not unless he leaves or dies. I mean, look."

She paged through the Pahrucii book, and another map appeared. This one was of the Protectorate. There were several golden footprints, and so many other prints like the ones that had led Sauer to this band that they crowded the map.

"Show me Fey only," he said, not to Fenwick, not really, but to the map itself.

When he said that, all of the other prints disappeared.

But there were prints scattered from here to Khēmía. There only appeared to be three different golden prints in all of Qavner—two in Trinovante, and the pair that was high-tailing it over the mountain.

"We can catch him," Fenwick said. "We don't have to do it tonight."

Sauer raised his head from the map. She was right. They would have time to figure out actual weapons and consider how to go after these Fey.

He'd had no idea what an essential tool these maps were. He'd seen them mentioned repeatedly in the old accounts of the attacks, but he had just thought that the maps would show where the battlefields were.

He had gravely misinterpreted what he had been read-ing. Gravely.

He let out a breath.

The sun was coming up over the mountains, sending diffuse light into the valley. He had been up all night, living a life he hadn't been able to imagine when the sun came up the day before.

He had a hunch he'd be living a completely different life now, one he couldn't entirely fathom.

But he was getting glimmers of it, the way that one caught glimmers of daylight before dawn actually broke.

He nodded. Fenwick was right. They could rest. They could figure out a plan.

They had tools. They just had to figure out how to use them—and use them well.

STORAGE
BUILDINGS

SIXTY

Cole and Xavier limped to the fields. The ground fog was completely gone, but the air had grown colder. Cole could see his breath. He was grateful for Xavier's warmth on his left side, and wondered if Xavier felt the same.

Xavier had been much too quiet. He was looking down as they walked as if holding his head up was nearly impossible. He had grown heavier too, leaning on Cole even more.

Cole had thought it wouldn't take them long to reach Volkovich and the carriages, but he hadn't counted on how depleted Xavier was. If Cole could have, he would have slung Xavier over his shoulder and carried him back.

But Cole didn't have the physical strength, not anymore. He had let himself grow soft with his love for books and his work and his regular routine. He was tired too, but not as depleted as Xavier. Cole's head still ached from that explosion, and he worried that there might be some kind of damage.

However, of the two of them, Cole was the one who was the strongest.

Still, when he saw that the carriages were in the same position at the edge of the field, his heart rose just a little. If he could have, he would have hurried forward. But he couldn't.

Xavier clearly hadn't seen them yet. His head was down, his movements had become little more than a trudge. Cole could almost hear Xavier's thoughts. *One more step. One more step. One more step.*

One foot in front of the other. That was what it took, and that had gotten them here.

The Fey that they had attacked near the barns had not followed them, nor had others appeared. Cole had half expected more attacks, and had worried that they would do something to him and Xavier that he couldn't stop.

If they had been approached, Cole would have had to let go of Xavier and prime the pistols. He wasn't even sure he could have done that, not and take care of Xavier at the same time.

One less worry, now that he could see the carriages.

The horses weren't bucking and moving like they had before. They seemed calmer. Cole was grateful for that as well. He couldn't deal with horses and Xavier and his own exhaustion.

Cole hoped that Volkovich was all right. If the horses weren't upset, then maybe it wouldn't be too much to assume that Volkovich had been the one to calm them.

Cole got close enough to smell the horses on the slight breeze. Volkovich appeared around the back end of the nearest carriage and let out something akin to a yelp.

Then he scurried down the path, and grabbed the other side of Xavier, helping him forward.

The extra help took some of Xavier's weight off Cole. They got to the carriages and Volkovich pulled open one of the doors, but Xavier couldn't climb up the small step to get inside.

Instead, he sank onto the step and leaned against the edge of the open door.

That was the moment when Cole realized that Xavier's robe was black. The silver was gone, and there was no writing at all.

Cole had no idea what that meant, but he had a hunch it wasn't good.

"They're dead," Cole said. "The ones near the barn. They're dead."

"I figured," Volkovich said, but he sounded as distracted as he looked. He had gripped Xavier's robe, then leaned him back, examining his face and his neck as if he was looking for some kind of injury.

"I think he used up every bit of his ability to stop them," Cole said.

Volkovich glanced sideways at Cole. "I don't have the skills to take care of him."

Cole smiled ruefully. "That's what he said. He said he wasn't a horse."

Volkovich let out an ironic chuckle, then patted Xavier on the cheek.

"Xavier," Volkovich said. "Xavier, do you know how we can help you?"

Xavier didn't respond. His eyes were closed, but he was obviously breathing.

"Maybe rest...?" Cole asked.

"That's probably our only choice," Volkovich said. "I'm not sure where to take him, though, if there are more Fey here."

"If we can get him to the conveyance," Cole said, "I can take him to the lodge. There's a back way that's wide enough for the conveyance."

"If it's that big," Volkovich said, "a carriage could get through."

"It could," Cole said, "but the conveyance can travel at higher speeds. If we see more Fey, I can get away from them."

He hoped. He had no idea what their magic could do, if it could help them move quickly.

But he was buoyed by the idea that magic here in Dorovich had different types. His was tied to technology, and from what little he knew of the Fey, they had no technology. So that might give the conveyance an edge.

It might give *him* an edge.

Volkovich turned ever so slightly, and looked up at the Serebro Mountains. Cole could almost read his mind as well.

Volkovich was weighing whether or it not it was wiser to return to Serebro.

"We have no idea how many are in Serebro," Cole said quietly. "Or if there are more explosions awaiting us there. We know that the Fey came here in two carriages. That can't be a lot of people."

Volkovich closed his eyes for a moment, then nodded. "You're right, of course. I hadn't thought it through."

"That's all right," Cole said. "This is new to all of us."

Volkovich touched Xavier's cheek, as if feeling for a fever. "He will need someone with him, someone who knows about the magic."

"That would be me," Cole said.

"You're exhausted too," Volkovich said.

"Right now," Cole said, "I don't think any of us have time for exhaustion. The question is, what do we do with these carriages? The Fey can't find them sitting out here."

"They won't." Xavier spoke, softly and very slowly. Cole had to lean forward to hear.

Then he glanced at Volkovich, who nodded. He seemed convinced, just by that one statement.

But Cole wasn't. He had seen things that he wouldn't have believed a week ago, and he had lost faith in the Regents. Now, things were different, and he wasn't sure how exactly to deal with any of that.

"How do you know they won't?" Cole asked.

"...feel..." Xavier said.

"You *feel* it?" Cole wasn't sure if feelings were enough, not after the night that they had had.

"It's all right," Volkovich said. "If he says they're not going to go after the carriages, then he knows what he's talking about. You have to trust him."

Cole let out a small sigh. He had trusted this far.

"Can we leave the carriages here, then?" Cole asked. He was talking to Volkovich, because he didn't want to tire Xavier even more than he already had.

"I'd prefer to get them to the barns," Volkovich said. "I'm not sure how to do that, though."

"I could help you," Cole said, even though he didn't want to. The last thing he wanted to try was driving a carriage even the short distance to the barns.

"...no..." Xavier again.

Cole put a hand on Xavier's shoulder. "We'll take care of this. Don't worry."

"...not..." Xavier's voice was little more than a sigh. Then he took a deep breath. "There's no danger here."

He was breathing hard.

"It's all right," Cole said.

Xavier shook his head, then closed his eyes. Cole empathized. Shaking his own head was difficult right now, because it still made him dizzy.

"Keep the carriages here...until dawn." Xavier was looking at Volkovich now. "Wait for dawn."

Volkovich didn't say anything, so Cole did.

"Should we all wait for dawn, then?"

Xavier opened his eyes. He smiled just a little. "I need sleep."

Didn't they all?

"...prefer a bed," Xavier said.

He was acting as if the crisis was past. But he said there were still Fey on campus. That meant the crisis wasn't past.

"What about the Fey?" Cole said.

"Don't worry," Xavier said. "They're gone. We're safe."

And then he passed out.

PART SEVEN
DAWN

THE
TURNOUT

SEREBRO
MOUNTAIN RANGE

CHAPTER
SIXTY-ONE

The carriages were gone. Weirdly, that was the first thing Lumin noticed. The carriages were no longer protected by Eerie's magick, but he had just seen her, so he knew her magic remained.

Someone else had broken the protection she had placed around the carriages, and taken the carriages away.

He stood, alone, at the turnout where not long ago, he had stood with his team. If Eerie was to be believed, they were all dead. All of them.

He had no idea how that happened.

He had Seen the deaths of Atrü's team in Trinovante, but he had thought them isolated. And on this long night, Lumin hadn't heard anyone speak of a Helia nor had he seen a woman in a long coat. No one had said *They're Fey*, like they had in his Vision.

Maybe it hadn't been a future Vision at all. Maybe he had seen a longer Open Vision.

He staggered forward, then caught himself. He looked at the valley below. Dawn was breaking, so the lights of the Academy were growing dim. Sunlight was marching across the valley, as the sun kept cresting the mountains.

The area where he had stood with Eerie not fifteen minutes earlier was still in darkness, but it wouldn't be for long.

He had no idea how long he should wait for her. She had sent him away knowing—what? That people who were coming for them would kill her? She had believed they had killed the rest of his team and he had no reason to doubt her.

No reason.

He didn't dare stay here. If they captured her, she would eventually tell them that she had sent him here. If he waited here too long, they would take one of their foul vehicles and find him, quicker than he expected.

He stepped back, shaking a little in the early morning chill. The sun wouldn't ease that chill. He was too high up, and the air in Qavner was just too damp.

He was going to have to figure out where he would go, how he would get there, and how he was going to get money.

He was going to have no choice but to go to the new rental that Gray had found for all of them. Lumin wouldn't be able to stay there either.

These Qavnerians knew about the Fey now, and they would be looking for him. He doubted they could find him, but he had lost his entire team because he had underestimated the magick the Qavnerians had.

He ran a shaking hand over his face.

He had a new mission now. He needed to get to Rugar. He needed to let the Black Family know just how dangerous Dorovich was. Dorovich might have lost some of its memory of magick, but it still had tools—and a lot of them—that could defeat the Fey.

He was going to have to tell Rugar that the defeat hundreds of years ago was not because of bad Fey leadership or even bad tactics. It was because the Dorovicians had power, a lot of it. They were a match to the Fey.

Rugar wouldn't believe him. Rugar would look at the failure. He would blame Lumin for being a bad leader.

For a brief moment, Lumin thought of disappearing into Dorovich, like so many Fey had centuries ago. But then he would condemn even more of his people to death.

And after this night, he couldn't do that. He couldn't be responsible for one more death, not if it could have been prevented.

Lumin shook himself. Eerie should have joined him by now.

He was going to have to trudge back to Serebro alone. He would have to hide from carriages and windstone vehicles. He was going to have to fade away like a Spy, so that no one noticed him.

He didn't really have that skill, but he was going to have to try.

He needed to get back to Nye, in whatever way possible.

LINGUISTICS

ARCHEOLOGY

HISTORY

REGENTS

TOWER

OLD

LIBRARY

ADV. STUDENT
WING

MAIN
ENTRANCE

CLOCK
TOWER

MEDICAL

SCIENCES

STORY

SCHOLAR'S
ENTRANCE

CAFETE

CHAPTER
SIXTY-TWO

Ludmilla's eyes burned. The dust in the Regent's Library was profound. She loosened some of it every single time she turned a page. She also released the smell of old paper into the air.

At least she wasn't smelling mildew. That was a death knell for any library.

She had no idea how long she had been sitting in the librarian's chair, reading the ancient bylaws. Croninshield had fallen asleep near the door, so she had to be feeling safer than she had been.

Good thing Croninshield slept too, because Ludmilla hadn't been able to hide some exclamations of shock. She had found so much. The Regents were not following the rules of the Board. She would have to do more reading to see if some of those rules had changed, but she doubted it.

The early bylaws, written centuries ago, were clear.

The Board of Regents weren't some random people

upholding education. The Board was designed to maintain the magic in Qavner. *All* of the magic in Qavner. And, she was beginning to see, the expansion of the Protectorate was less about political power than protecting—yes, protecting—all of Dorovich.

That it had gone awry, that other groups were not allowed into the Regents or that the magic of other cultures clashed, was not foreseen by the original founders.

They had written all of this, developed it all, after the first Fey attack all those years ago. The Board had seen themselves as the protectors of the continent, of everyone, for all time.

They weren't just self-chosen people. They were all members of the Old Families, and those families had chosen the member who had the most magical ability.

Serebro Academy was initially designed to train mages in magic. That it had lost its mission long ago confused her, made her unable to understand what had gone wrong.

Devin Chaban's tampering with the Board tampered with magic, almost more than the Purges had. Getting rid of the right members of the Old Families would destroy the last of the protections the Board had established hundreds of years before.

She leaned back in her chair and rubbed her eyes, a move she instantly regretted. It felt like she had forced more dust into them.

At that moment, the door banged.

Croninshield jumped to her feet, grabbing one of the lanterns. Maybe Croninshield hadn't been as sound asleep as Ludmilla thought.

The lights were still bright here, though. She felt safer than she had in the corridor.

The door banged again, and then the lock turned.

Croninshield held up the lantern as if it were a sword. Ludmilla stood, ready to grab her lantern as well, when the door slammed open.

A man stumbled inside. He was blood-covered, his hair messed, his eyes wild. He was wearing a silver campus security guard's uniform. and he looked familiar.

"Herbert?" Croninshield said. "Herbert Jaxon?"

Ludmilla stiffened even more. Was he another of those fake people, the ones who looked like a real person but had a Fey inside of them?

She picked up her lantern and stepped around the desk.

But the light didn't flare toward him. Neither did the light from Croninshield's lantern nor the lamps on the walls.

"May?" The man's voice was little more than a croak. "Oh May, after I found that body in the corridor, I thought you were dead."

"We've had an interesting night," Croninshield said. She waved a hand at Ludmilla. "Meet one of our newest Regents, Ludmilla Odenkirk."

The man looked at Ludmilla, but didn't really see her. He was more concerned with Croninshield.

"The library was attacked," he said. "There were Fey everywhere. But we think we got all of them. Except maybe one. I'm not clear on that."

He sounded breathless. He kept the door open, which was making Ludmilla nervous.

"Then I realized you were missing, and one of the librarians said she saw you take a Regent toward the back, and that Louella followed, and we found Louella or what was left of her."

"That wasn't Louella," Croninshield said.

"I figured that out. It was a suit or something. We had another in the library. That horrible visiting professor, Bascherini."

Croninshield grunted, whether in acknowledgement or what, Ludmilla didn't know.

"I..." The man stopped talking, then he looked around the room. "What are you doing in here?"

This last he directed at Ludmilla.

"Reading the bylaws for the Board of Regents," she said. She felt oddly calm. She was beginning to think all of the answers they needed to every question they had, about magic, about the Fey, about the Academy, were in this room.

"Why?" he asked.

She didn't know how to explain that meeting the day before or the terror in that corridor or the relief she was feeling as she looked through the books.

"Let's just say there was a need," she said.

Croninshield looked at her as if trying to understand what Ludmilla said. Then Croninshield said to the man—this Jaxon, "You said there were Fey. There aren't any now?"

"Not on campus," he said. "But there's a bigger problem in the Protectorate, at least that's what Professor Sauer says."

"Wolfgang Sauer? What does he have to do with it?" Croninshield asked.

The man shook his head. "It's all confusing. And strange. I don't pretend to understand it."

Croninshield walked toward him. She lifted the edge of the lantern, directing the light at him. It grew slightly brighter, but only because she had opened one of the panels.

"I don't know how to prove that I'm not one of those suit-people, May," Jaxon said. "But I'm not."

Ludmilla opened her lantern all the way too, but nothing happened. The man seemed to be who he said he was.

She swallowed against a dry throat. Her stomach growled. She hadn't slept or eaten in—she had no idea how long.

"What time is it?" she asked.

"I don't know exactly," the man said. "A few hours after dawn. Everyone is dealing with the aftermath. There's a lot of strange damage, sightings, dead. The Administration is sending someone to Serebro to alert their Constabulary."

A few hours after dawn. Morning. They were supposed to have a Board meeting in the morning. Ludmilla wondered if that would happen now.

Either way, it didn't dare happen without her.

"Is there any way I can come back here?" she asked Croninshield.

Croninshield nodded. "You know how now. I can give you a key."

"Thank you." Ludmilla was still unwilling to admit that she had a key. She wasn't sure why. And she wasn't sure if she wanted to walk those corridors alone. Not for a long time.

She looked at the bylaws, wondering if she should take them with her.

But that was too risky. She didn't trust her fellow Regents. She no longer trusted anyone except Croninshield.

"We need to deal with these," Ludmilla said to her, indicating the bylaws. "Let's do that. Mr.—Jaxon?—we will catch up with you."

He raised his eyebrows, as if startled she would dismiss him. She was a little startled too. She had never spoken to anyone like that in her entire life.

"It's okay, Herbert," Croninshield said. "Give us a few minutes. We'll meet you outside."

He nodded, then slipped out the door, pulling it closed.

"You don't trust him," Croninshield said.

Yes, that was true, but not why Ludmilla wanted him gone.

"These bylaws are important," she said. "I need to put them where no one else can find them easily. Can you help me with that?"

Croninshield stared at her for a moment. "What did you find?" she asked.

Did she deserve to know? Ludmilla wasn't sure, but she was sure of one thing. There were Croninshields in the original bylaws, even if there wasn't one on the Board.

She tapped the parchment in front of her. More dust rose.

"We have answers in here," Ludmilla said.

"To what?" Croninshield asked.

"To everything," Ludmilla said, letting the awe she'd been feeling in the last few hours into her voice. "To everything we need to know."

SEREBRO
MOUNTAIN RANGE

SEREBRO
ACADEMY

TO TRINOVANTE

SEREBRO
MOUNTAIN RANGE

SEREBRO
ACADEMY

TO TRINOVANTE

HEAR DIRECTLY
FROM KRIS

Sign up for the Kristine Kathryn Rusch newsletter and hear from Kris herself.

Go to kriswrites.com.

Get the latest news and releases from all of the WMG authors and lines, including Kristine Kathryn Rusch, Kristine Grayson, Kris Nelscott, Dean Wesley Smith, *Pulphouse Fiction Magazine*, and so much more.

Go to wmgbooks.com.

You can also follow Kris on Bookbub.

We value honest feedback, and would love to hear your opinion in a review, if you're so inclined, on your favorite book retailer's site.

ABOUT THE AUTHOR

International bestseller Kristine Kathryn Rusch wrote seven books featuring the Fey before traditional publishing issues in the United States stymied her. The extremely popular series became a bestseller in multiple languages, including French, Italian, German, Polish, and Czech. When the first book, *The Sacrifice,* first appeared in the United States, it was hailed as one of the best fantasy novels of the year. Rusch took an unintended twenty-plus year hiatus from the Fey after completing the second full mini-saga. Spurred by a successful Kickstarter for a novella featuring the Fey, she dove back into the project. She explains her journey back to the Fey in *Lessons from the Writing of The Fey.* All seven of the books are back in print through WMG Publishing, and have garnered new readers worldwide. Rusch recently published the novella, *The Reflection on Mount Vitaki,* and has completed three new novels, with a fourth underway.

Rusch writes in many genres, from science fiction to mystery, from western to romance. She has written under a pile of pen names, but most of her work appears as Kristine Kathryn Rusch. Her Kris Nelscott pen name has won or been nominated for most of the awards in the mystery genre, and her Kristine Grayson pen name became a bestseller in romance. Her science fiction novels set in the bestselling Diving Universe have won dozens of awards and are in development for a major TV show. She also writes the Retrieval Artist sf series and several major series that mostly appear as short fiction.

Rusch broke a number of barriers in the sf/f field, including being the first female editor of *The Magazine of Fantasy & Science Fiction*. She has owned two different publishing companies, and writes a highly regarded publishing industry blog on Patreon. She also writes a highly regarded weekly publishing industry blog. Find out more about her work at kriswrites.com, and more about the Fey at WorldoftheFey.com.

f facebook.com/kristinekathrynruschwriter

P patreon.com/kristinekathrynrusch

BB bookbub.com/authors/kristine-kathryn-rusch

www.ingramcontent.com/pod-product-compliance
Lightning Source LLC
Chambersburg PA
CBHW010725100726
47899CB00009B/2922

* 9 7 8 1 5 6 1 4 6 1 5 8 5 *